Emily®
the Strange

ROCK, DEATH, FAKE, REVENGE & ALONE

Volume 2

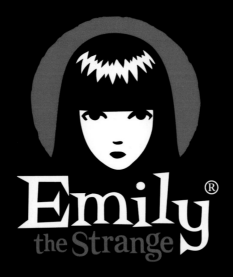

Emily® the Strange

Created by   Rob Reger

Illustration by   Buzz Parker
Ryan Hill
Derek Fridolfs
Nicomi 'Nix' Turner

Writers   Rob Reger
Jessica Gruner
Kitty Remington
Buzz Parker
Nicomi 'Nix' Turner
Brian Brooks

Trip Out Artists   Winston Smith
Tim Biskup
Jason Mecier
Turo 'Scissorhands'
Fawn Gehweiler

Editor   Shawna Gore

Publisher   Mike Richardson

Dedicated to everyone's My Strange Cat

Published by Dark Horse Books
A division of Dark Horse Comics, Inc.

Dark Horse Comics
10956 SE Main Street
Milwaukie, OR 97222

www.darkhorse.com
www.emilystrange.com

NEECHEE

COSMIC*DEBRIS*

DARK HORSE BOOKS

First Edition: September 2009
ISBN: 978-1-59582-221-5

1 3 5 7 9 10 8 6 4 2

Publisher Mike Richardson—Executive Vice President Neil Hankerson—Chief Financial Officer Tom Weddle—Vice President Of Publishing Randy Stradley—Vice President Of Business Development Michael Martens—Vice President Of Marketing, Sales, And Licensing Anita Nelson—Vice President Of Product Development David Scroggy—Vice President Of Information Technology Dale LaFountain—Director Of Purchasing Darlene Vogel—General Counsel Ken Lizzi—Editorial Director Davey Estrada—Senior Managing Editor Scott Allie—Senior Books Editor, Dark Horse Books Chris Warner—Executive Editor Diana Schutz—Director Of Design And Production Cary Grazzini—Art Director Lia Ribacchi—Director Of Scheduling Cara Niece

TABLE OF CONTEMPT

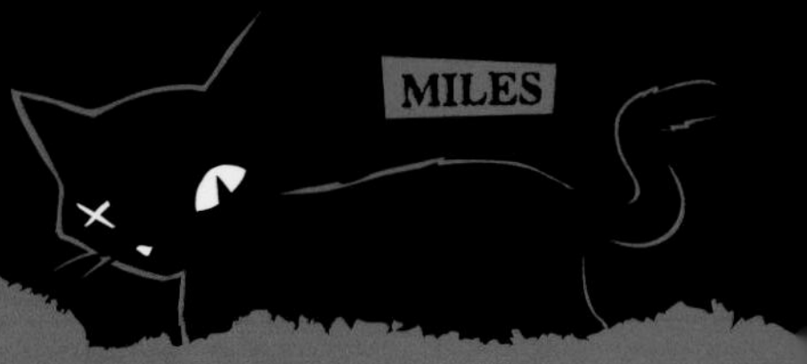
MILES

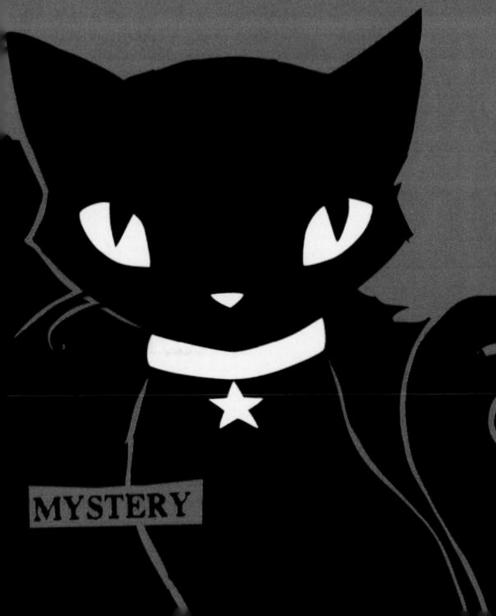
MYSTERY

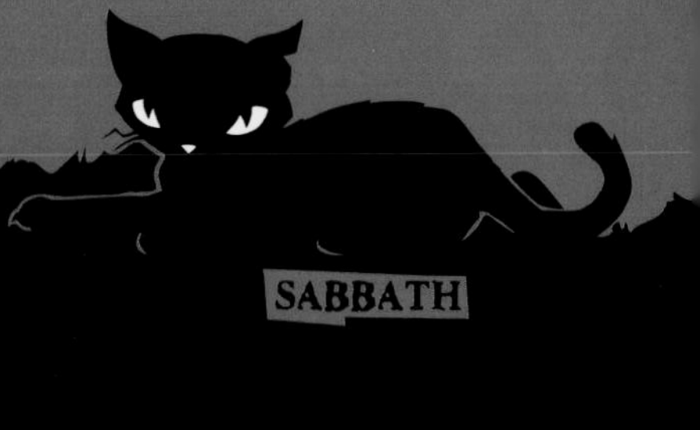
SABBATH

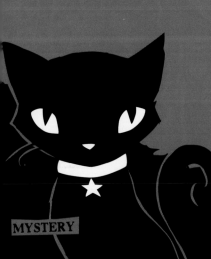

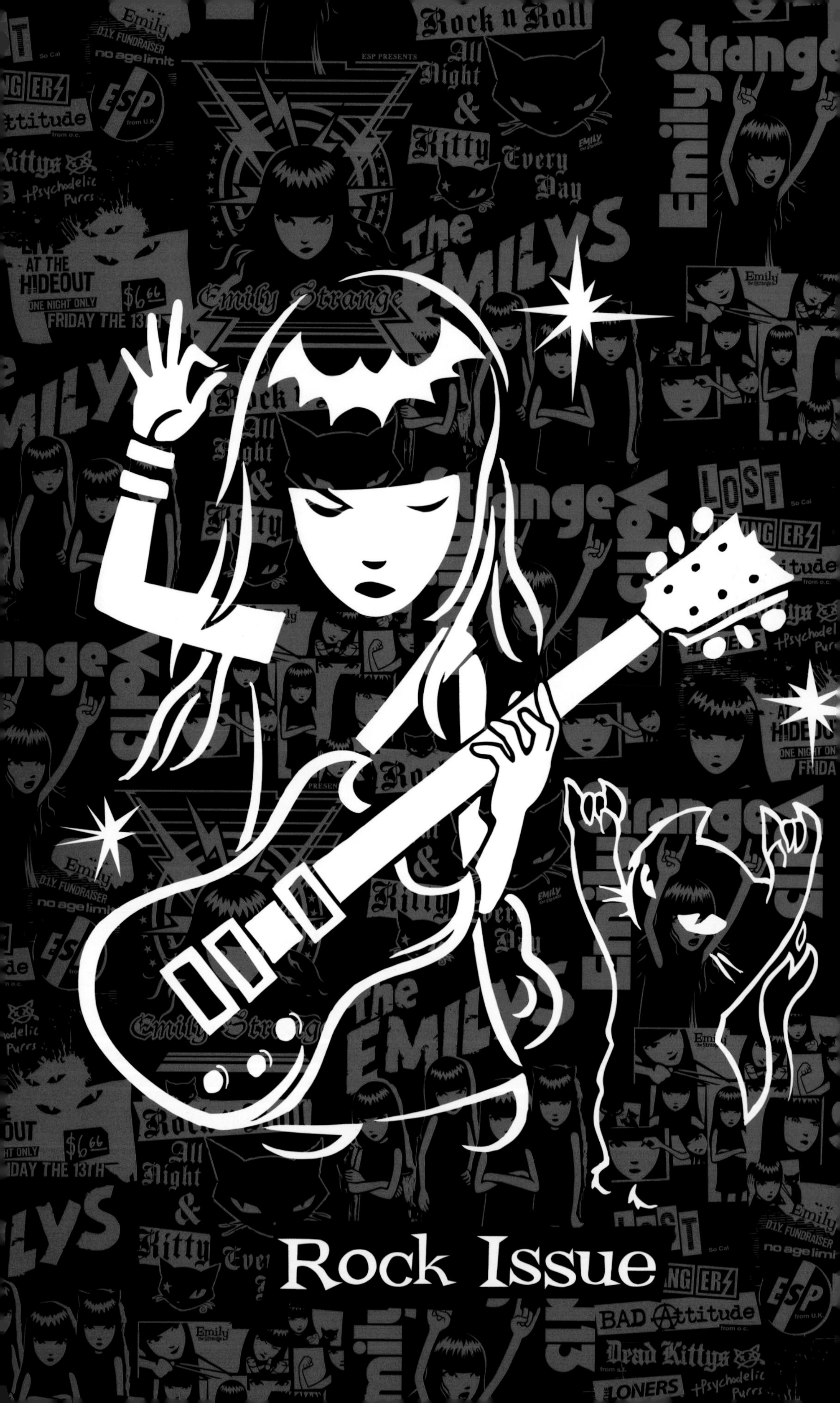
Rock Issue

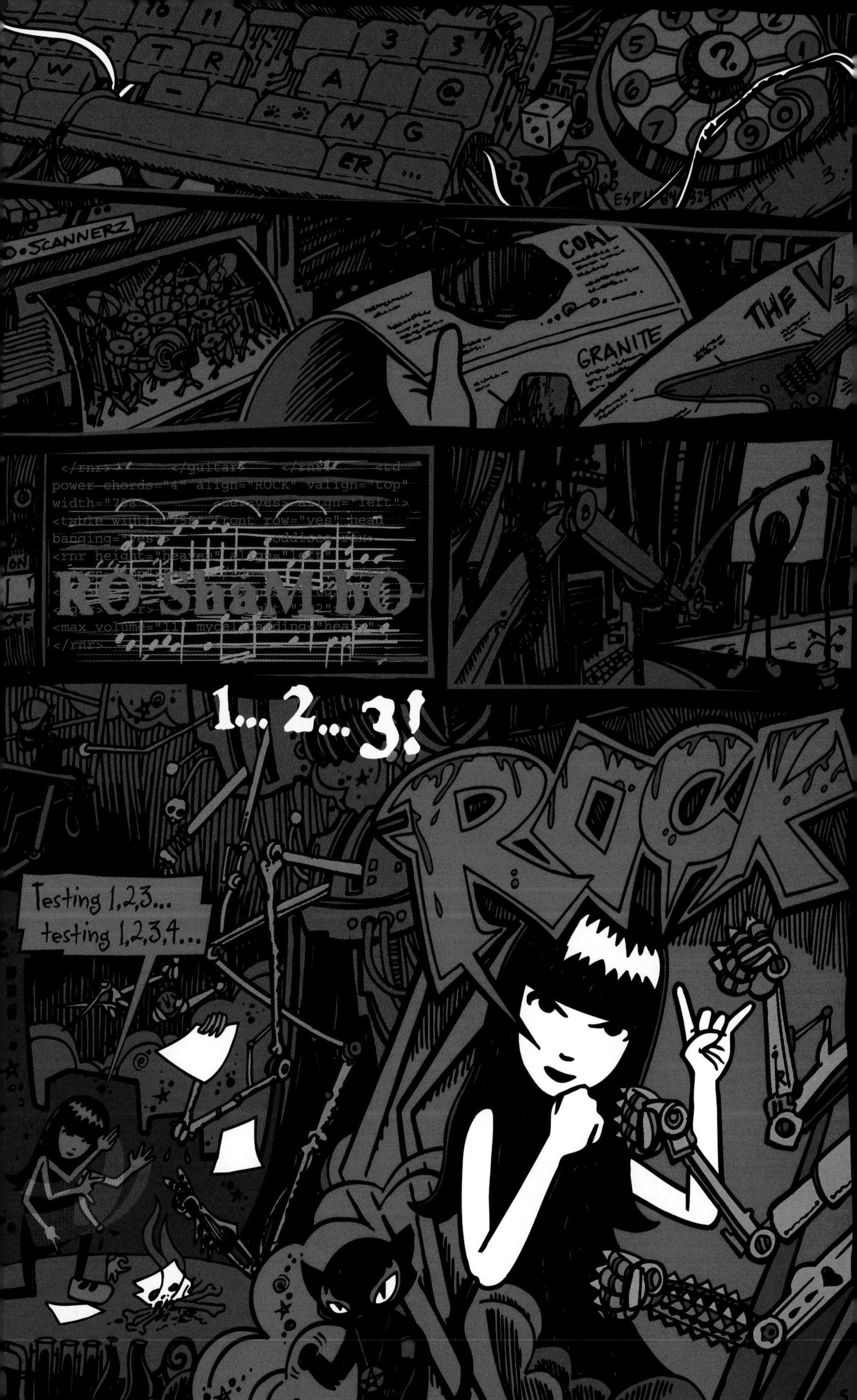
SCANNERZ
COAL
GRANITE
THE V.
power-chords="4" align="ROCK" valign="top"
RO ShaM bO
1... 2... 3!
ROCK
Testing 1,2,3...
testing 1,2,3,4...

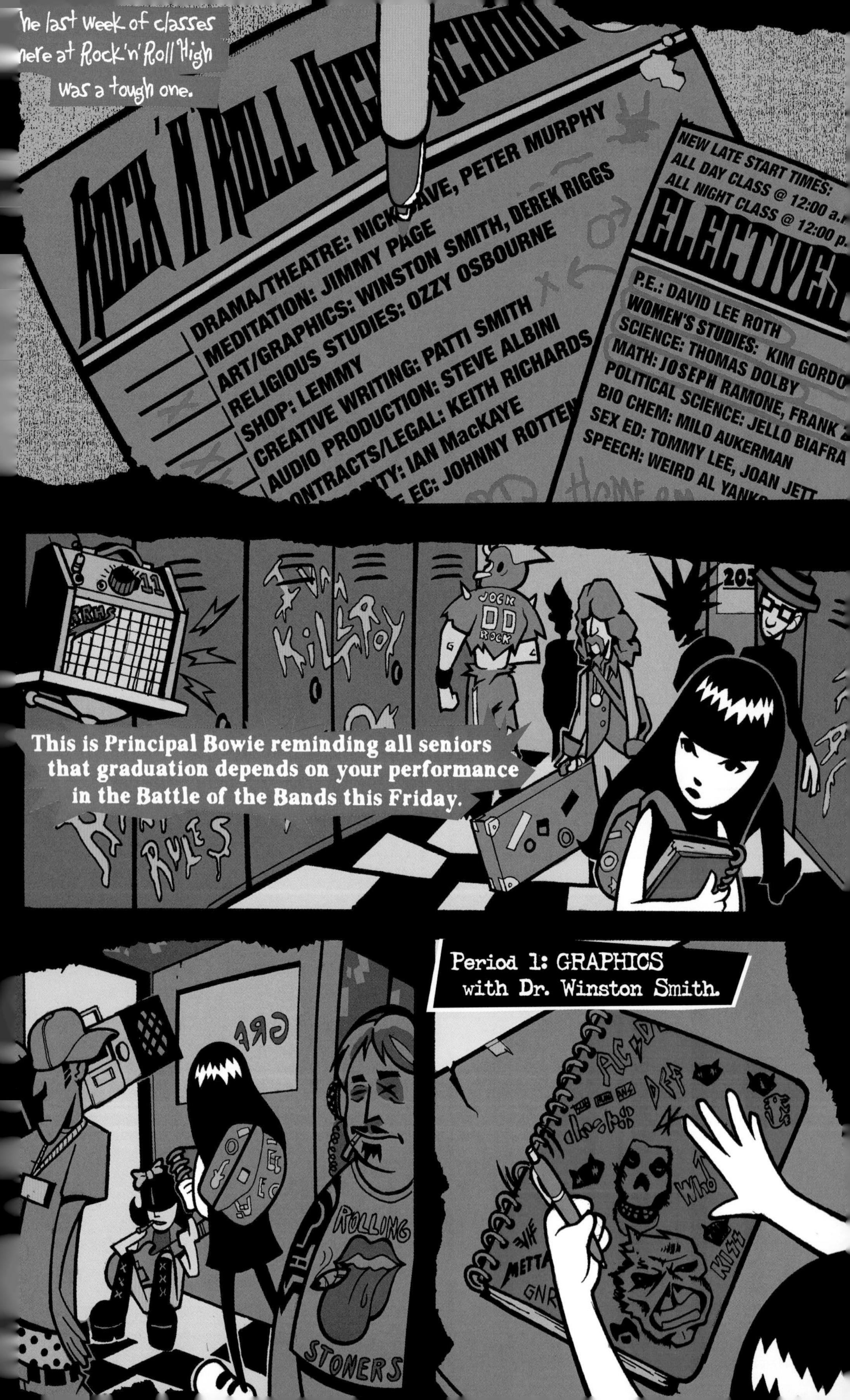

The last week of classes here at Rock'n' Roll High was a tough one.
DRAMA/THEATRE: NICK CAVE, PETER MURPHY
MEDITATION: JIMMY PAGE
ART/GRAPHICS: WINSTON SMITH, DEREK RIGGS
RELIGIOUS STUDIES: OZZY OSBOURNE
SHOP: LEMMY
CREATIVE WRITING: PATTI SMITH
AUDIO PRODUCTION: STEVE ALBINI
CONTRACTS/LEGAL: KEITH RICHARDS
IAN MacKAYE
EC: JOHNNY ROTTEN
NEW LATE START TIMES:
ALL DAY CLASS @ 12:00 a.
ALL NIGHT CLASS @ 12:00 p.
ELECTIVES
P.E.: DAVID LEE ROTH
WOMEN'S STUDIES: KIM GORDO
SCIENCE: THOMAS DOLBY
MATH: JOSEPH RAMONE, FRANK
POLITICAL SCIENCE: JELLO BIAFRA
BIO CHEM: MILO AUKERMAN
SEX ED: TOMMY LEE, JOAN JETT
SPEECH: WEIRD AL YANK
JOCK ROCK
KILLROY
RULES
This is Principal Bowie reminding all seniors that graduation depends on your performance in the Battle of the Bands this Friday.
Period 1: GRAPHICS with Dr. Winston Smith.
ROLLING STONERS
KISS

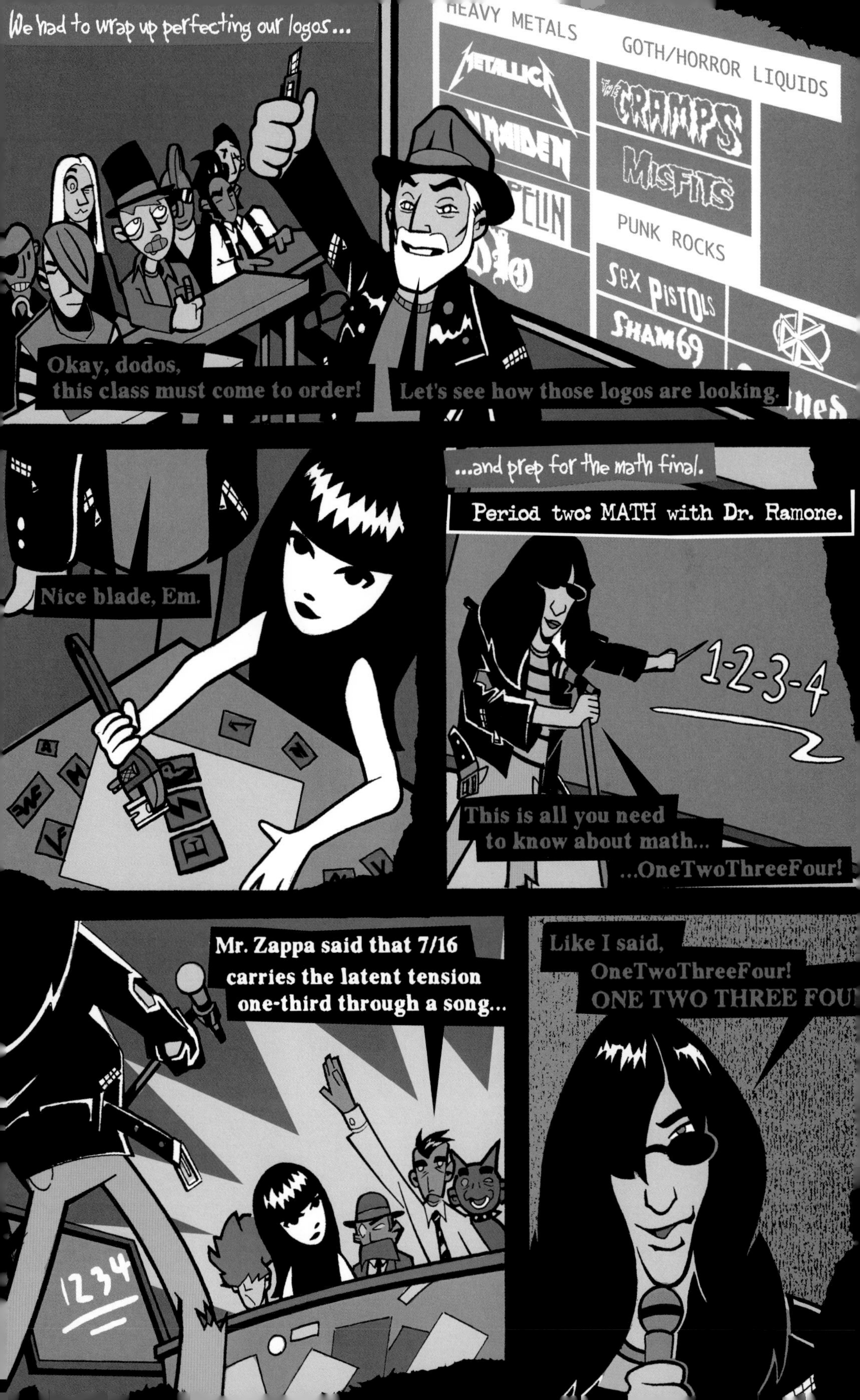
We had to wrap up perfecting our logos...
HEAVY METALS
METALLICA
GOTH/HORROR LIQUIDS
THE CRAMPS
MISFITS
PUNK ROCKS
SEX PISTOLS
SHAM 69
Okay, dodos,
this class must come to order!
Let's see how those logos are looking.
Nice blade, Em.
...and prep for the math final.
Period two: MATH with Dr. Ramone.
1-2-3-4
This is all you need
to know about math...
...OneTwoThreeFour!
Mr. Zappa said that 7/16
carries the latent tension
one-third through a song...
1234
Like I said,
OneTwoThreeFour!
ONE TWO THREE FOU

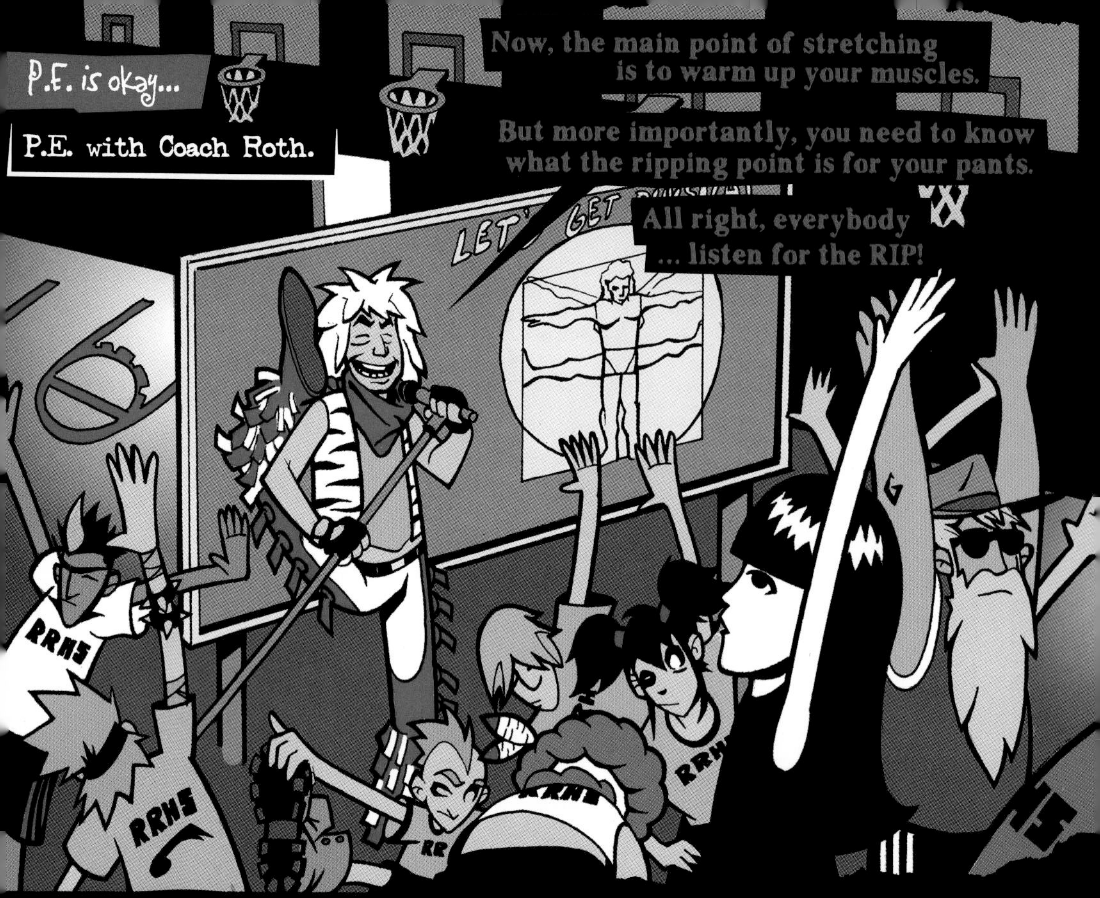
P.E. is okay...
P.E. with Coach Roth.
Now, the main point of stretching is to warm up your muscles.
But more importantly, you need to know what the ripping point is for your pants.
All right, everybody ... listen for the RIP!
RRHS

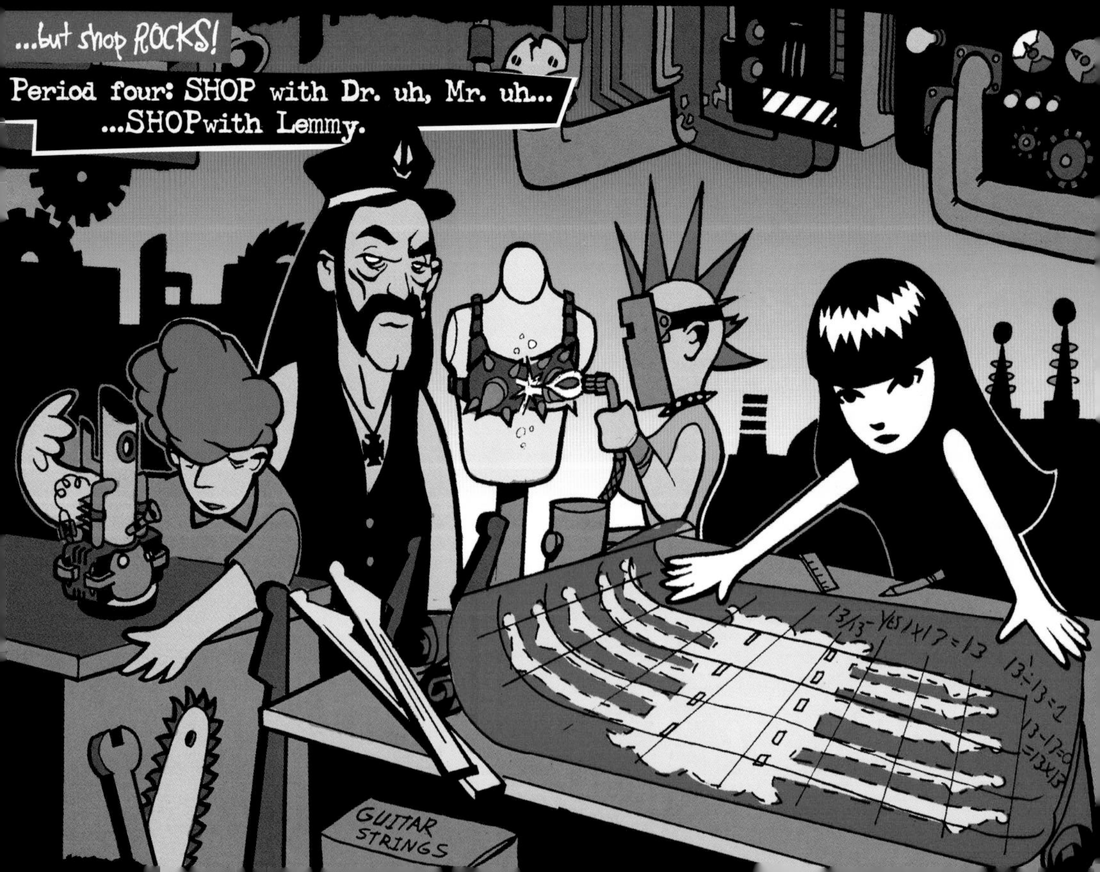
...but shop ROCKS!
Period four: SHOP with Dr. uh, Mr. uh...
...SHOPwith Lemmy.
13/13=YES!×17=13
13÷13=1
13-17=0
=13×13
GUITAR STRINGS

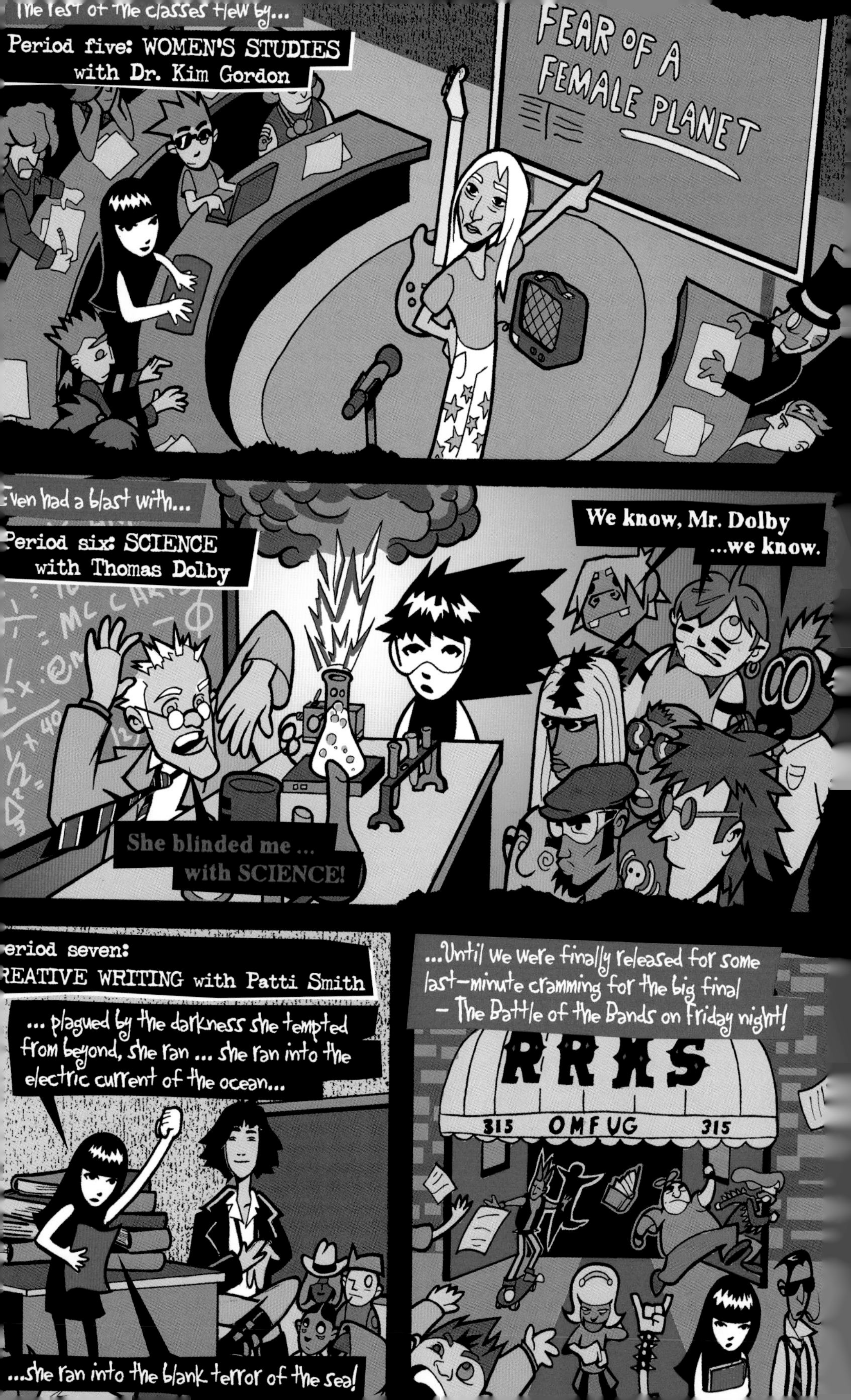
The rest of the classes flew by...
Period five: WOMEN'S STUDIES with Dr. Kim Gordon
FEAR OF A FEMALE PLANET
Even had a blast with...
Period six: SCIENCE with Thomas Dolby
We know, Mr. Dolby ...we know.
She blinded me ... with SCIENCE!
eriod seven: REATIVE WRITING with Patti Smith
... plagued by the darkness she tempted from beyond, she ran ... she ran into the electric current of the ocean...
...she ran into the blank terror of the sea!
...Until we were finally released for some last-minute cramming for the big final – The Battle of the Bands on Friday night!
315 OMFUG 315

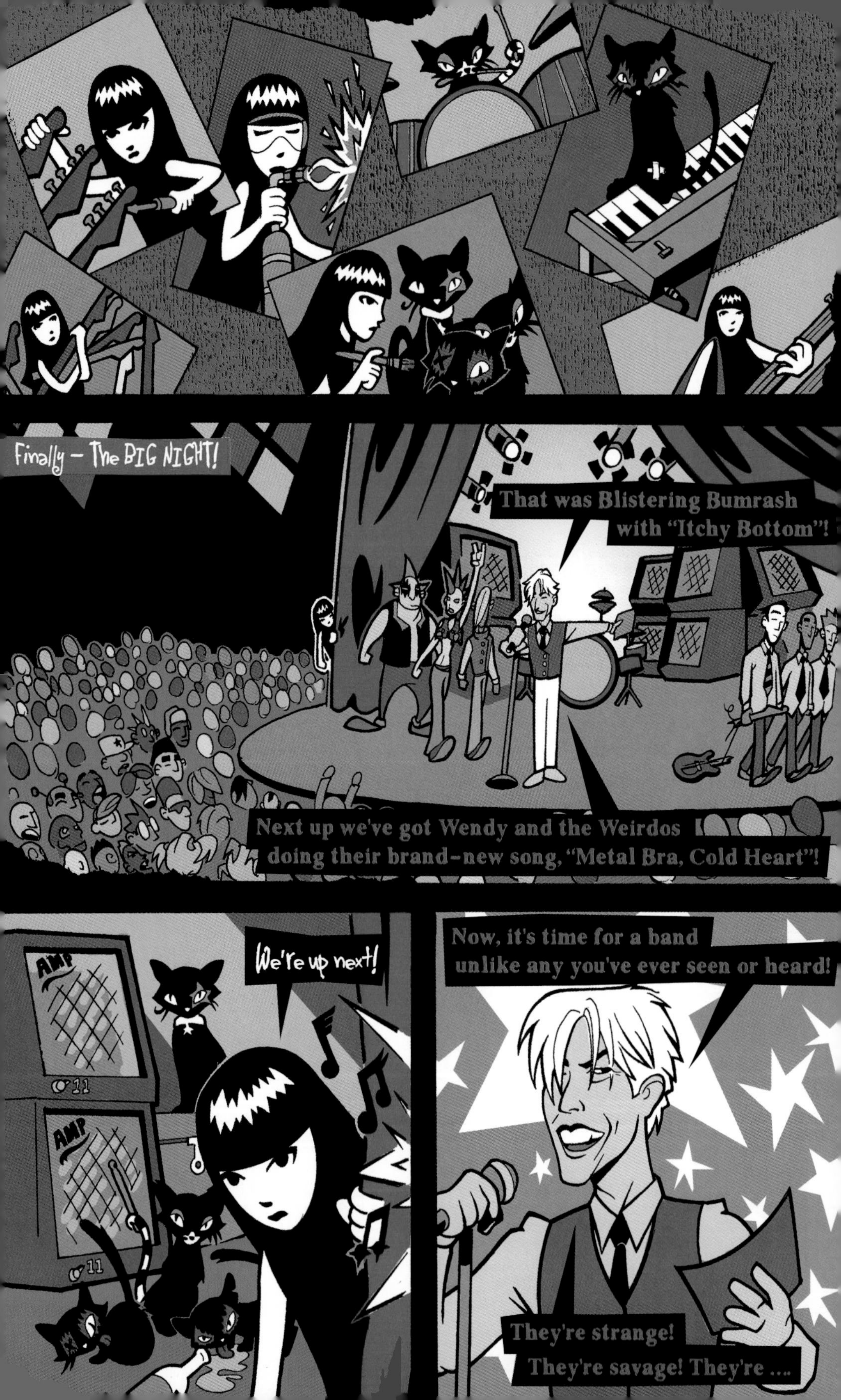
Finally – The BIG NIGHT!
That was Blistering Bumrash with "Itchy Bottom"!
Next up we've got Wendy and the Weirdos doing their brand-new song, "Metal Bra, Cold Heart"!
We're up next!
AMP
11
AMP
11
Now, it's time for a band unlike any you've ever seen or heard!
They're strange!
They're savage! They're ...

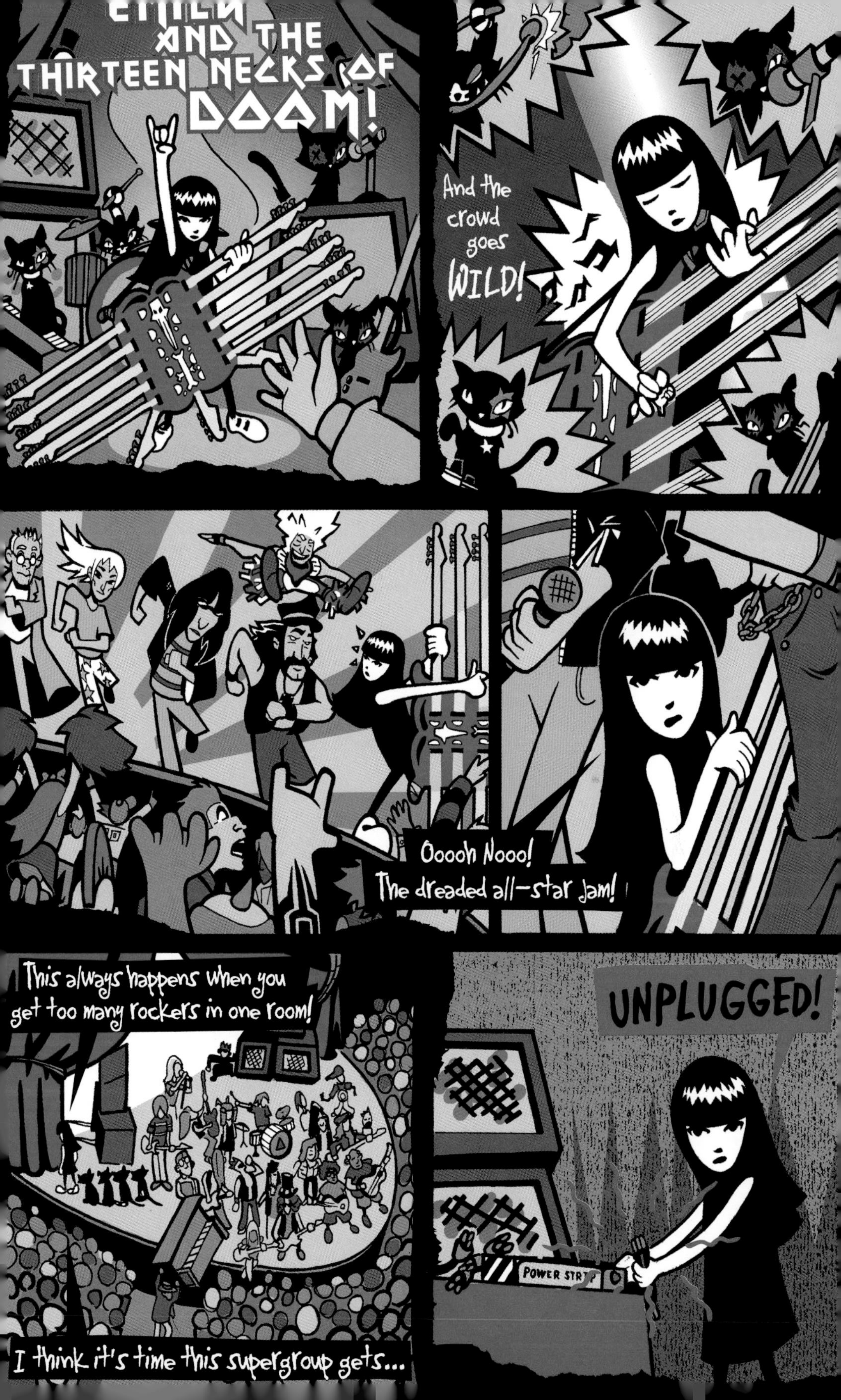
AND THE
THIRTEEN NECKS OF
DOOM!
And the crowd goes WILD!
Ooooh Nooo!
The dreaded all-star jam!
This always happens when you get too many rockers in one room!
I think it's time this supergroup gets...
UNPLUGGED!

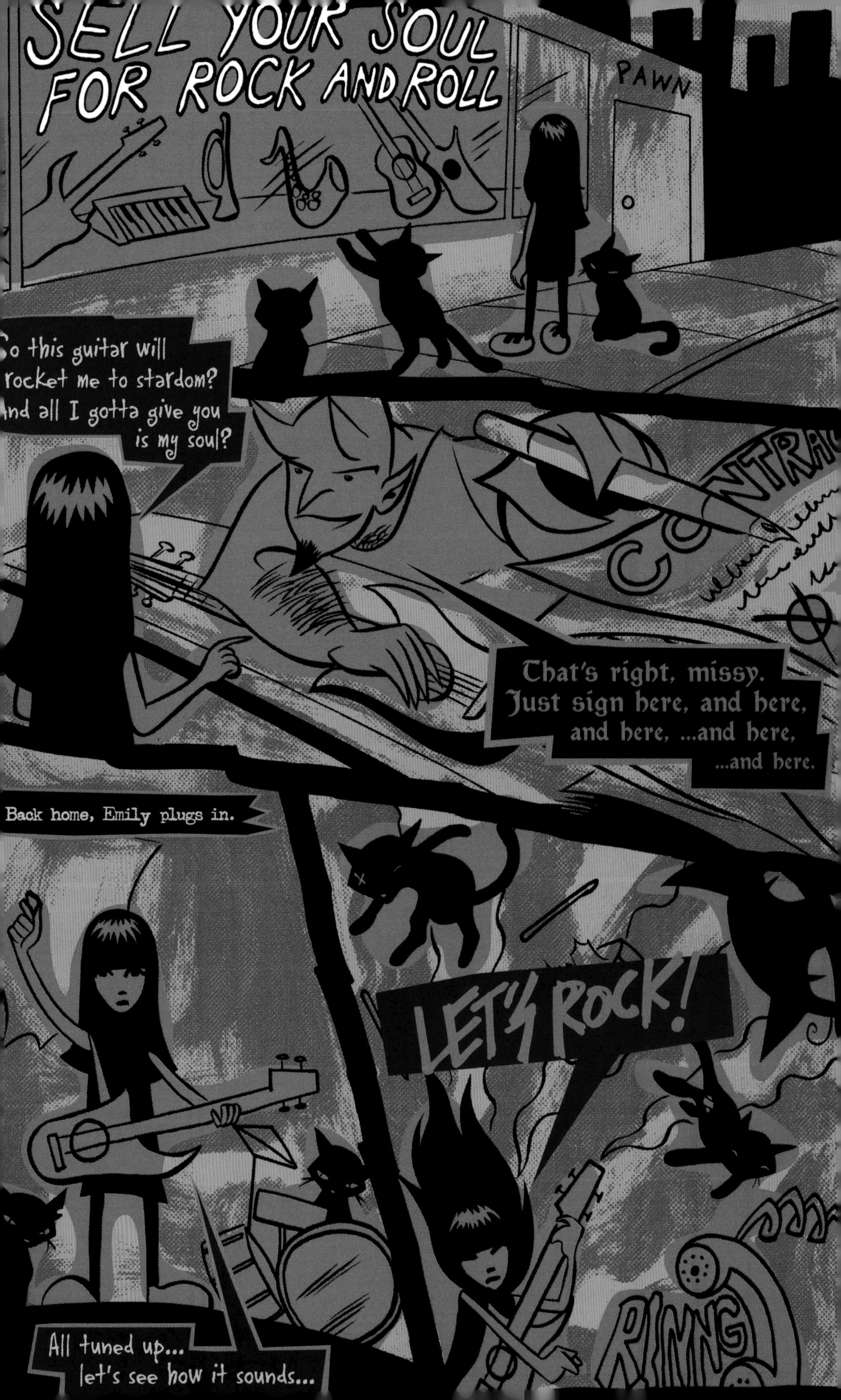
SELL YOUR SOUL FOR ROCK AND ROLL
PAWN
So this guitar will rocket me to stardom? And all I gotta give you is my soul?
CONTRACT
That's right, missy. Just sign here, and here, and here, ...and here, ...and here.
Back home, Emily plugs in.
LET'S ROCK!
RINNG
All tuned up... let's see how it sounds...

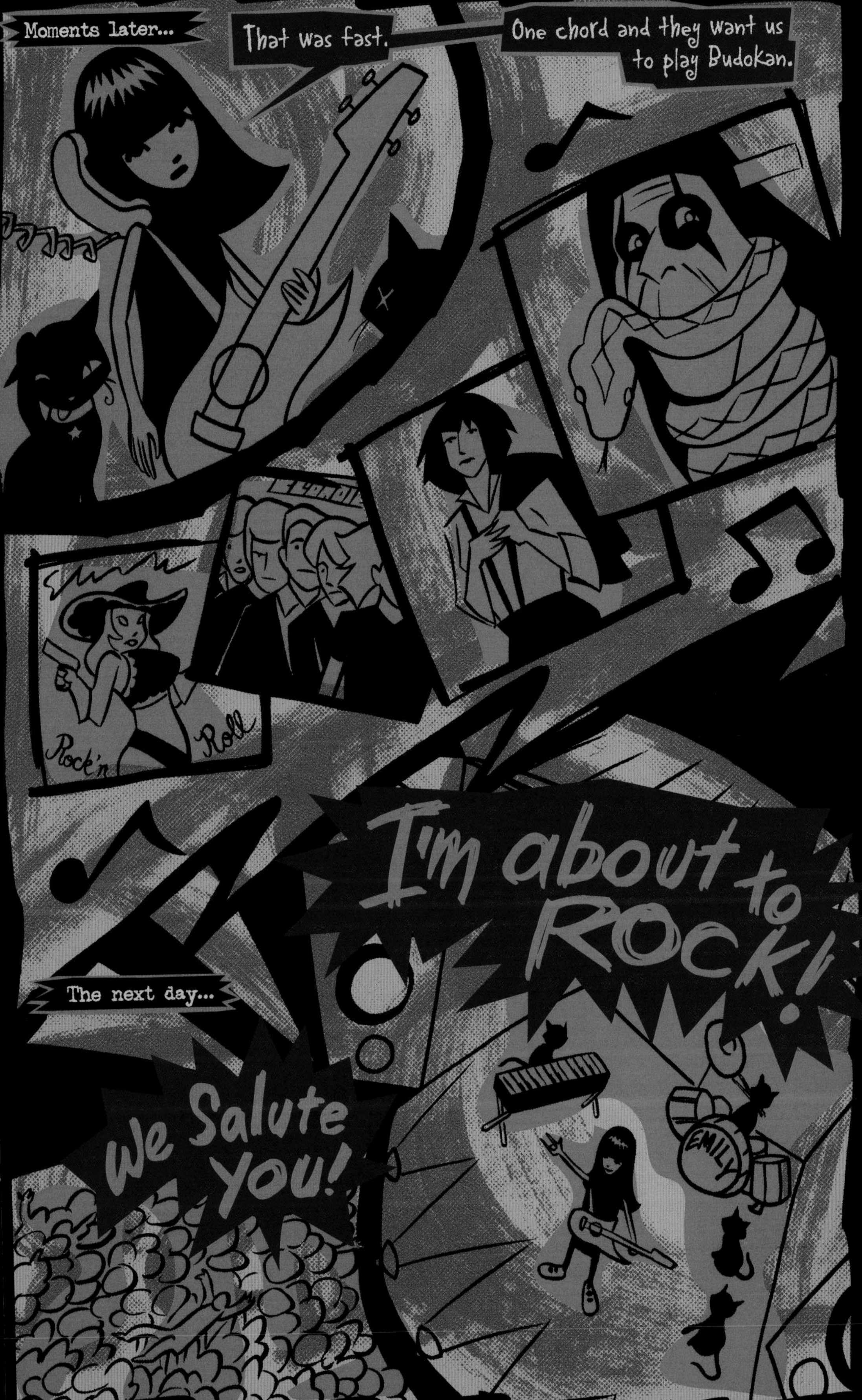
Moments later...
That was fast.
One chord and they want us to play Budokan.
Rock'n Roll
I'm about to ROCK!
The next day...
We Salute you!
EMILY

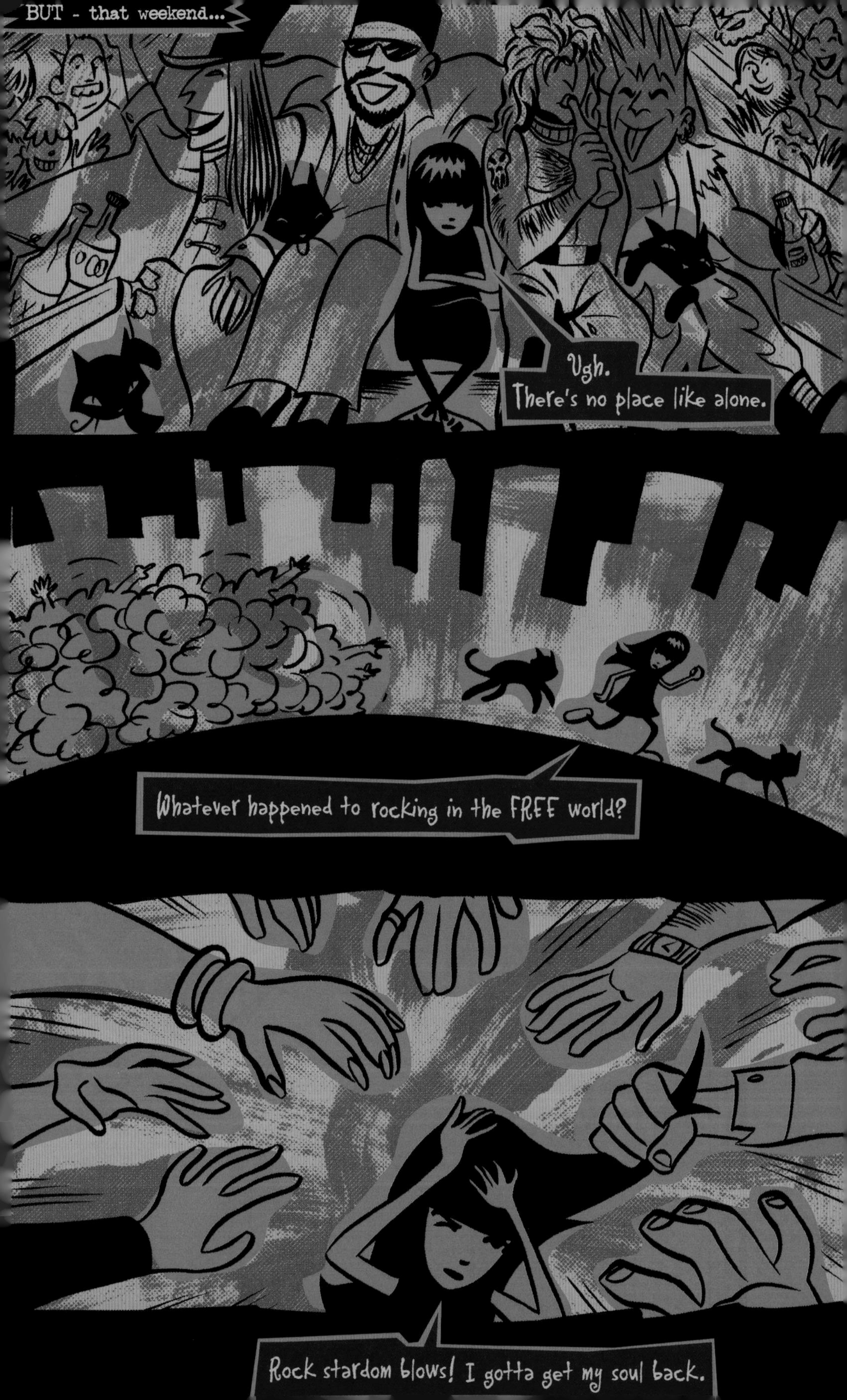

BUT - that weekend...
Ugh.
There's no place like alone.
Whatever happened to rocking in the FREE world?
Rock stardom blows! I gotta get my soul back.

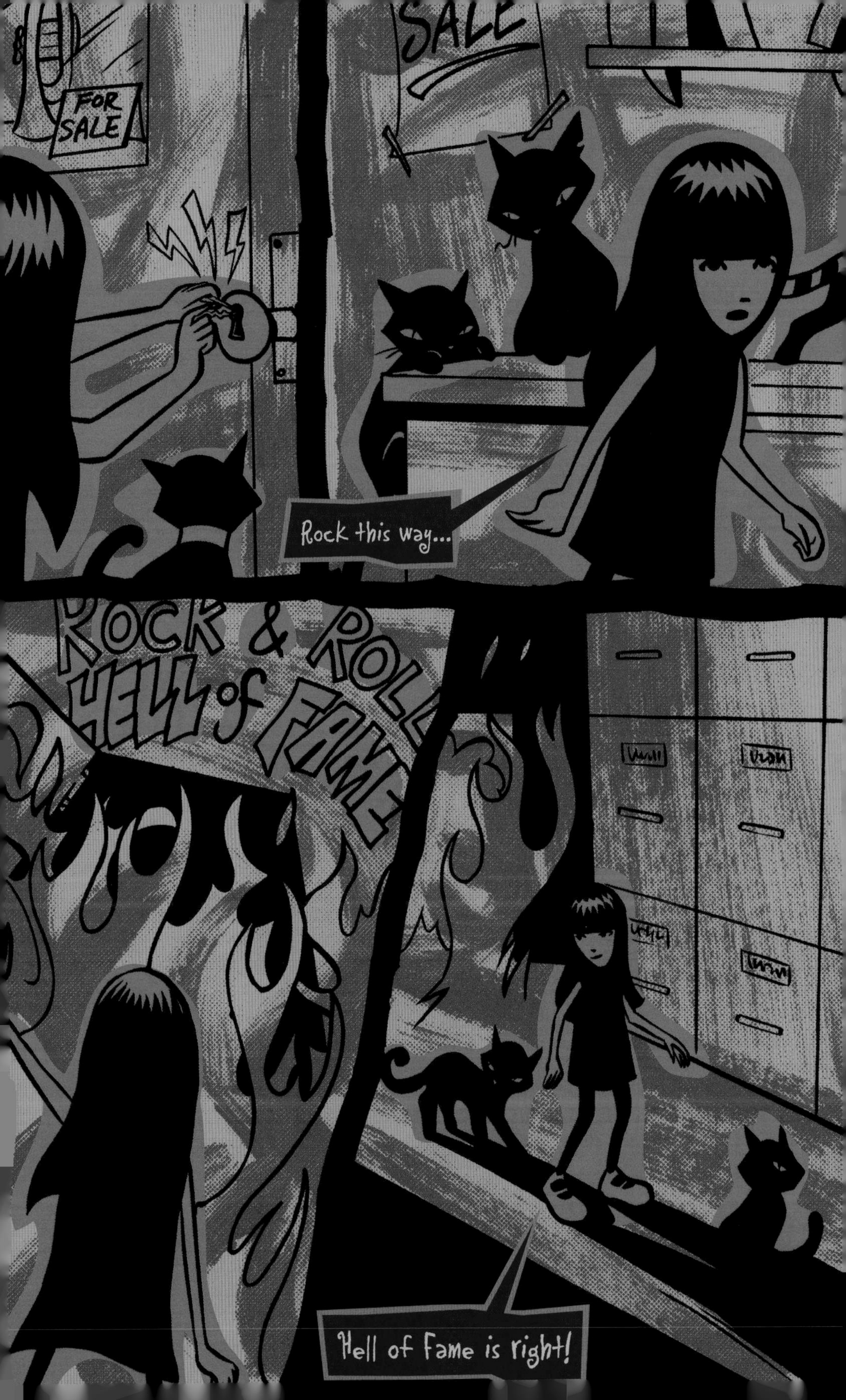
FOR SALE
SALE
Rock this way...
ROCK & ROLL HELL of FAME
Hell of Fame is right!

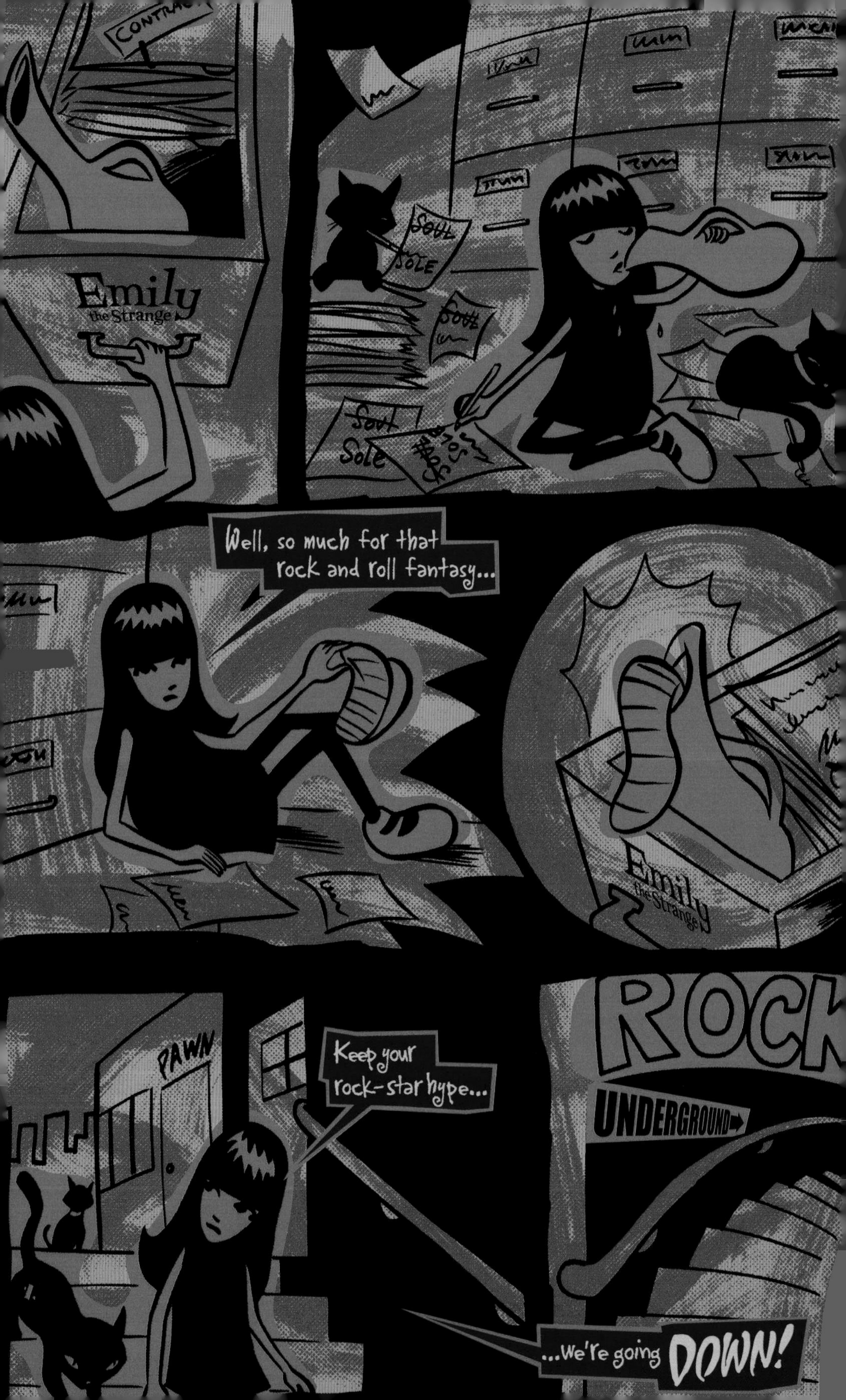
Emily the Strange
SOLE
Well, so much for that rock and roll fantasy...
PAWN
Keep your rock-star hype...
ROCK
UNDERGROUND
...we're going DOWN!

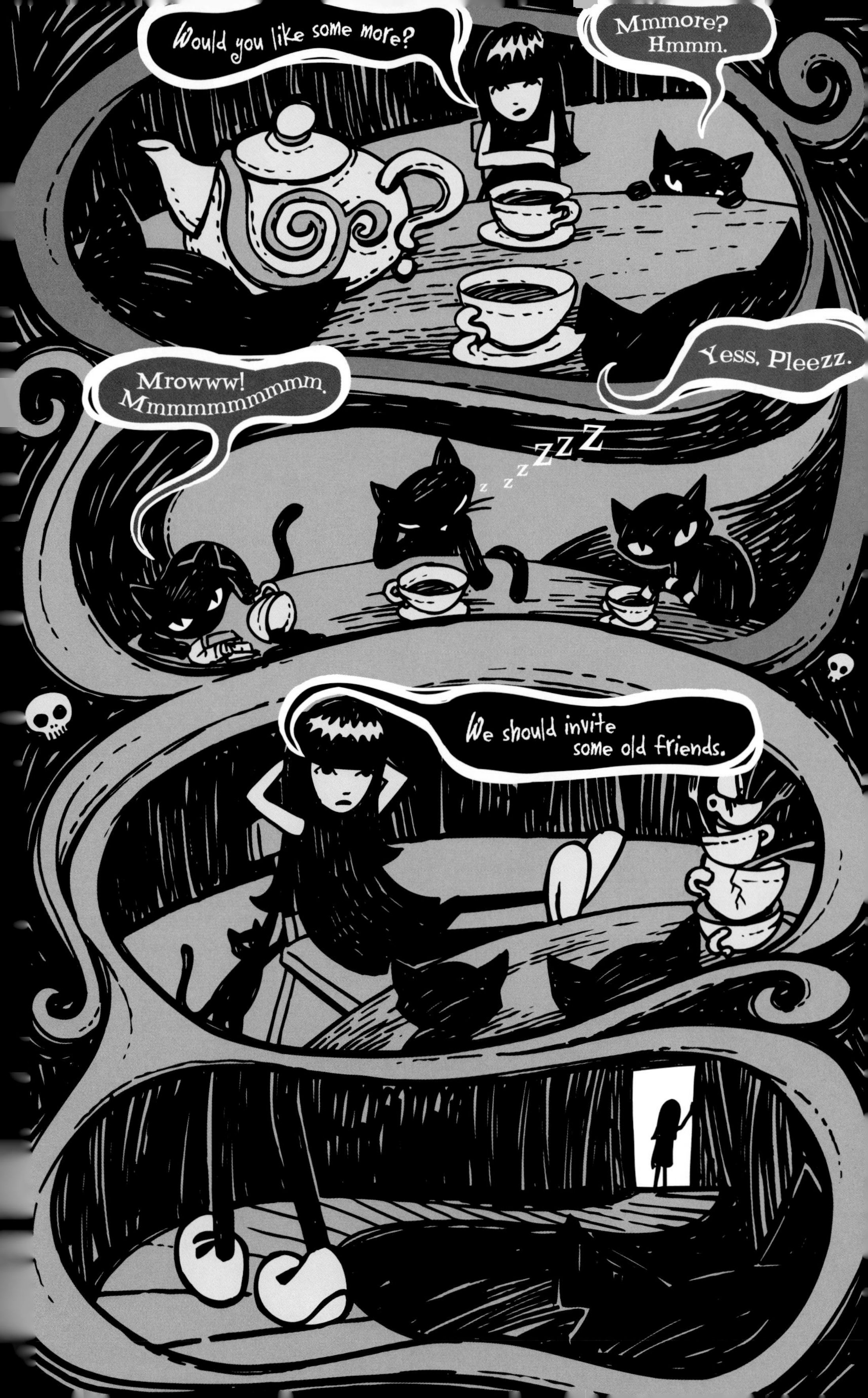
Would you like some more?
Mmmore? Hmmm.
Yess. Pleezz.
Mrowww! Mmmmmmmmm.
zzzZZZ
We should invite some old friends.

DINNER GHOSTS

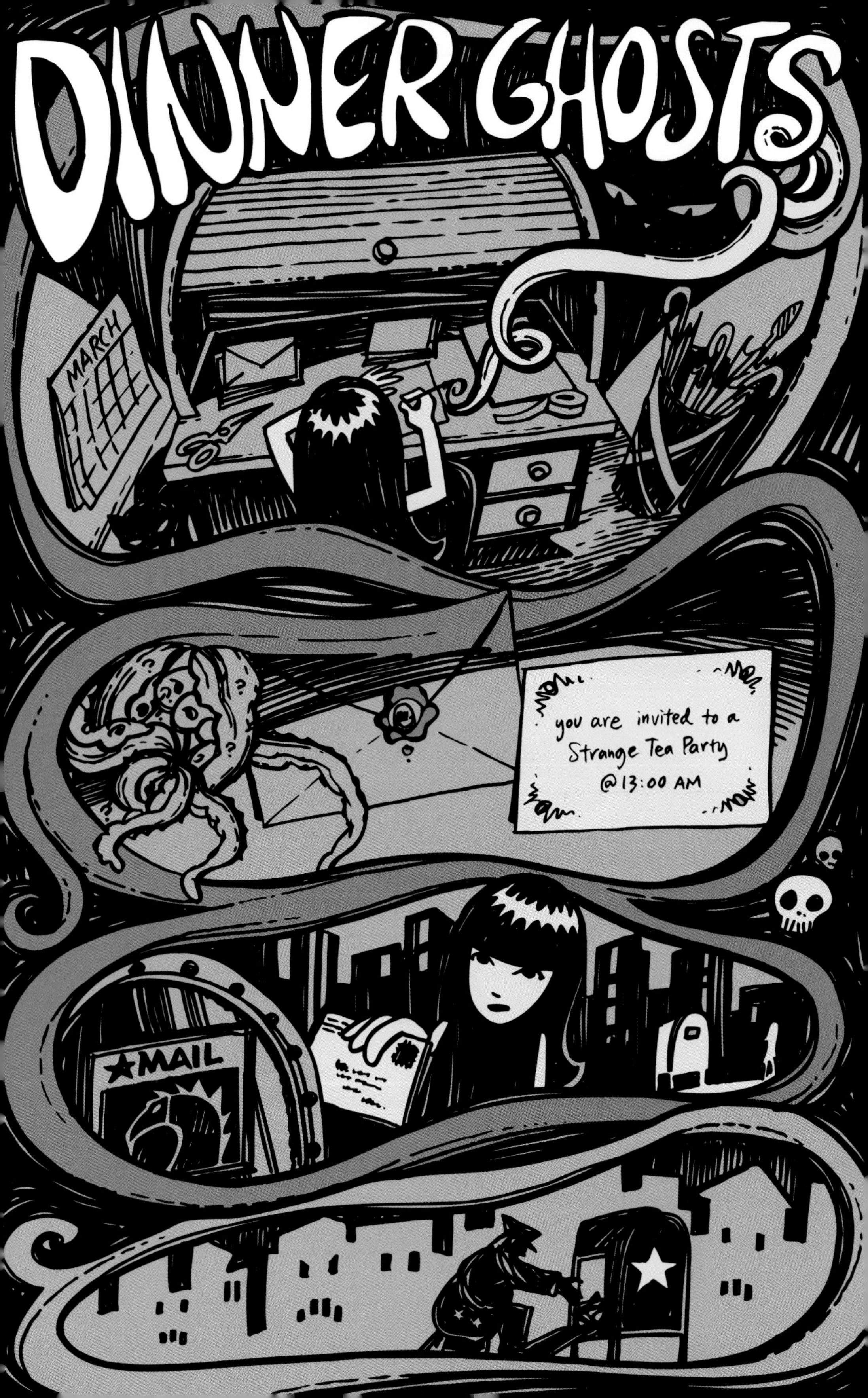

MARCH
you are invited to a
Strange Tea Party
@13:00 AM
MAIL

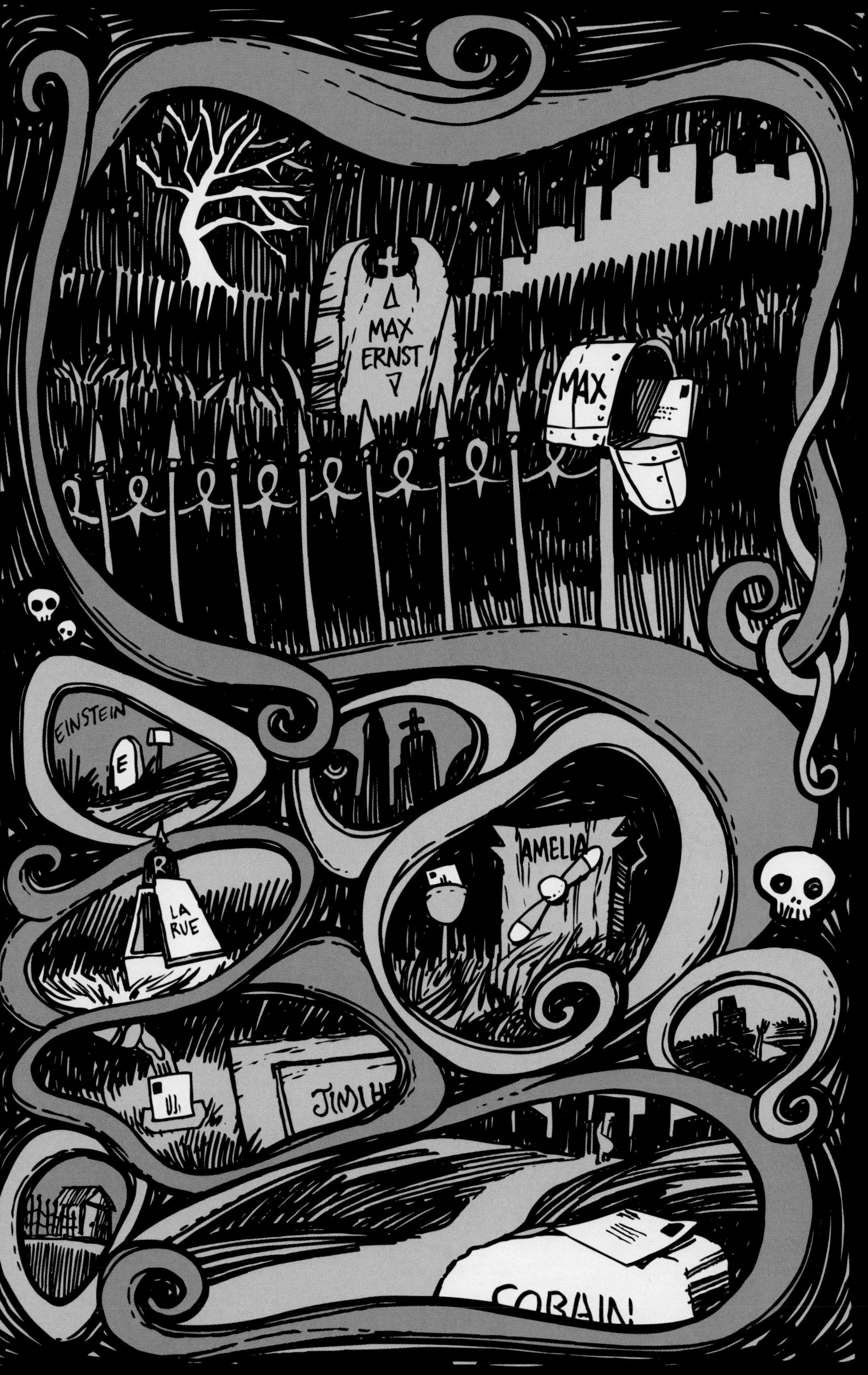
MAX
ERNST
MAX
EINSTEIN
E
LA
RUE
AMELIA
COBAIN

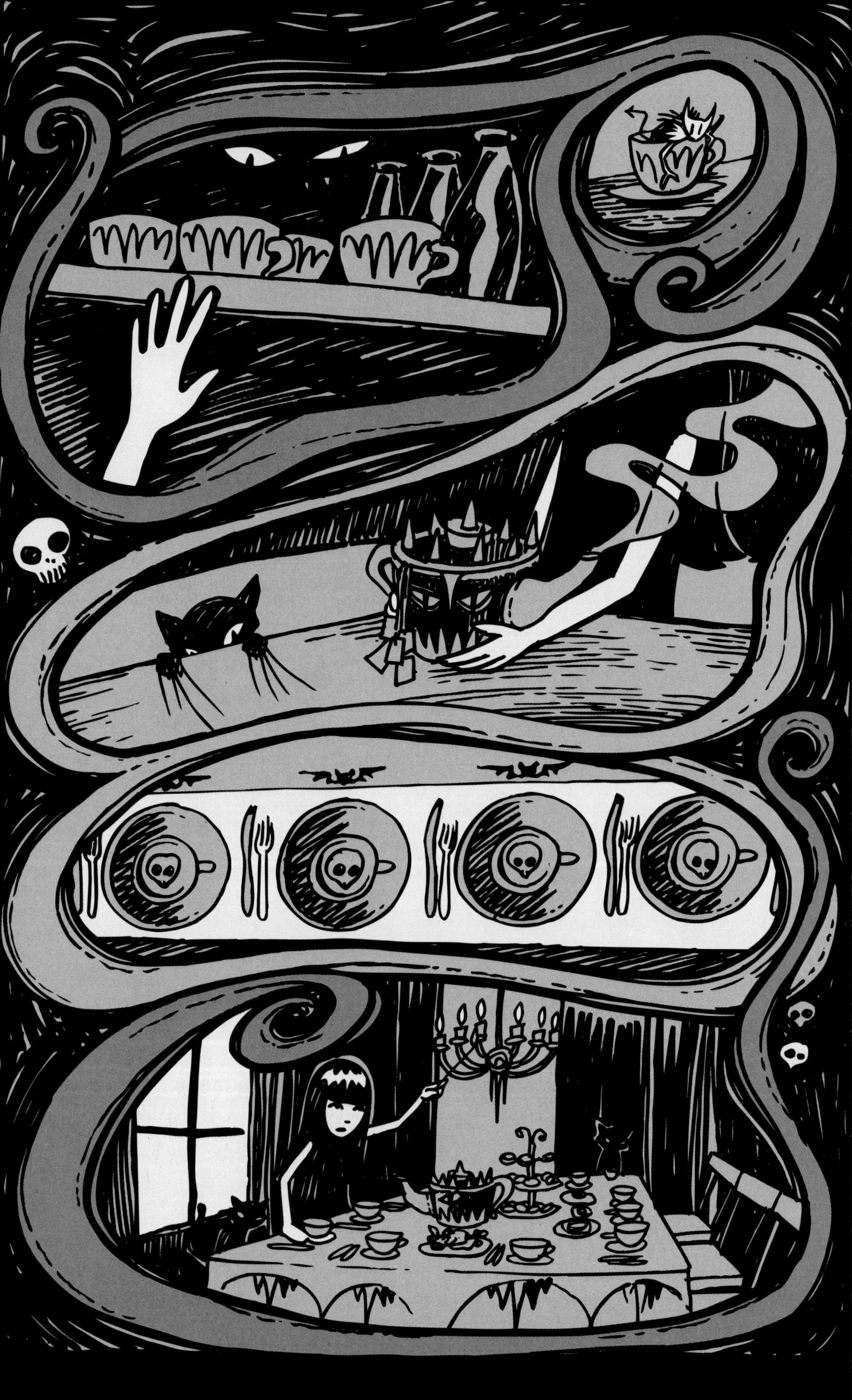

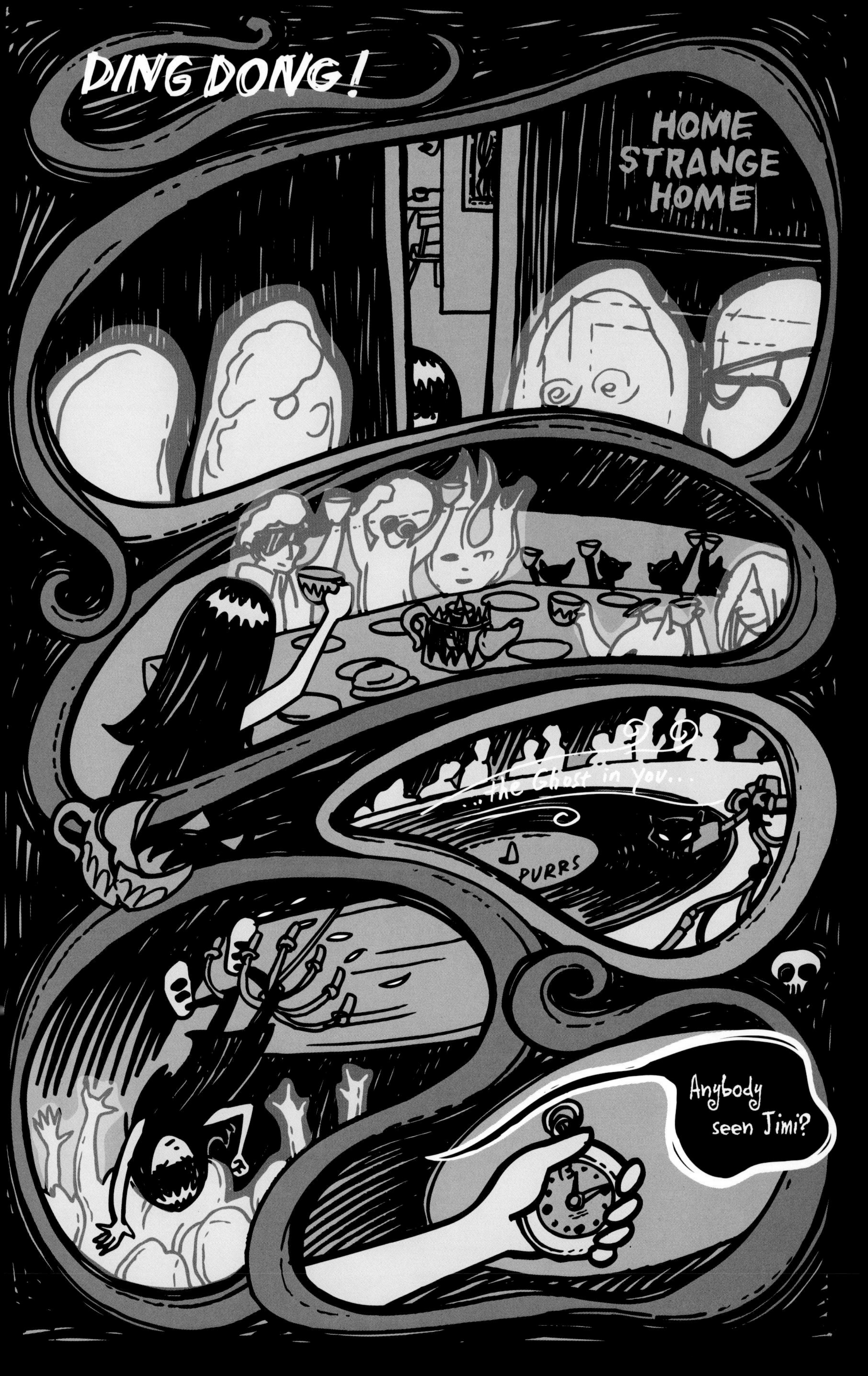
DING DONG!
HOME STRANGE HOME
...the Ghost in you...
PURRS
Anybody seen Jimi?

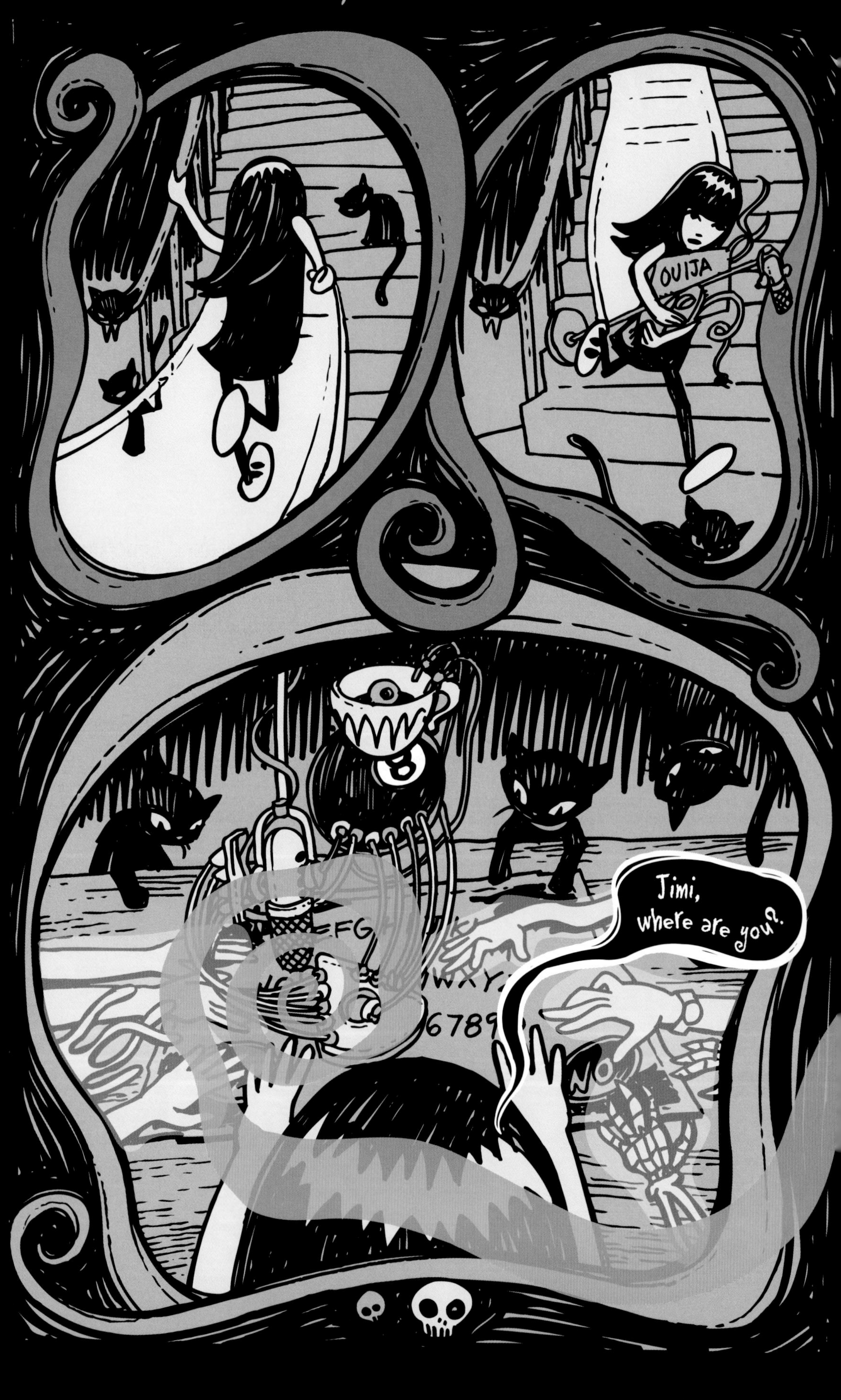
OUIJA
Jimi, where are you?

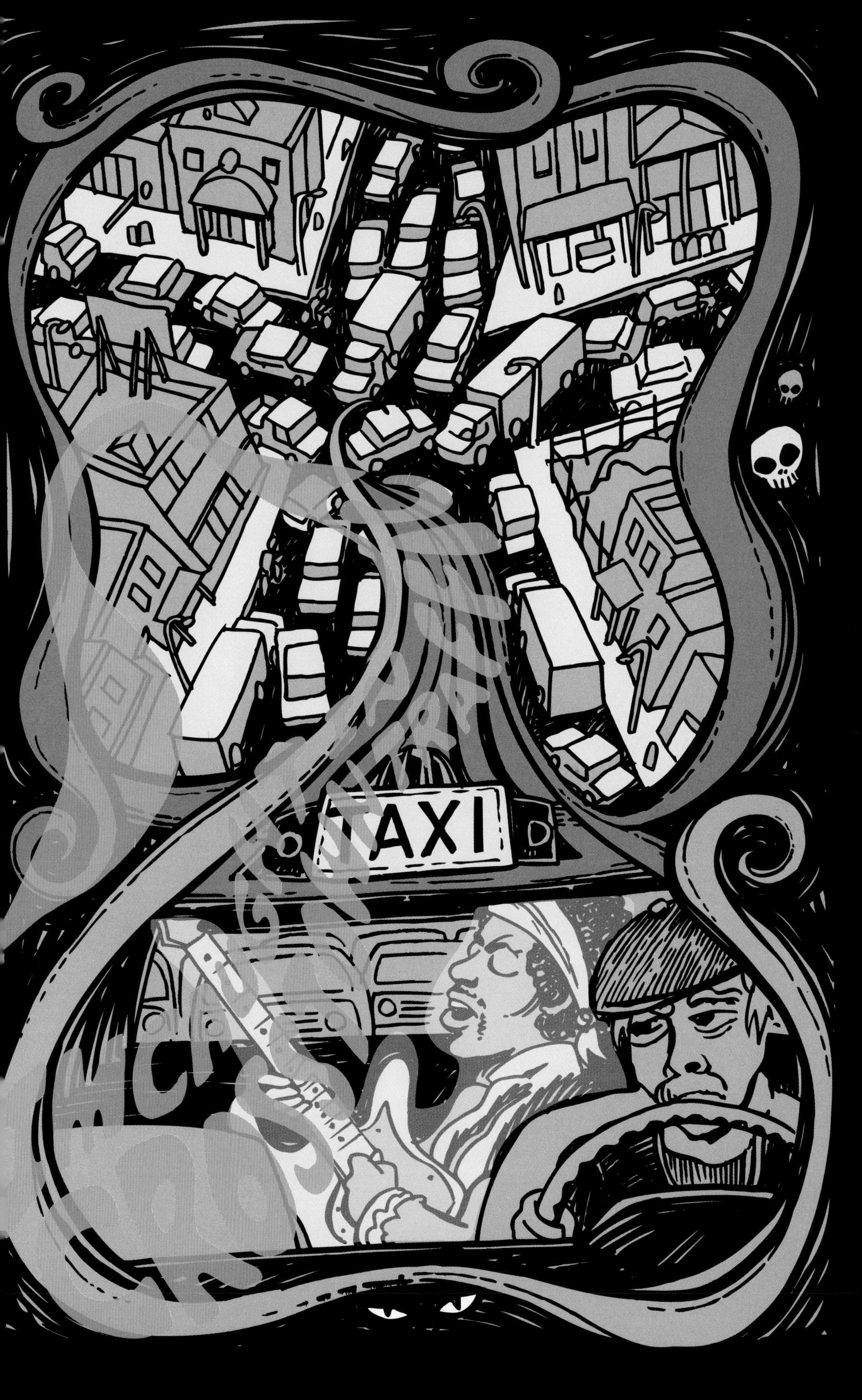
TAXI

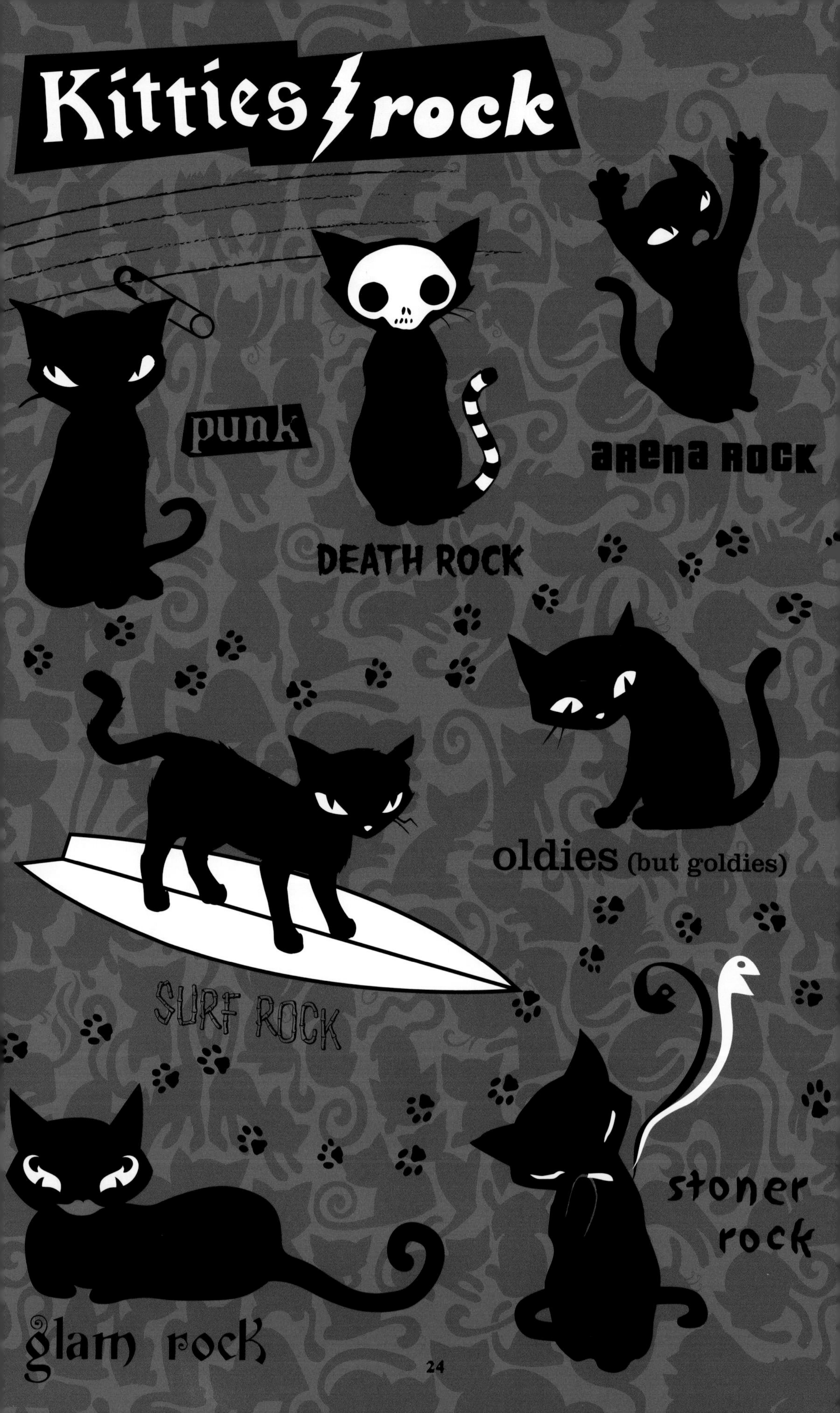
Kitties rock
punk
DEATH ROCK
arena ROCK
oldies (but goldies)
SURF ROCK
glam rock
stoner rock

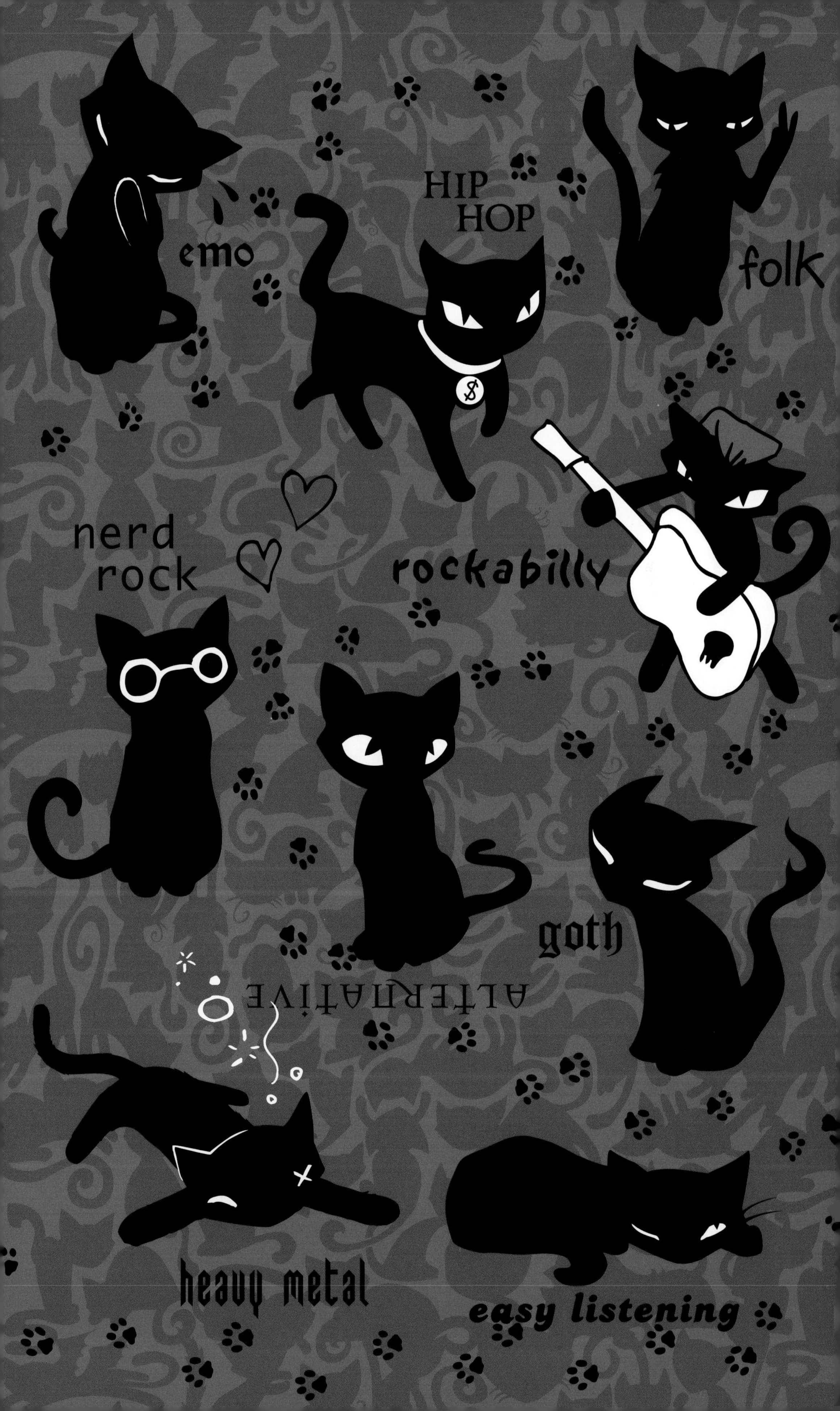
emo
HIP HOP
folk
nerd rock
rockabilly
goth
alternative
heavy metal
easy listening

EMILY ROCKS

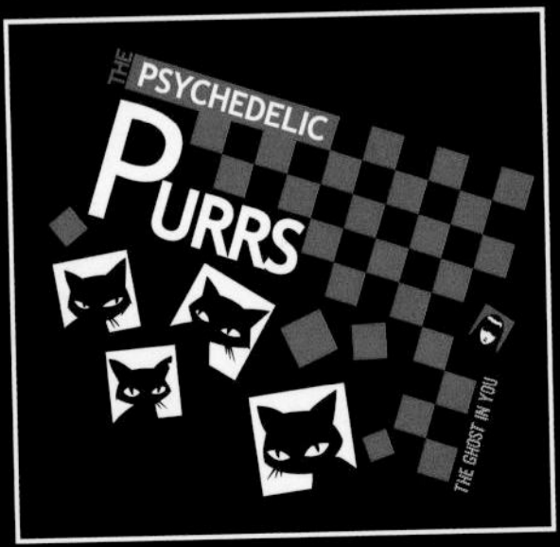
THE PSYCHEDELIC
PURRS
THE GHOST IN YOU

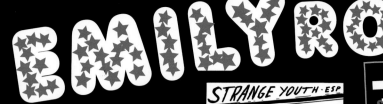

Psychedelic Purrs
"The Ghost in You"

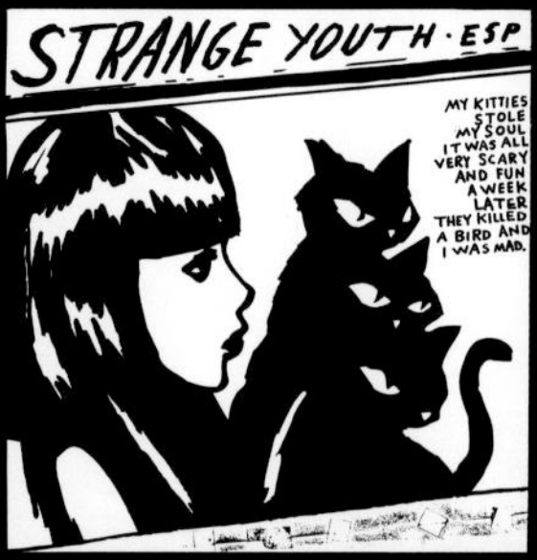
STRANGE YOUTH · ESP
MY KITTIES STOLE MY SOUL IT WAS ALL VERY SCARY AND FUN A WEEK LATER THEY KILLED A BIRD AND I WAS MAD.

Strange Youth
"ESP"

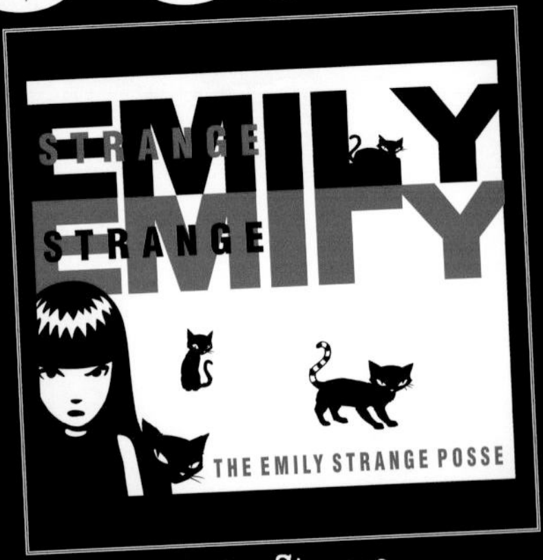
STRANGE
EMILY
STRANGE
EMILY
THE EMILY STRANGE POSSE

Emily Strange
"Stranger with Candy"

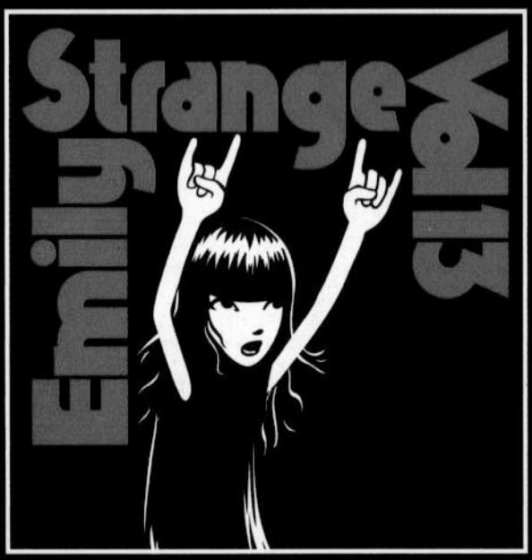
Emily Strange Vol 13

Emily Strange
"Volume 13"

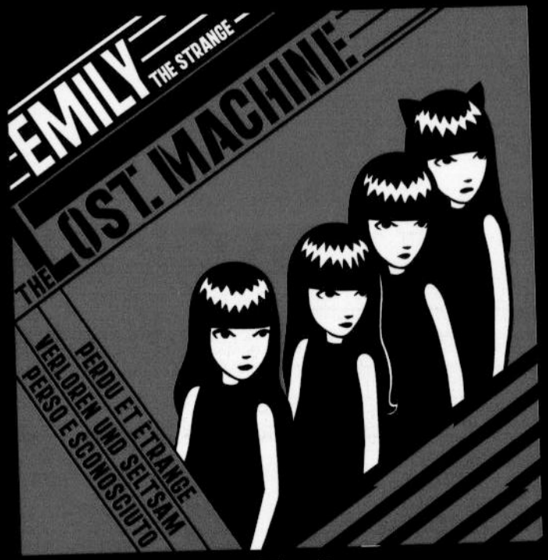
EMILY THE STRANGE
THE LOST MACHINE
PERDU ET ETRANGE
VERLOREN UND SELTSAM
PERSO E SCONOSCIUTO

The Emilys
"The Lost Machine"

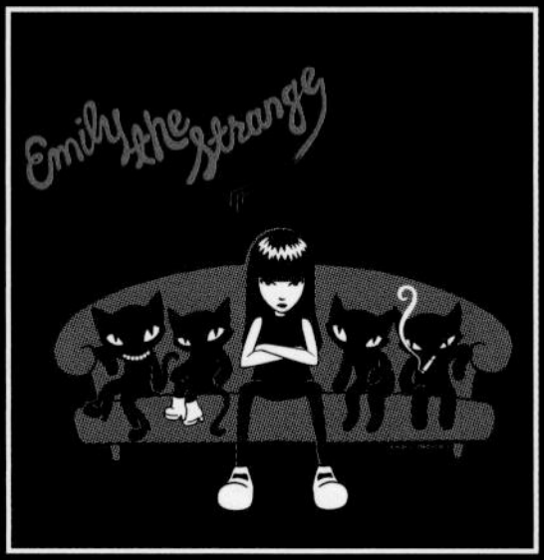
Emily the Strange

Emily the Strange
"New York Paws"

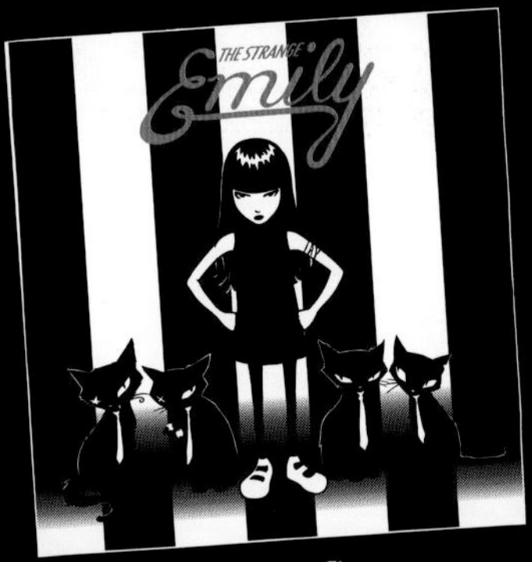
THE STRANGE
Emily

Emily the Strange
"Parallel Felines"

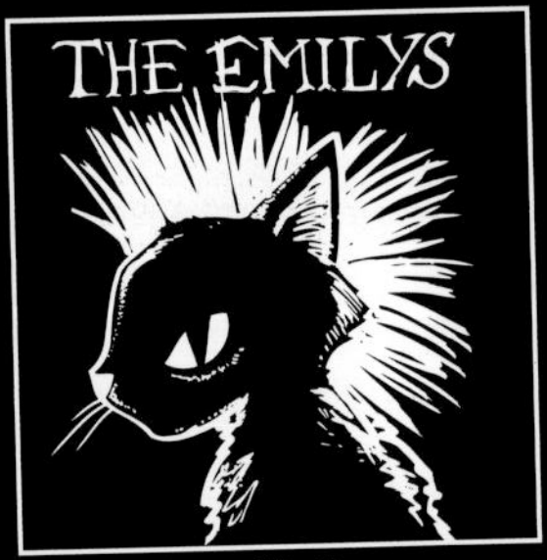
THE EMILYS

The Emilys
"Strange Not Dead"

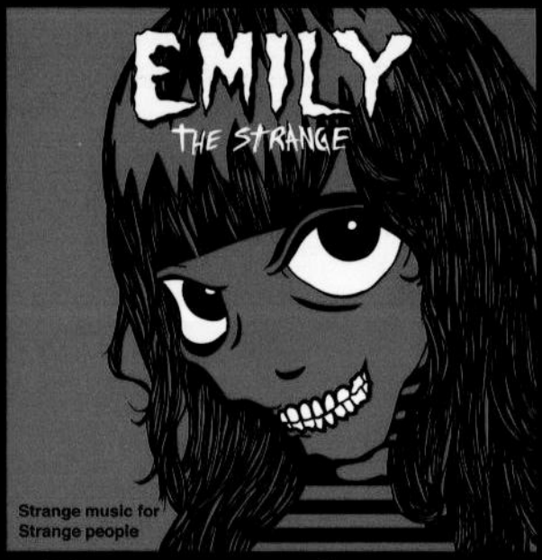
EMILY
THE STRANGE
Strange music for
Strange people

Emily the Strange
"Strange Music for
Strange People"

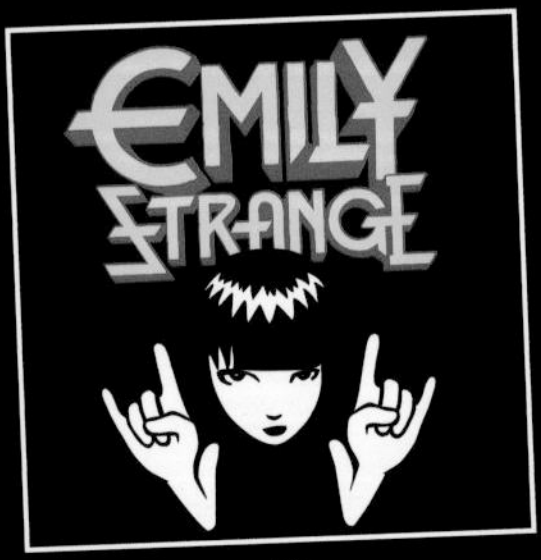
EMILY
STRANGE

Emily Strange
"Crazy Strange"

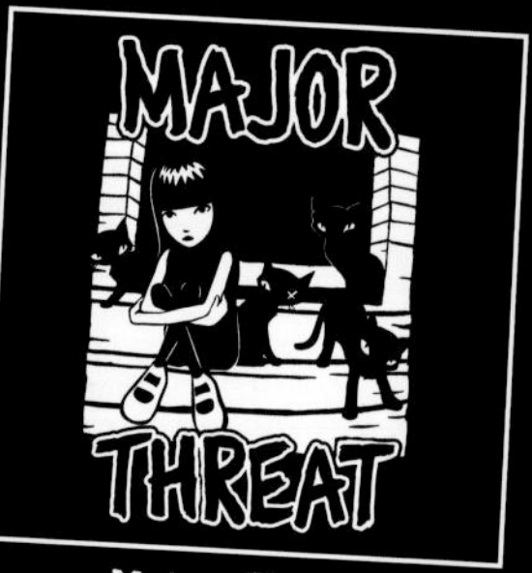
MAJOR
THREAT

Major Threat
"Strange Days"

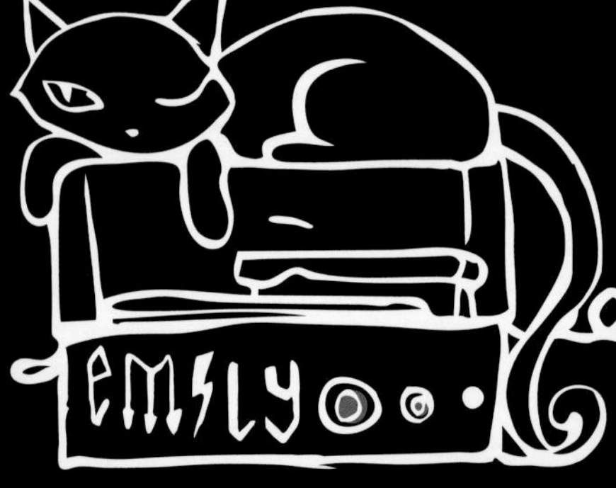
EMILY

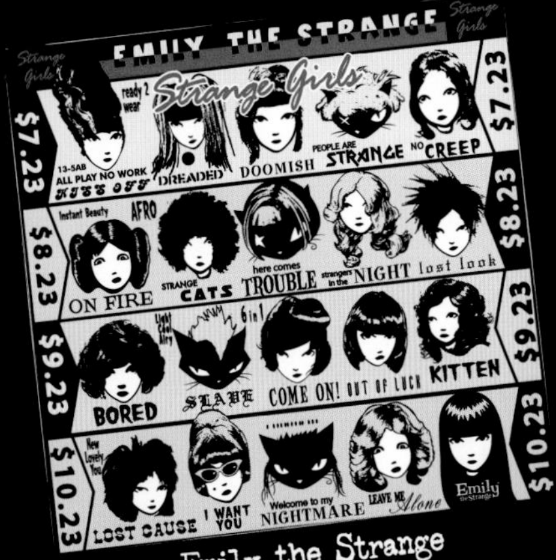
EMILY THE STRANGE
Strange Girls
$7.23
$8.23
$9.23
$10.23
ready 2 wear
DOOMISH
PEOPLE ARE STRANGE
NO CREEP
ALL PLAY NO WORK
DREADED
Instant Beauty
AFRO
ON FIRE
STRANGE CATS
here comes TROUBLE
strangers in the NIGHT
lost look
BORED
SLAVE
6 in 1
COME ON!
OUT OF LUCK
KITTEN
LOST CAUSE
I WANT YOU
Welcome to my NIGHTMARE
LEAVE ME Alone

Emily the Strange
"Strange Girls"

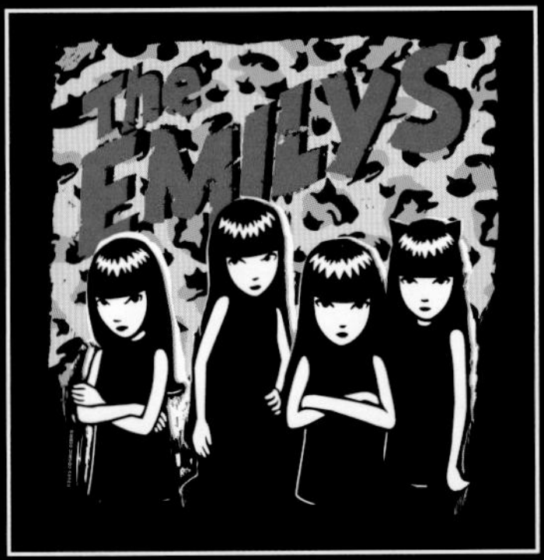
The EMILYS

The Emilys
"The Emilys"

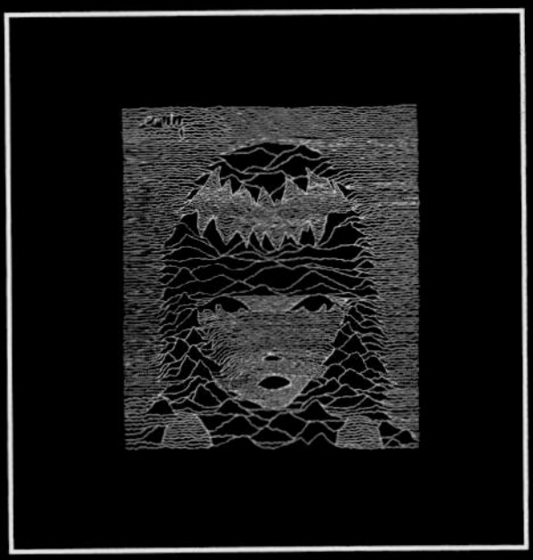

Emily the Strange
"Unknown Stranger"

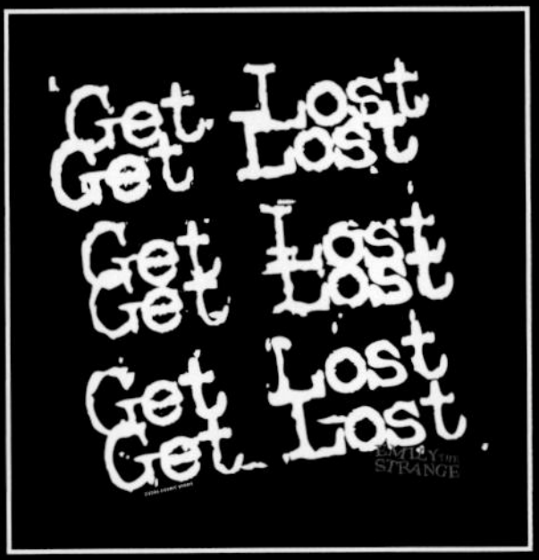
Get Lost
Get Lost
Get Lost
Get Lost
Get Lost
Get Lost

Emily the Strange
"Get Lost" EP

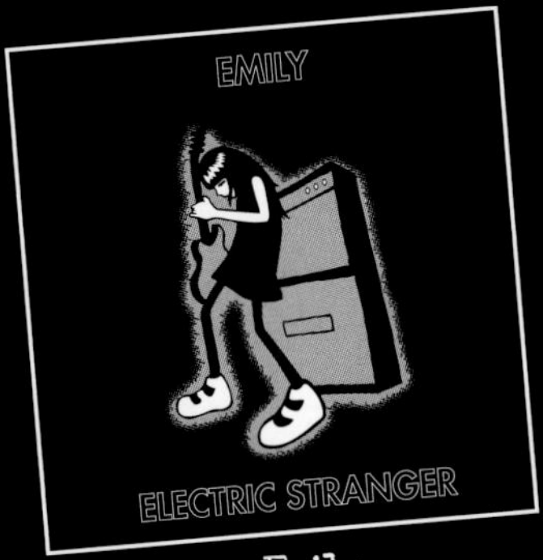
EMILY
ELECTRIC STRANGER

Emily
"Electric Stranger"

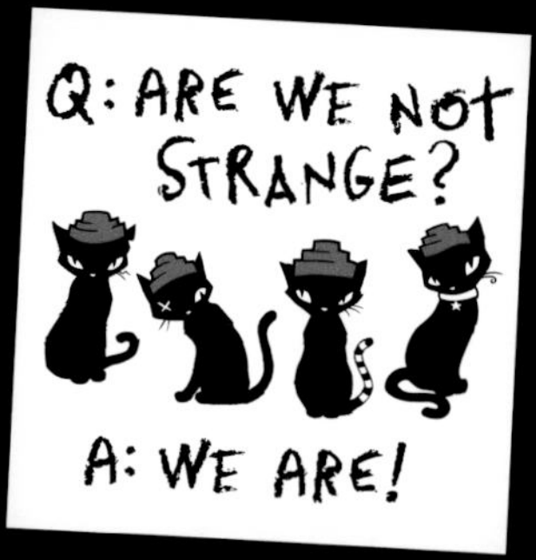
Q: ARE WE NOT STRANGE?
A: WE ARE!

Emily Strange Posse
"Are We Not Strange?"

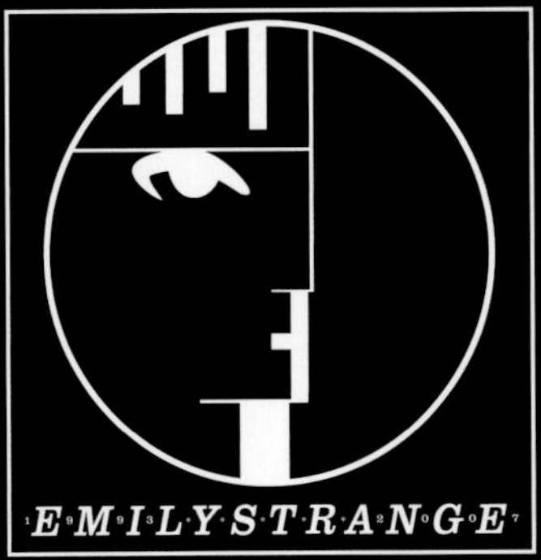
E·M·I·L·Y·S·T·R·A·N·G·E

Emily Strange
"Boo House 1993-2007"

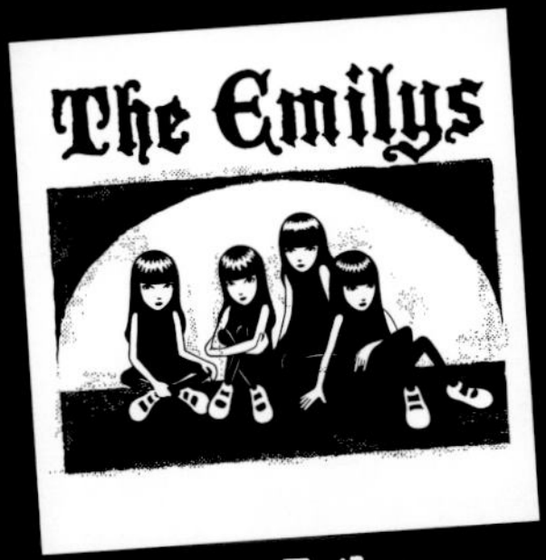
The Emilys

The Emilys
"Strange but Not Forgotten"

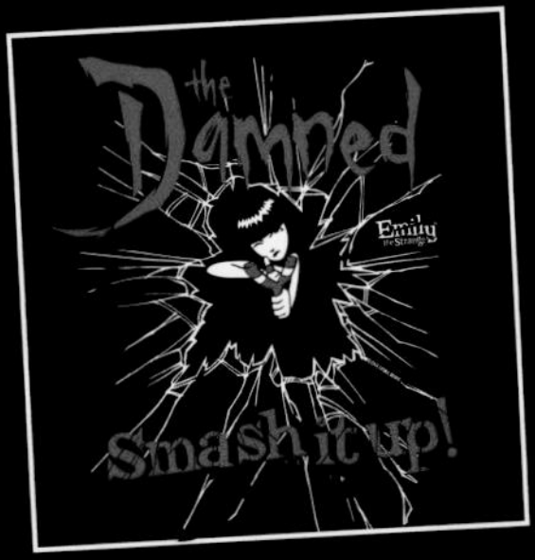
the Damned
Smash it up!

The Damned
featuring Emily the Strange
"Smash It Up"

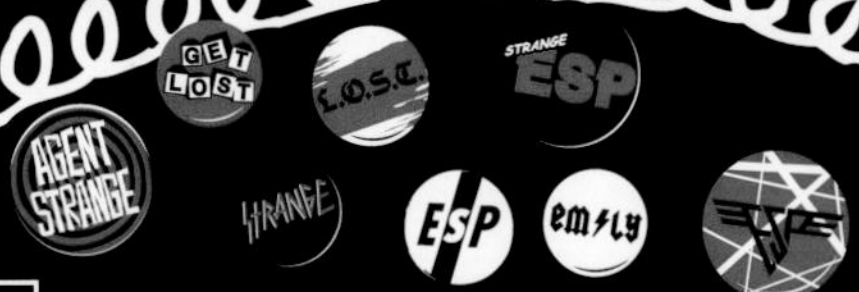
GET LOST
L.O.S.T.
STRANGE ESP
AGENT STRANGE
STRANGE
ESP
emily

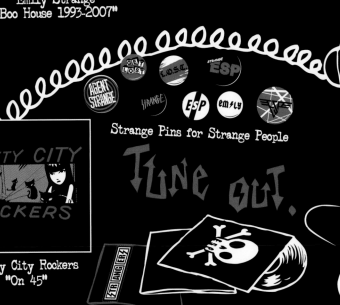

Strange Pins for Strange People

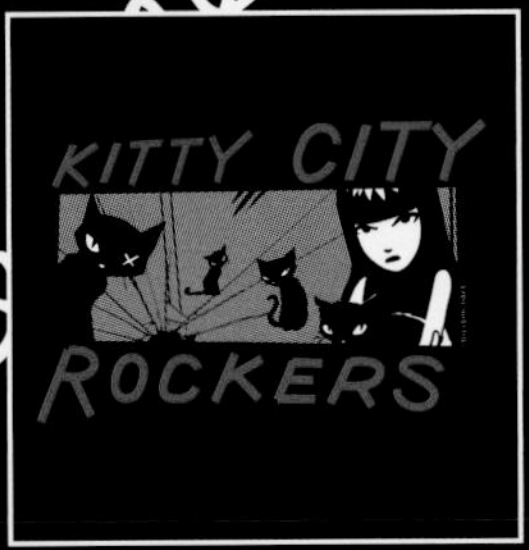
KITTY CITY
ROCKERS

Kitty City Rockers
"On 45"

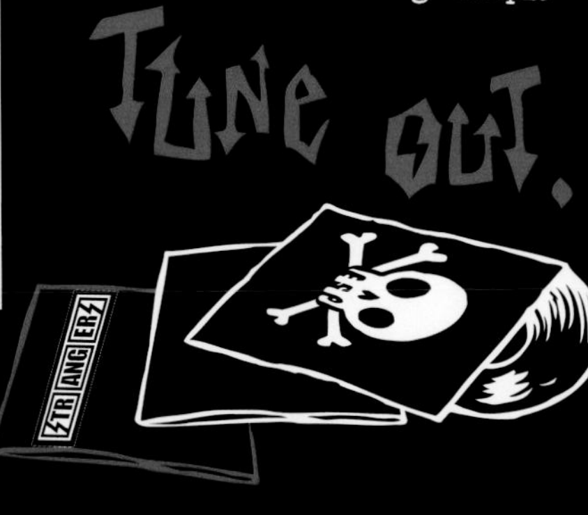
TUNE OUT.
STRANGERS

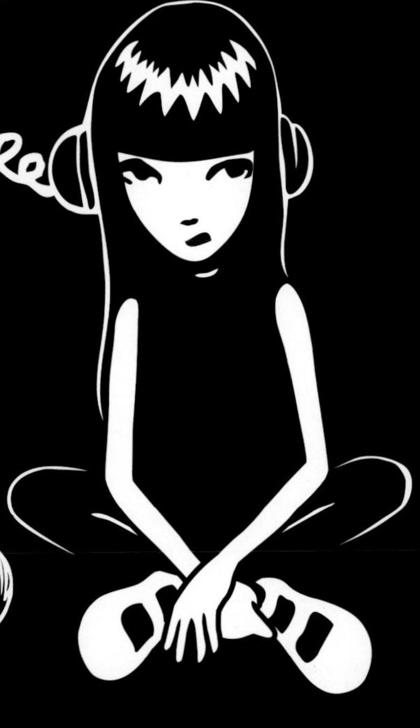

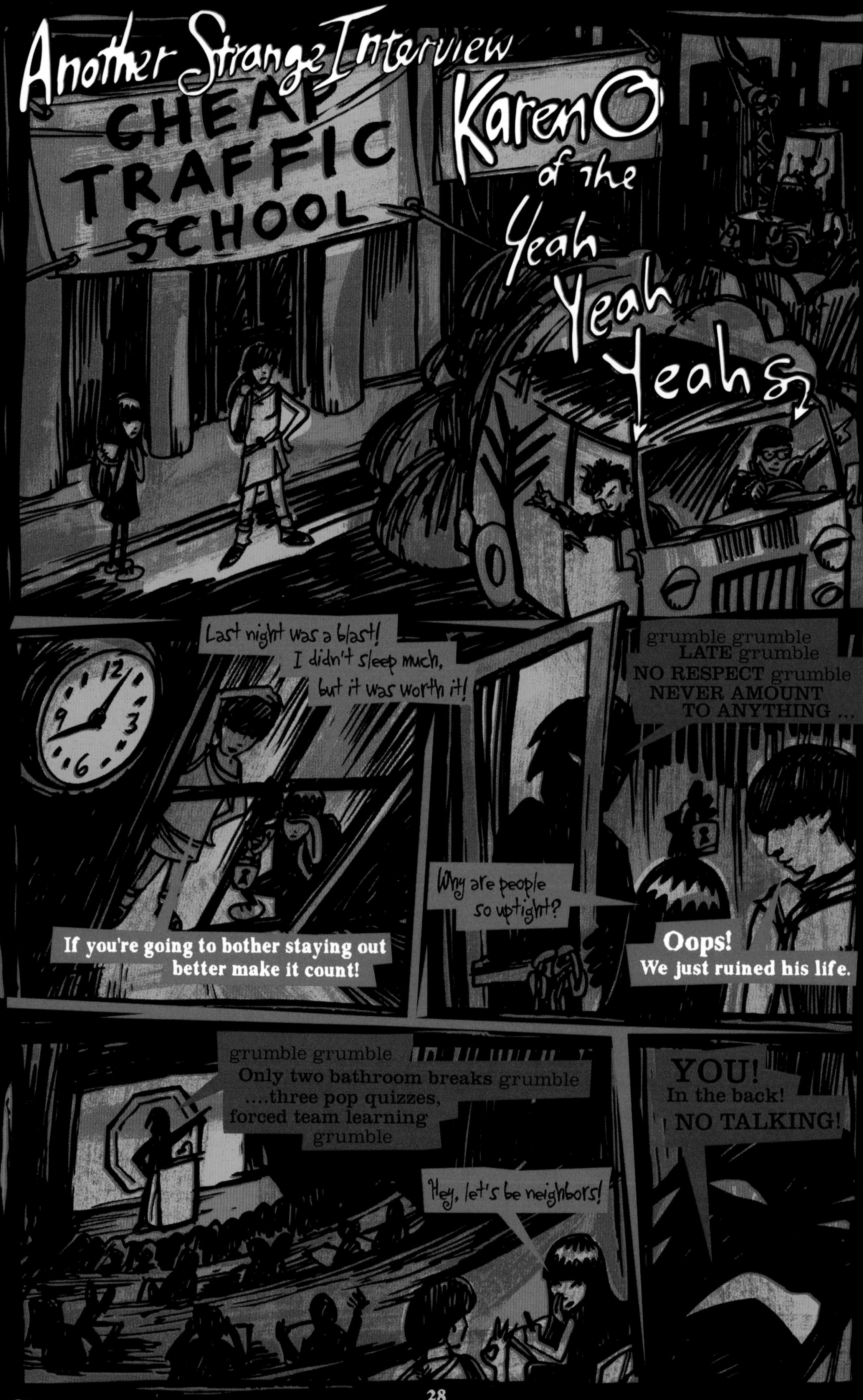
Another Strange Interview
Karen O
of the Yeah Yeah Yeahs
CHEAP TRAFFIC SCHOOL
Last night was a blast! I didn't sleep much, but it was worth it!
If you're going to bother staying out better make it count!
grumble grumble LATE grumble NO RESPECT grumble NEVER AMOUNT TO ANYTHING ...
Why are people so uptight?
Oops! We just ruined his life.
grumble grumble Only two bathroom breaks grumble ....three pop quizzes, forced team learning grumble
Hey, let's be neighbors!
YOU! In the back! NO TALKING!

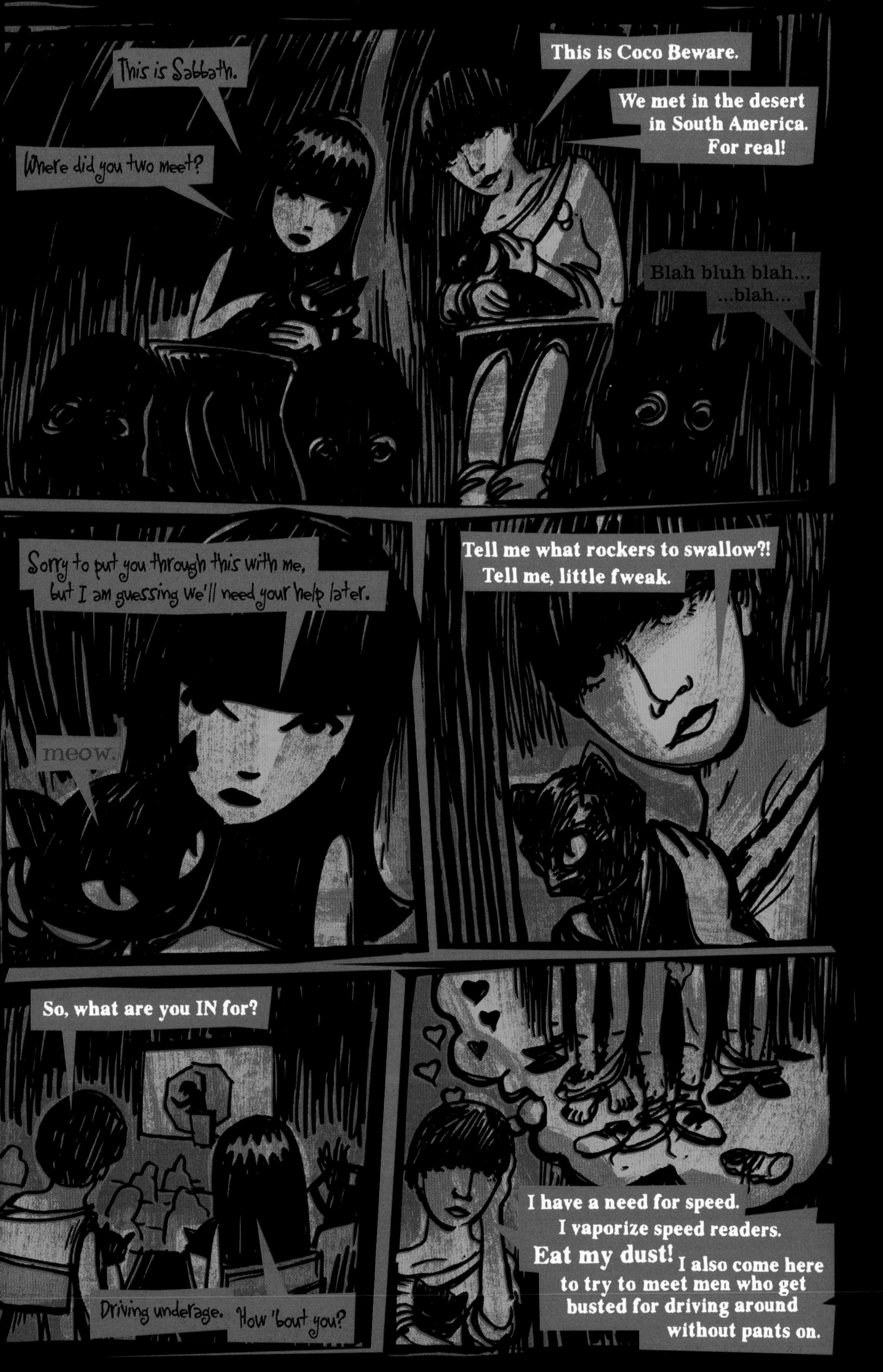
This is Sabbath.
Where did you two meet?
This is Coco Beware.
We met in the desert in South America. For real!
Blah bluh blah... ...blah...
Sorry to put you through this with me, but I am guessing we'll need your help later.
meow.
Tell me what rockers to swallow?! Tell me, little fweak.
So, what are you IN for?
Driving underage.
How 'bout you?
I have a need for speed. I vaporize speed readers.
Eat my dust!
I also come here to try to meet men who get busted for driving around without pants on.

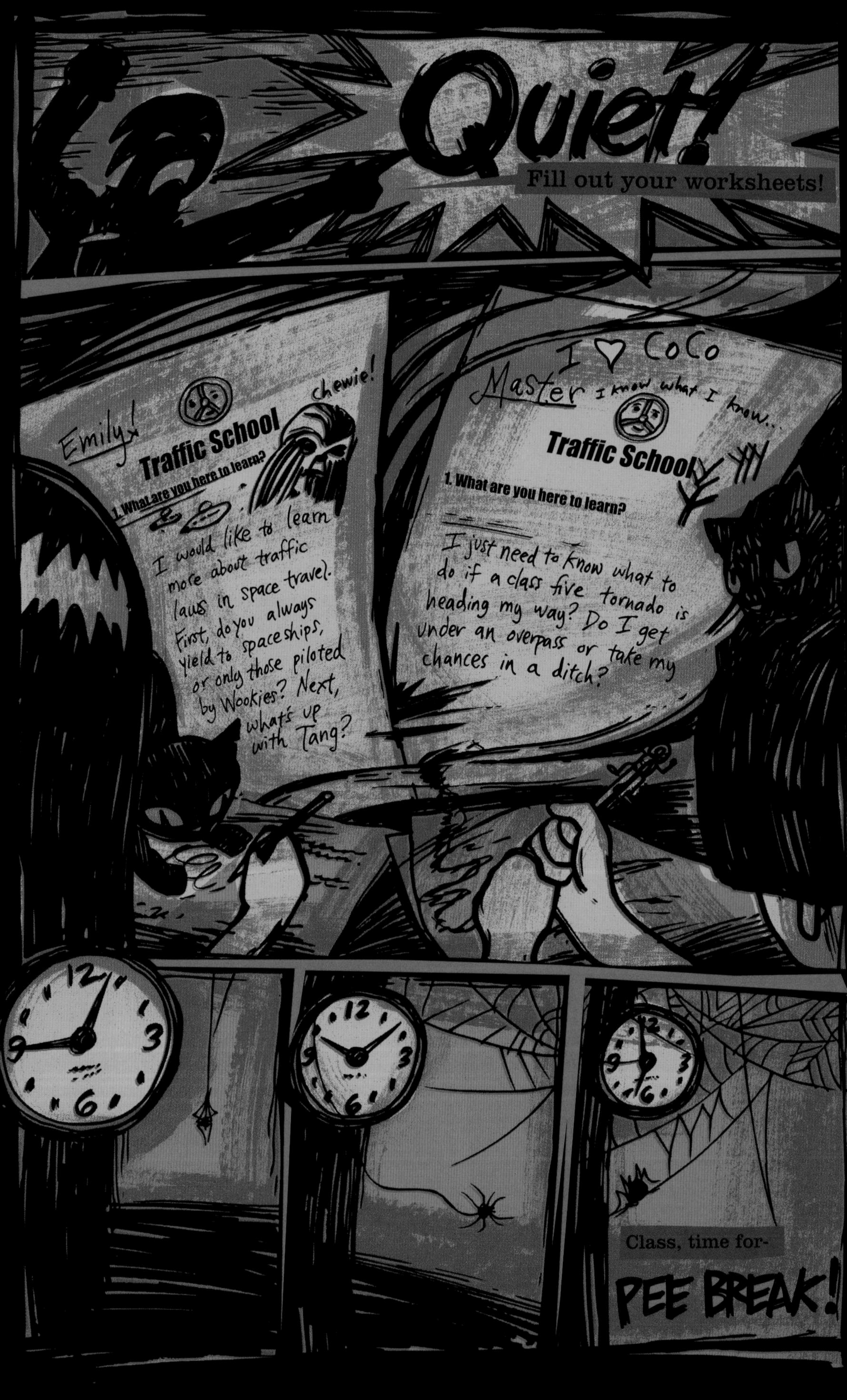
Quiet!
Fill out your worksheets!
Emily!
chewie!
Traffic School
1. What are you here to learn?
I would like to learn more about traffic laws in space travel. First, do you always yield to spaceships, or only those piloted by Wookies? Next, what's up with Tang?
I ♡ CoCo
Master I know what I know..
Traffic School
1. What are you here to learn?
I just need to know what to do if a class five tornado is heading my way? Do I get under an overpass or take my chances in a ditch?
Class, time for-
PEE BREAK!

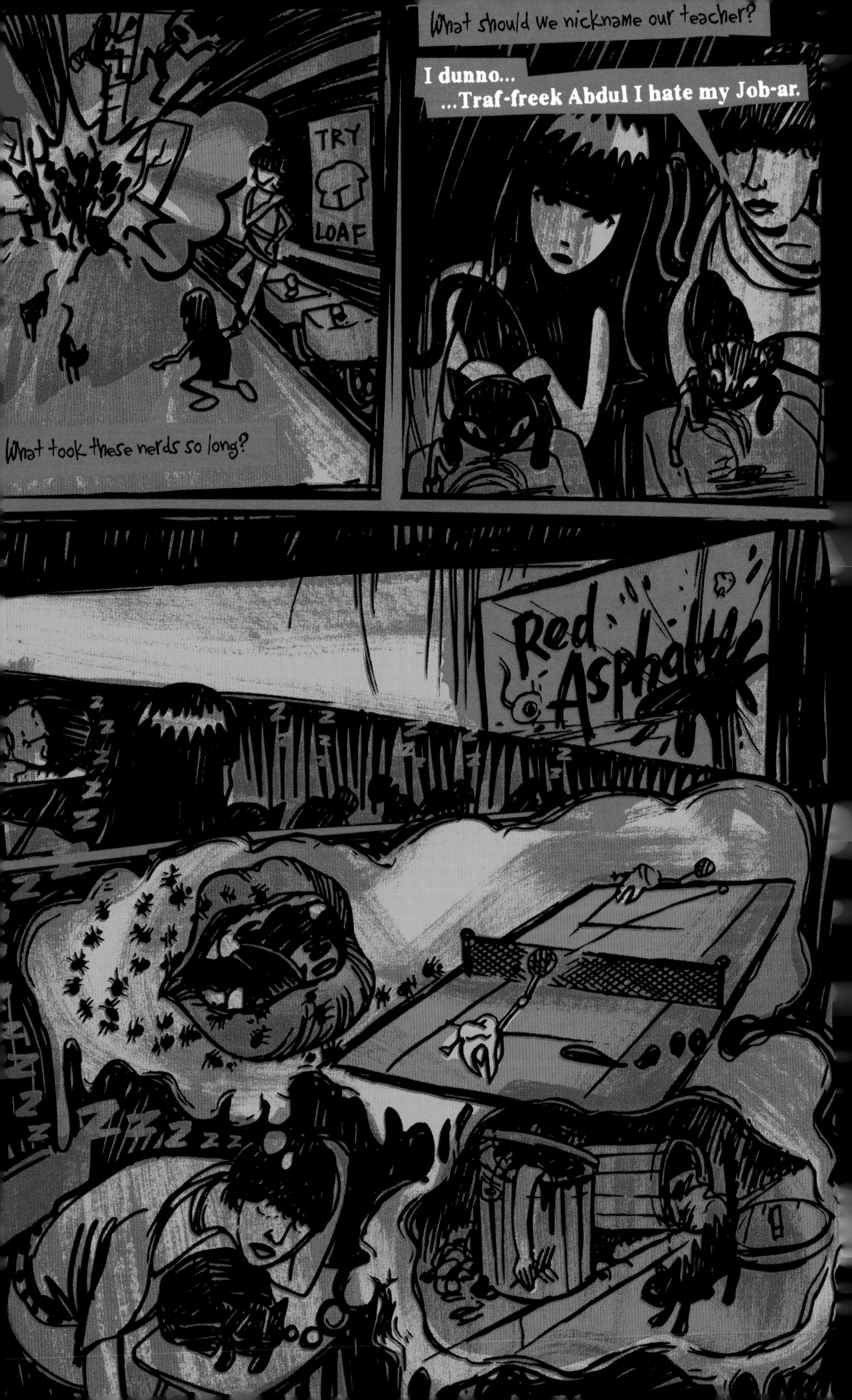
TRY LOAF
What took these nerds so long?
What should we nickname our teacher?
I dunno...
...Traf-freek Abdul I hate my Job-ar.
Red Asphalt

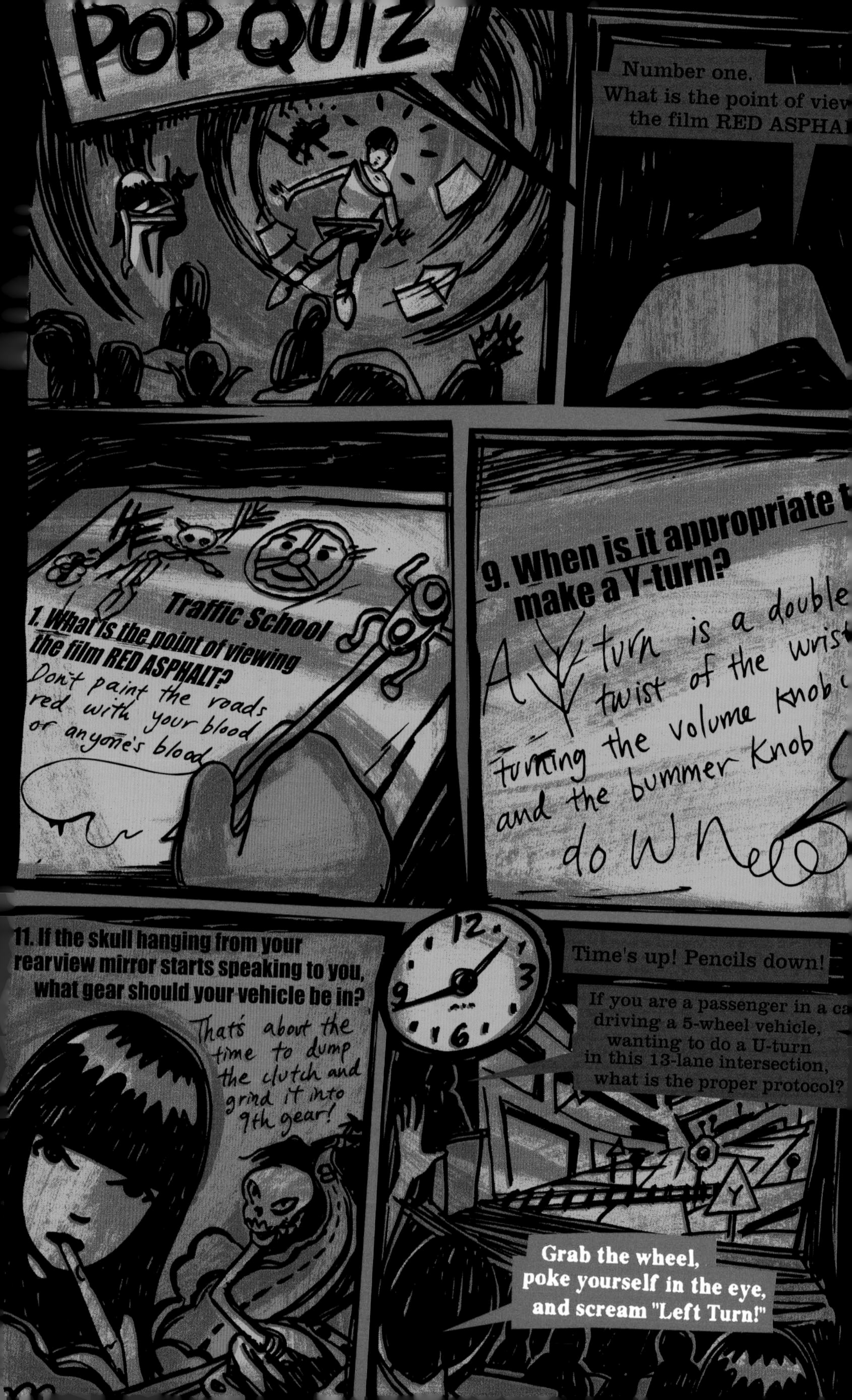
POP QUIZ
Number one.
What is the point of view
the film RED ASPHA
Traffic School
1. What is the point of viewing the film RED ASPHALT?
Don't paint the roads red with your blood or anyone's blood
9. When is it appropriate t make a Y-turn?
A turn is a double twist of the wris
turning the volume knob
and the bummer knob
down
11. If the skull hanging from your rearview mirror starts speaking to you, what gear should your vehicle be in?
That's about the time to dump the clutch and grind it into 9th gear!
Time's up! Pencils down!
If you are a passenger in a ca
driving a 5-wheel vehicle,
wanting to do a U-turn
in this 13-lane intersection,
what is the proper protocol?
Grab the wheel,
poke yourself in the eye,
and scream "Left Turn!"

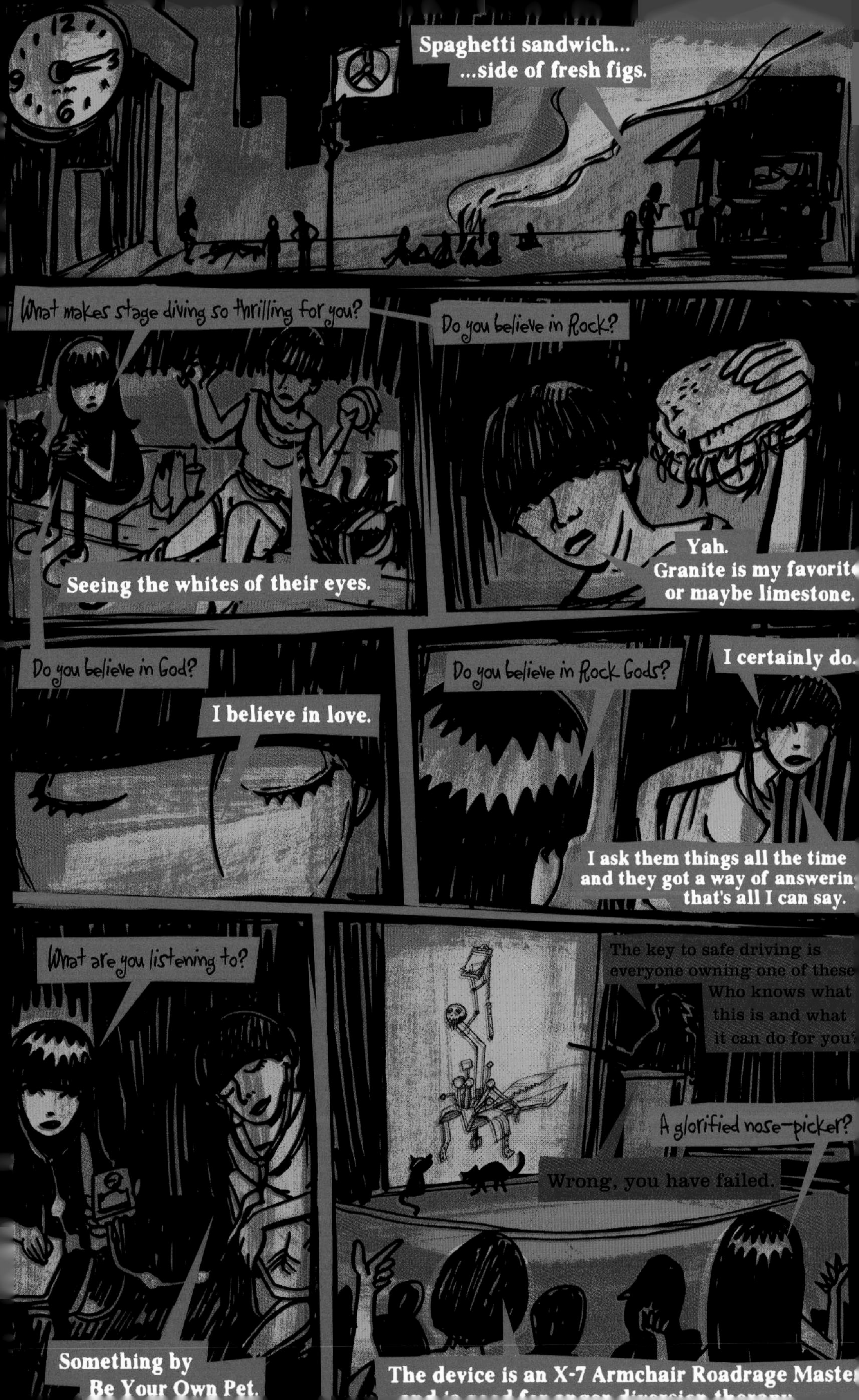

Spaghetti sandwich...
...side of fresh figs.
What makes stage diving so thrilling for you?
Seeing the whites of their eyes.
Do you believe in Rock?
Yah.
Granite is my favorit
or maybe limestone.
Do you believe in God?
I believe in love.
Do you believe in Rock Gods?
I certainly do.
I ask them things all the time
and they got a way of answerin
that's all I can say.
What are you listening to?
Something by
Be Your Own Pet.
The key to safe driving is
everyone owning one of these
Who knows what
this is and what
it can do for you?
A glorified nose-picker?
Wrong, you have failed.
The device is an X-7 Armchair Roadrage Maste

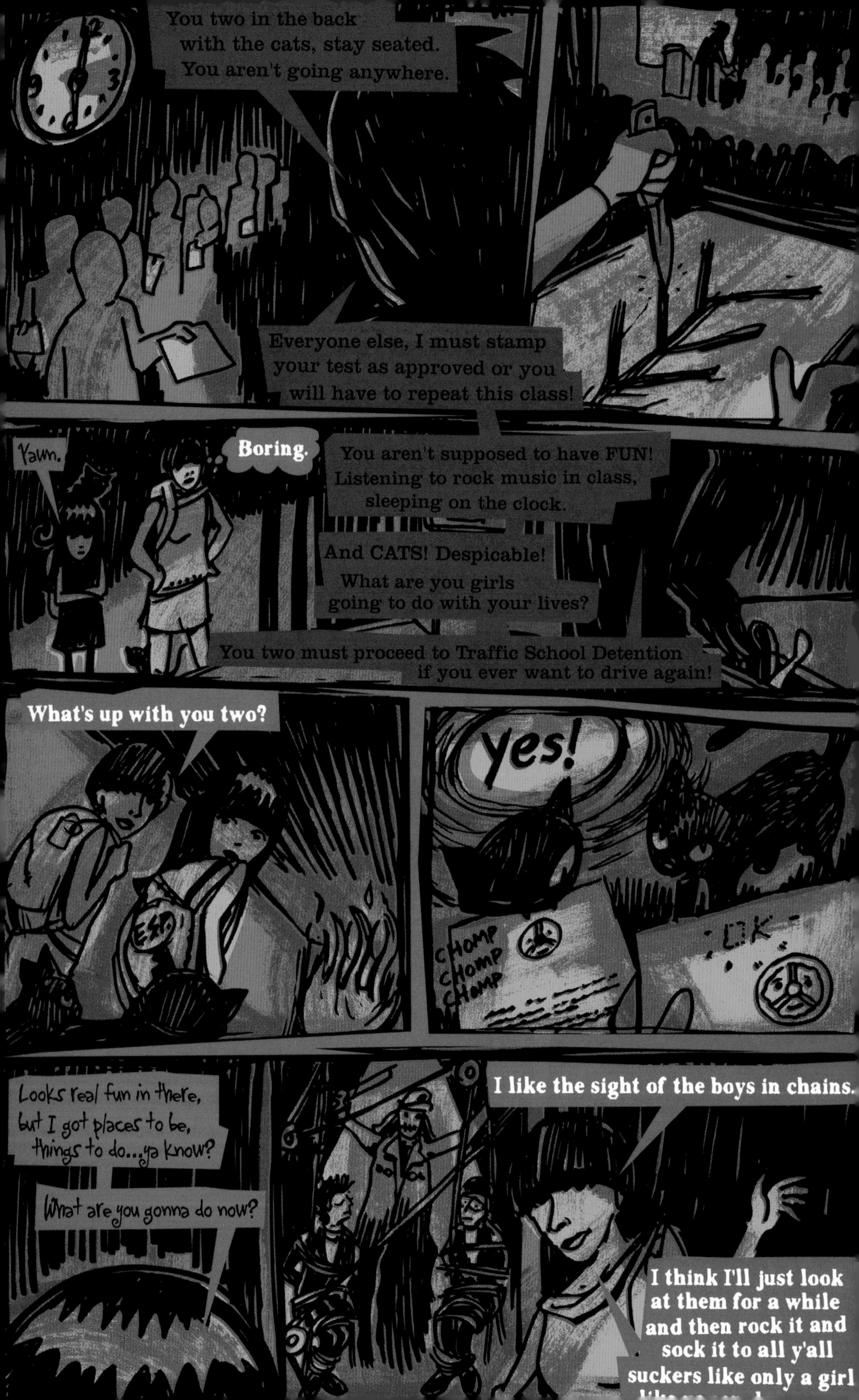
You two in the back with the cats, stay seated. You aren't going anywhere.
Everyone else, I must stamp your test as approved or you will have to repeat this class!
Yawn.
Boring.
You aren't supposed to have FUN! Listening to rock music in class, sleeping on the clock.
And CATS! Despicable!
What are you girls going to do with your lives?
You two must proceed to Traffic School Detention if you ever want to drive again!
What's up with you two?
yes!
CHOMP
CHOMP
CHOMP
OK
Looks real fun in there, but I got places to be, things to do...ya know?
What are you gonna do now?
I like the sight of the boys in chains.
I think I'll just look at them for a while and then rock it and sock it to all y'all suckers like only a girl

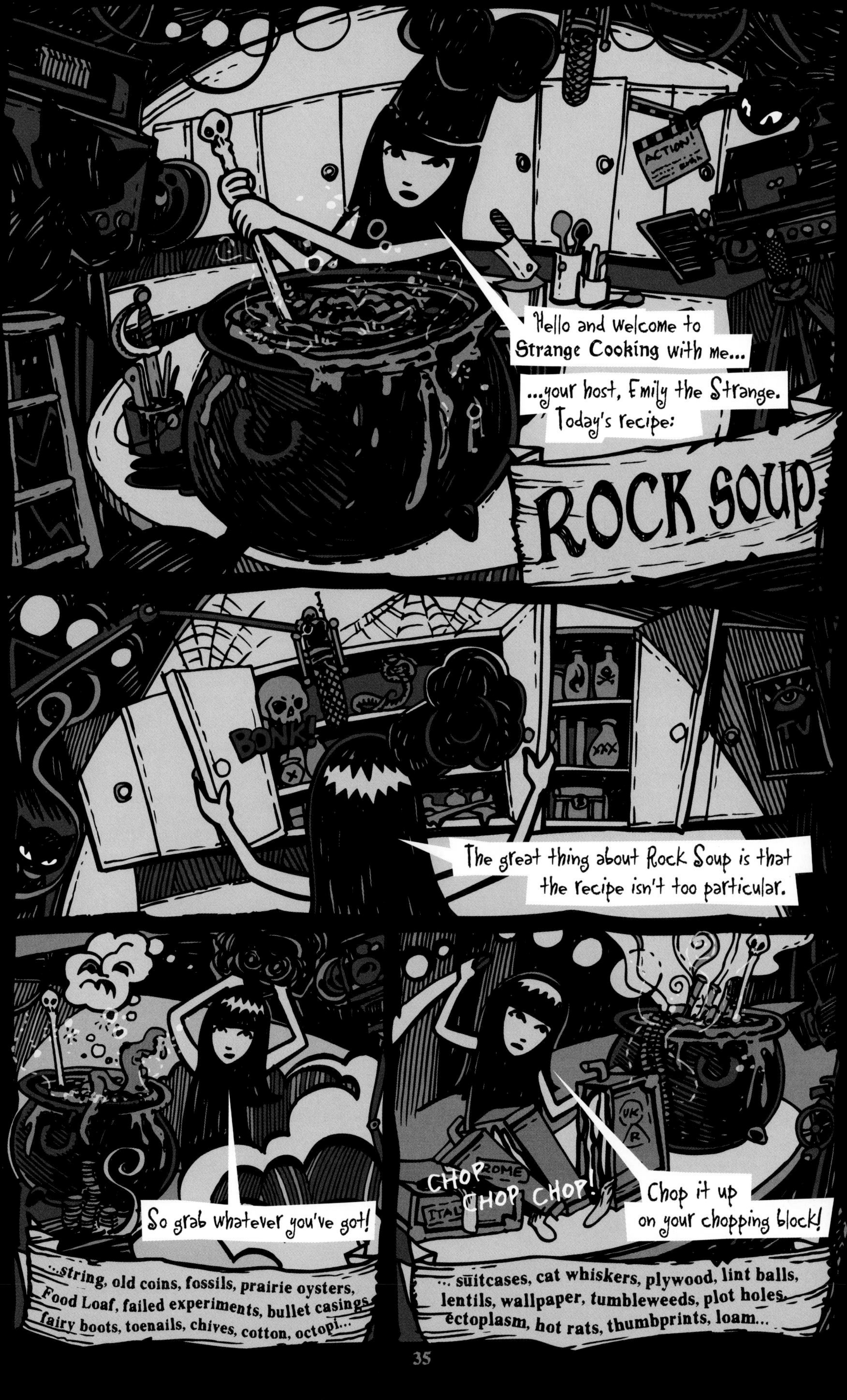
Hello and welcome to
Strange Cooking with me...
...your host, Emily the Strange.
Today's recipe:
ROCK SOUP
ACTION!
BONK!
The great thing about Rock Soup is that
the recipe isn't too particular.
So grab whatever you've got!
...string, old coins, fossils, prairie oysters,
Food Loaf, failed experiments, bullet casings,
fairy boots, toenails, chives, cotton, octopi...
CHOP CHOP CHOP!
Chop it up
on your chopping block!
... suitcases, cat whiskers, plywood, lint balls,
lentils, wallpaper, tumbleweeds, plot holes,
ectoplasm, hot rats, thumbprints, loam...

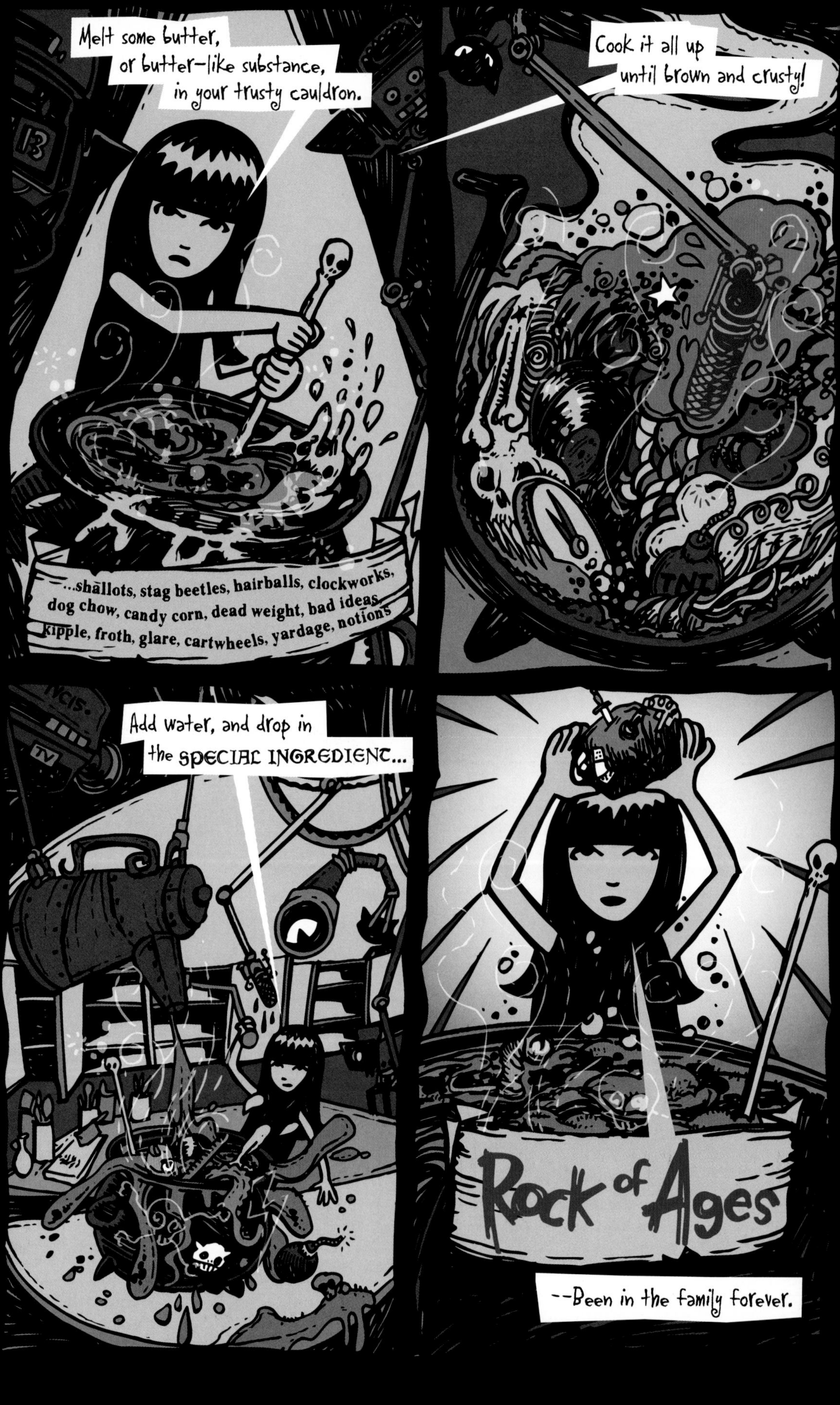
Melt some butter,
or butter-like substance,
in your trusty cauldron.
...shallots, stag beetles, hairballs, clockworks, dog chow, candy corn, dead weight, bad ideas, kipple, froth, glare, cartwheels, yardage, notions
Cook it all up
until brown and crusty!
TNT
Add water, and drop in
the SPECIAL INGREDIENT...
TV
Rock of Ages
--Been in the family forever.

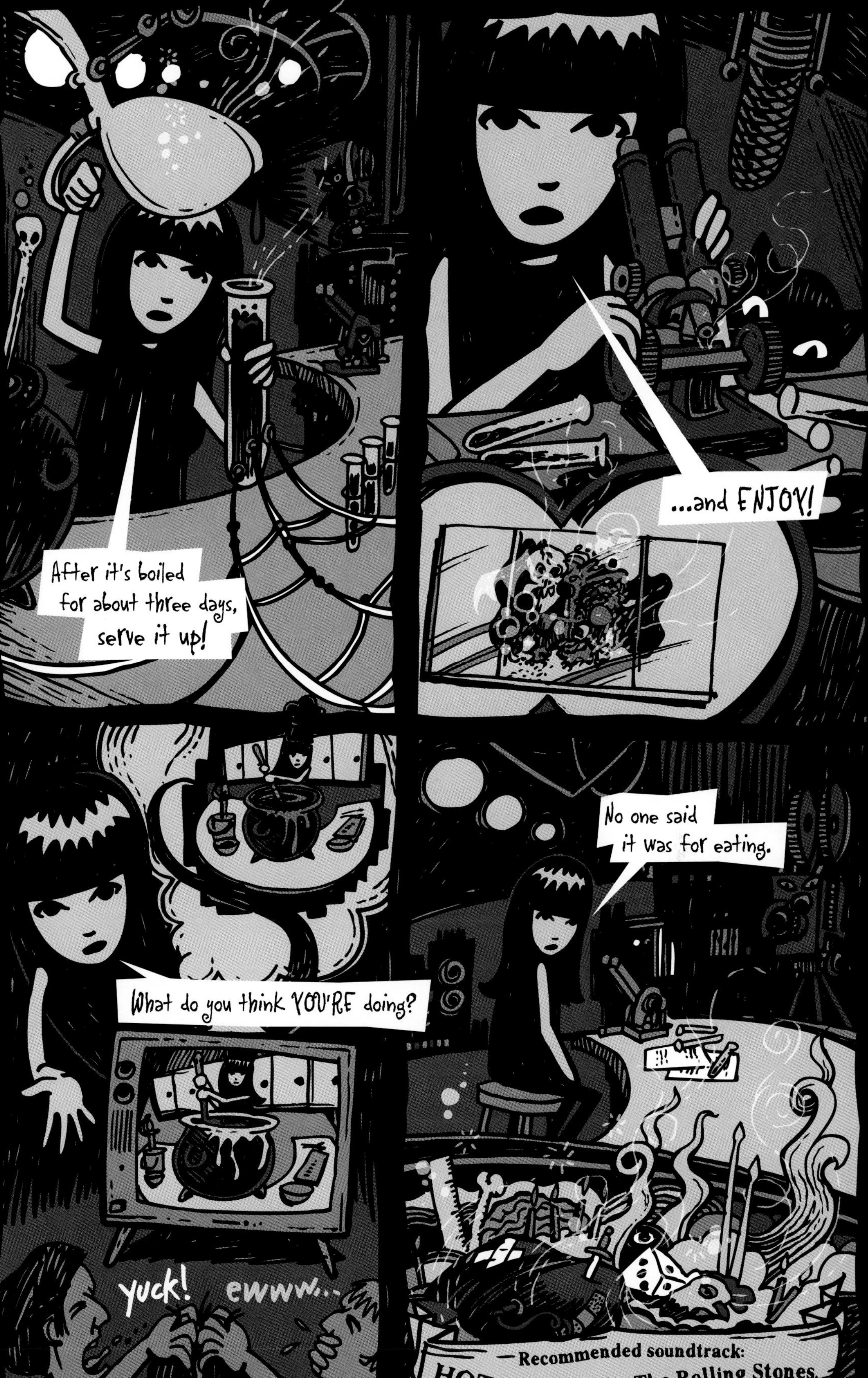
After it's boiled for about three days, serve it up!
...and ENJOY!
What do you think YOU'RE doing?
yuck!
ewww...
No one said it was for eating.
—Recommended soundtrack:
HOT ROCKS by The Rolling Stones.

EMILY'S TOP 13

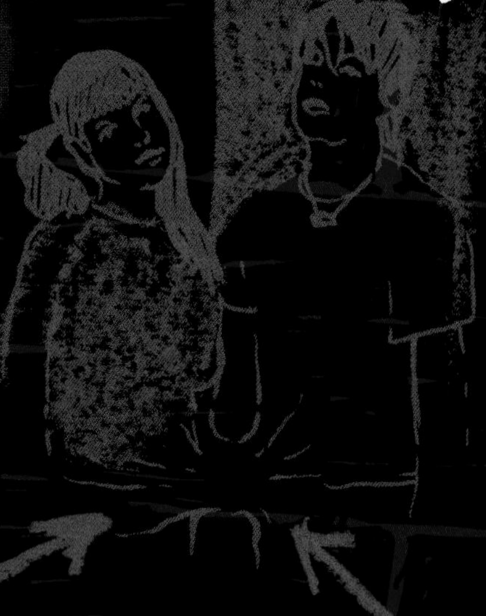

1. Pete Townshend holds the record for the most broken necks: 515.

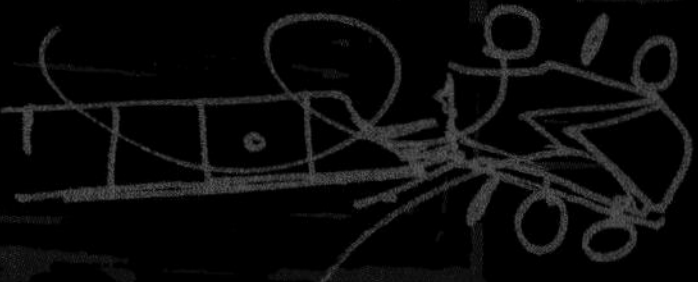

2. Jimi Hendrix once kissed some guy.

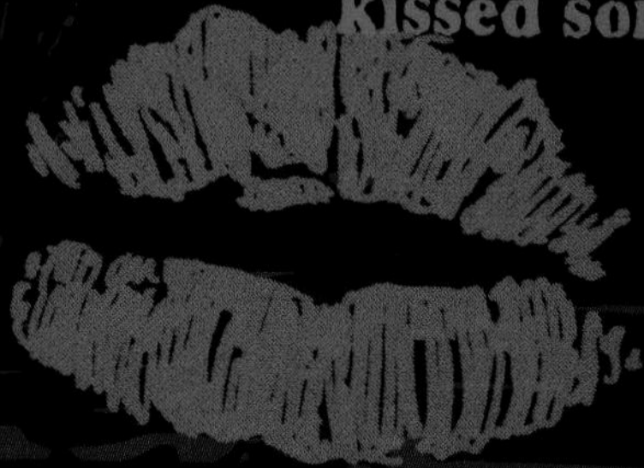

3. Jack and Meg White were born conjoined twins and have never been separated.

4. Blondie was arrested for eating guitars in bars with candy cars on Mars.

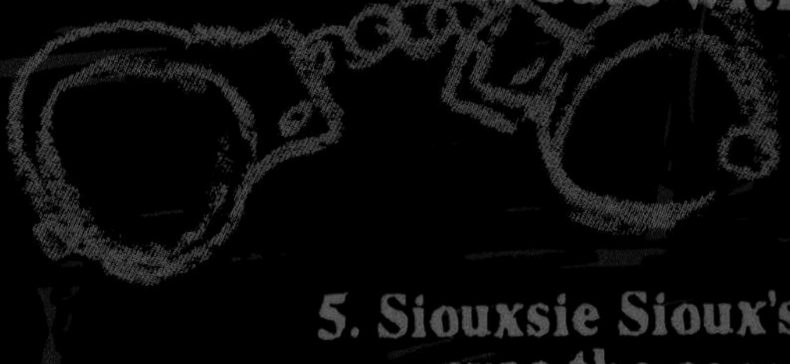

5. Siouxsie Sioux's maternal grandmother was the second cousin to the paternal great-great-great-grandfather of Sabbath Trillium of the Woods.

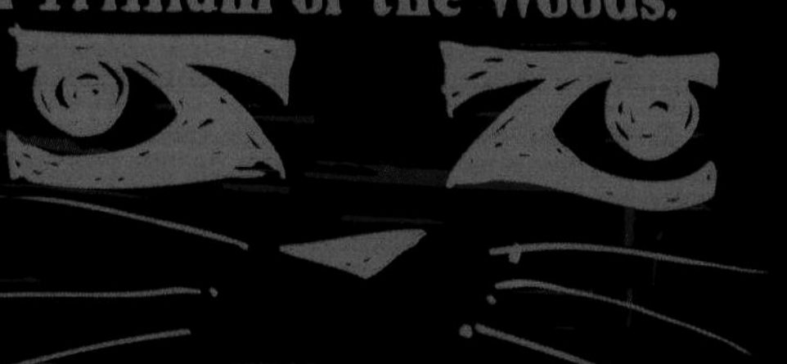

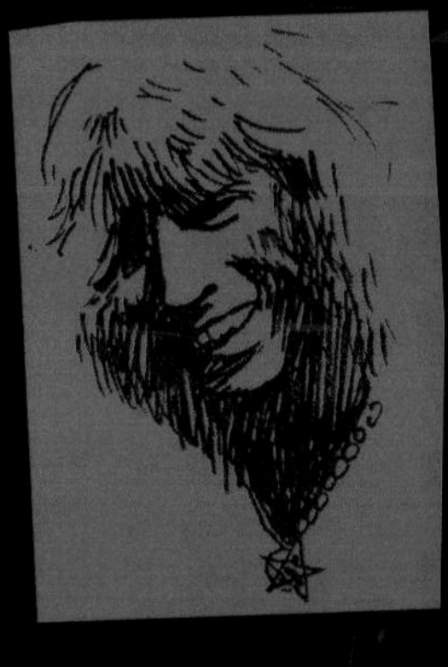

6. Bon Scott had "Highway to Hell" performed at his funeral.

ROCK RUMORS

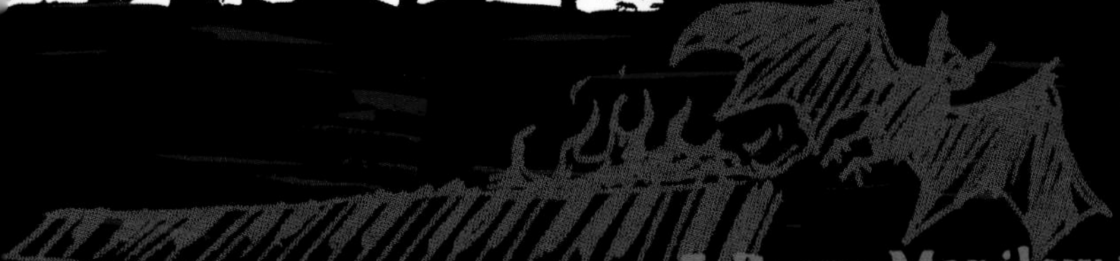

7. Barry Manilow taught Ozzy everything he knows.

8. Rodney really was on the rock!

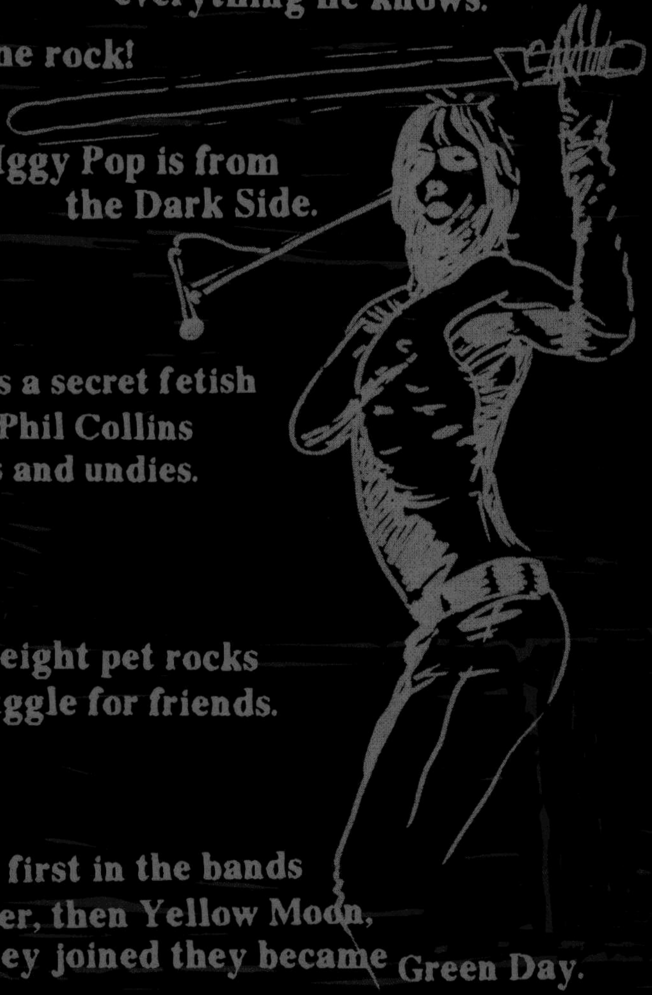

9. Iggy Pop is from the Dark Side.

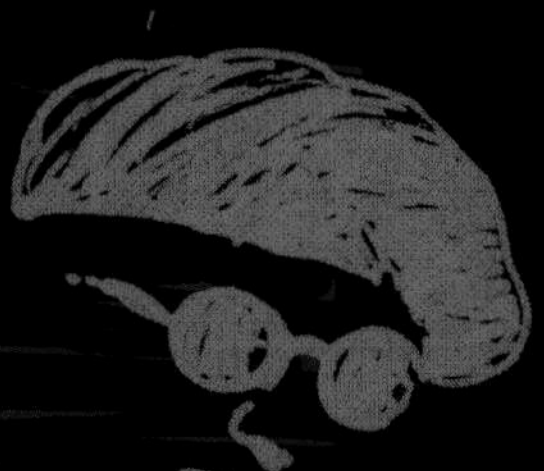

10. Captain Sensible has a secret fetish for performing with Phil Collins wearing only tube socks and undies.

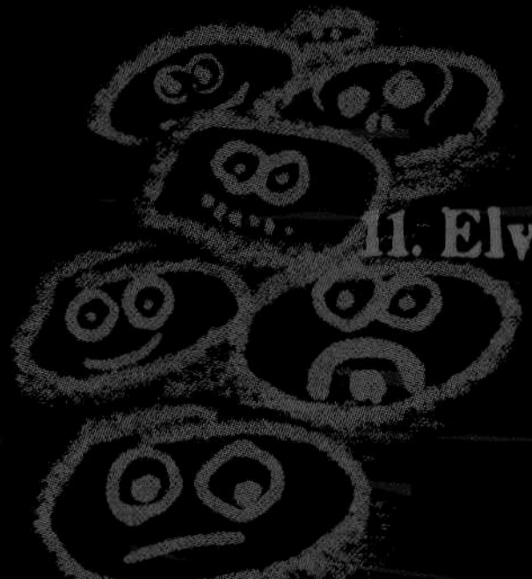

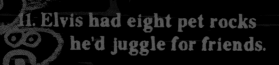

11. Elvis had eight pet rocks he'd juggle for friends.

12. Green Day was first in the bands Blue Water, then Yellow Moon, then when they joined they became Green Day.

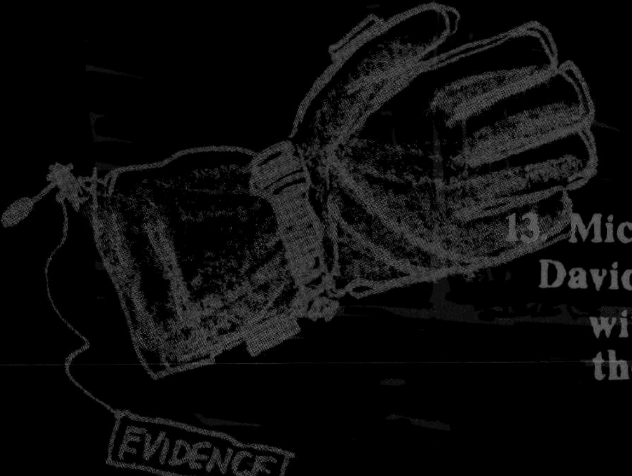
EVIDENCE

13. Mick Jagger once slapped David Bowie across the face with a ski glove, then made him drink soda pop and eat pop rocks.

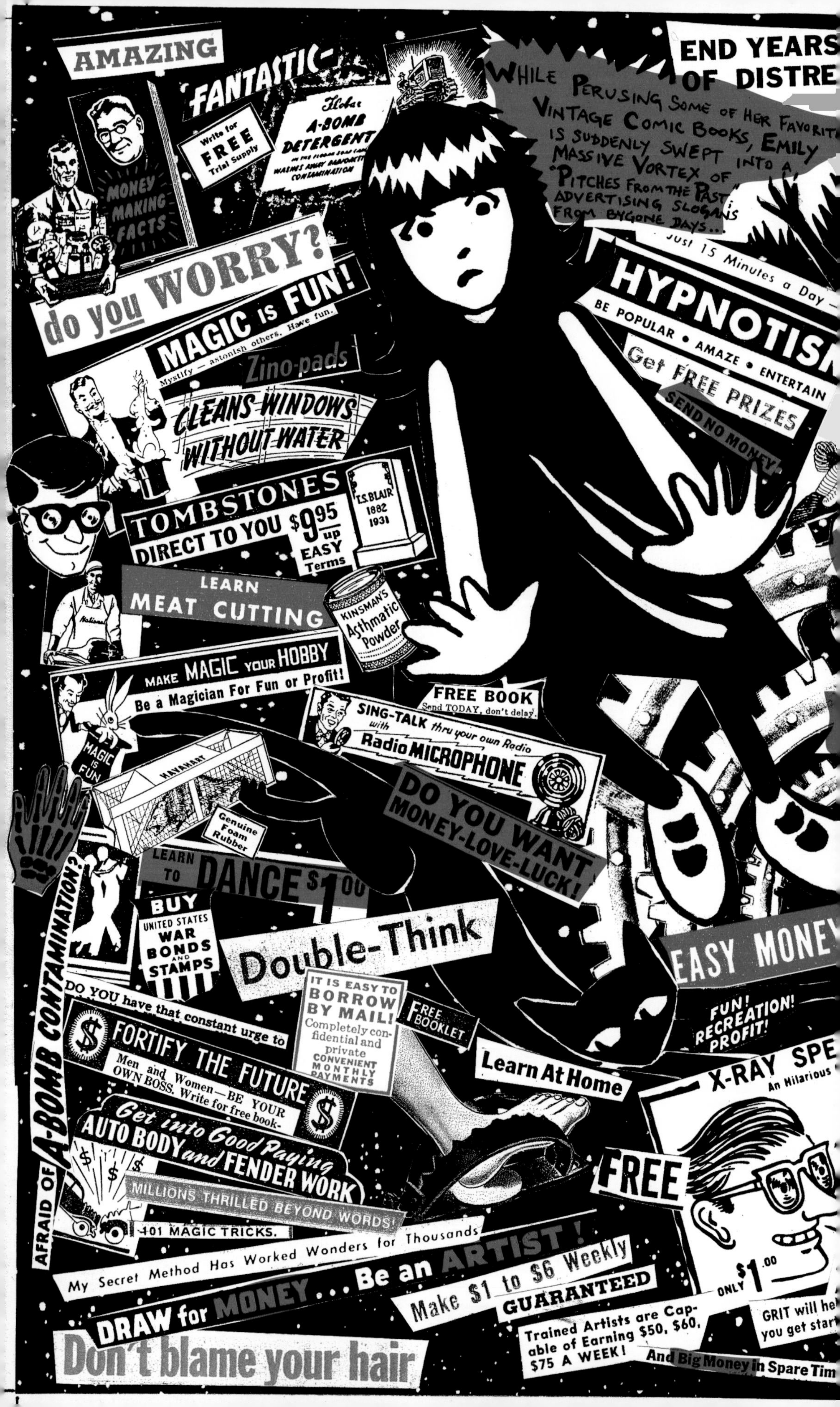

WHILE PERUSING SOME OF HER FAVORITE VINTAGE COMIC BOOKS, EMILY IS SUDDENLY SWEPT INTO A MASSIVE VORTEX OF "PITCHES FROM THE PAST," ADVERTISING SLOGANS FROM BYGONE DAYS...
AMAZING
FANTASTIC-
END YEARS OF DISTRE
MONEY MAKING FACTS
Write for FREE Trial Supply
A-BOMB DETERGENT
WASHES AWAY RADIOACTIVE CONTAMINATION
do you WORRY?
MAGIC IS FUN!
Mystify — astonish others. Have fun.
Zino-pads
CLEANS WINDOWS WITHOUT WATER
Just 15 Minutes a Day
HYPNOTISM
BE POPULAR • AMAZE • ENTERTAIN
Get FREE PRIZES
SEND NO MONEY
TOMBSTONES DIRECT TO YOU $9.95 up EASY Terms
T.S. BLAIR 1882 1931
LEARN MEAT CUTTING
KINSMAN'S Asthmatic Powder
MAKE MAGIC YOUR HOBBY
Be a Magician For Fun or Profit!
FREE BOOK
Send TODAY, don't delay.
SING-TALK thru your own Radio with Radio MICROPHONE
MAGIC IS FUN
HAVAHART
Genuine Foam Rubber
DO YOU WANT MONEY-LOVE-LUCK!
LEARN TO DANCE $1.00
BUY UNITED STATES WAR BONDS AND STAMPS
Double-Think
EASY MONEY
AFRAID OF A-BOMB CONTAMINATION?
DO YOU have that constant urge to
FORTIFY THE FUTURE
Men and Women—BE YOUR OWN BOSS. Write for free book-
IT IS EASY TO BORROW BY MAIL! Completely confidential and private CONVENIENT MONTHLY PAYMENTS
FREE BOOKLET
FUN! RECREATION! PROFIT!
Learn At Home
X-RAY SPE
An Hilarious
Get into Good Paying AUTO BODY and FENDER WORK
MILLIONS THRILLED BEYOND WORDS!
101 MAGIC TRICKS.
FREE
My Secret Method Has Worked Wonders for Thousands
Be an ARTIST!
Make $1 to $6 Weekly
GUARANTEED
ONLY $1.00
DRAW for MONEY...
Trained Artists are Capable of Earning $50, $60, $75 A WEEK!
GRIT will he you get star
And Big Money in Spare Tim
Don't blame your hair

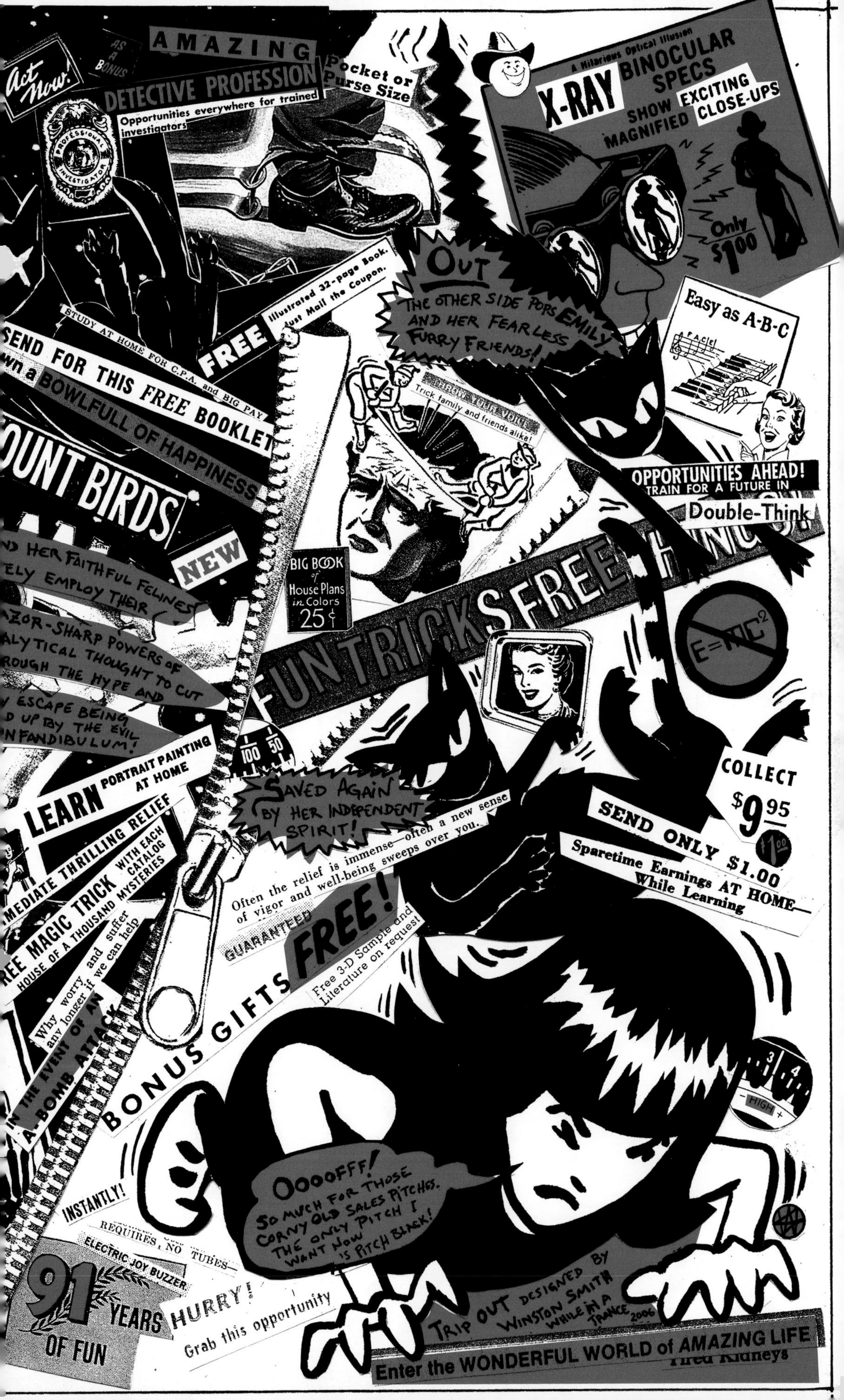

Act Now!
AS A BONUS
AMAZING
DETECTIVE PROFESSION
Opportunities everywhere for trained investigators
PROFESSIONAL INVESTIGATOR
Pocket or Purse Size
A Hilarious Optical Illusion
X-RAY BINOCULAR SPECS
SHOW EXCITING MAGNIFIED CLOSE-UPS
Only $1.00
OUT THE OTHER SIDE POPS EMILY AND HER FEARLESS FURRY FRIENDS!
Illustrated 32-page Book. Just Mail the Coupon.
FREE
STUDY AT HOME FOR C.P.A. and BIG PAY
SEND FOR THIS FREE BOOKLET
wn a BOWLFULL OF HAPPINESS
OUNT BIRDS
NEW
ND HER FAITHFUL FELINES
ELY EMPLOY THEIR
AZOR-SHARP POWERS OF
ALYTICAL THOUGHT TO CUT
ROUGH THE HYPE AND
ESCAPE BEING
D UP BY THE EVIL
NFANDIBULUM!
Easy as A-B-C
Trick family and friends alike!
OPPORTUNITIES AHEAD!
TRAIN FOR A FUTURE IN
Double-Think
BIG BOOK of House Plans in Colors 25¢
FUN TRICKS FREE
E=MC²
LEARN PORTRAIT PAINTING AT HOME
IMMEDIATE THRILLING RELIEF
REE MAGIC TRICK WITH EACH CATALOG
HOUSE OF A THOUSAND MYSTERIES
Why worry and suffer any longer if we can help
IN THE EVENT OF AN A-BOMB ATTACK
SAVED AGAIN BY HER INDEPENDENT SPIRIT!
Often the relief is immense—often a new sense of vigor and well-being sweeps over you.
GUARANTEED
FREE!
Free 3-D Sample and Literature on request
BONUS GIFTS
COLLECT $9.95
SEND ONLY $1.00
Sparetime Earnings AT HOME—While Learning
HIGH
INSTANTLY!
REQUIRES NO TUBES
ELECTRIC JOY BUZZER
91 YEARS OF FUN
HURRY!
Grab this opportunity
OOOOFFF! SO MUCH FOR THOSE CORNY OLD SALES PITCHES. THE ONLY PITCH I WANT NOW IS PITCH BLACK!
TRIP OUT DESIGNED BY WINSTON SMITH WHILE IN A TRANCE 2006
Enter the WONDERFUL WORLD of AMAZING LIFE
Tired Kidneys

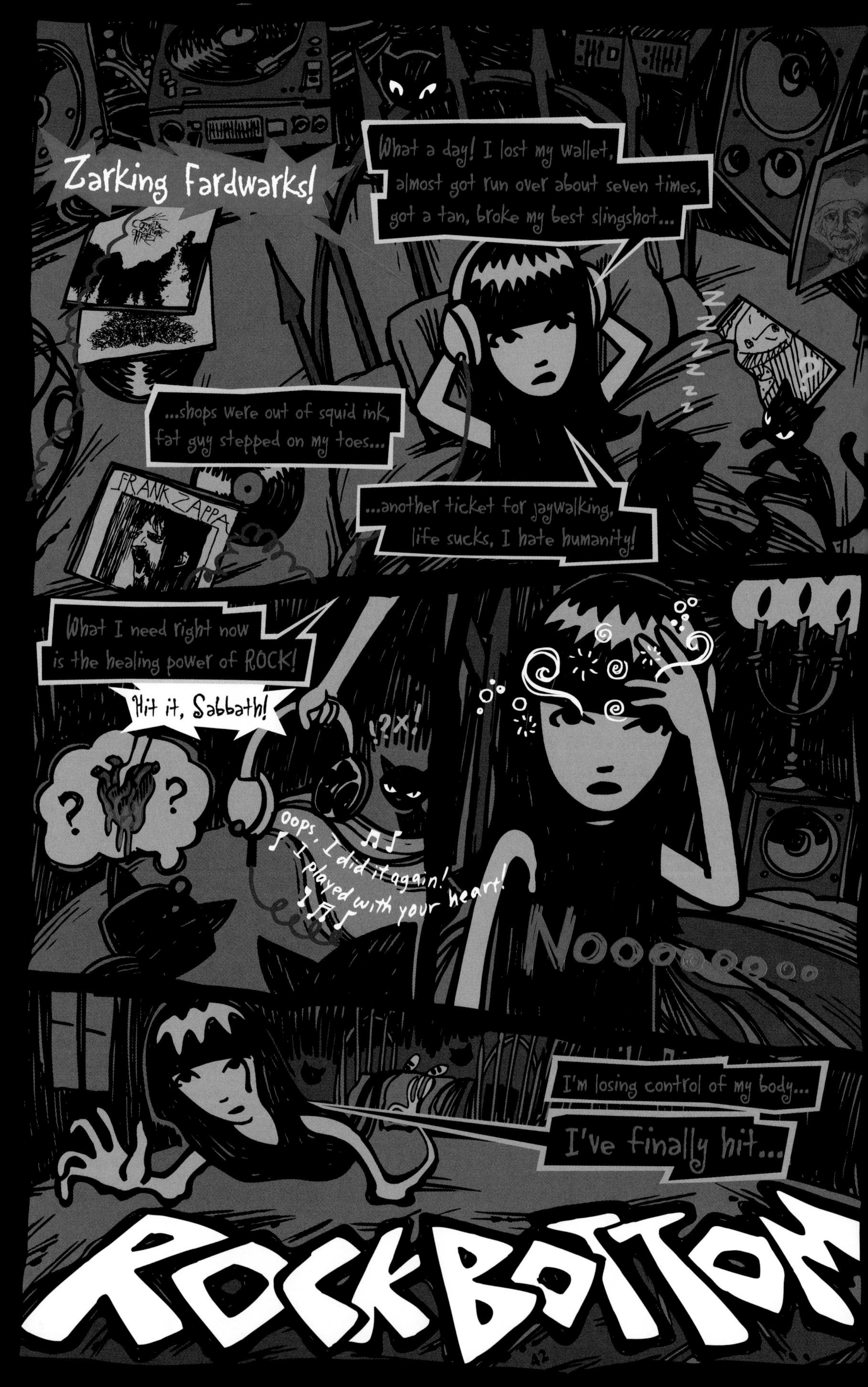

Zarking Fardwarks!
What a day! I lost my wallet, almost got run over about seven times, got a tan, broke my best slingshot...
...shops were out of squid ink, fat guy stepped on my toes...
...another ticket for jaywalking, life sucks, I hate humanity!
FRANK ZAPPA
What I need right now is the healing power of ROCK!
Hit it, Sabbath!
!?X!
Oops, I did it again! I played with your heart!
Nooooooooo
I'm losing control of my body...
I've finally hit...
ROCK BOTTOM

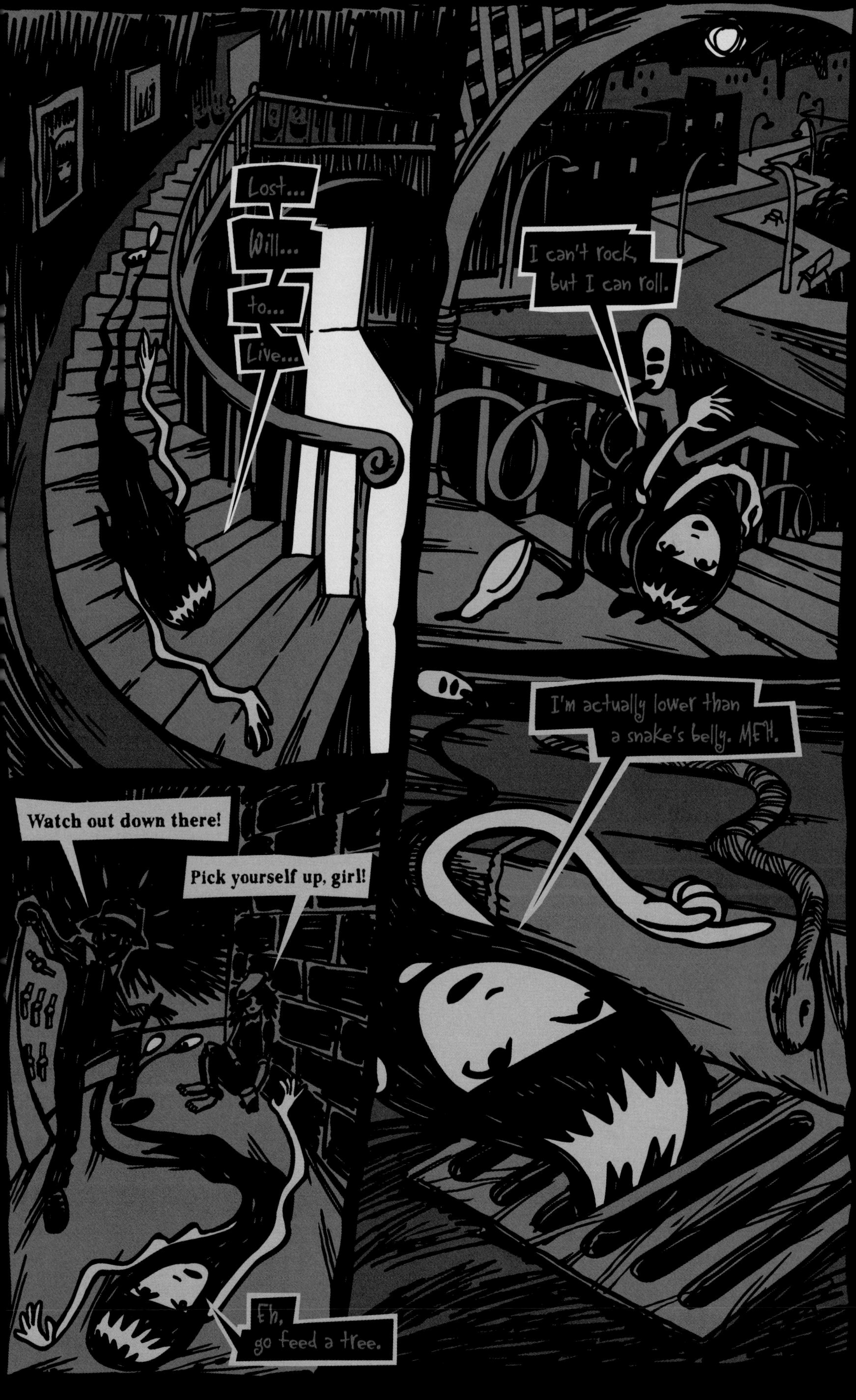
Lost...
Will...
to...
Live...
I can't rock, but I can roll.
Watch out down there!
Pick yourself up, girl!
Eh, go feed a tree.
I'm actually lower than a snake's belly. MEH.

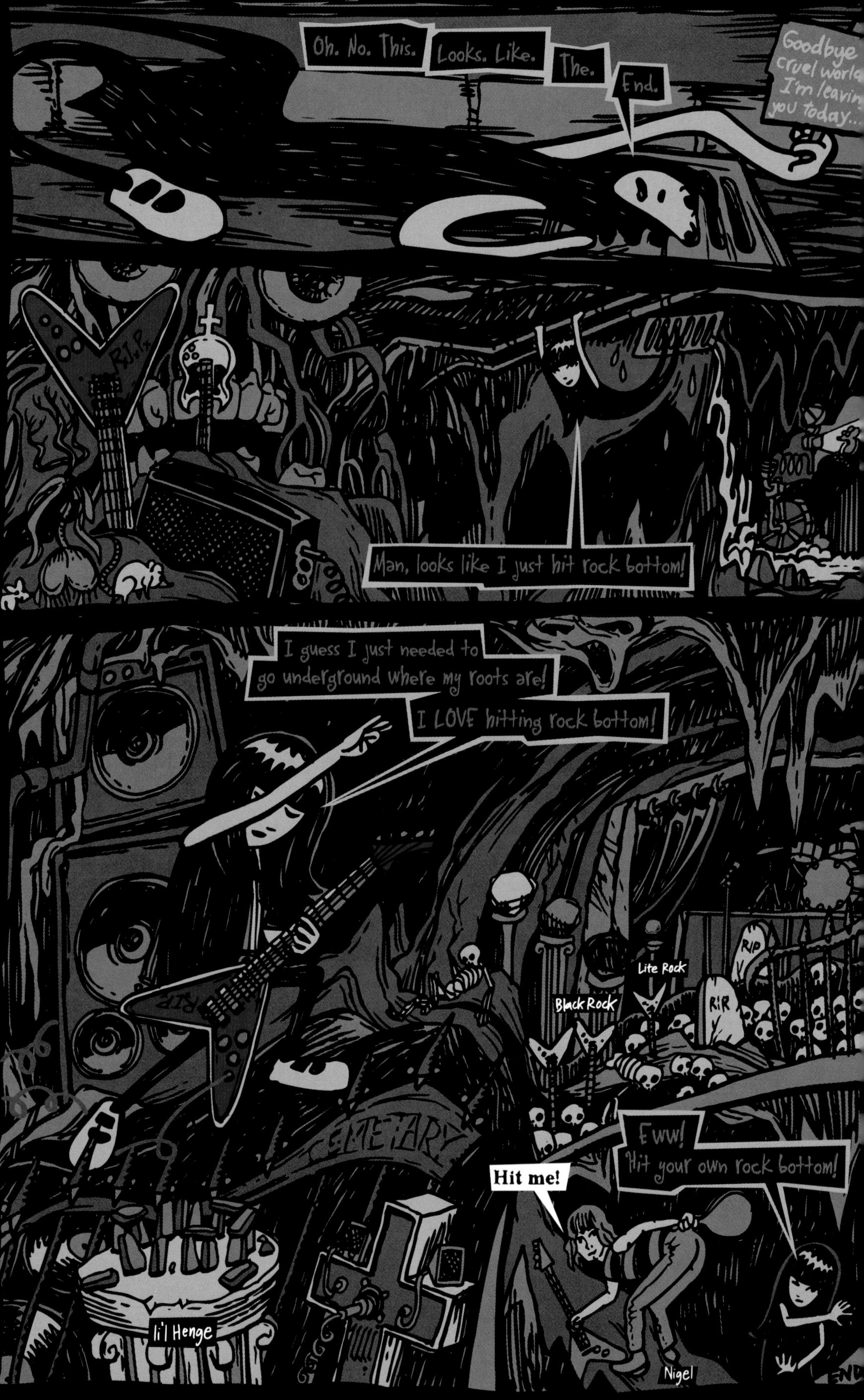

Oh. No. This.
Looks. Like.
The.
End.
Goodbye
cruel worl
I'm leavin
you today...
Man, looks like I just hit rock bottom!
I guess I just needed to go underground where my roots are!
I LOVE hitting rock bottom!
Lite Rock
Black Rock
CEMETARY
Hit me!
Eww! Hit your own rock bottom!
li'l Henge
Nigel

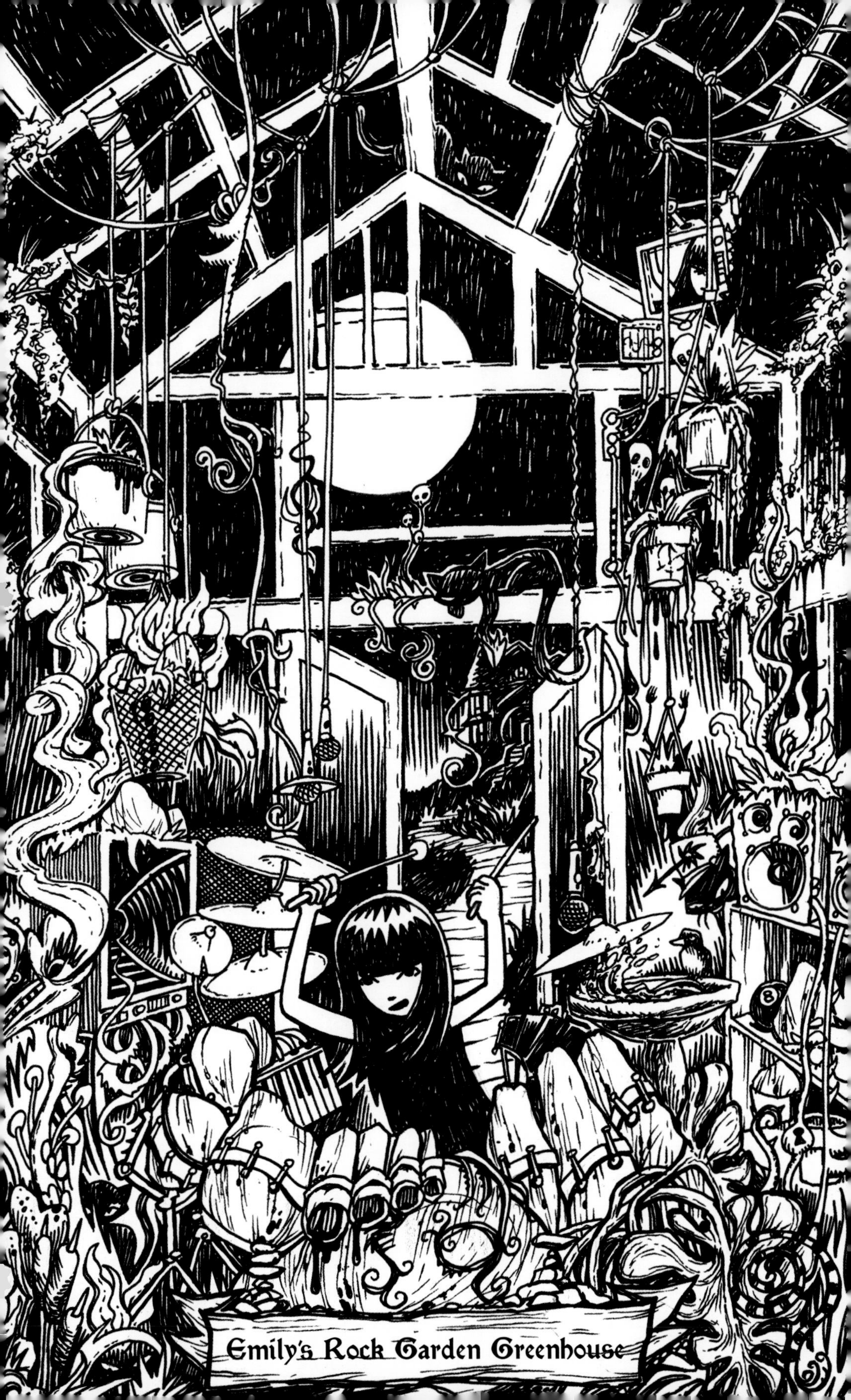
Emily's Rock Garden Greenhouse

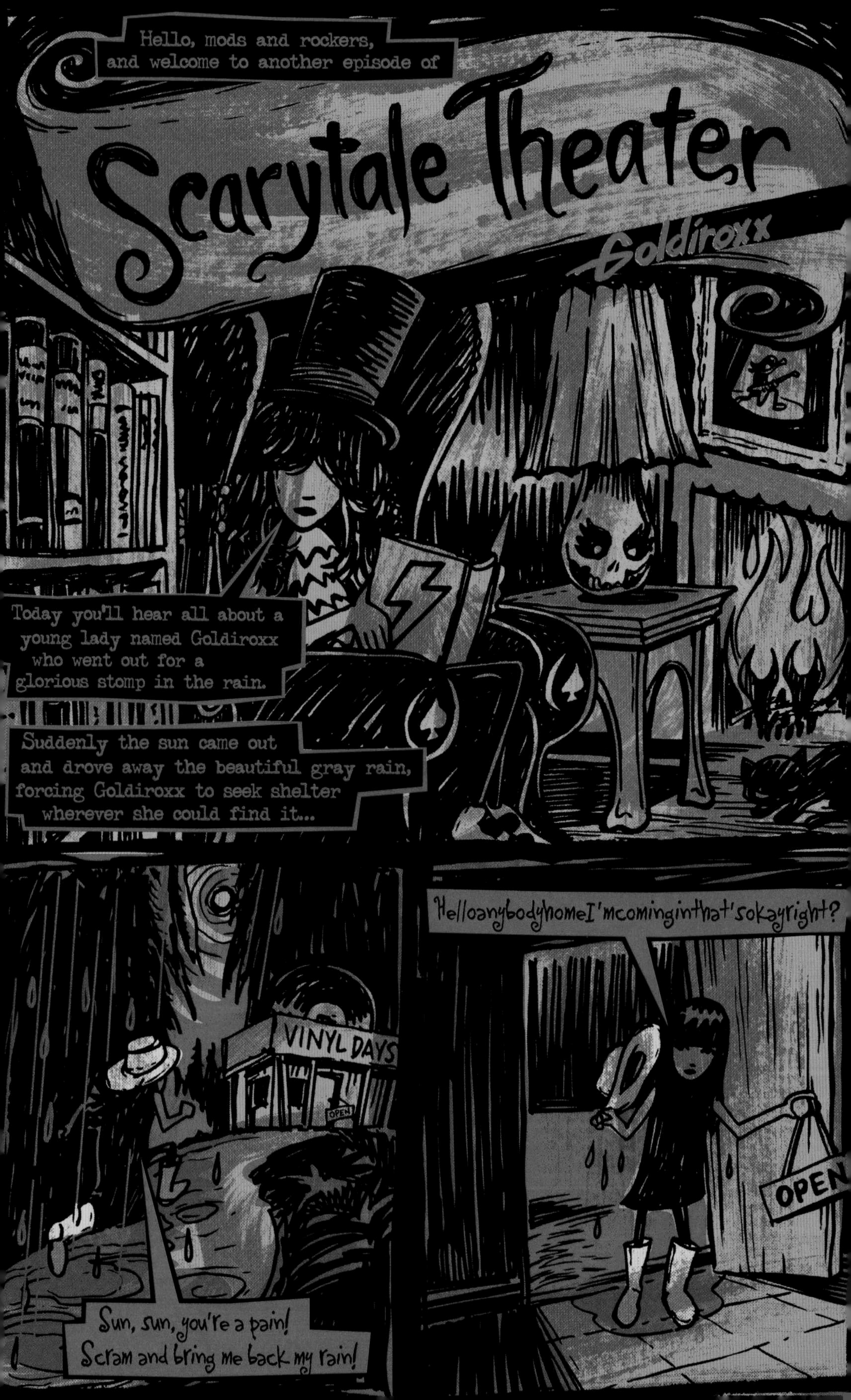
Hello, mods and rockers, and welcome to another episode of
Scarytale Theater
Goldiroxx
Today you'll hear all about a young lady named Goldiroxx who went out for a glorious stomp in the rain.
Suddenly the sun came out and drove away the beautiful gray rain, forcing Goldiroxx to seek shelter wherever she could find it...
VINYL DAYS
OPEN
Sun, sun, you're a pain! Scram and bring me back my rain!
HelloanybodyhomeI'mcominginthat'sokayright?
OPEN

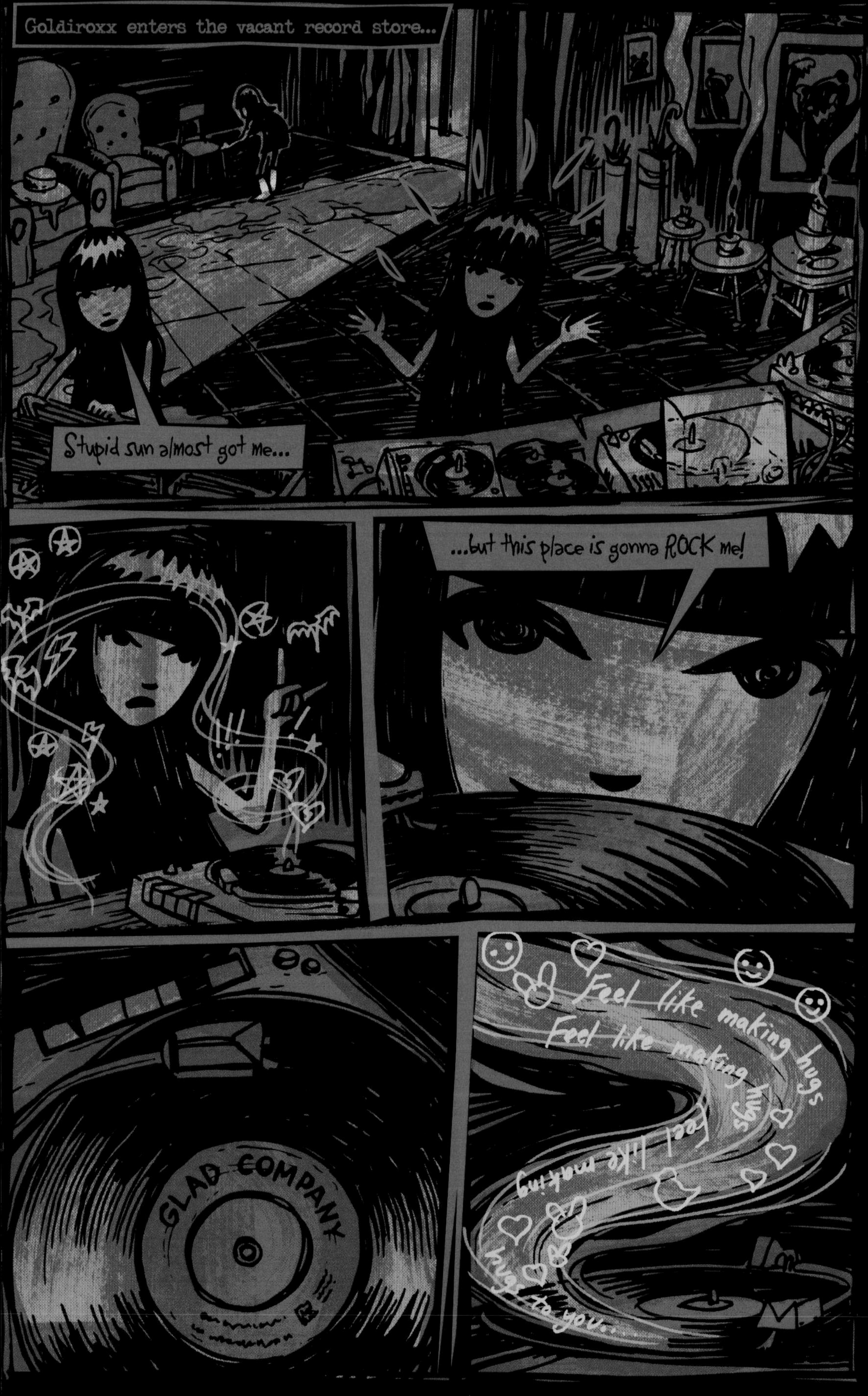
Goldiroxx enters the vacant record store...
Stupid sun almost got me...
...but this place is gonna ROCK me!
GLAD COMPANY
Feel like making hugs
Feel like making hugs
Feel like making hugs to you...

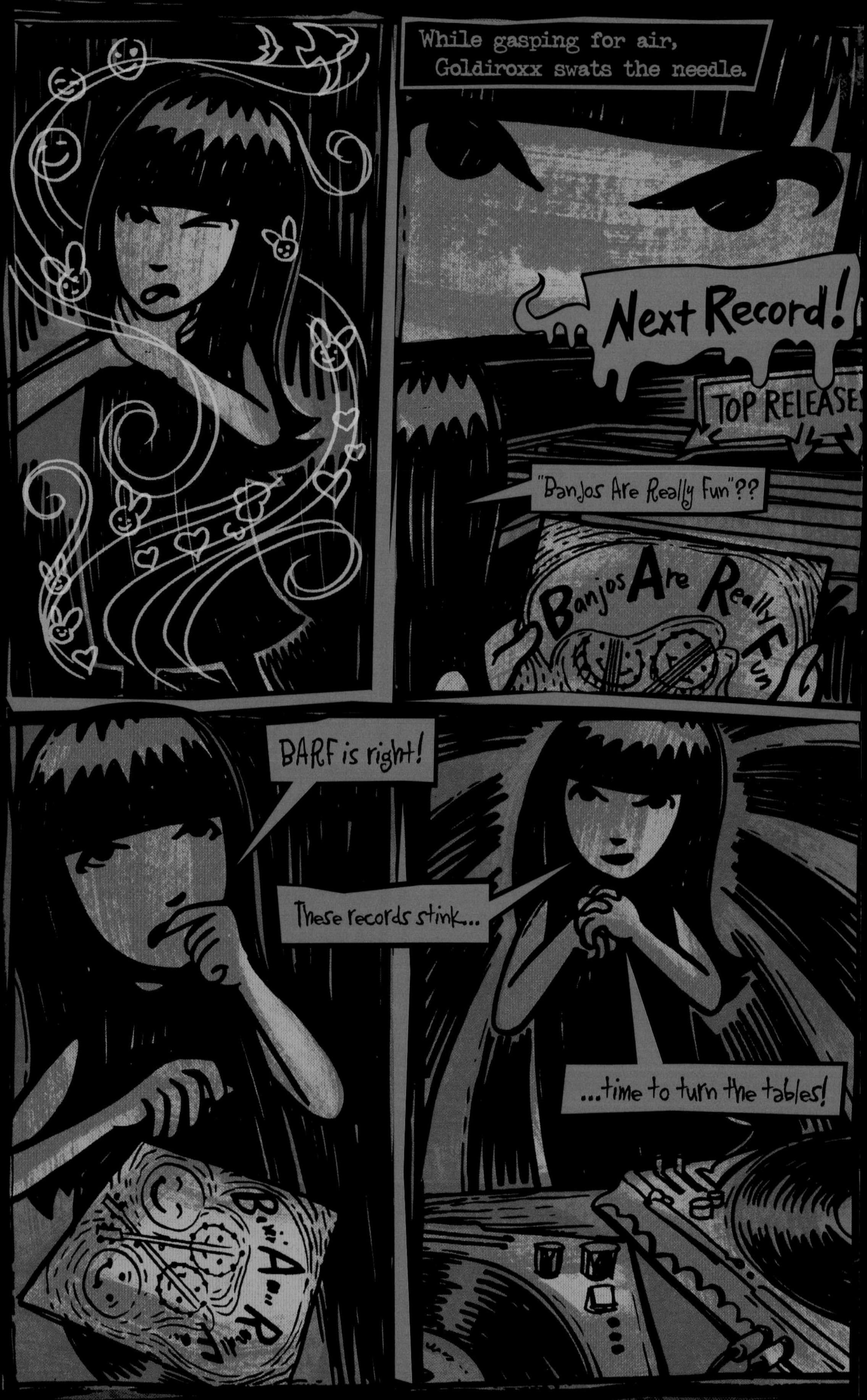

While gasping for air, Goldiroxx swats the needle.
Next Record!
TOP RELEASE
"Banjos Are Really Fun"??
Banjos Are Really Fun
BARF is right!
These records stink...
...time to turn the tables!

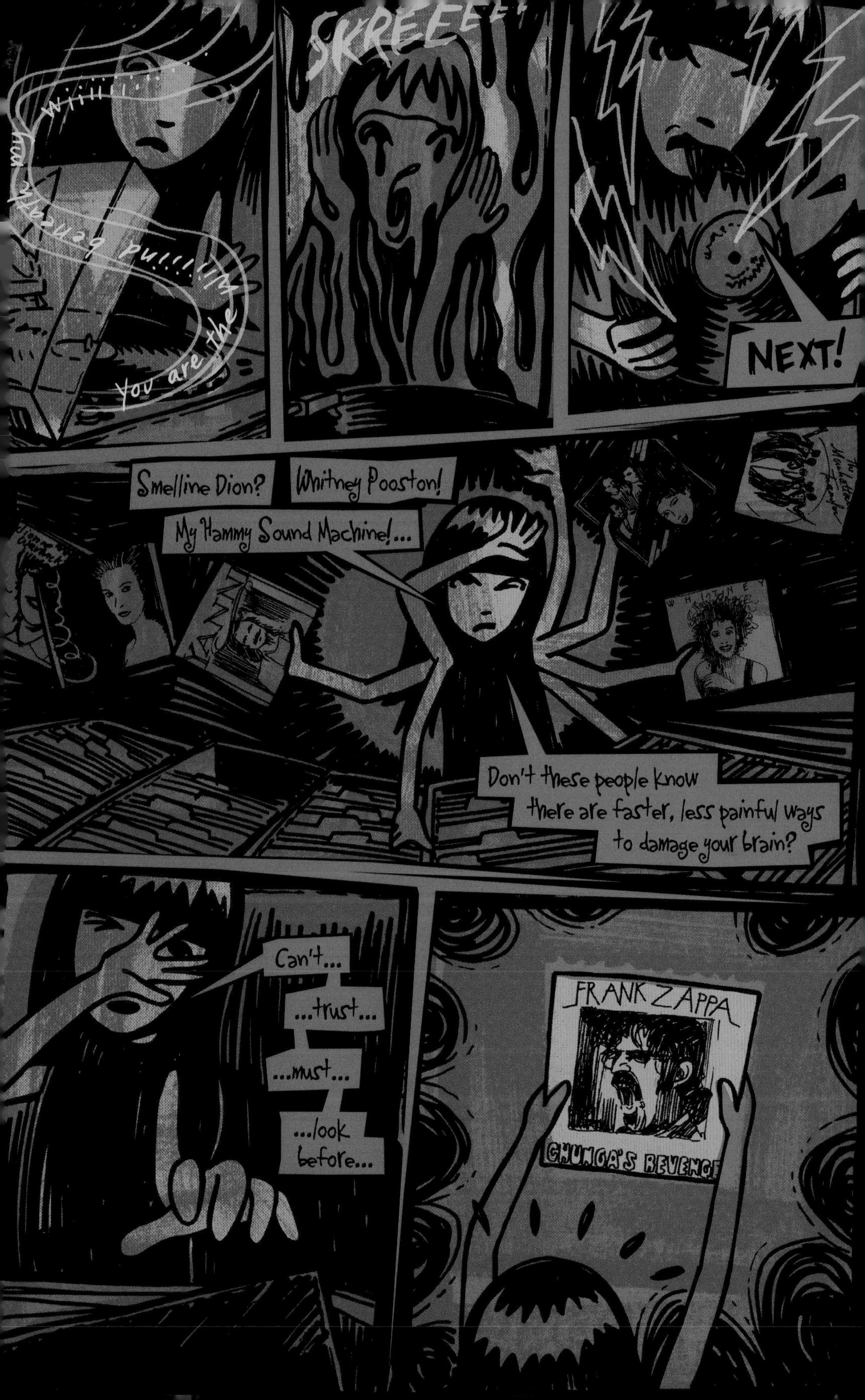
You are the wiiiiind beneath my wiiiiii...
SKREEEE
NEXT!
Smelline Dion?
Whitney Pooston!
My Hammy Sound Machine!...
WHITNEY
Don't these people know there are faster, less painful ways to damage your brain?
Can't...
...trust...
...must...
...look before...
FRANK ZAPPA
CHUNGA'S REVENGE

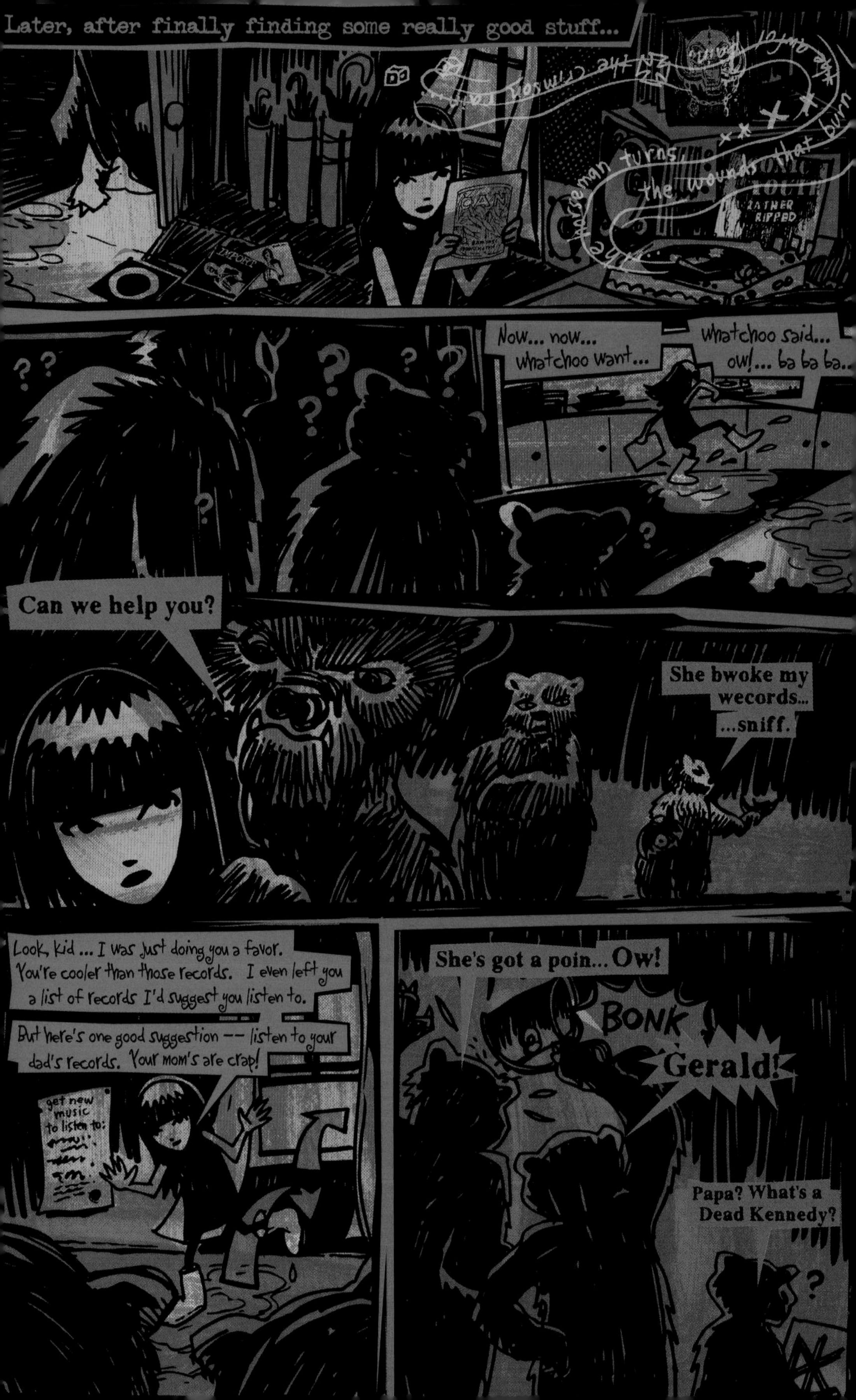

Later, after finally finding some really good stuff...
CAN
IMPORT
RATHER RIPPED
the horseman turns the wounds that burn
Now... now... whatchoo want...
whatchoo said... ow!... ba ba ba...
Can we help you?
She bwoke my wecords... ...sniff.
Look, kid ... I was just doing you a favor. You're cooler than those records. I even left you a list of records I'd suggest you listen to.
But here's one good suggestion -- listen to your dad's records. Your mom's are crap!
get new music to listen to:
She's got a poin... Ow!
BONK
Gerald!
Papa? What's a Dead Kennedy?

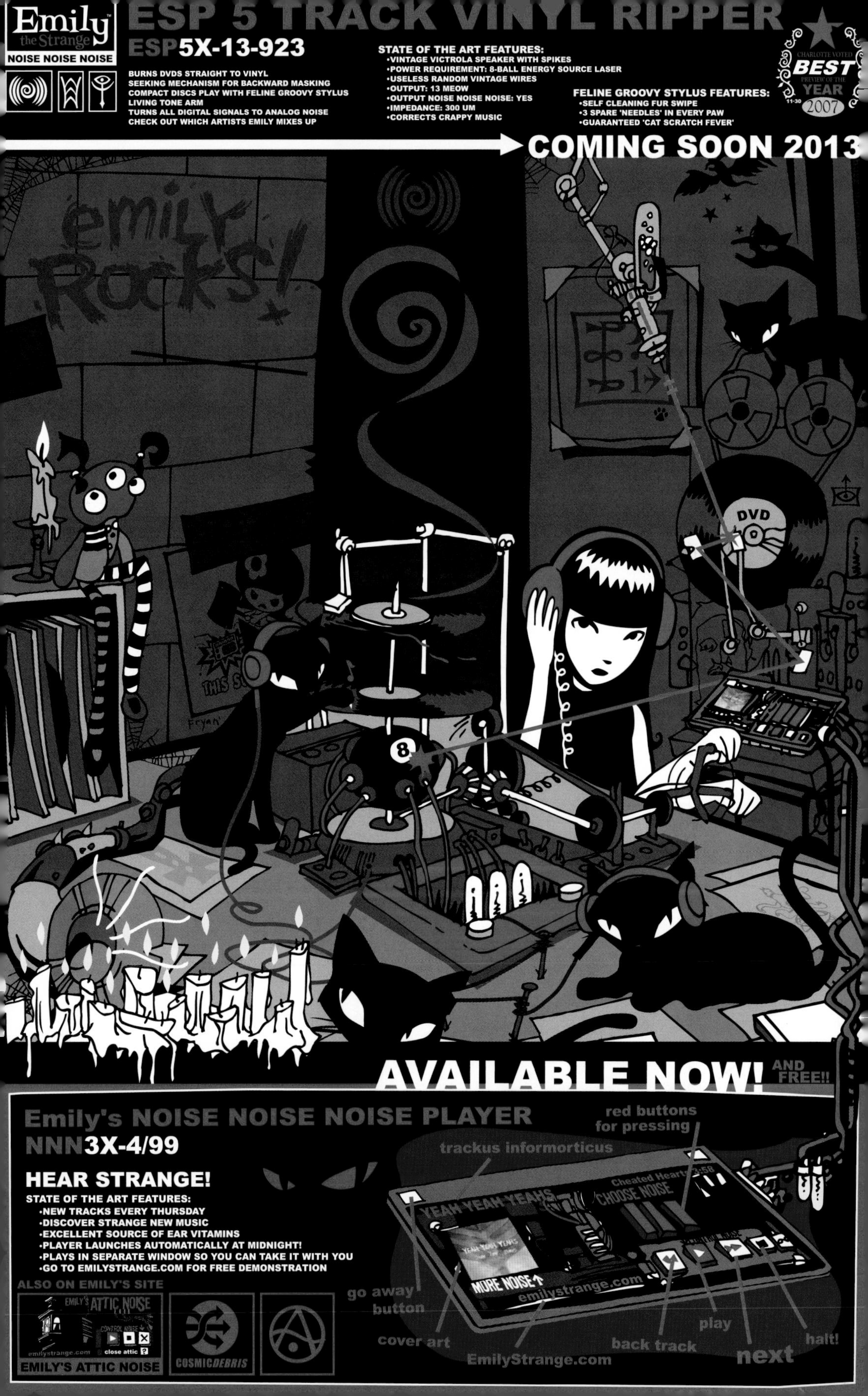
Emily the Strange
NOISE NOISE NOISE
ESP 5 TRACK VINYL RIPPER
ESP5X-13-923
BURNS DVDS STRAIGHT TO VINYL
SEEKING MECHANISM FOR BACKWARD MASKING
COMPACT DISCS PLAY WITH FELINE GROOVY STYLUS
LIVING TONE ARM
TURNS ALL DIGITAL SIGNALS TO ANALOG NOISE
CHECK OUT WHICH ARTISTS EMILY MIXES UP
STATE OF THE ART FEATURES:
•VINTAGE VICTROLA SPEAKER WITH SPIKES
•POWER REQUIREMENT: 8-BALL ENERGY SOURCE LASER
•USELESS RANDOM VINTAGE WIRES
•OUTPUT: 13 MEOW
•OUTPUT NOISE NOISE NOISE: YES
•IMPEDANCE: 300 UM
•CORRECTS CRAPPY MUSIC
FELINE GROOVY STYLUS FEATURES:
•SELF CLEANING FUR SWIPE
•3 SPARE 'NEEDLES' IN EVERY PAW
•GUARANTEED 'CAT SCRATCH FEVER'
CHARLOTTE VOTED BEST PREVIEW OF THE YEAR 11-30 2007
COMING SOON 2013
emily Rocks!
DVD
8
AVAILABLE NOW! AND FREE!!
Emily's NOISE NOISE NOISE PLAYER
NNN3X-4/99
HEAR STRANGE!
STATE OF THE ART FEATURES:
•NEW TRACKS EVERY THURSDAY
•DISCOVER STRANGE NEW MUSIC
•EXCELLENT SOURCE OF EAR VITAMINS
•PLAYER LAUNCHES AUTOMATICALLY AT MIDNIGHT!
•PLAYS IN SEPARATE WINDOW SO YOU CAN TAKE IT WITH YOU
•GO TO EMILYSTRANGE.COM FOR FREE DEMONSTRATION
ALSO ON EMILY'S SITE
EMILY'S ATTIC NOISE
emilystrange.com
close attic
EMILY'S ATTIC NOISE
COSMICDEBRIS
red buttons for pressing
trackus informorticus
Cheated Hearts 3:58
YEAH YEAH YEAHS
CHOOSE NOISE
MORE NOISE
emilystrange.com
go away button
cover art
EmilyStrange.com
back track
play
next
halt!

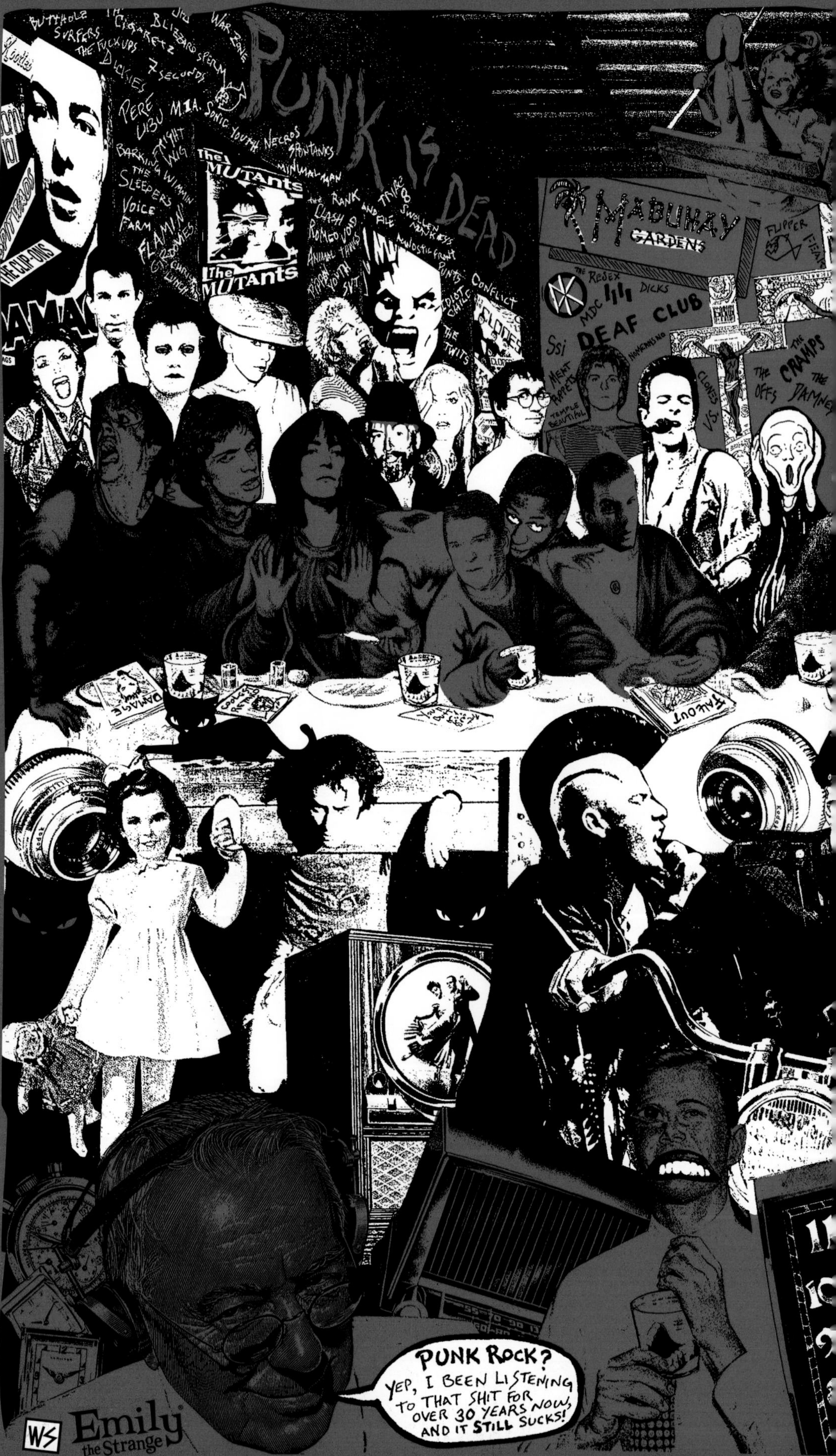
PUNK IS DEAD
BUTTHOLE SURFERS
THE FUCKUPS
CIGARETZ
BLIZZARD SPERM
WAR ZONE
DICKIES
7 SECONDS
PERE UBU
M.I.A.
SONIC YOUTH
NECROS
SPONTANEOUS
RIGHT WIG
BARKING WIMMIN
THE SLEEPERS
VOICE FARM
FLAMIN' GROOVIES
The MUTANTS
The MUTANTS
MINIMAL MAN
THE RANK AND FILE
THE CLASH
ROMEO VOID
ANIMAL TRAVIS
SWOLLEN MONKEYS
AGNOSTIC FRONT
CONFLICT
IDIOT CHILD
THE TWITS
THE CLIP-ONS
MABUHAY GARDENS
FLIPPER
THE RESEX
DICKS
MDC
DEAF CLUB
Ssi
MEAT PUPPETS
TEMPLE BEAUTIFUL
CLONES
THE CRAMPS
THE OFFS
THE DAMNED
FALLOUT
PUNK ROCK?
YEP, I BEEN LISTENING TO THAT SHIT FOR OVER 30 YEARS NOW, AND IT STILL SUCKS!
WS
Emily the Strange

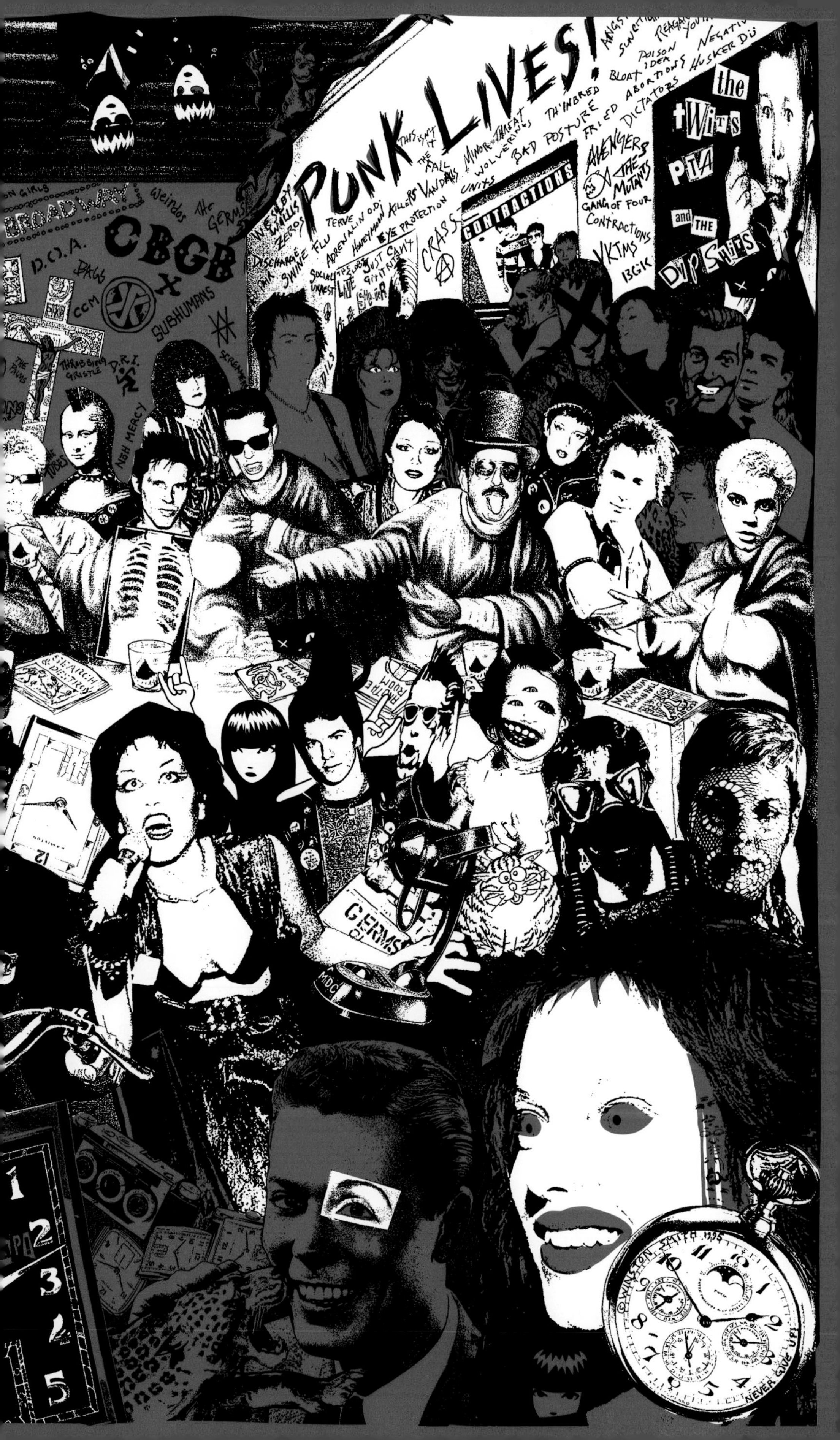

PUNK LIVES!
THIS isn't IT
THE FALL
MINOR THREAT
WOLVERINES
TH'INBRED
BAD POSTURE
FRIED ABORTIONS
DICTATORS
BLOAT
POISON IDEA
HUSKER DÜ
REAGAN YOUTH
WESLEY WILLIS
ZEROS
TERVE
DISCHARGE
SWINE FLU
ADRENALIN O.D.
KILLERS
VANDALS
EYE PROTECTION
UNITS
CRASS
CONTRACTIONS
AVENGERS
THE MUTANTS
GANG OF FOUR
CONTRACTIONS
VKTMS
BGK
the TWITS PTA and THE DIPSHITS
BROADWAY
Weirdos
the GERMS
CBGB
D.O.A.
BAGS
CCM
SUBHUMANS
THROBBING GRISTLE
D.R.I.
SCREAMERS
SEARCH & DESTROY
GERMS
MDC
WINSTON SMITH
NEVER GIVE UP!

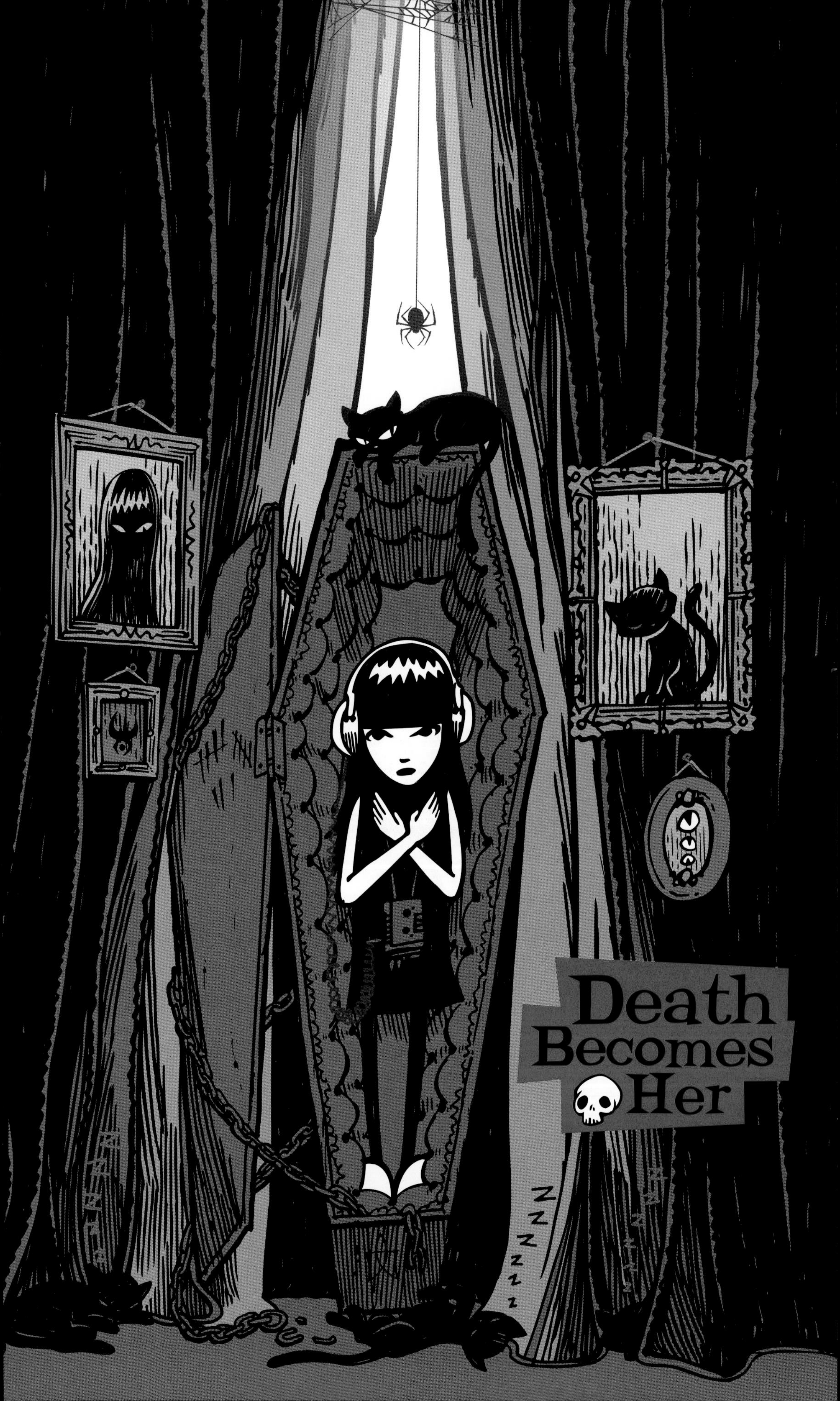
Death
Becomes
Her
Z
Z
Z
z
z
z
z

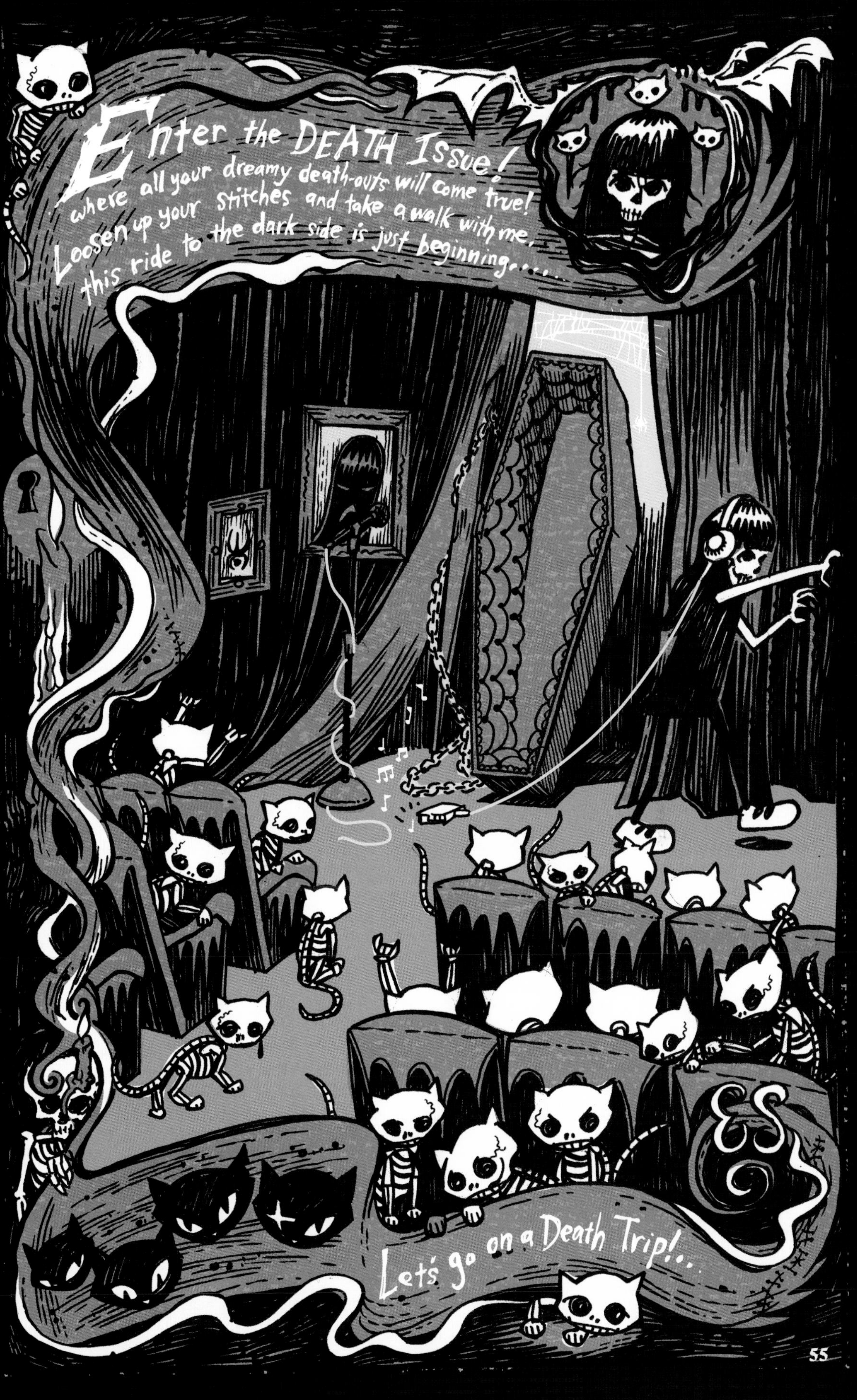
Enter the DEATH Issue!
where all your dreamy death-outs will come true!
Loosen up your stitches and take a walk with me,
this ride to the dark side is just beginning.....
Let's go on a Death Trip!..

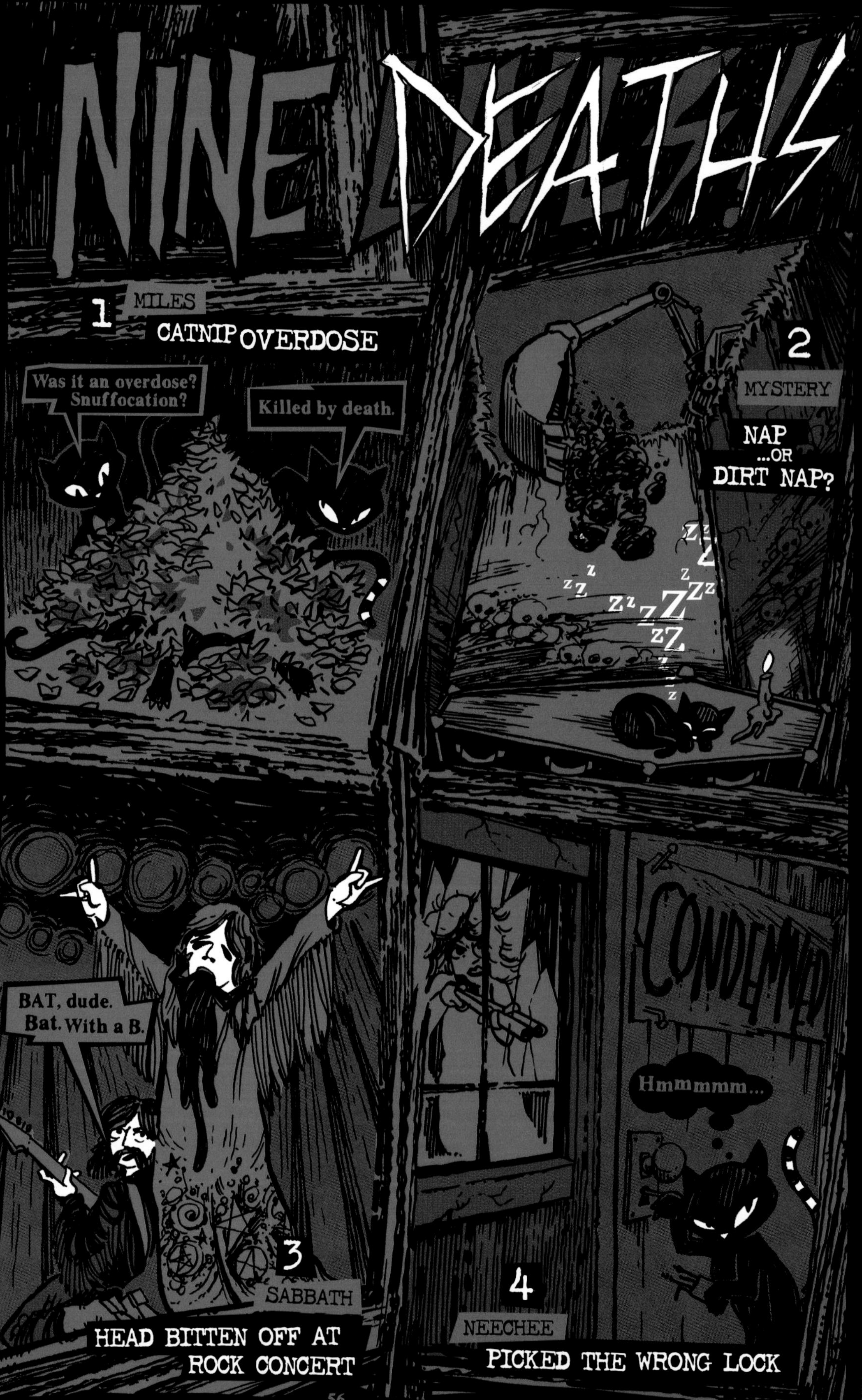
NINE DEATHS
1
MILES
CATNIP OVERDOSE
Was it an overdose? Snuffocation?
Killed by death.
2
MYSTERY
NAP ...OR DIRT NAP?
3
SABBATH
BAT, dude. Bat. With a B.
HEAD BITTEN OFF AT ROCK CONCERT
4
NEECHEE
CONDEMNED
Hmmmmm...
PICKED THE WRONG LOCK

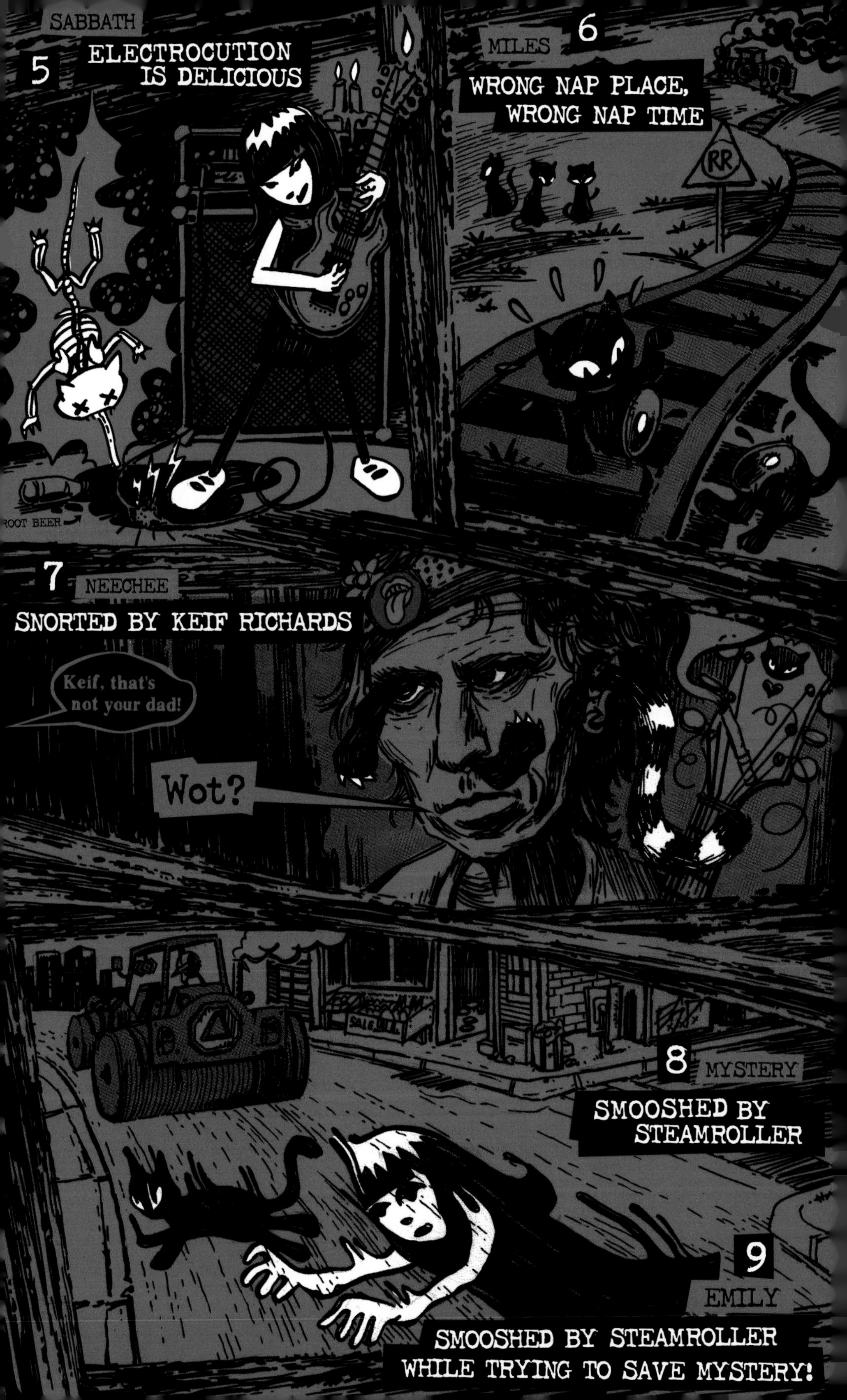

SABBATH
5
ELECTROCUTION IS DELICIOUS
ROOT BEER
MILES
6
WRONG NAP PLACE, WRONG NAP TIME
RR
7
NEECHEE
SNORTED BY KEIF RICHARDS
Keif, that's not your dad!
Wot?
SALE
8
MYSTERY
SMOOSHED BY STEAMROLLER
9
EMILY
SMOOSHED BY STEAMROLLER WHILE TRYING TO SAVE MYSTERY!

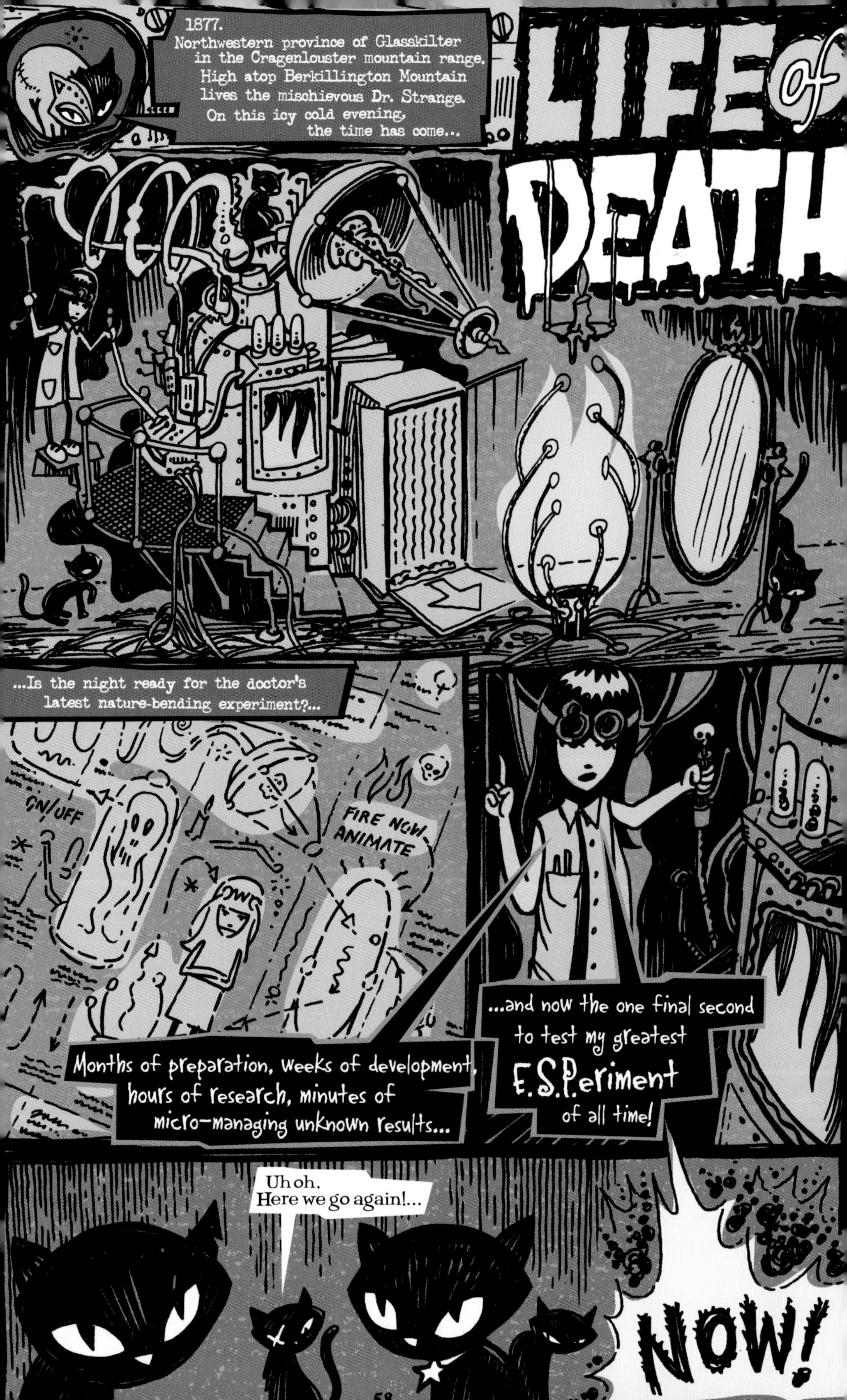

1877.
Northwestern province of Glasskilter in the Cragenlouster mountain range. High atop Berkillington Mountain lives the mischievous Dr. Strange. On this icy cold evening, the time has come...
LIFE of DEATH
...Is the night ready for the doctor's latest nature-bending experiment?...
ON/OFF
FIRE NOW ANIMATE
Months of preparation, weeks of development, hours of research, minutes of micro-managing unknown results...
...and now the one final second to test my greatest E.S.P.eriment of all time!
Uh oh. Here we go again!...
NOW!

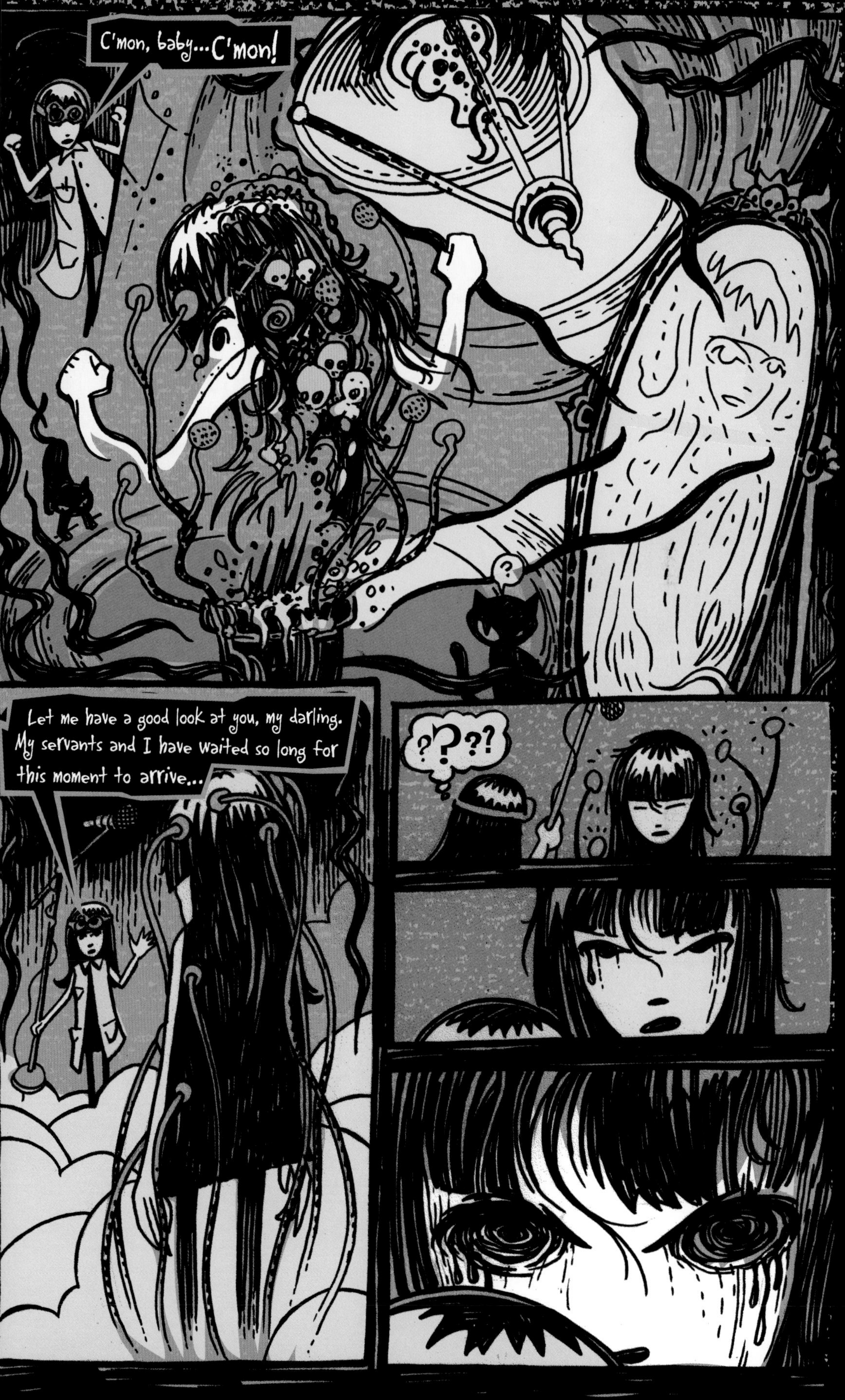
C'mon, baby...C'mon!
?
Let me have a good look at you, my darling. My servants and I have waited so long for this moment to arrive...
??????

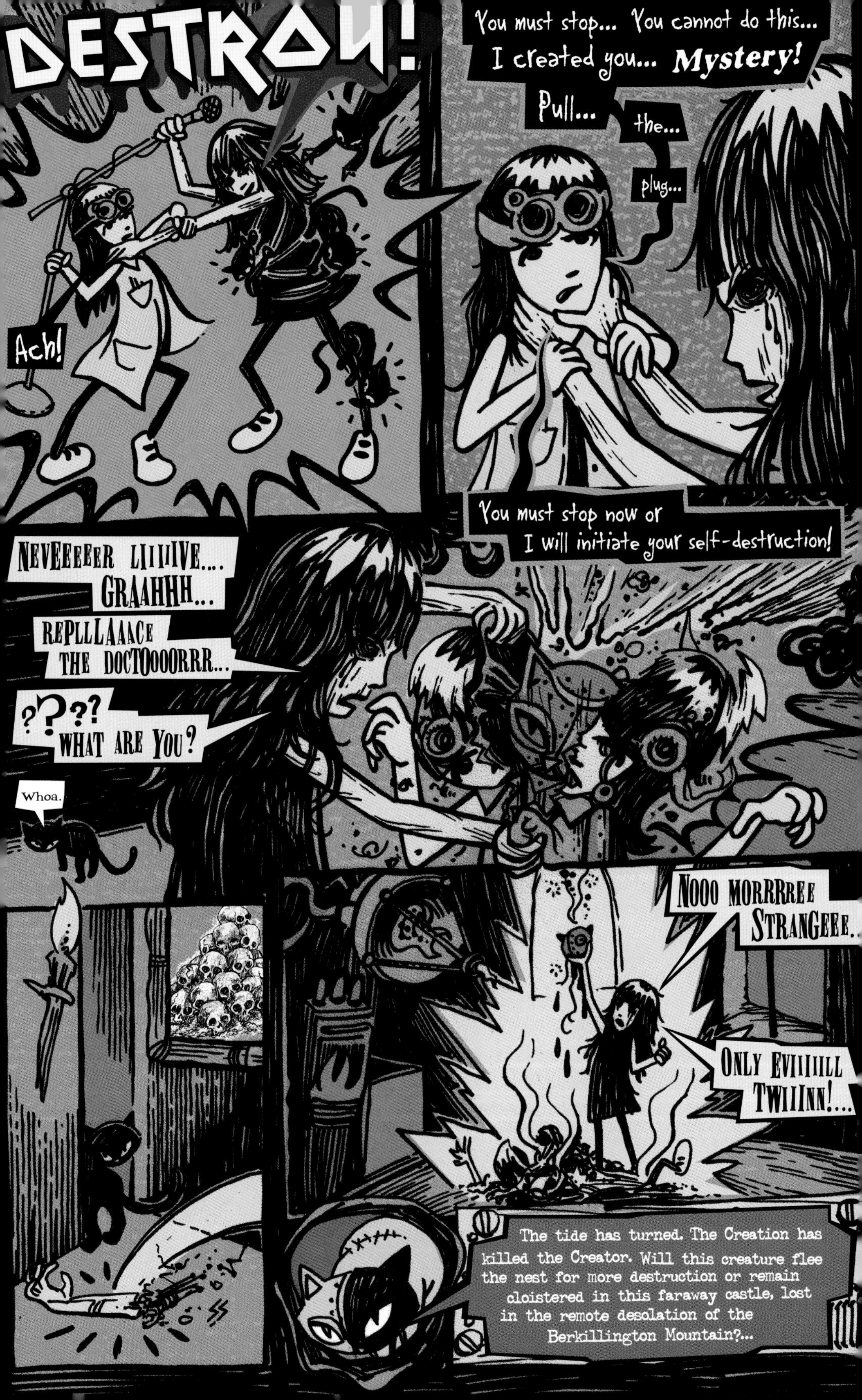
DESTROY!
Ach!
You must stop... You cannot do this... I created you... Mystery!
Pull...
the...
plug...
You must stop now or I will initiate your self-destruction!
NEVEEEEER LIIIIIVE.... GRAAHHH... REPLLLAAACE THE DOCTOOOORRR...
???? WHAT ARE YOU?
Whoa.
NOOO MORRRREE STRANGEEE..
ONLY EVIIIIILL TWIIINN!...
The tide has turned. The Creation has killed the Creator. Will this creature flee the nest for more destruction or remain cloistered in this faraway castle, lost in the remote desolation of the Berkillington Mountain?...

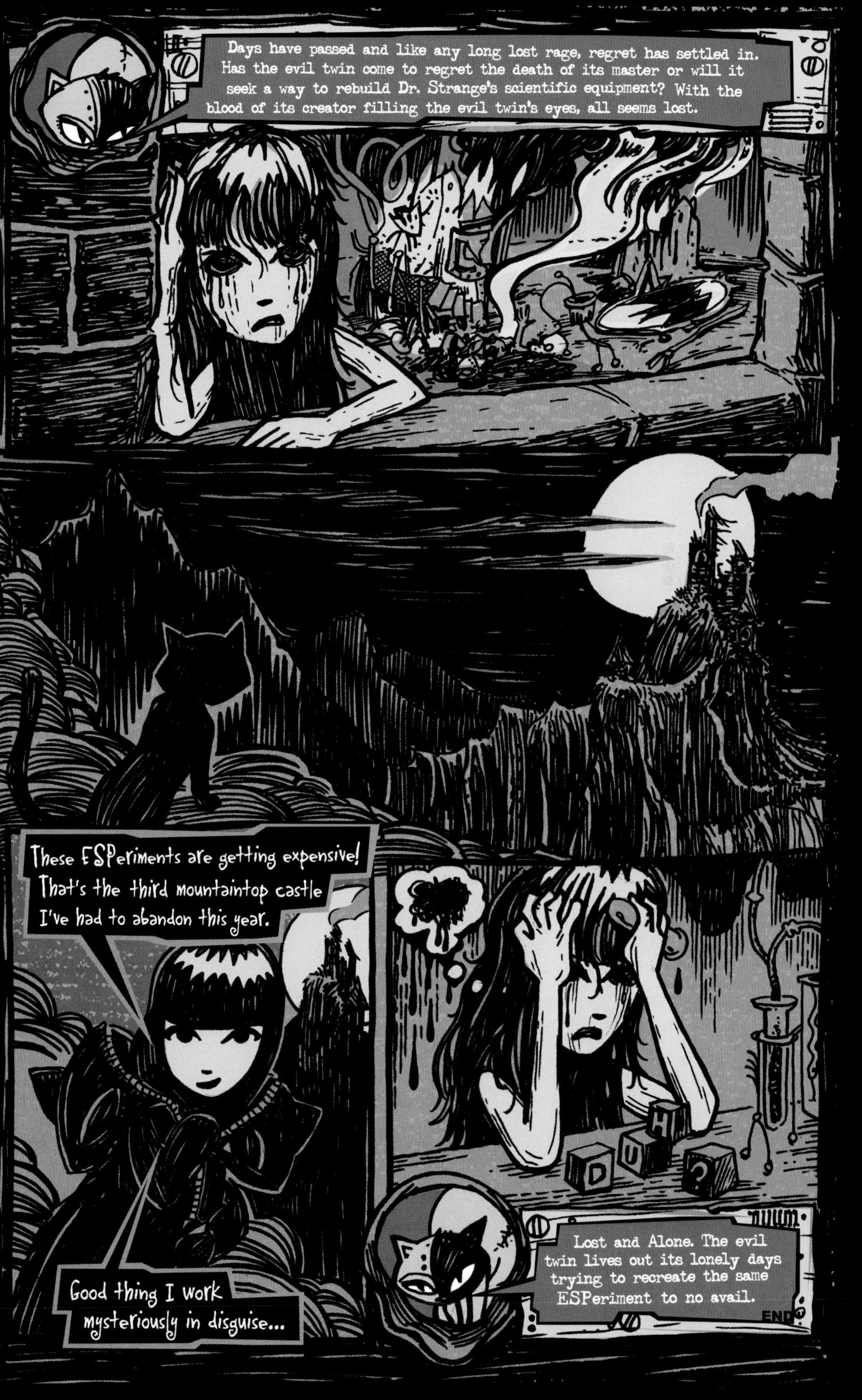
Days have passed and like any long lost rage, regret has settled in. Has the evil twin come to regret the death of its master or will it seek a way to rebuild Dr. Strange's scientific equipment? With the blood of its creator filling the evil twin's eyes, all seems lost.
These ESPeriments are getting expensive! That's the third mountaintop castle I've had to abandon this year.
Good thing I work mysteriously in disguise...
H
D U ?
Lost and Alone. The evil twin lives out its lonely days trying to recreate the same ESPeriment to no avail.
END

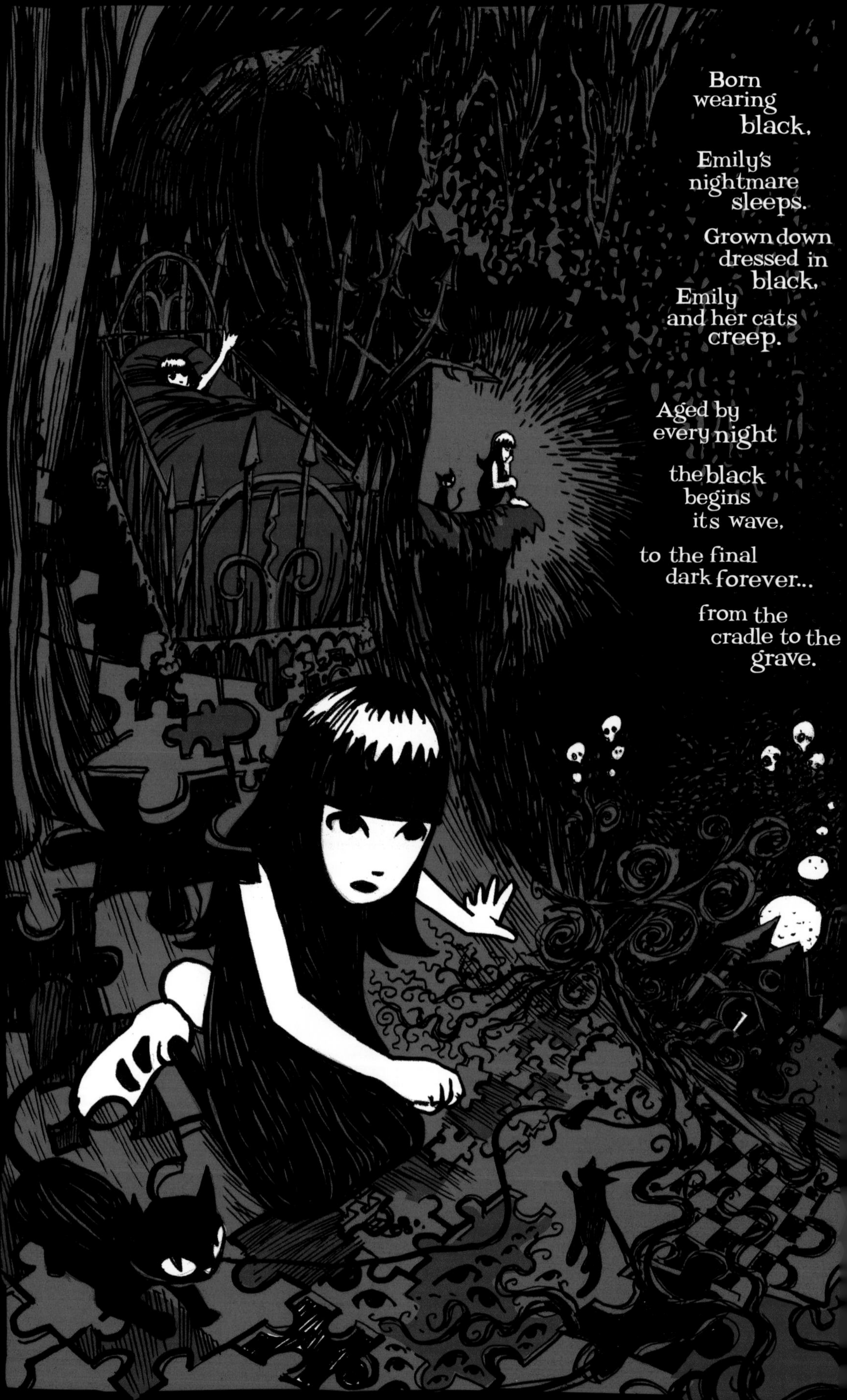
Born
wearing
black.
Emily's
nightmare
sleeps.
Grown down
dressed in
black.
Emily
and her cats
creep.
Aged by
every night
the black
begins
its wave.
to the final
dark forever...
from the
cradle to the
grave.

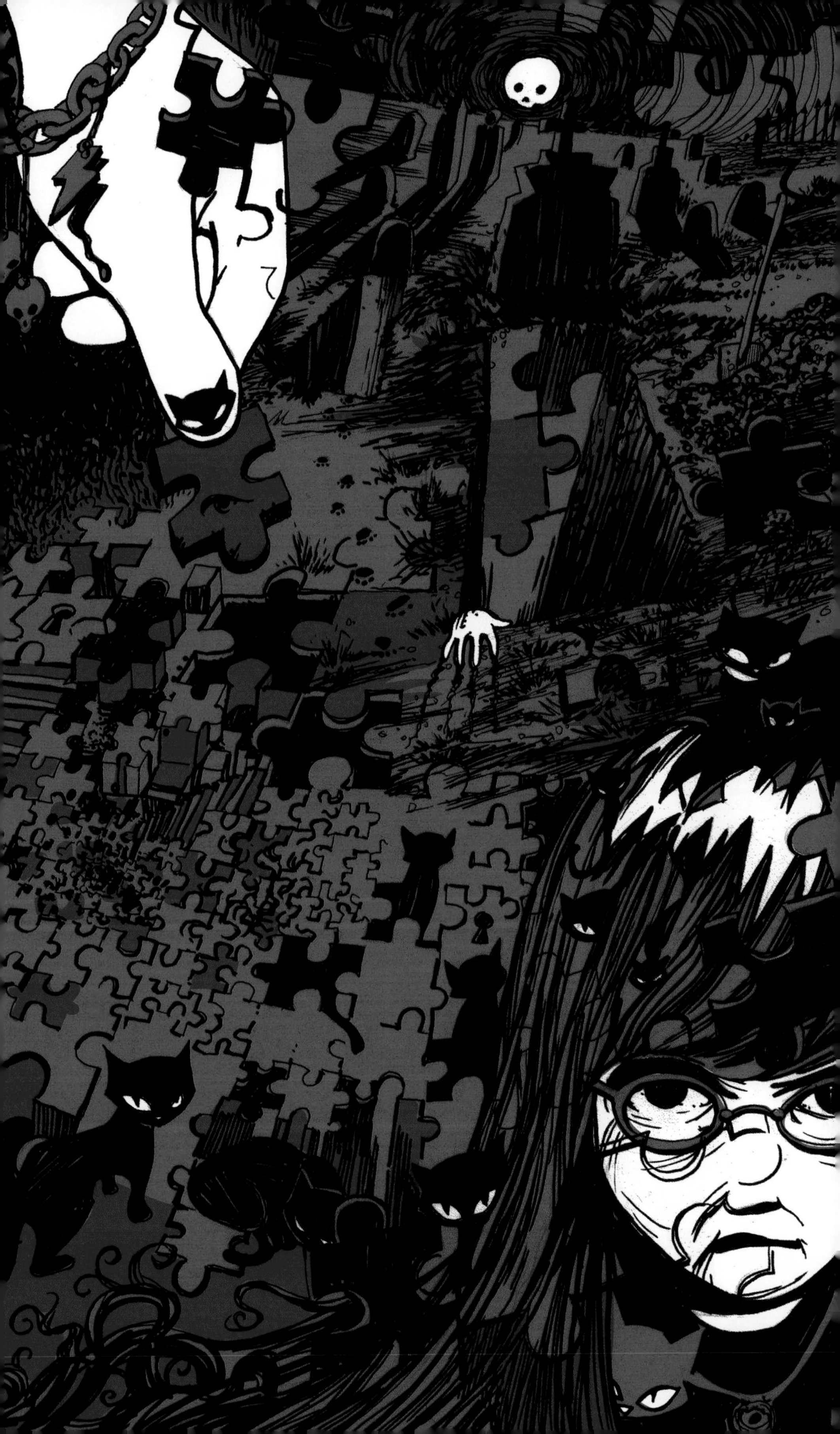

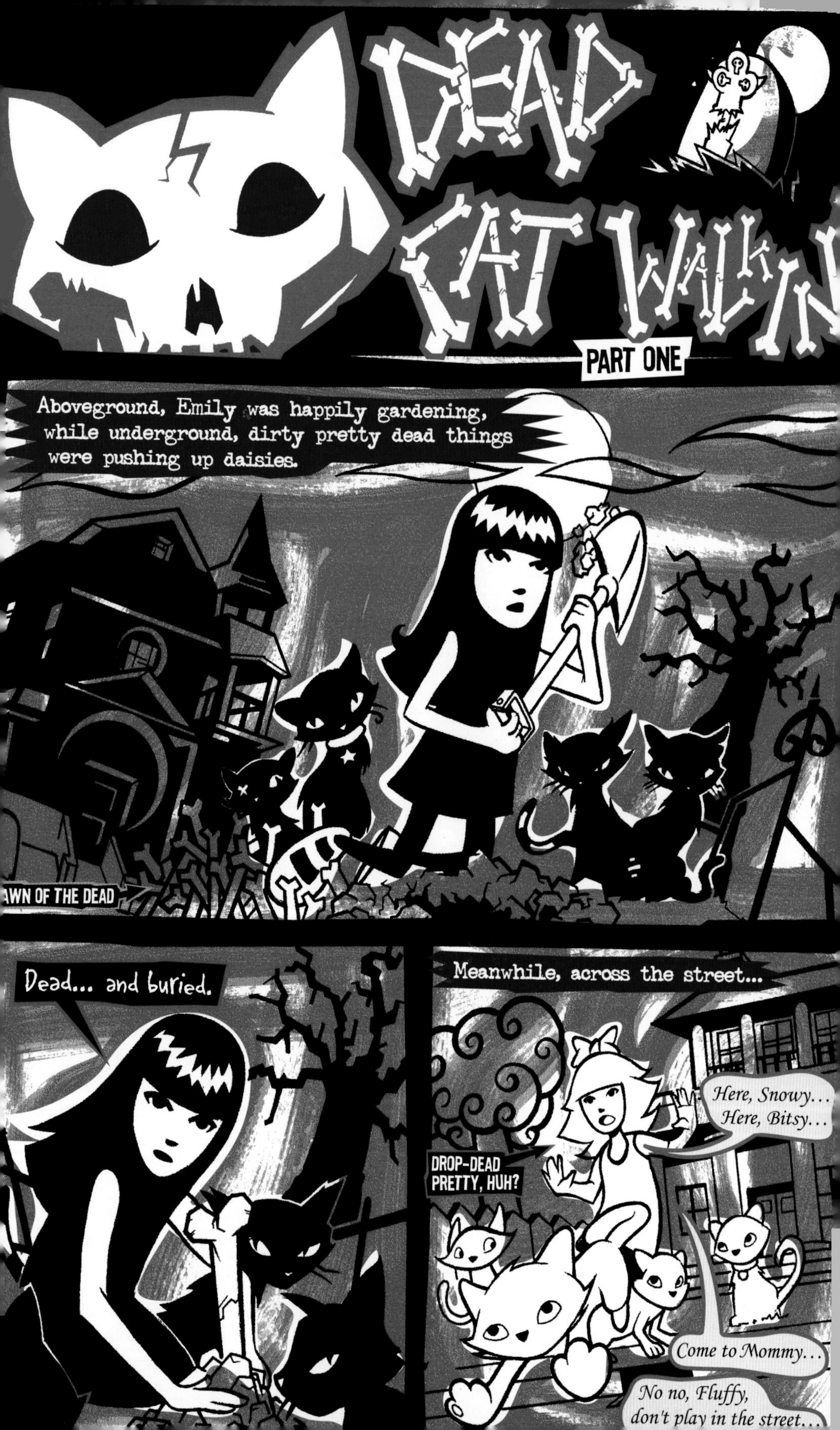
DEAD CAT WALKIN
PART ONE
Aboveground, Emily was happily gardening, while underground, dirty pretty dead things were pushing up daisies.
AWN OF THE DEAD
Dead... and buried.
Meanwhile, across the street...
DROP-DEAD PRETTY, HUH?
Here, Snowy... Here, Bitsy...
Come to Mommy...
No no, Fluffy, don't play in the street...

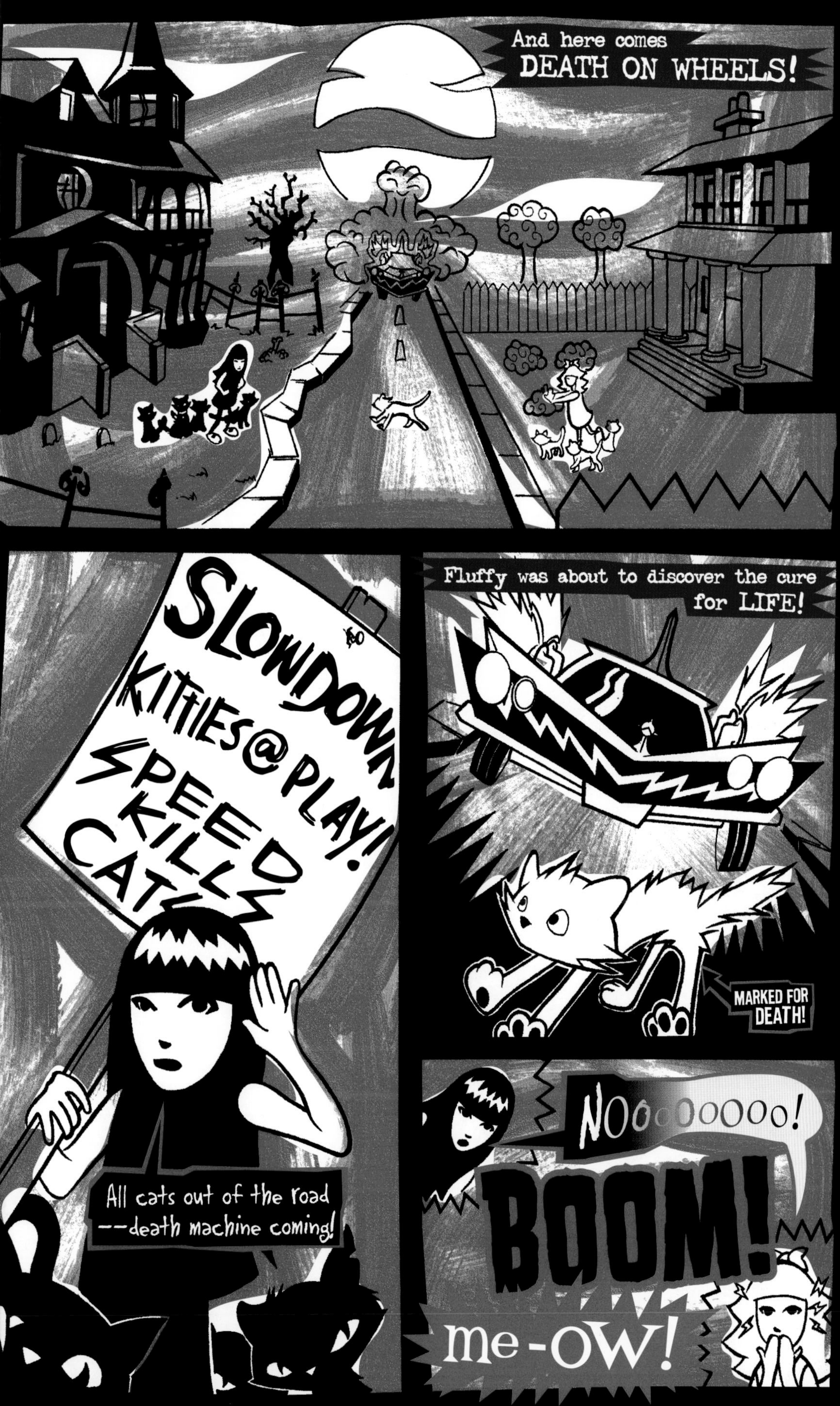

And here comes DEATH ON WHEELS!
SLOWDOWN
KITTIES@PLAY!
SPEED KILLS CATS
All cats out of the road --death machine coming!
Fluffy was about to discover the cure for LIFE!
MARKED FOR DEATH!
NOOoOOOOo!
BOOM!
me-OW!

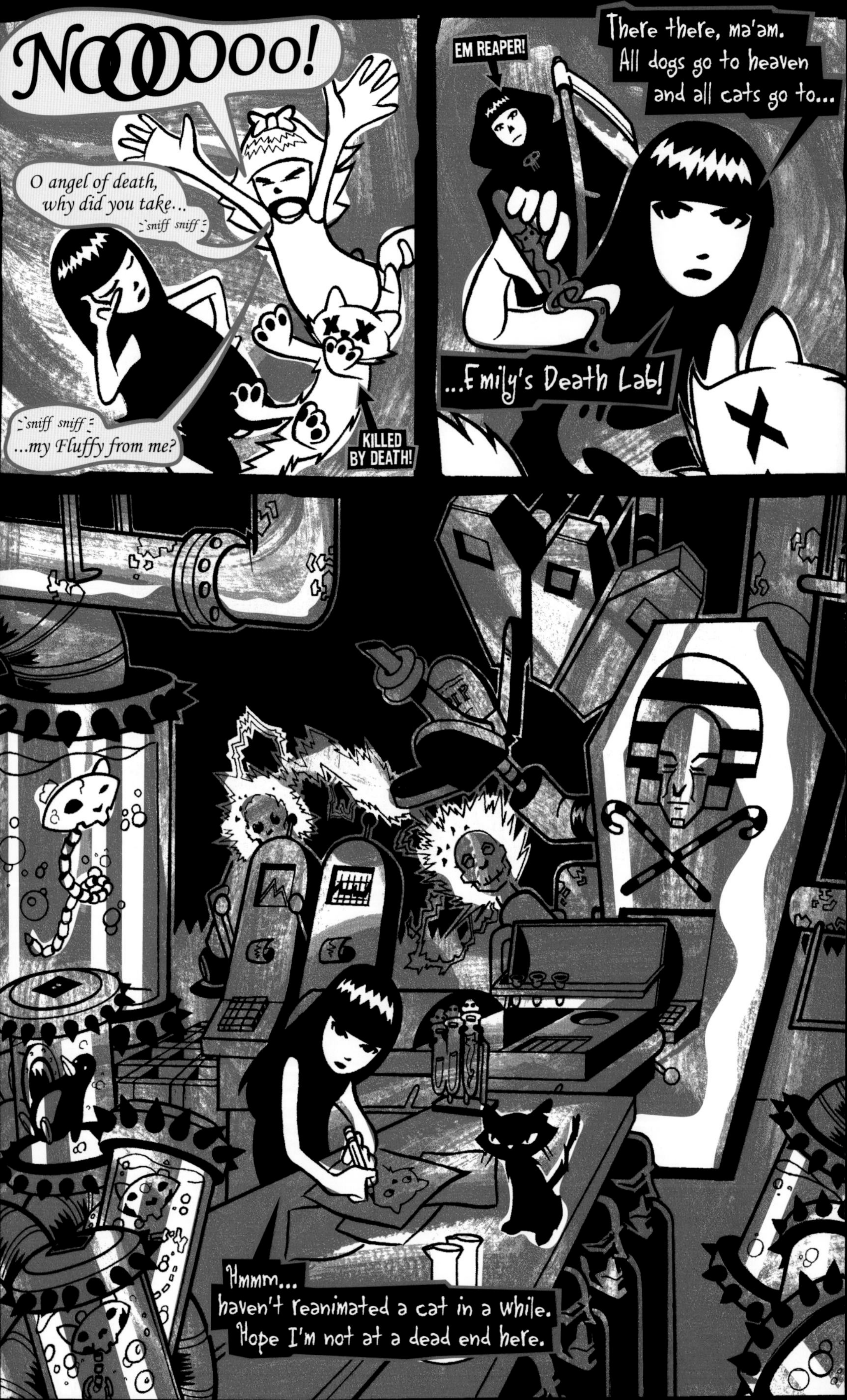
NOOOOoo!
O angel of death, why did you take...
sniff sniff
sniff sniff
...my Fluffy from me?
KILLED BY DEATH!
EM REAPER!
There there, ma'am. All dogs go to heaven and all cats go to...
...Emily's Death Lab!
R.I.P.
Hmmm... haven't reanimated a cat in a while. Hope I'm not at a dead end here.

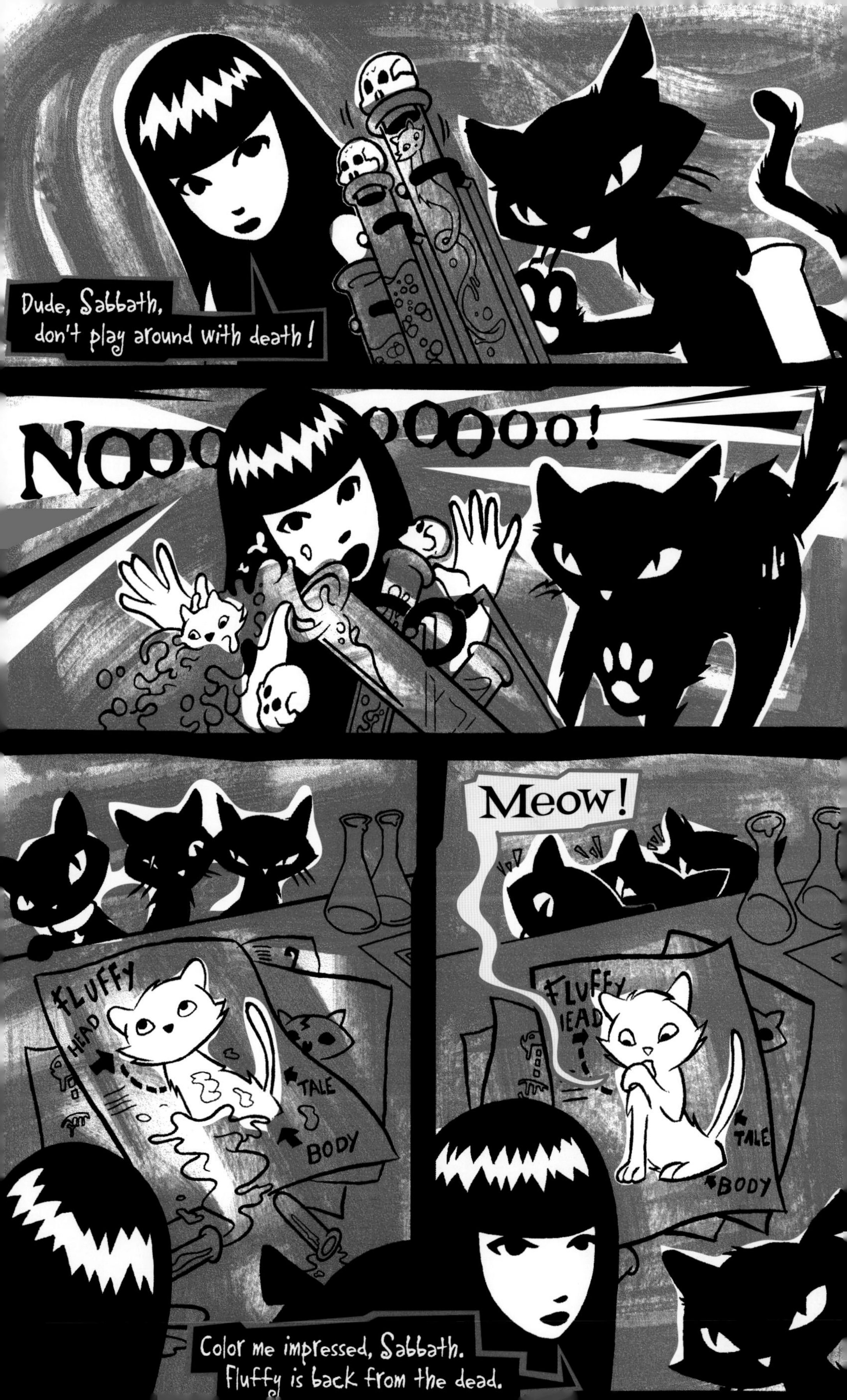
Dude, Sabbath, don't play around with death!
NOOOOOOOOOo!
FLUFFY
HEAD
TALE
BODY
Meow!
FLUFFY
HEAD
TALE
BODY
Color me impressed, Sabbath. Fluffy is back from the dead.

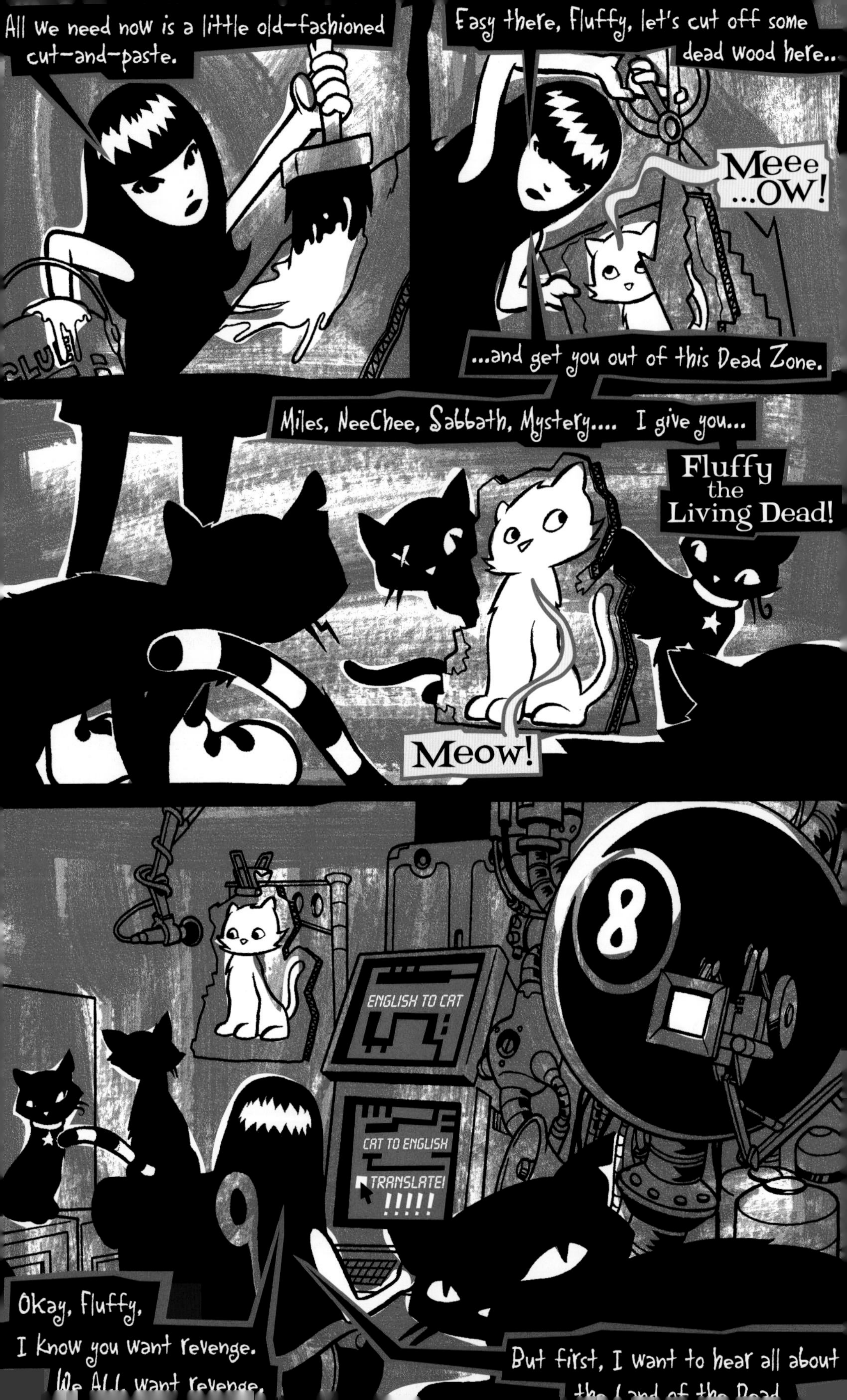
All we need now is a little old-fashioned cut-and-paste.
GLUE
Easy there, Fluffy, let's cut off some dead wood here..
Meee ...OW!
...and get you out of this Dead Zone.
Miles, NeeChee, Sabbath, Mystery.... I give you...
Fluffy the Living Dead!
Meow!
ENGLISH TO CAT
CAT TO ENGLISH
TRANSLATE!
!!!!!
8
Okay, Fluffy,
I know you want revenge.
We ALL want revenge.
But first, I want to hear all about

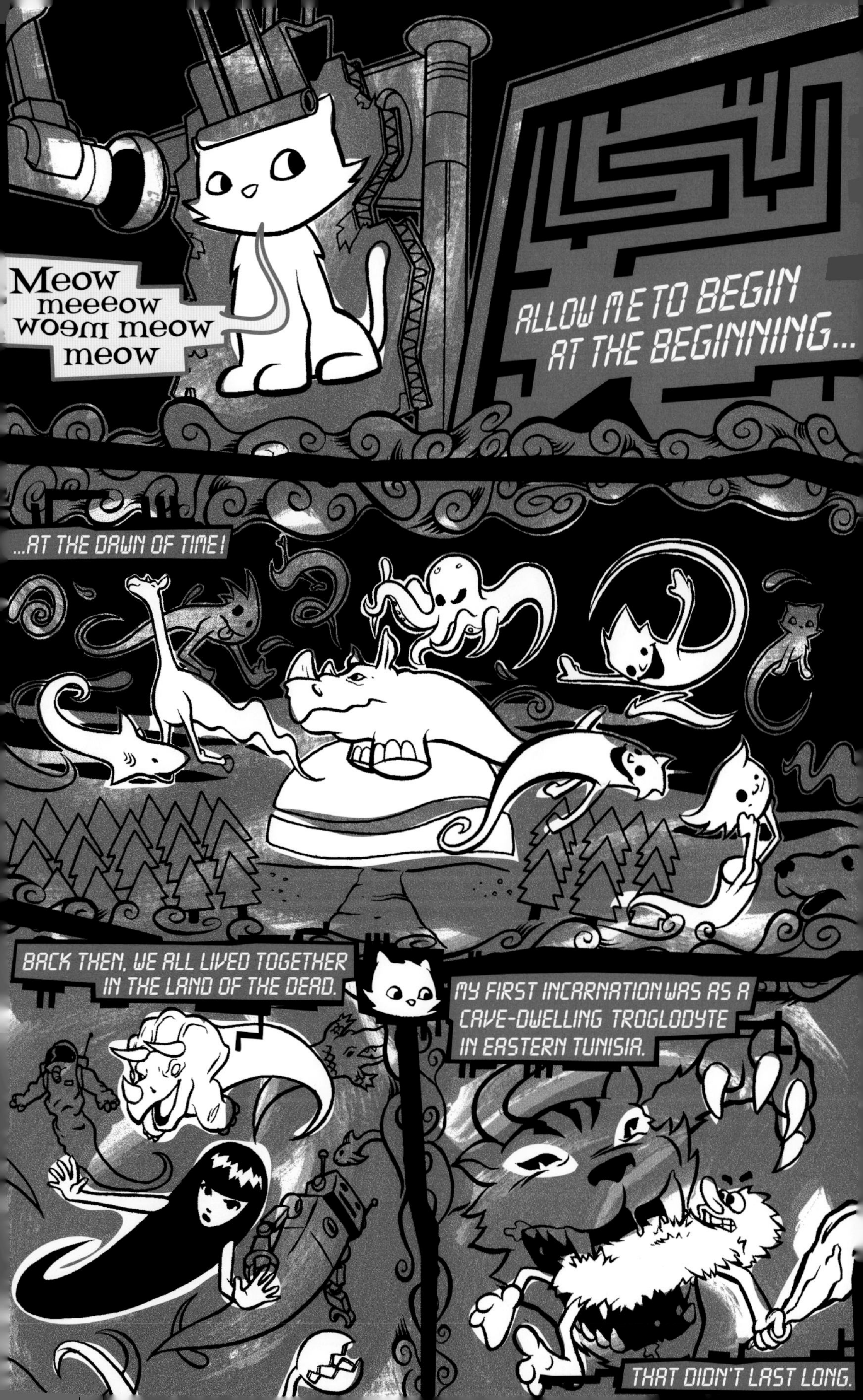
Meow meeeow woem meow meow
ALLOW ME TO BEGIN AT THE BEGINNING...
...AT THE DAWN OF TIME!
BACK THEN, WE ALL LIVED TOGETHER IN THE LAND OF THE DEAD.
MY FIRST INCARNATION WAS AS A CAVE-DWELLING TROGLODYTE IN EASTERN TUNISIA.
THAT DIDN'T LAST LONG.

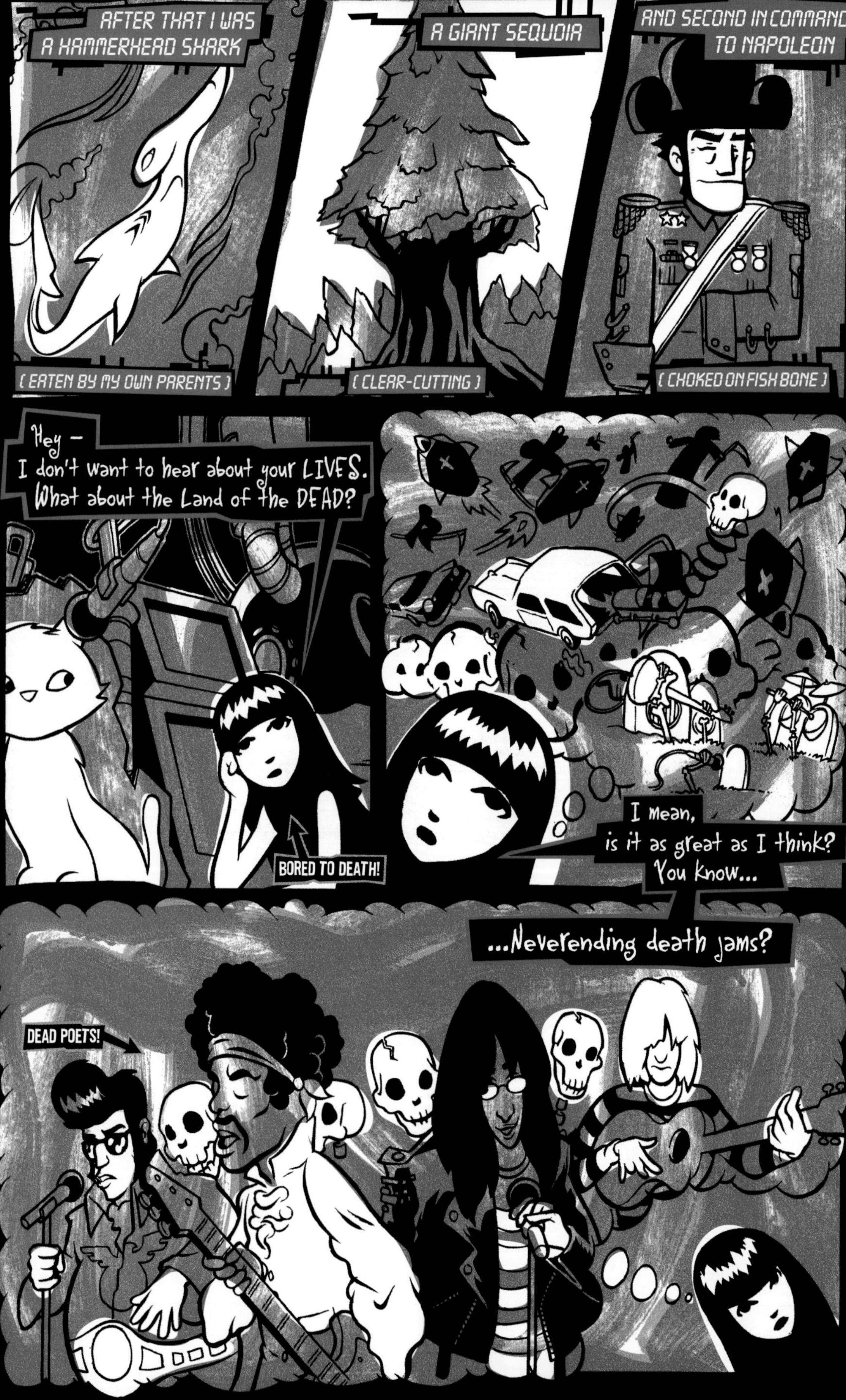
AFTER THAT I WAS A HAMMERHEAD SHARK
(EATEN BY MY OWN PARENTS)
A GIANT SEQUOIA
(CLEAR-CUTTING)
AND SECOND IN COMMAND TO NAPOLEON
(CHOKED ON FISH BONE)
Hey — I don't want to hear about your LIVES. What about the Land of the DEAD?
BORED TO DEATH!
I mean, is it as great as I think? You know...
...Neverending death jams?
DEAD POETS!

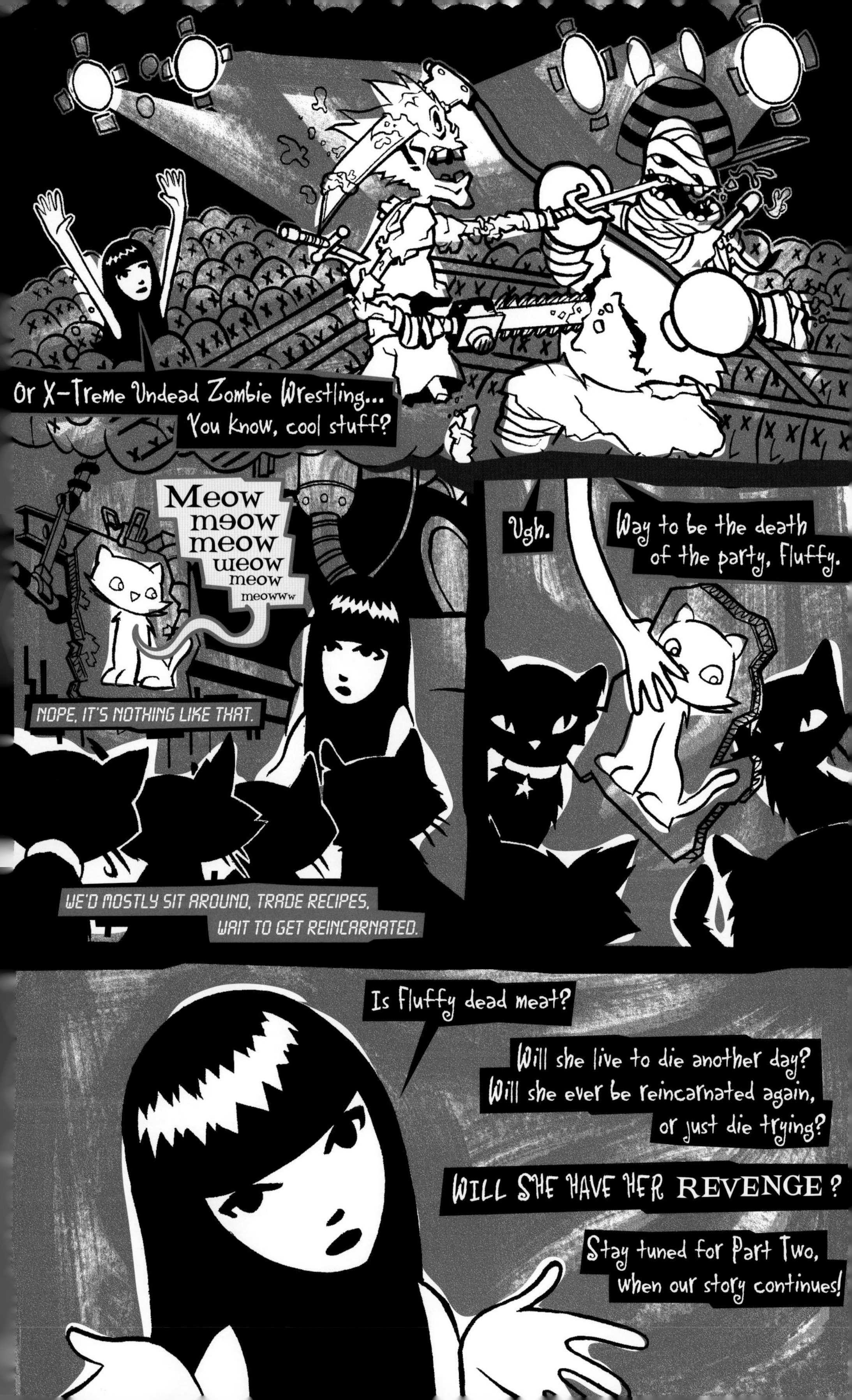
Or X-Treme Undead Zombie Wrestling... You know, cool stuff?
Meow meow meow meow meow meowww
NOPE, IT'S NOTHING LIKE THAT.
WE'D MOSTLY SIT AROUND, TRADE RECIPES, WAIT TO GET REINCARNATED.
Ugh.
Way to be the death of the party, Fluffy.
Is Fluffy dead meat?
Will she live to die another day? Will she ever be reincarnated again, or just die trying?
WILL SHE HAVE HER REVENGE?
Stay tuned for Part Two, when our story continues!

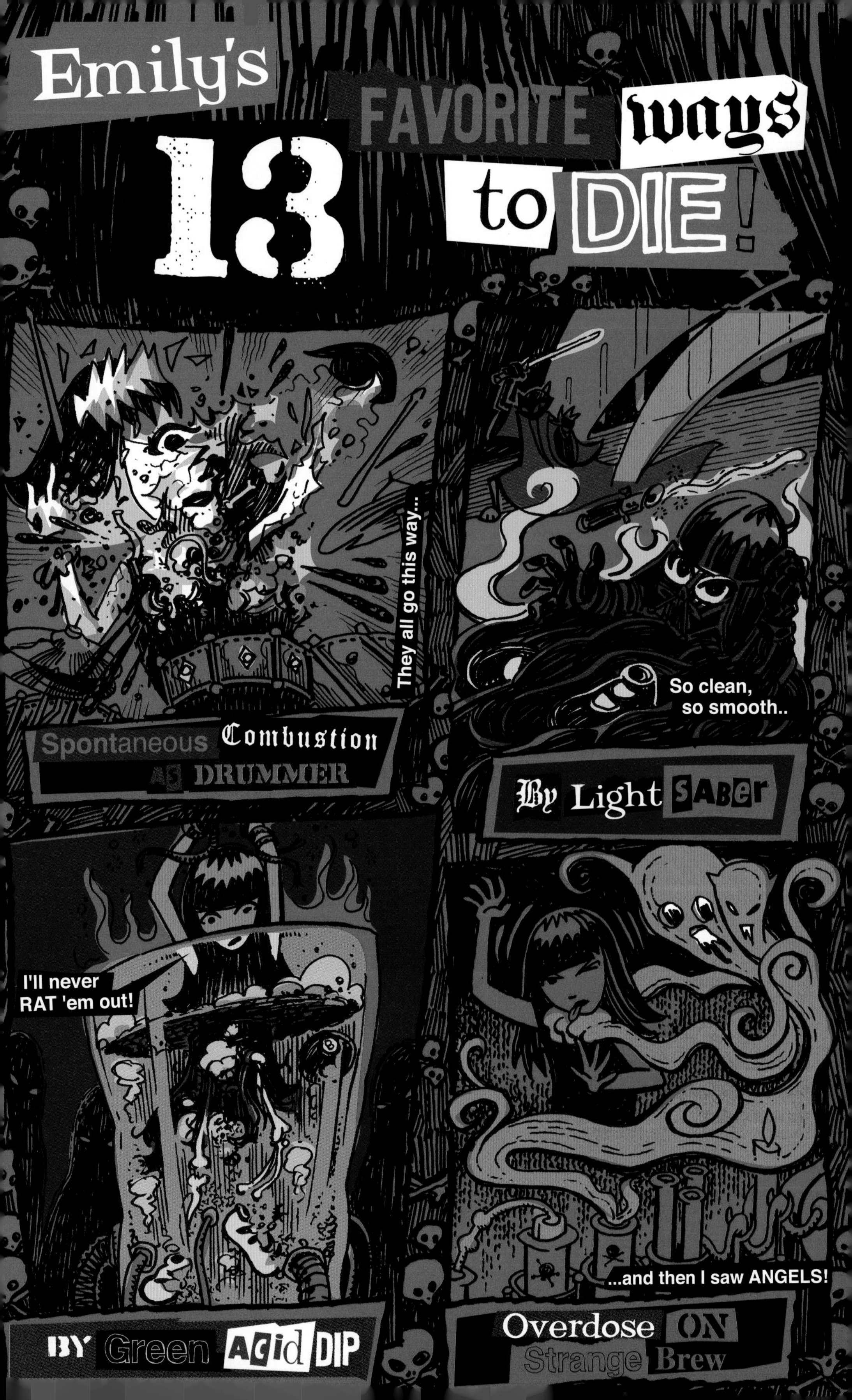
Emily's 13 FAVORITE ways to DIE!
They all go this way...
Spontaneous Combustion AS DRUMMER
So clean, so smooth..
By Light SABer
I'll never RAT 'em out!
BY Green Acid DIP
...and then I saw ANGELS!
Overdose ON Strange Brew

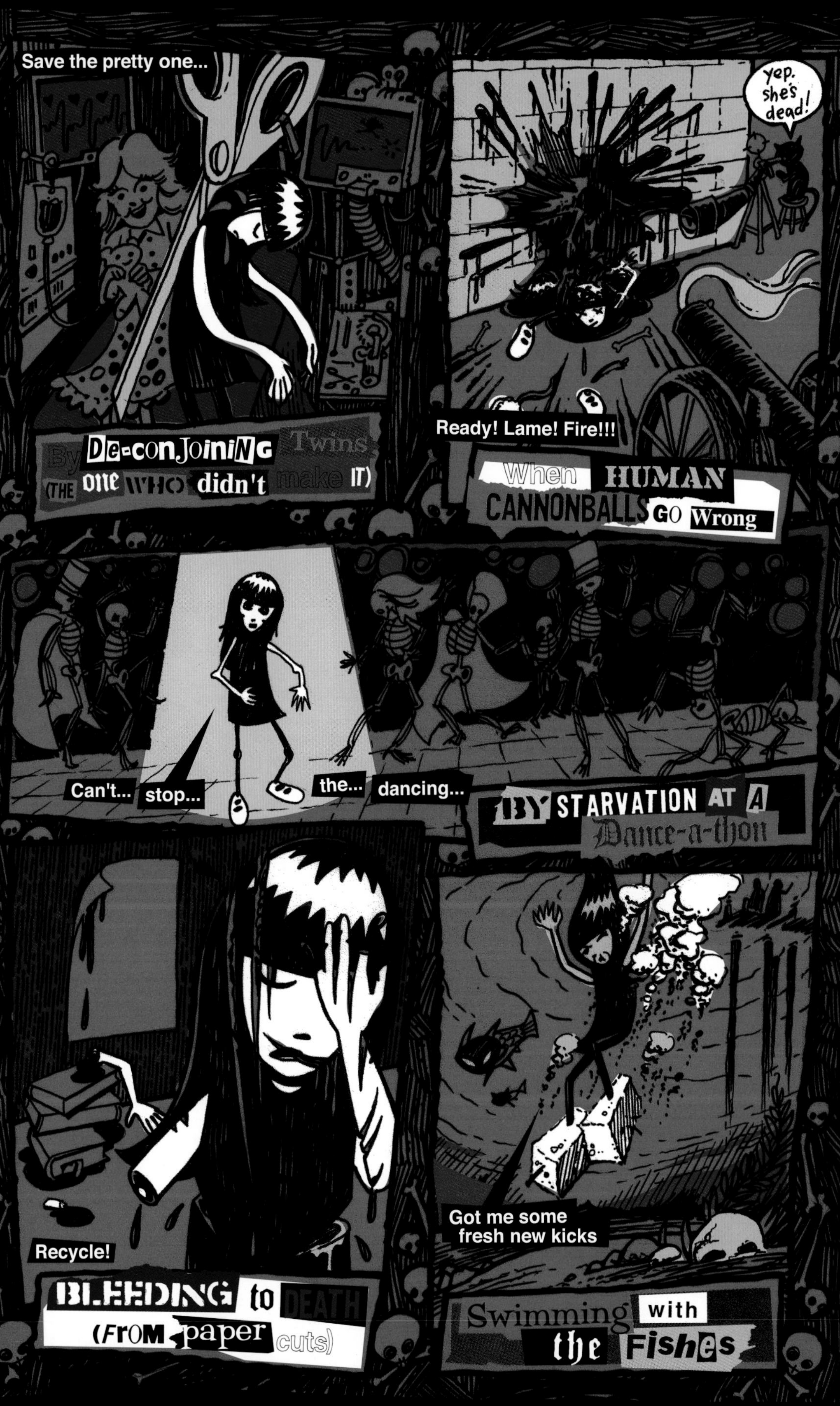
Save the pretty one...
By De-conJoiniNG Twins
(THE one WHO didn't make IT)
yep. she's dead!
Ready! Lame! Fire!!!
When HUMAN CANNONBALLS GO Wrong
Can't... stop... the... dancing...
BY STARVATION AT A Dance-a-thon
Recycle!
BLEEDING to DEATH
(FrOM paper cuts)
Got me some fresh new kicks
Swimming with the Fishes

C'mon guys, it's in heeeeeerrrre!
IMPALED by SPIKES
Hello.
MEDUSA'S glare (turned TO stone)
I need more dots, must have more dots...
BEING eaten in PACMAN
Can't people just properly dispose of themselves?
Stepped on by GODZILLA

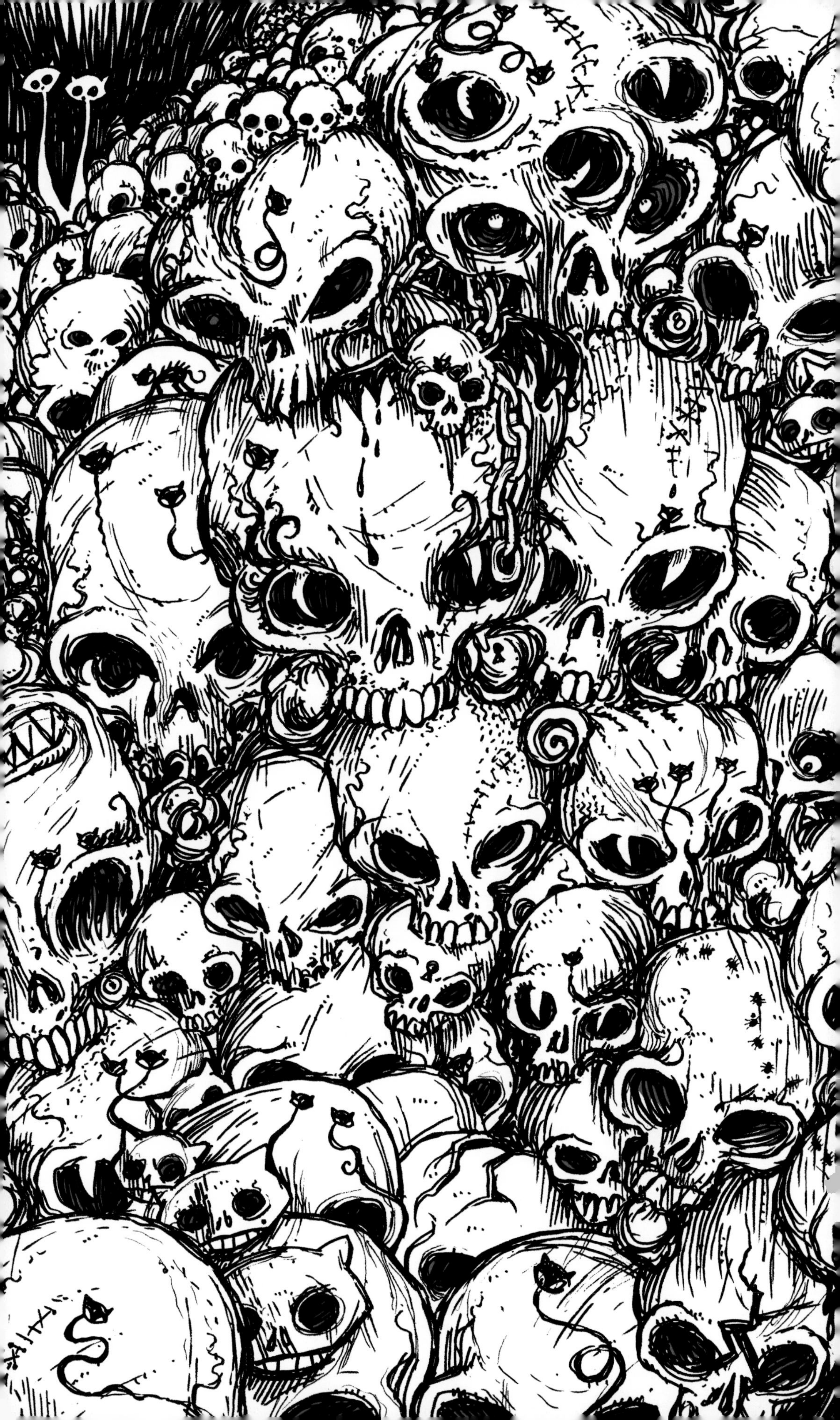

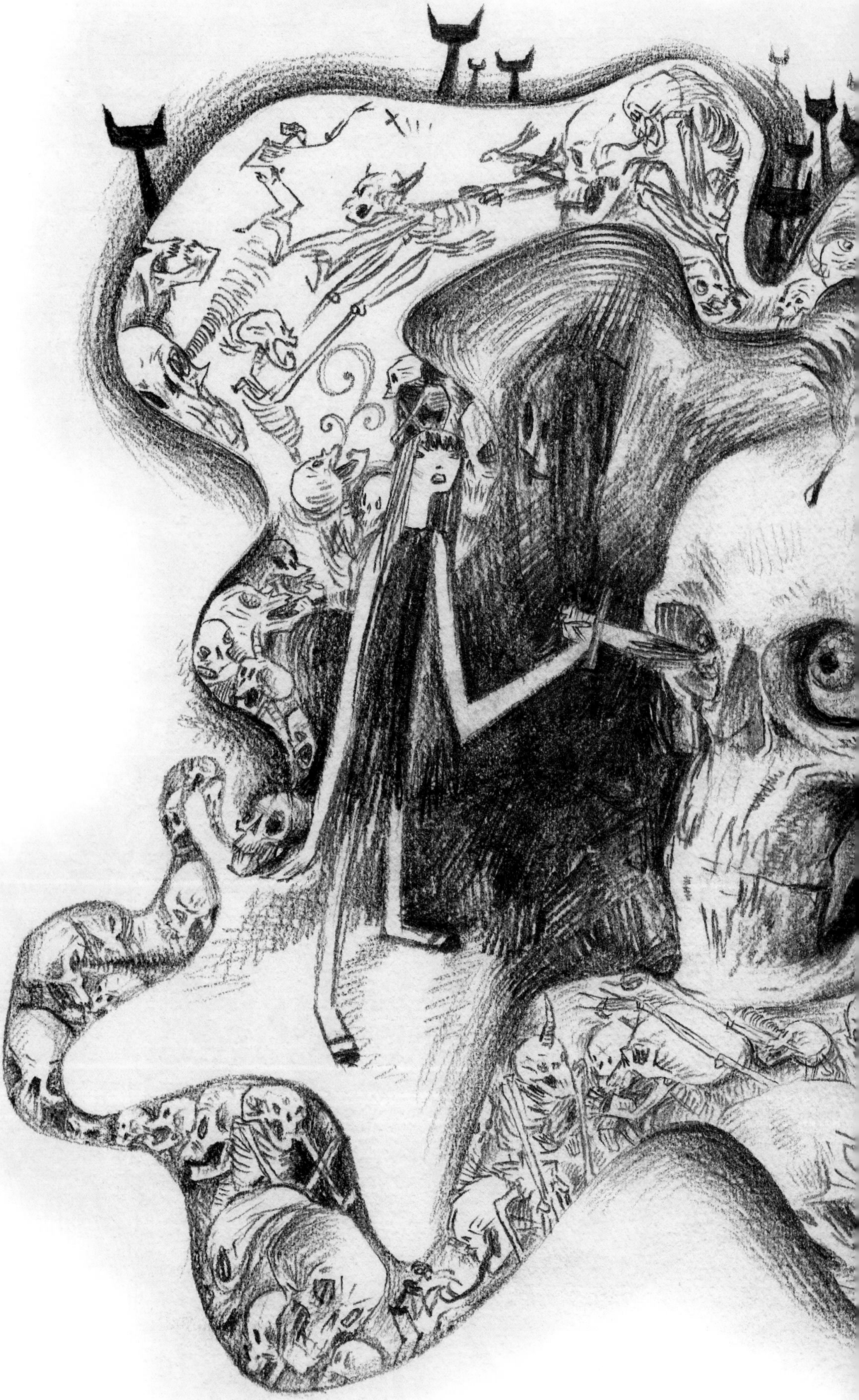

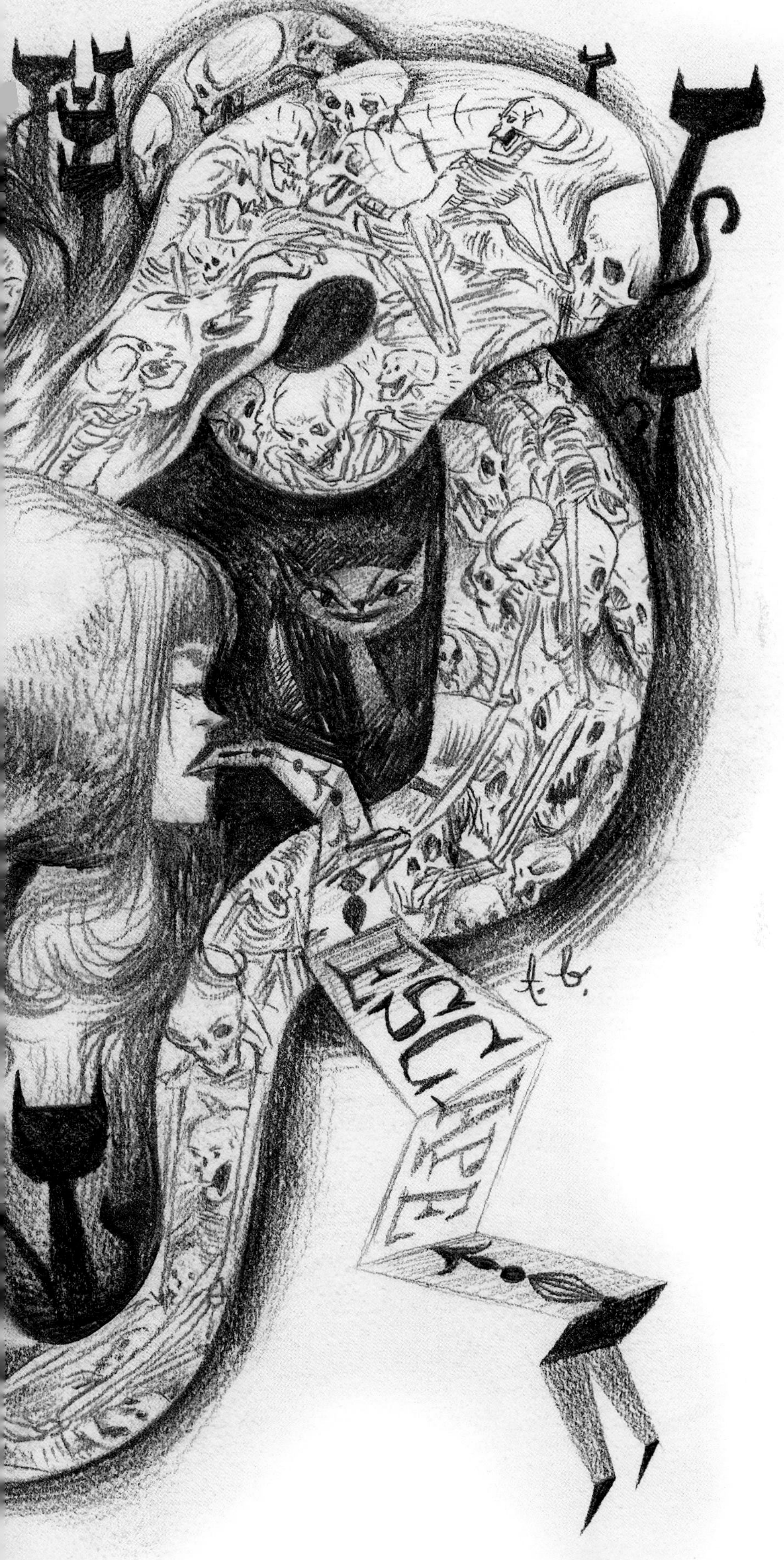

TRIP OUT #5 by Tim Biskup

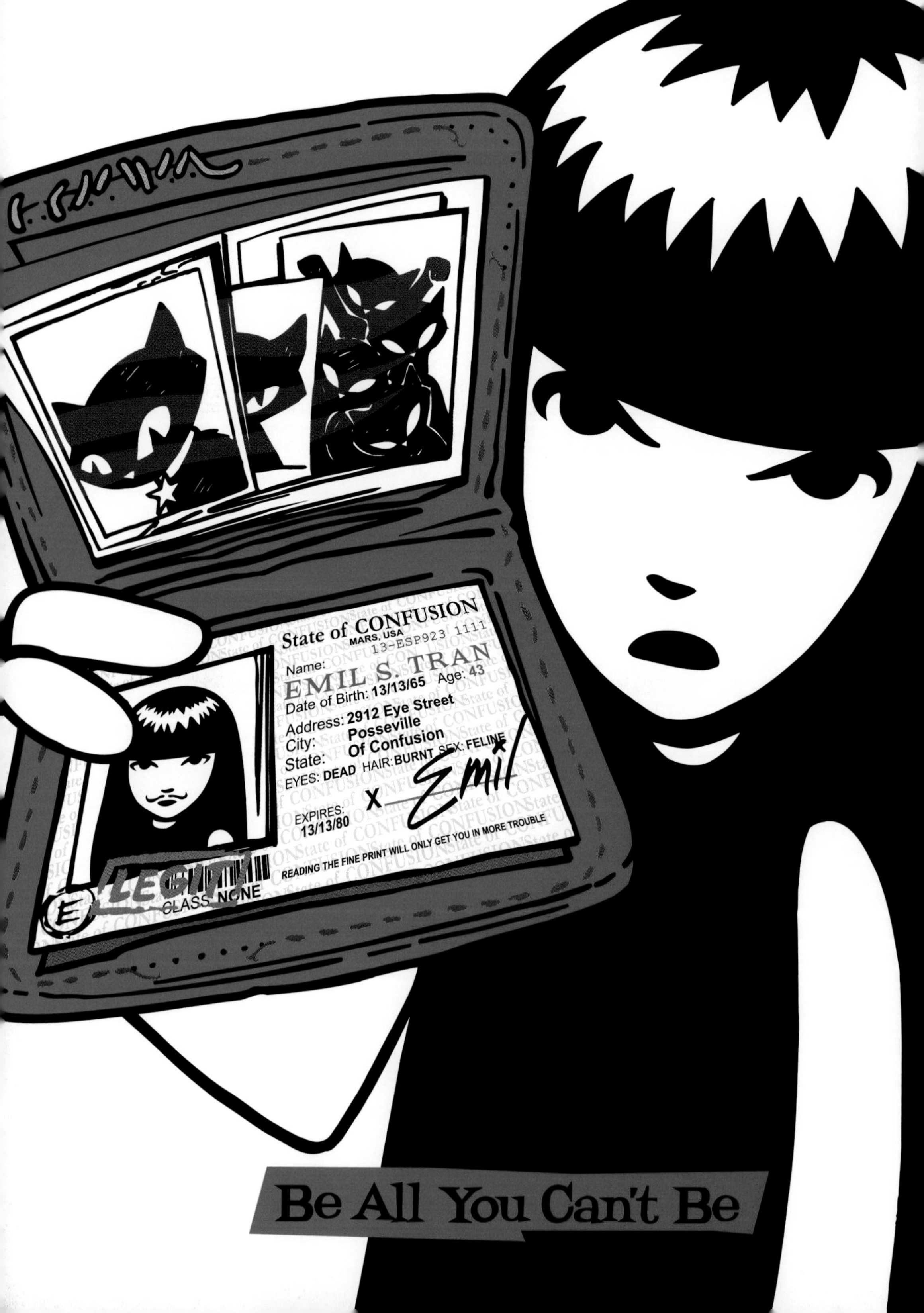
State of CONFUSION
MARS, USA
13-ESP923 1111
Name:
EMIL S. TRAN
Date of Birth: 13/13/65 Age: 43
Address: 2912 Eye Street
City: Posseville
State: Of Confusion
EYES: DEAD HAIR: BURNT SEX: FELINE
X Emil
EXPIRES: 13/13/80
READING THE FINE PRINT WILL ONLY GET YOU IN MORE TROUBLE
LEGIT!
CLASS: NONE
Be All You Can't Be

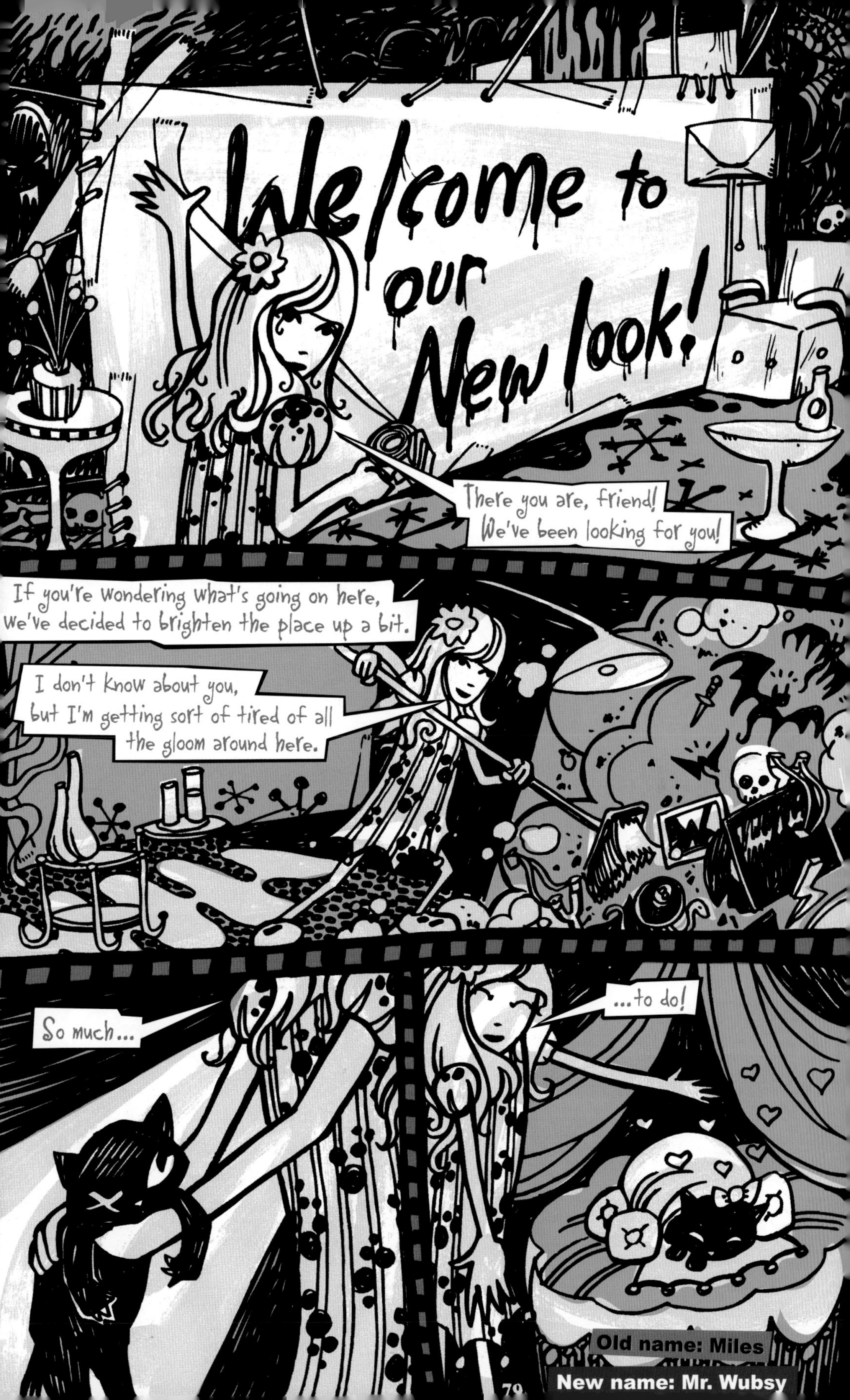
Welcome to our New look!
There you are, friend! We've been looking for you!
If you're wondering what's going on here, we've decided to brighten the place up a bit.
I don't know about you, but I'm getting sort of tired of all the gloom around here.
So much...
...to do!
Old name: Miles
New name: Mr. Wubsy

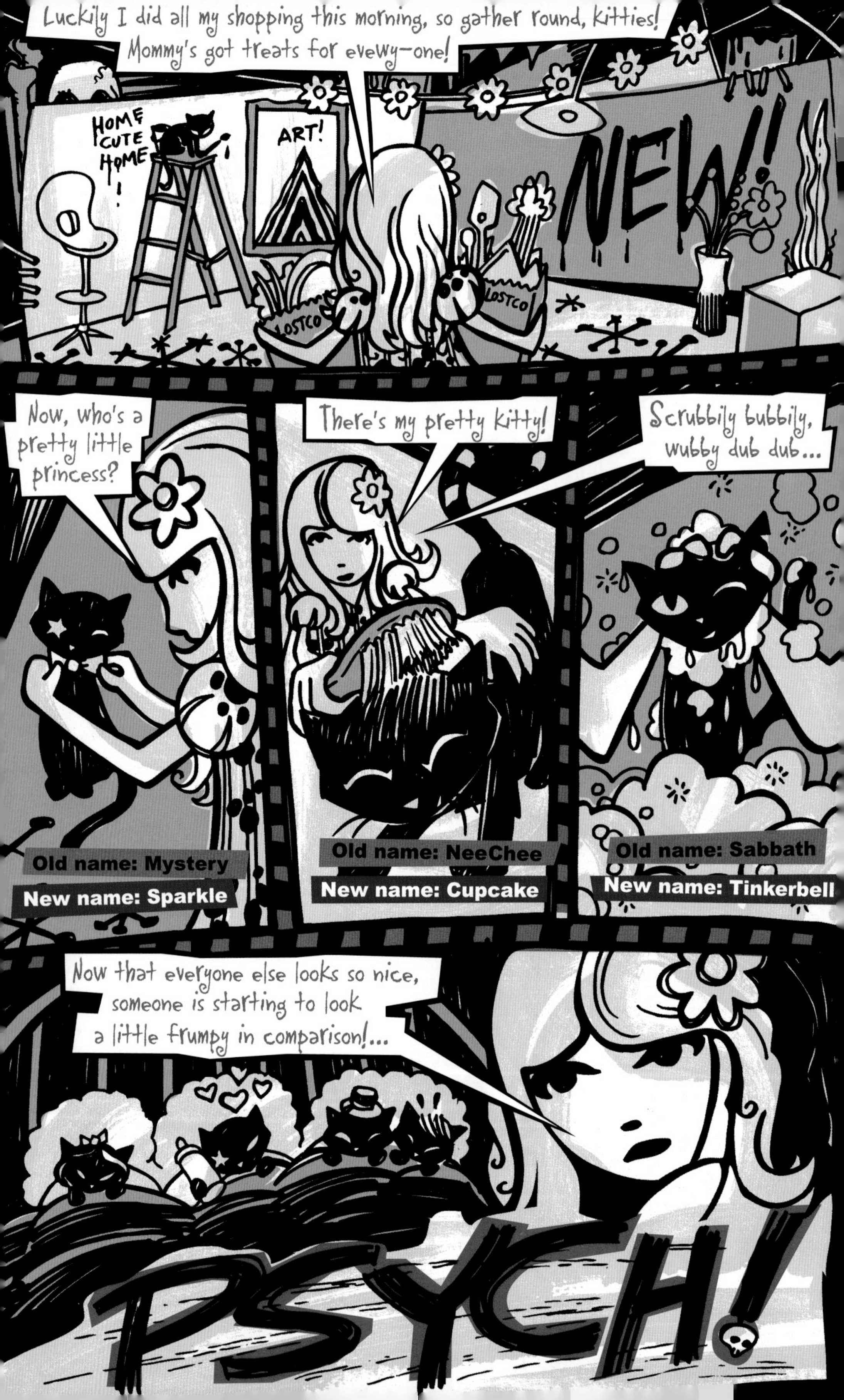

Luckily I did all my shopping this morning, so gather round, kitties! Mommy's got treats for evewy-one!
HOME CUTE HOME!
ART!
LOSTCO
LOSTCO
NEW!!
Now, who's a pretty little princess?
Old name: Mystery
New name: Sparkle
There's my pretty kitty!
Old name: NeeChee
New name: Cupcake
Scrubbily bubbily, wubby dub dub...
Old name: Sabbath
New name: Tinkerbell
Now that everyone else looks so nice, someone is starting to look a little frumpy in comparison!...
PSYCH!

FAKE I.D.

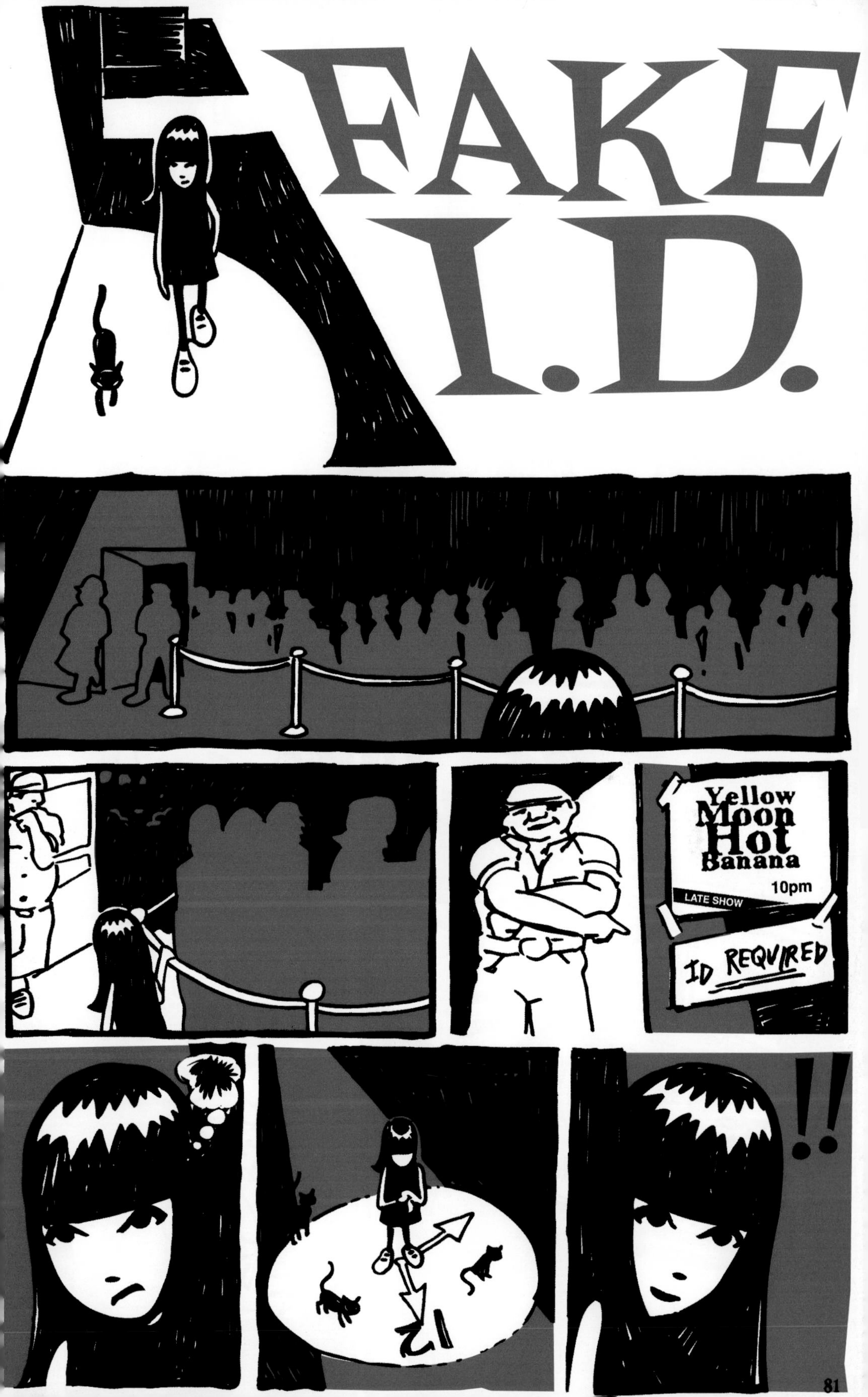
Yellow Moon Hot Banana
10pm
LATE SHOW
ID REQUIRED

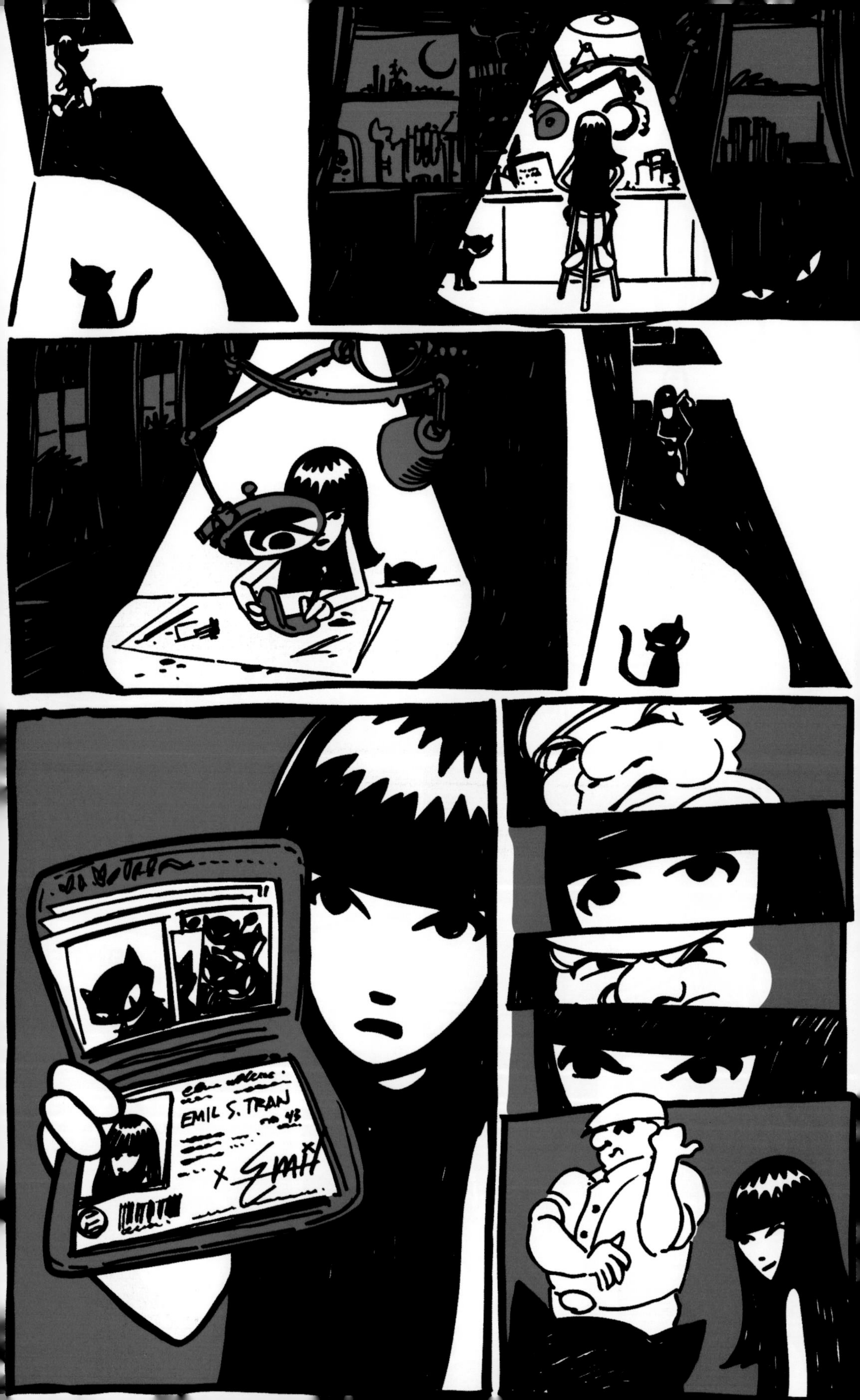
EMIL S. TRAN

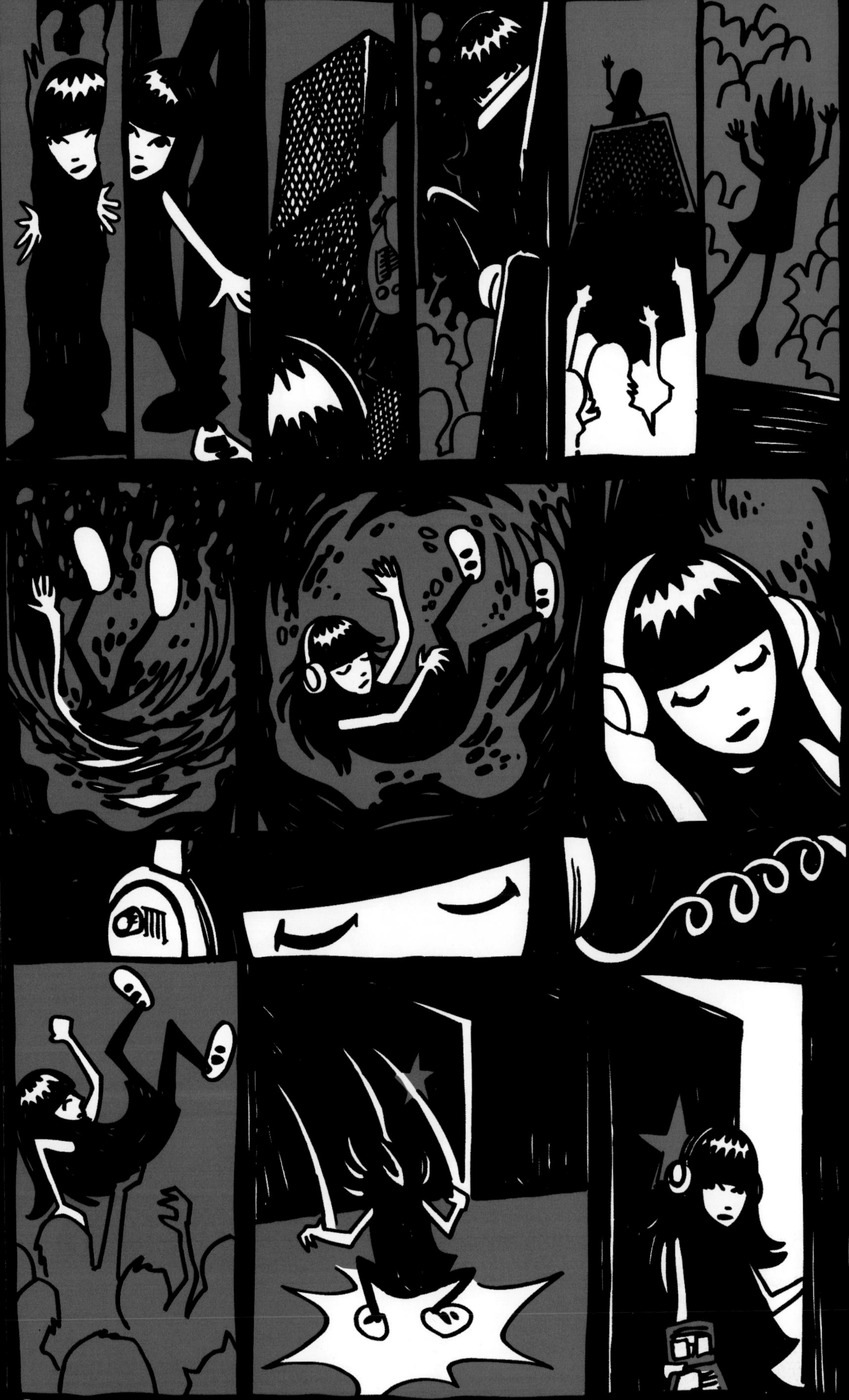

EMILYS TOP 13 FAKE

TRIP TO THE MOON
(It's all Hollyweird
smoke 'n' mirrors)

FAKE BLOOD
(There's no such thing
as fake blood!)
Muwa ha ha ha!!

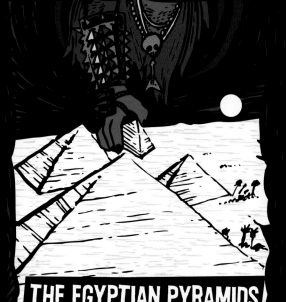

THE EGYPTIAN PYRAMIDS
(Were really built by
The God of Metal)

THE MAN OF 1000 FACES
(Seeing is deceiving!)

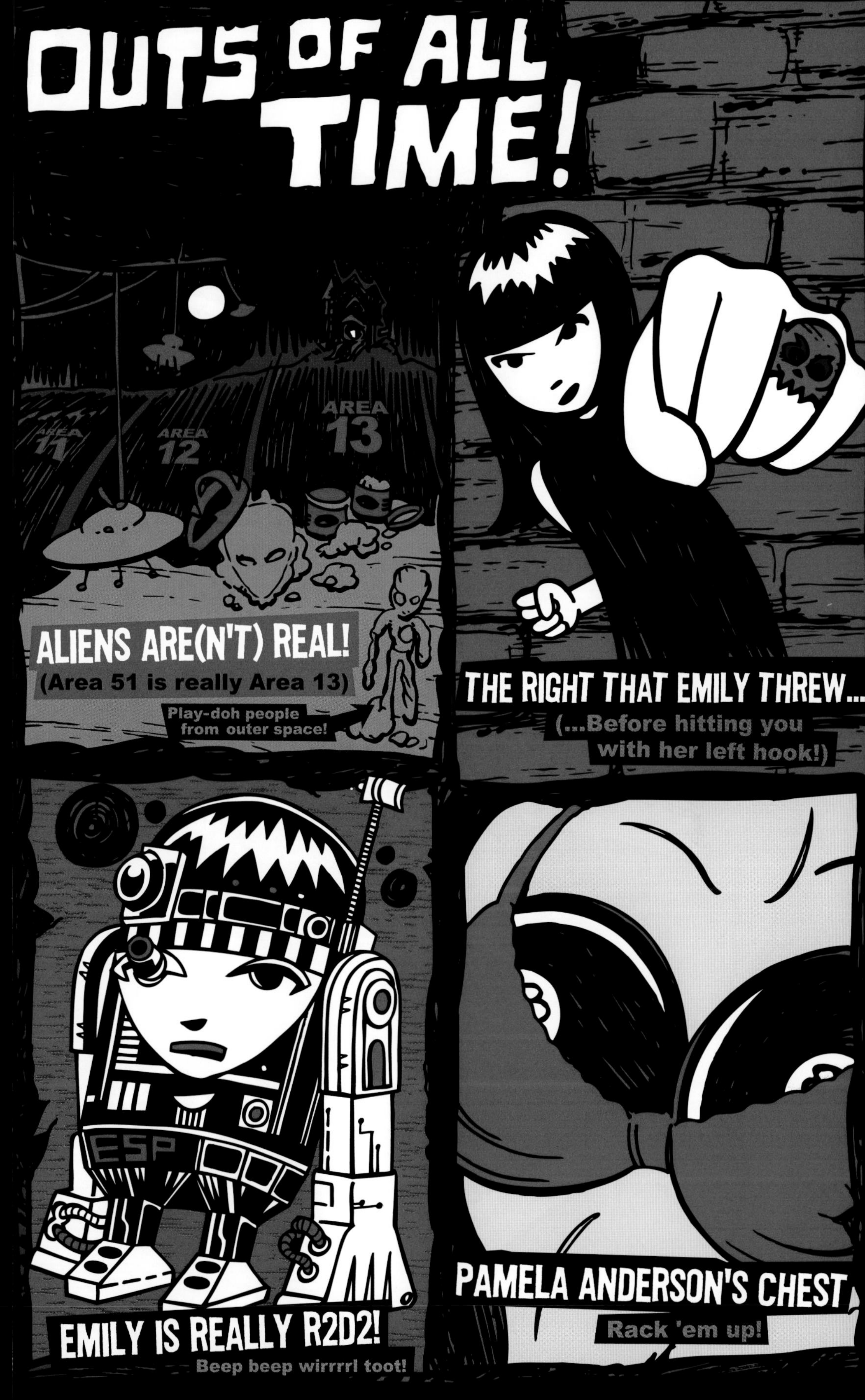
OUTS OF ALL TIME!
AREA 11
AREA 12
AREA 13
ALIENS ARE(N'T) REAL!
(Area 51 is really Area 13)
Play-doh people from outer space!
THE RIGHT THAT EMILY THREW...
(...Before hitting you with her left hook!)
ESP
EMILY IS REALLY R2D2!
Beep beep wirrrrl toot!
PAMELA ANDERSON'S CHEST
Rack 'em up!

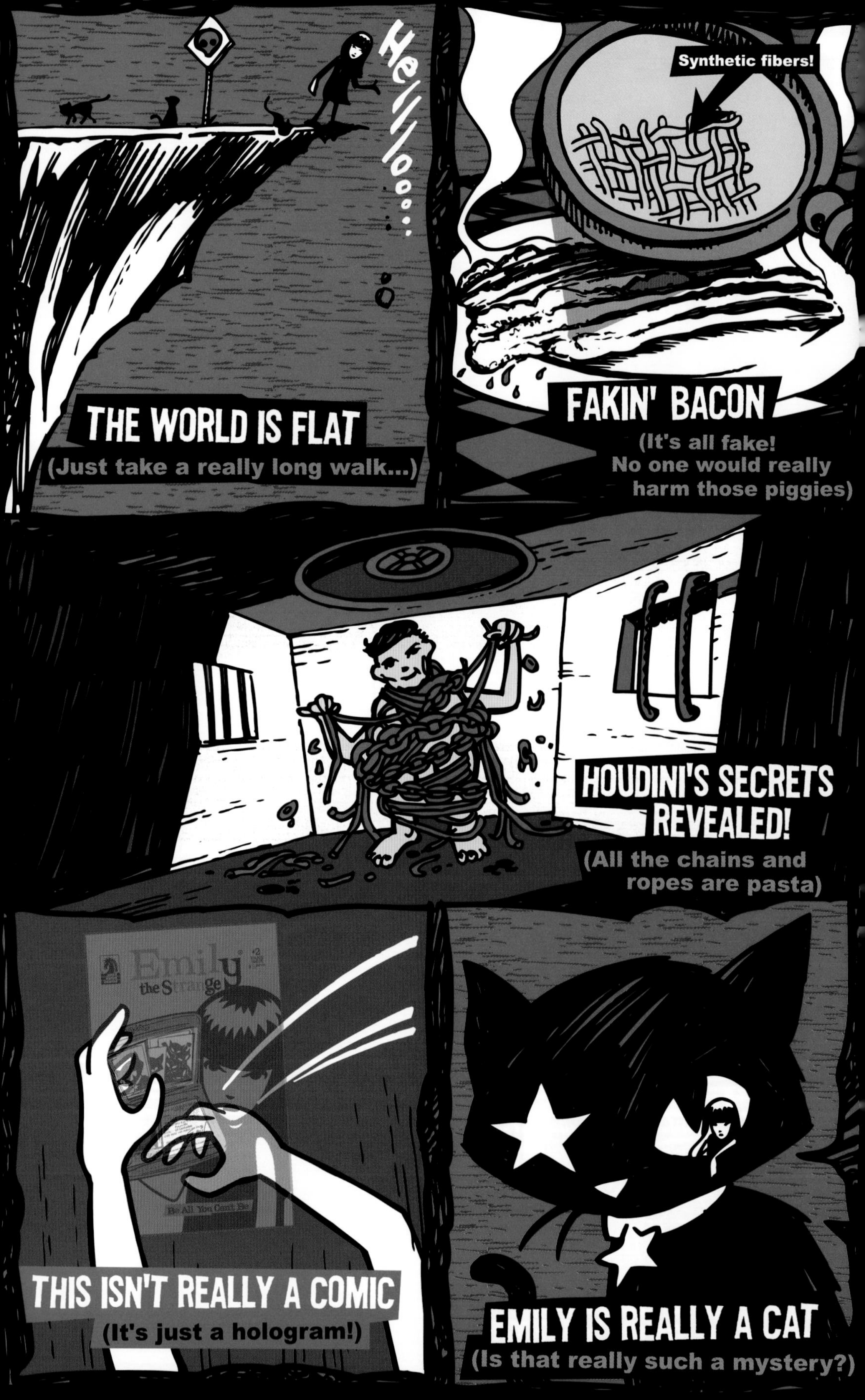

Hellllooo...
THE WORLD IS FLAT
(Just take a really long walk...)
Synthetic fibers!
FAKIN' BACON
(It's all fake!
No one would really
harm those piggies)
HOUDINI'S SECRETS
REVEALED!
(All the chains and
ropes are pasta)
Emily the Strange
Be All You Can't Be
THIS ISN'T REALLY A COMIC
(It's just a hologram!)
EMILY IS REALLY A CAT
(Is that really such a mystery?)

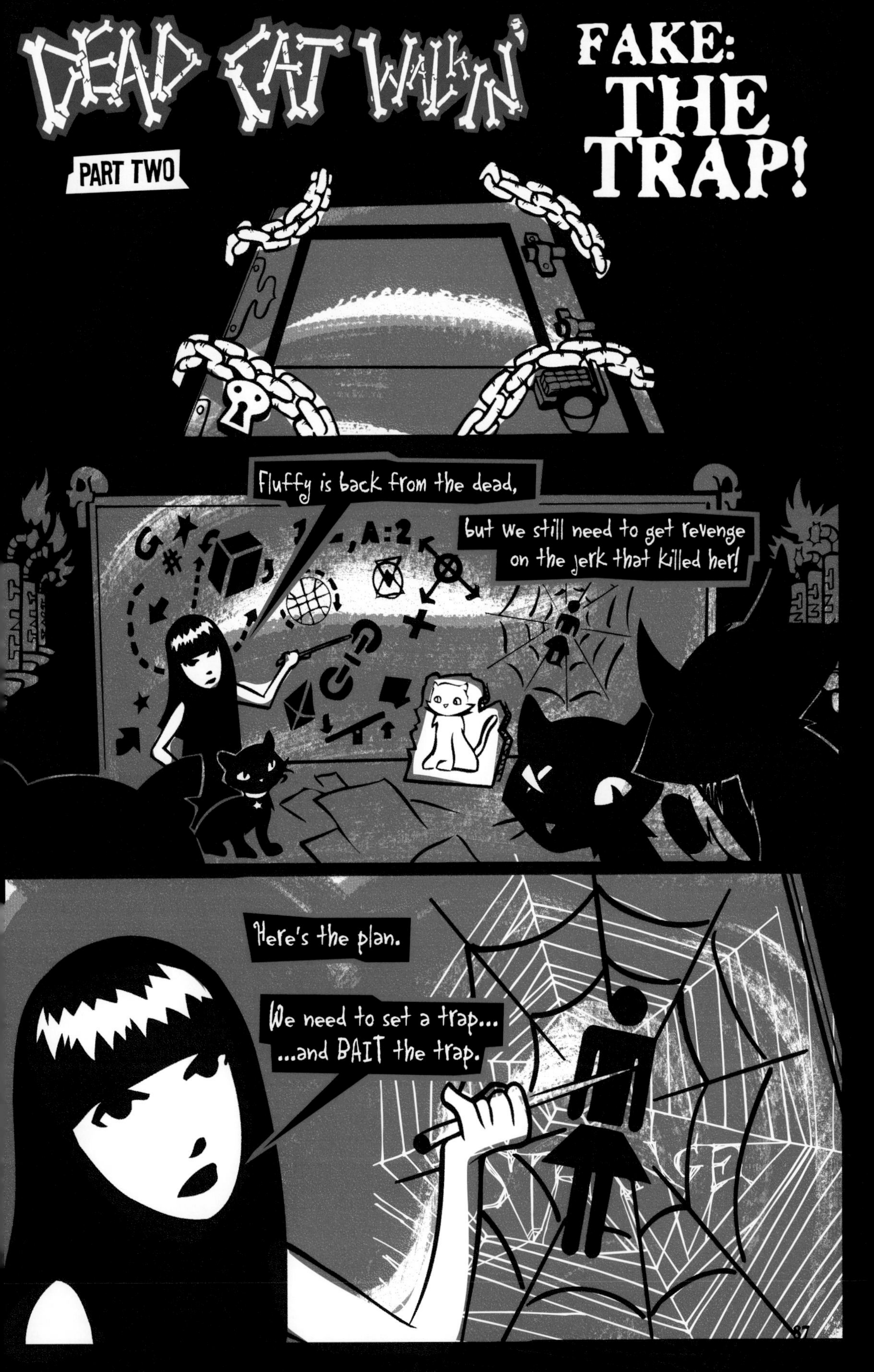
DEAD CAT WALKIN'
PART TWO
FAKE: THE TRAP!
Fluffy is back from the dead,
but we still need to get revenge on the jerk that killed her!
Here's the plan.
We need to set a trap...
...and BAIT the trap.

EMILY'S FAKETORY
a Remote Controlled Fully Functioning
a Artificial Woman Patent Pending
We have the technology.
We can create her.
Bring that simulation to life!
Aha ah hah ha hah
ha ha hah haha ha!
I give you...

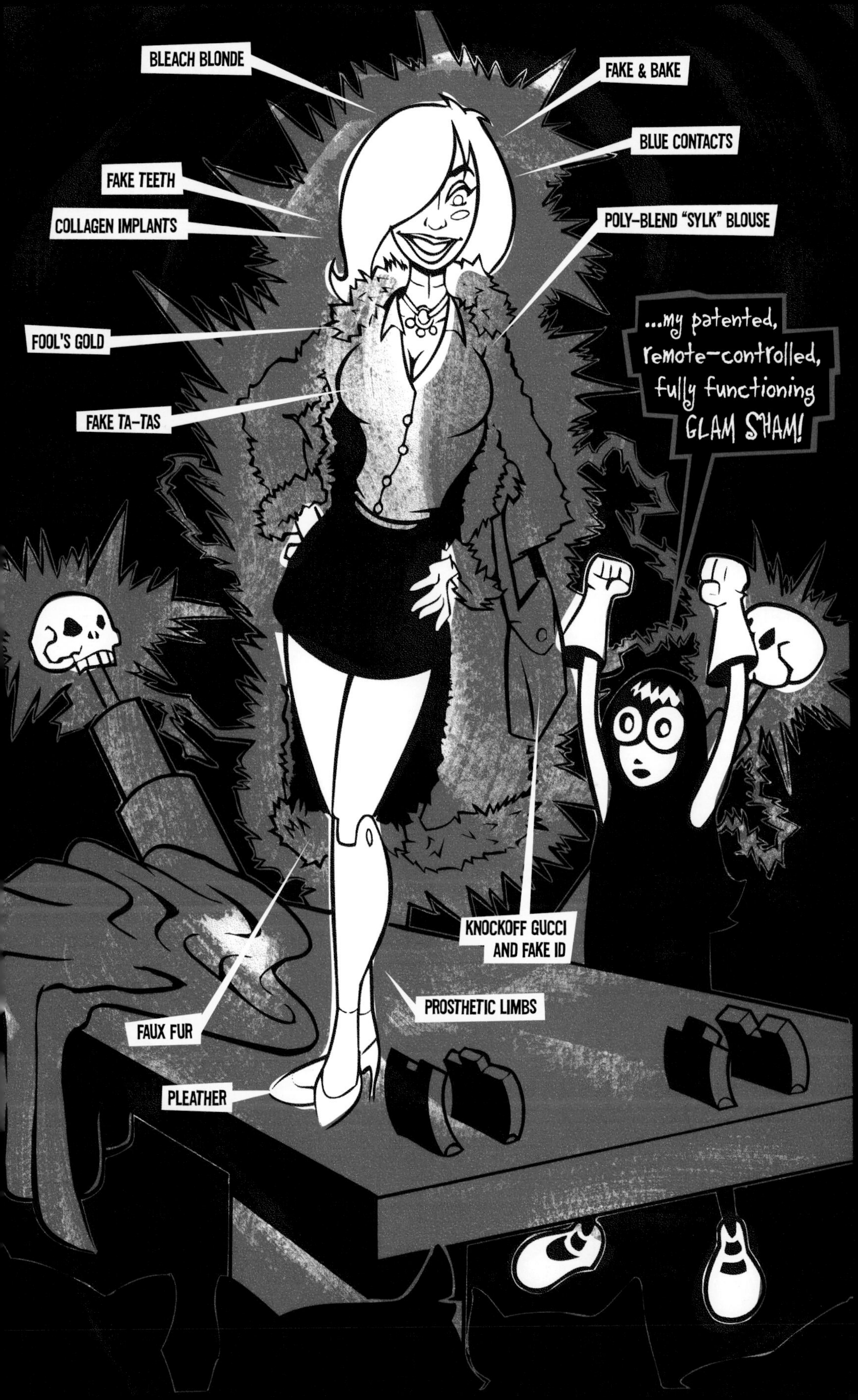
BLEACH BLONDE
FAKE & BAKE
BLUE CONTACTS
FAKE TEETH
COLLAGEN IMPLANTS
POLY-BLEND "SYLK" BLOUSE
FOOL'S GOLD
FAKE TA-TAS
...my patented, remote-controlled, fully functioning GLAM SHAM!
KNOCKOFF GUCCI AND FAKE ID
PROSTHETIC LIMBS
FAUX FUR
PLEATHER

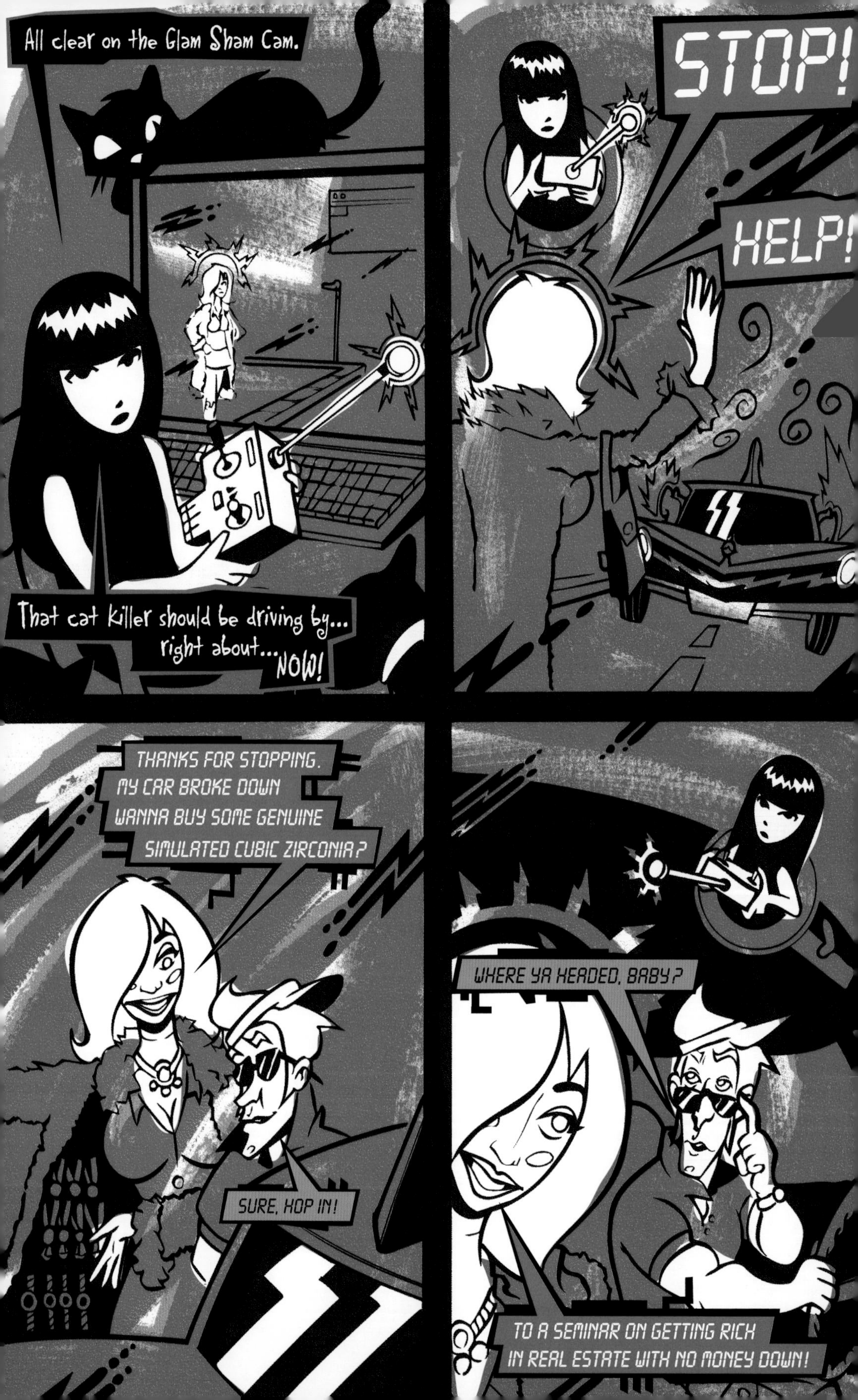
All clear on the Glam Sham Cam.
That cat killer should be driving by... right about... NOW!
STOP!
HELP!
THANKS FOR STOPPING. MY CAR BROKE DOWN WANNA BUY SOME GENUINE SIMULATED CUBIC ZIRCONIA?
SURE, HOP IN!
WHERE YA HEADED, BABY?
TO A SEMINAR ON GETTING RICH IN REAL ESTATE WITH NO MONEY DOWN!

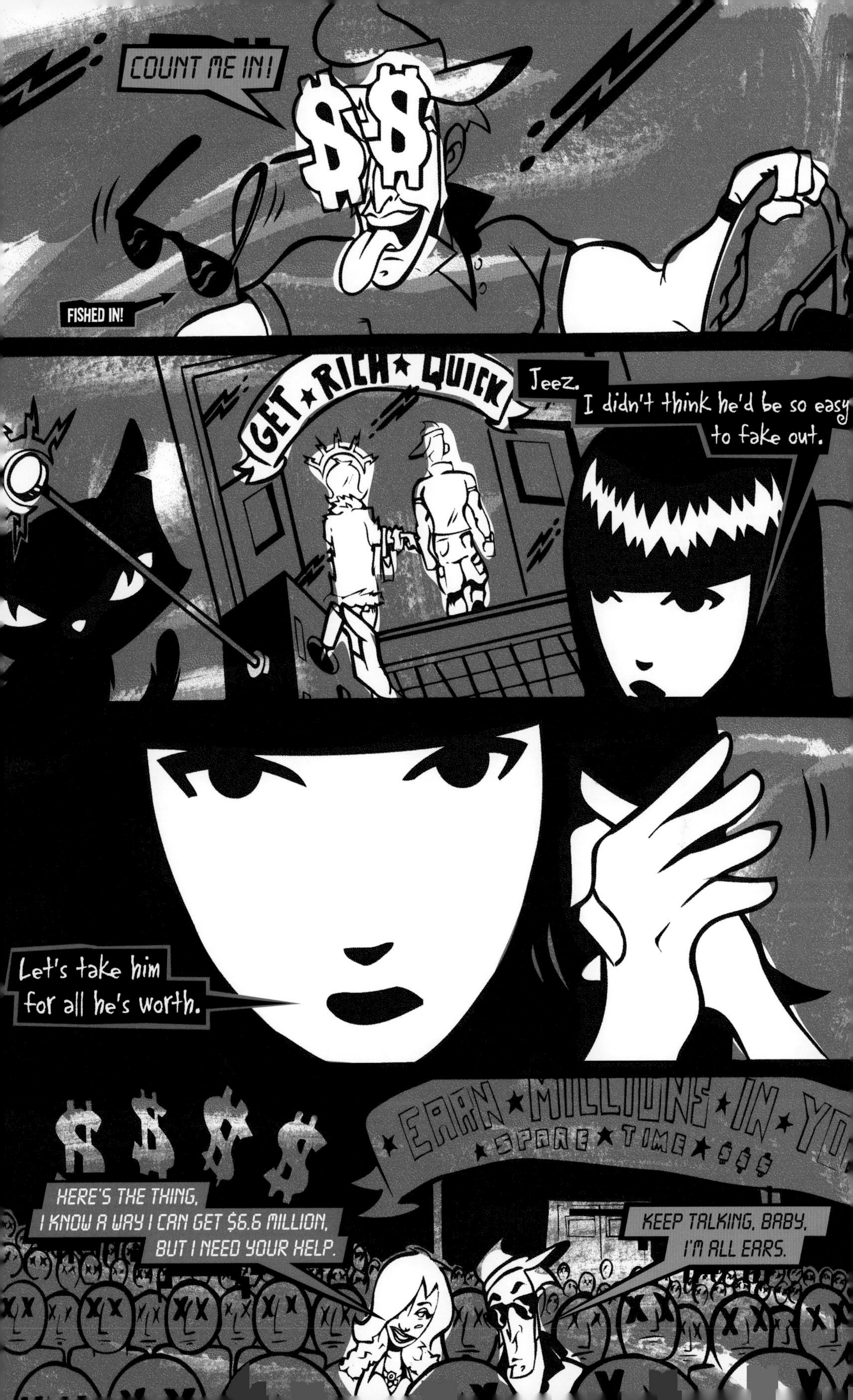
COUNT ME IN!
FISHED IN!
GET ★ RICH ★ QUICK
Jeez.
I didn't think he'd be so easy to fake out.
Let's take him for all he's worth.
HERE'S THE THING, I KNOW A WAY I CAN GET $6.6 MILLION, BUT I NEED YOUR HELP.
KEEP TALKING, BABY. I'M ALL EARS.

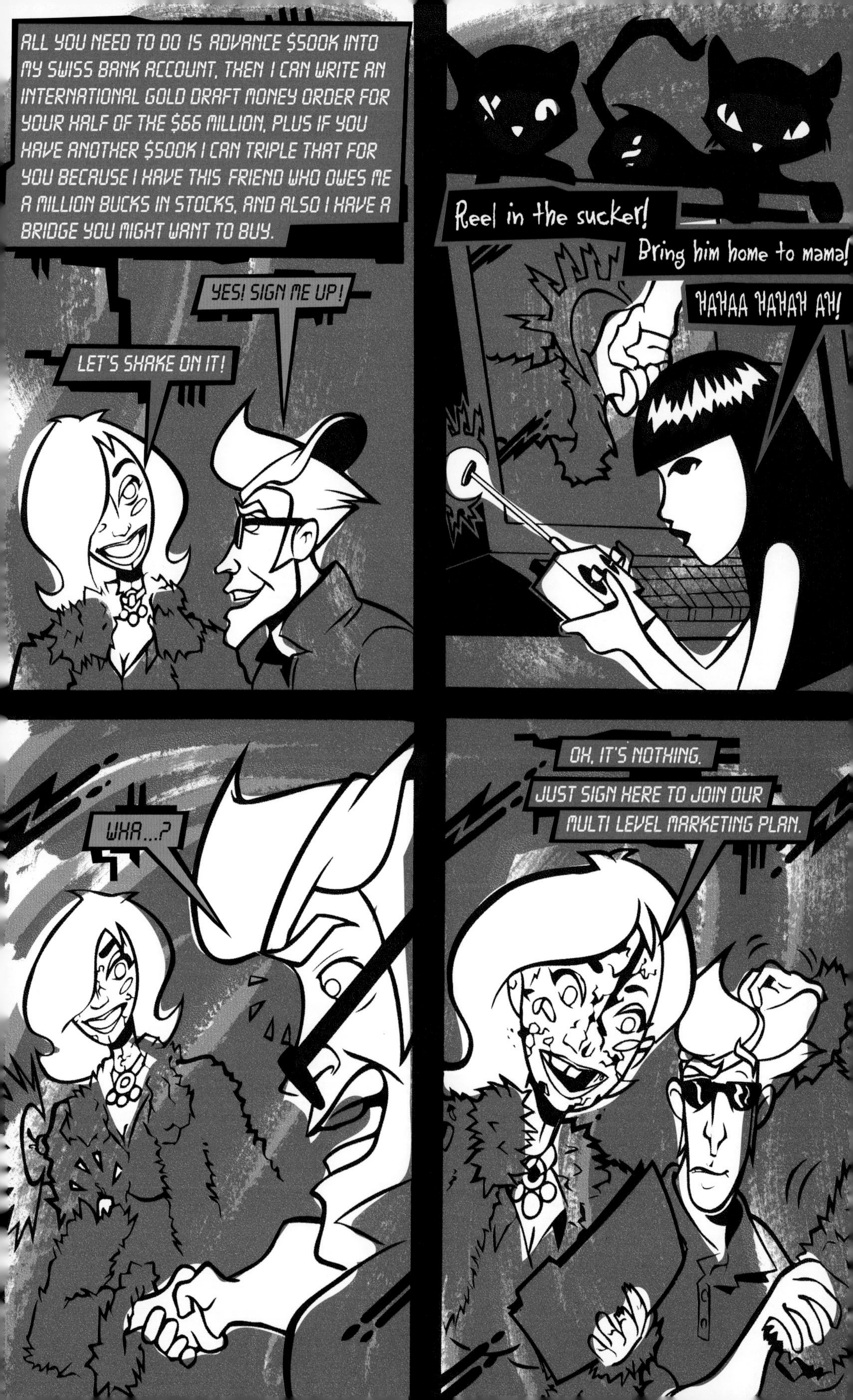
ALL YOU NEED TO DO IS ADVANCE $500K INTO MY SWISS BANK ACCOUNT, THEN I CAN WRITE AN INTERNATIONAL GOLD DRAFT MONEY ORDER FOR YOUR HALF OF THE $66 MILLION, PLUS IF YOU HAVE ANOTHER $500K I CAN TRIPLE THAT FOR YOU BECAUSE I HAVE THIS FRIEND WHO OWES ME A MILLION BUCKS IN STOCKS, AND ALSO I HAVE A BRIDGE YOU MIGHT WANT TO BUY.
YES! SIGN ME UP!
LET'S SHAKE ON IT!
Reel in the sucker!
Bring him home to mama!
HAHAA HAHAH AH!
WHA...?
OH, IT'S NOTHING.
JUST SIGN HERE TO JOIN OUR
MULTI LEVEL MARKETING PLAN.

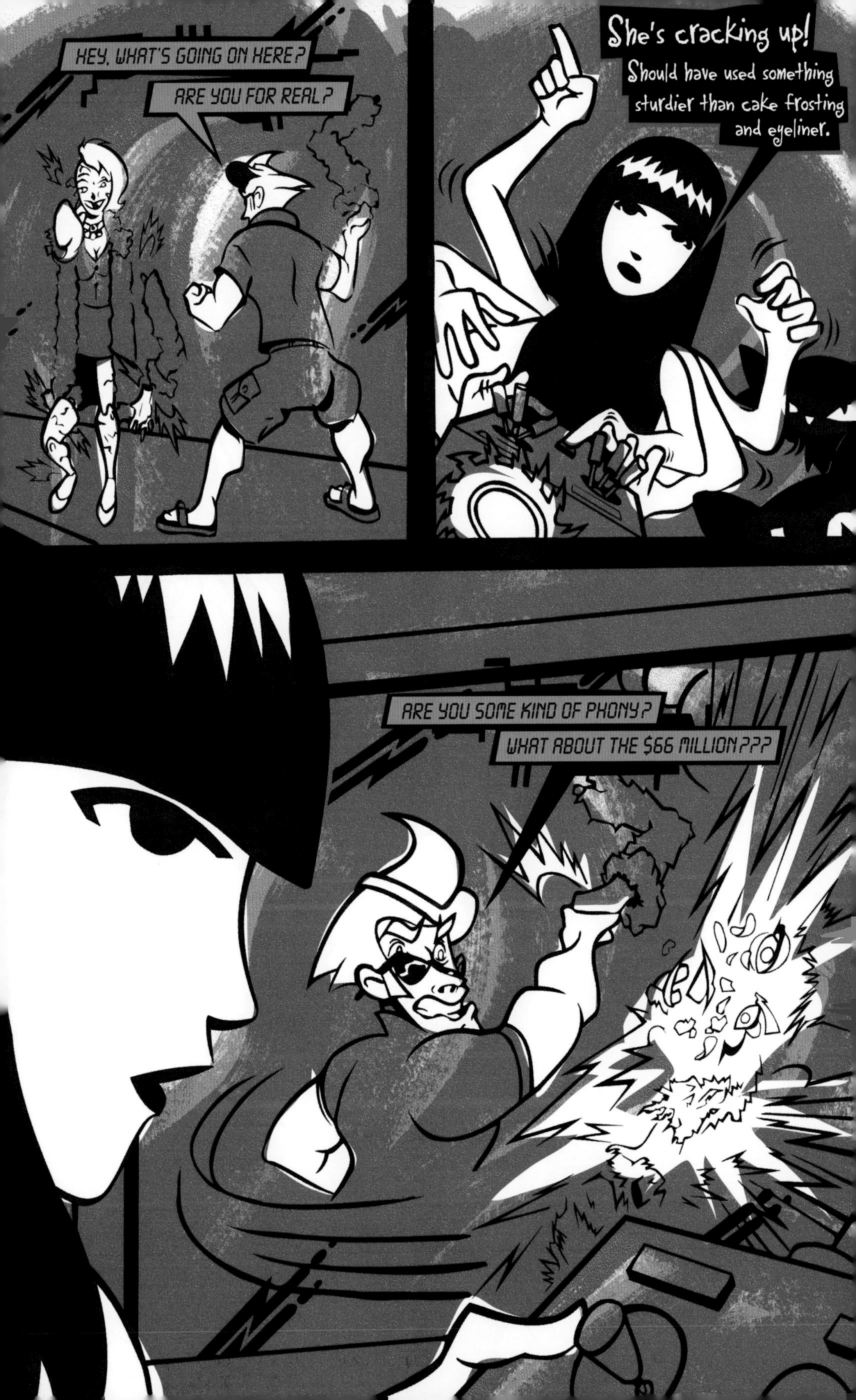
HEY, WHAT'S GOING ON HERE?
ARE YOU FOR REAL?
She's cracking up!
Should have used something sturdier than cake frosting and eyeliner.
ARE YOU SOME KIND OF PHONY?
WHAT ABOUT THE $66 MILLION???

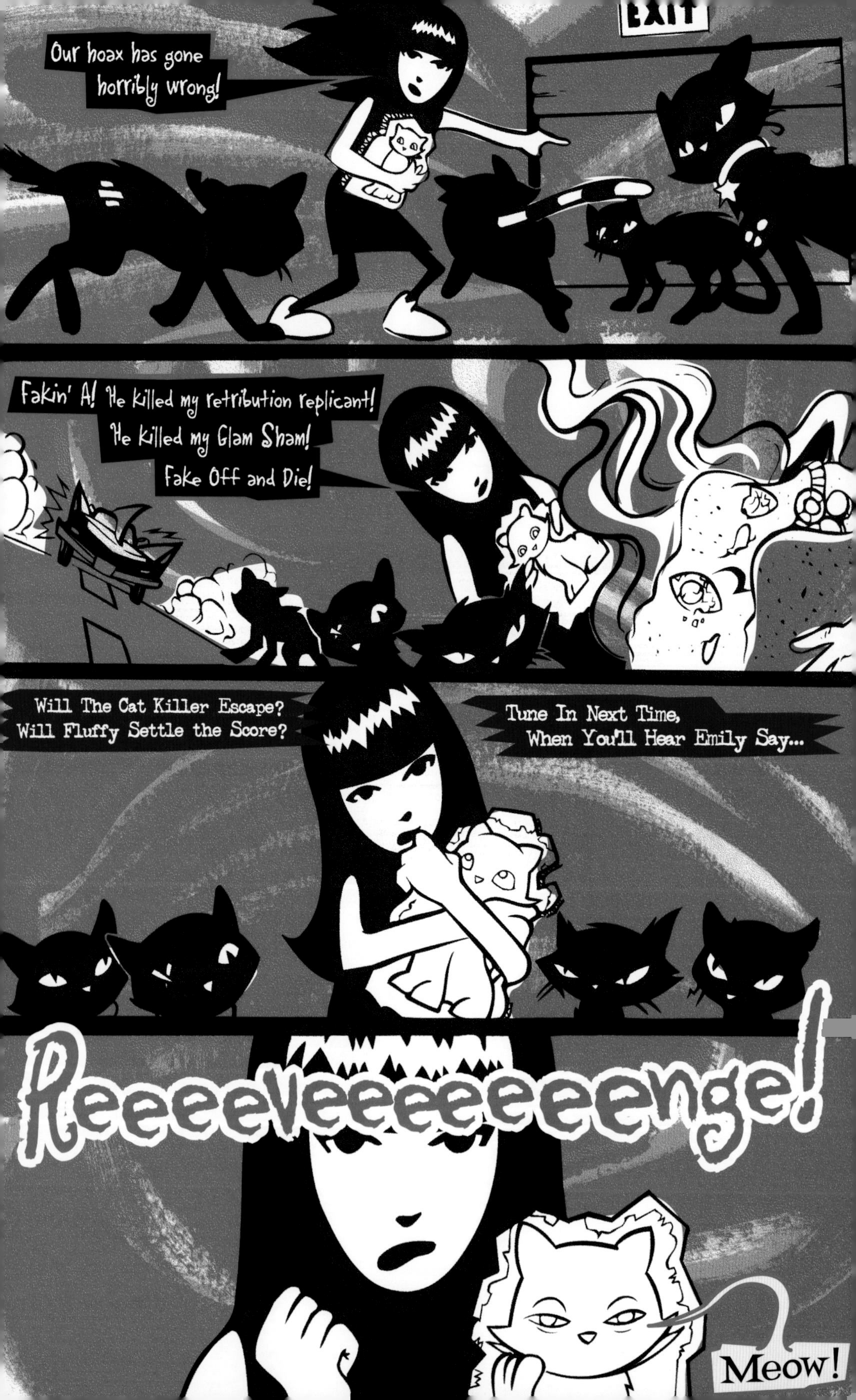
EXIT
Our hoax has gone horribly wrong!
Fakin' A! He killed my retribution replicant!
He killed my Glam Sham!
Fake Off and Die!
Will The Cat Killer Escape?
Will Fluffy Settle the Score?
Tune In Next Time, When You'll Hear Emily Say...
Reeeeveeeeeeeeenge!
Meow!

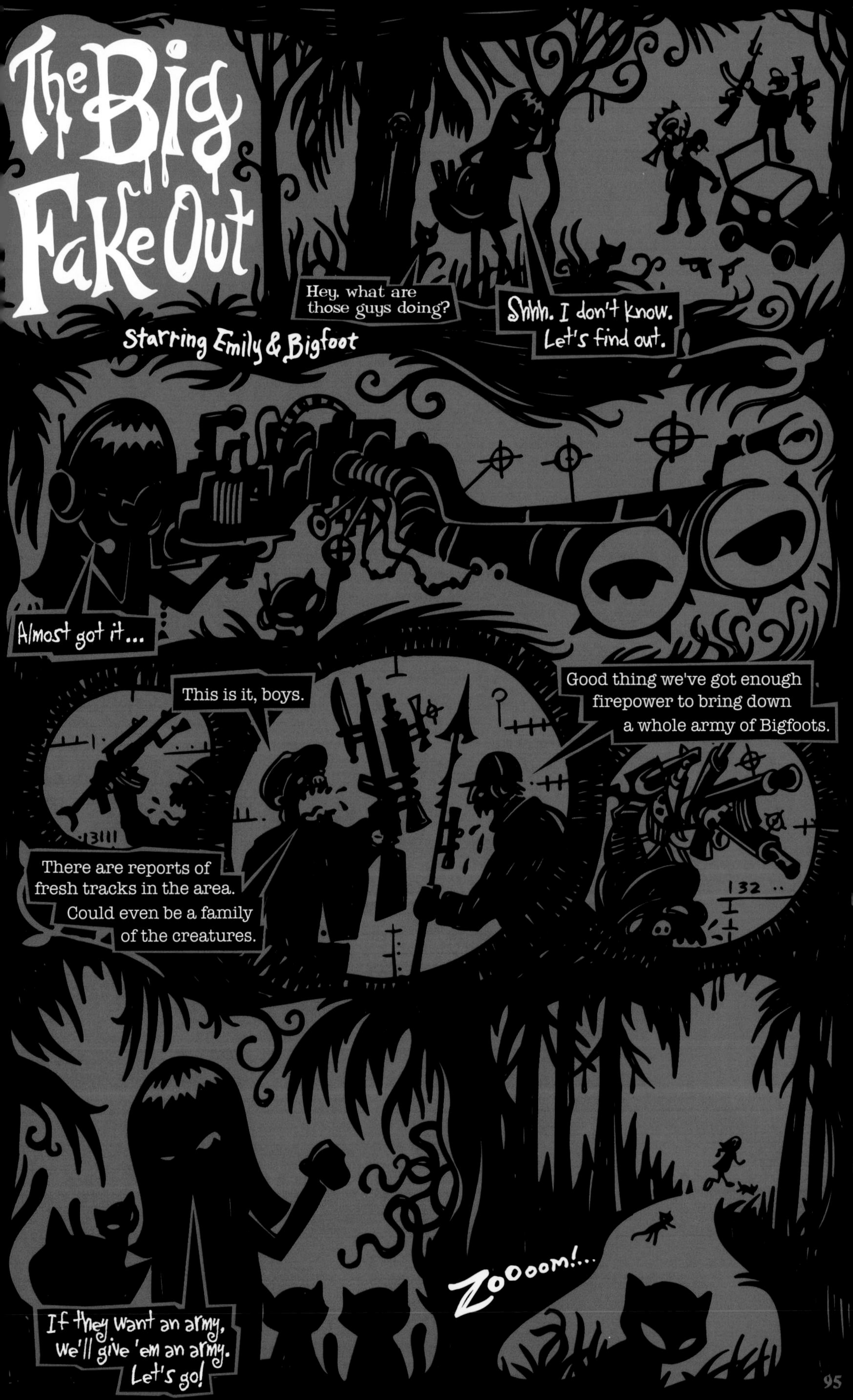

The Big Fake Out
Starring Emily & Bigfoot
Hey, what are those guys doing?
Shhh. I don't know. Let's find out.
Almost got it...
This is it, boys.
Good thing we've got enough firepower to bring down a whole army of Bigfoots.
There are reports of fresh tracks in the area. Could even be a family of the creatures.
If they want an army, we'll give 'em an army. Let's go!
ZOOoom!...

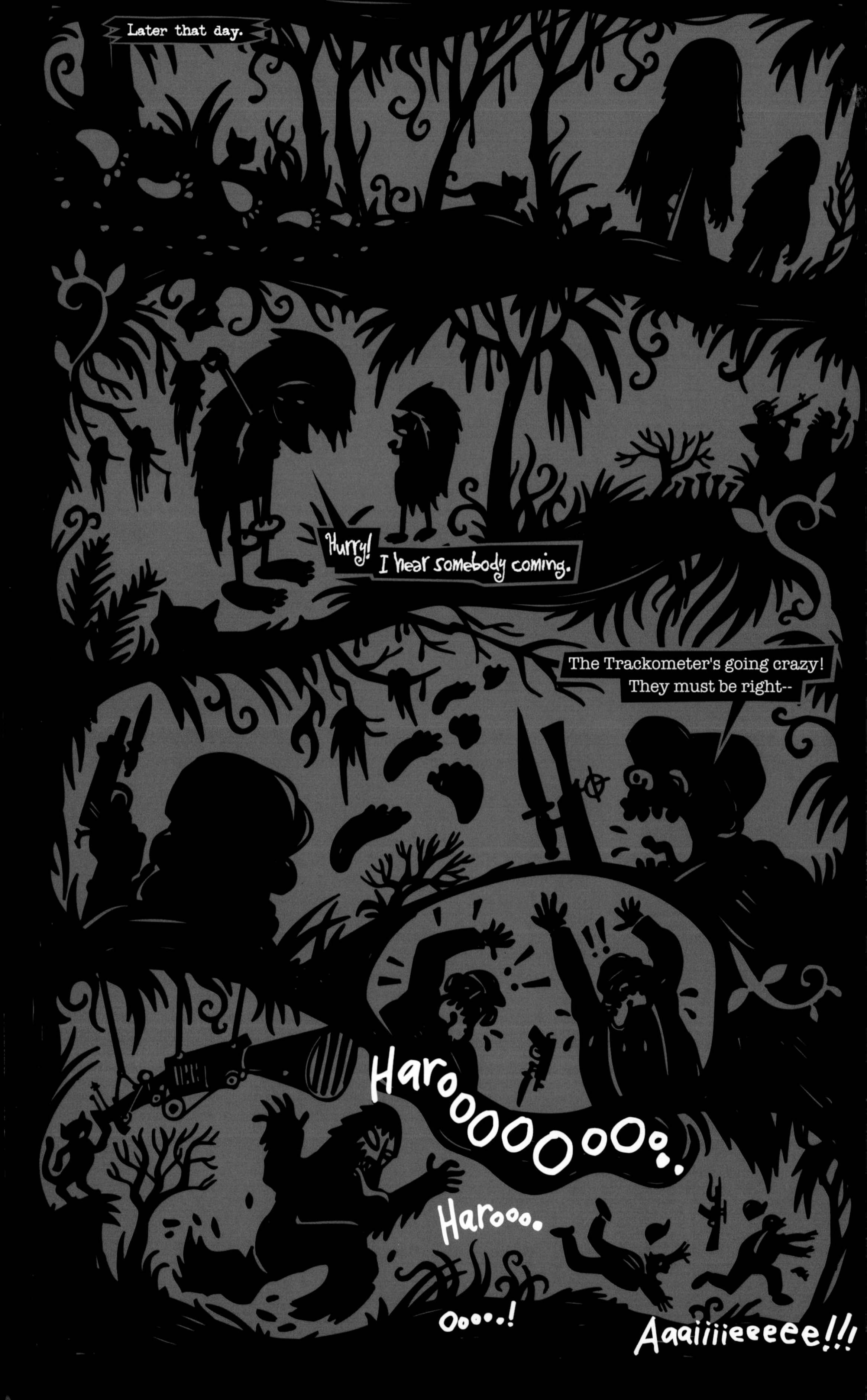
Later that day.
Hurry! I hear somebody coming.
The Trackometer's going crazy! They must be right--
!!
Haroooooooo..
Harooo.
Oooo..!
Aaaiiiieeeee!!!

RRRrrr...
RRRrroooWww!!
He He He He!
It worked, guys!
Hawoooo...
Now let's pack up and get back to your neck of the woods. I saw some blackberries there earlier that need to be picked.
These Halloween props came in handy!
Har Har Rrrrrow!
You're right – forest berries DO make the most delicious jam...

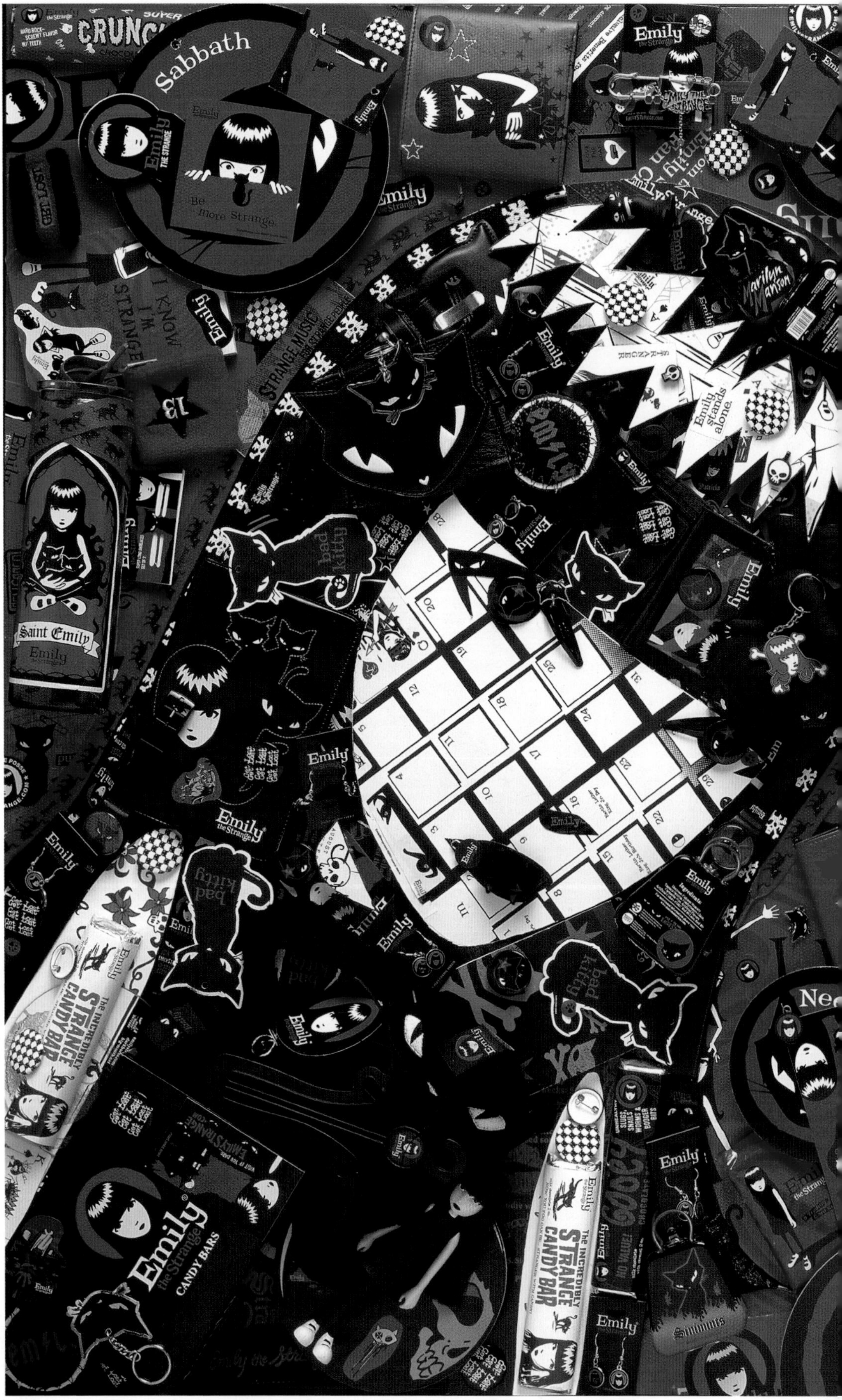
CRUNCH
Sabbath
Emily THE STRANGE
Be more Strange.
I KNOW I'M STRANGE
13
STRANGE MUSIC
Saint Emily
Emily the Strange
bad kitty
Get Lost
Emily stands alone.
Marilyn Manson
THE INCREDIBLY STRANGE CANDY BAR
Emily the Strange CANDY BARS
Sinmints

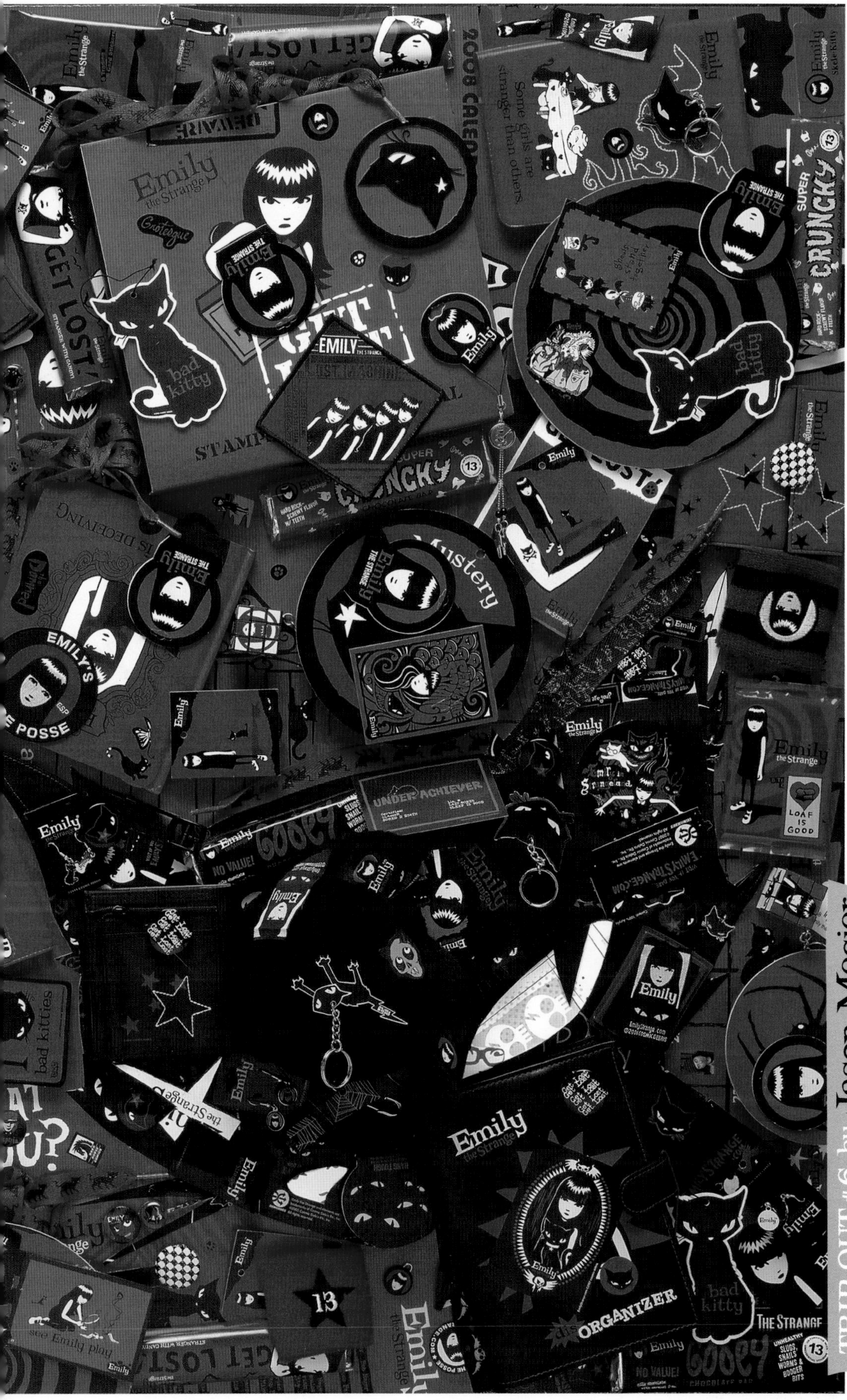

Emily the Strange
GET LOST
2008 CALEN
Some girls are stranger than others.
Grotesque
bad kitty
SUPER CRUNCHY
EMILY'S POSSE
Mystery
UNDER ACHIEVER
GOOEY
NO VALUE!
bad kitties
LOAF IS GOOD
ORGANIZER
THE STRANGE
see Emily play
13
STAMP

TRIP OUT #6 by Jason Mecier

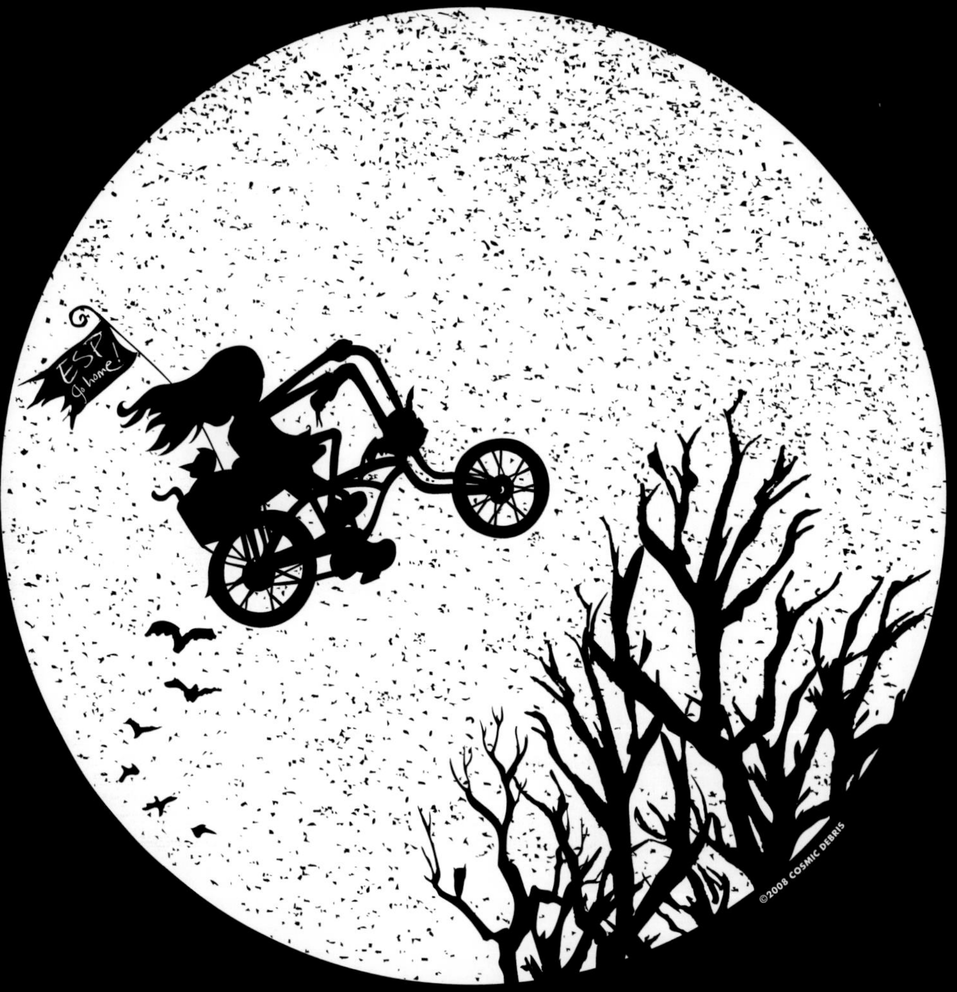
ESP go home!
©2008 COSMIC DEBRIS

STRANGER BY NIGHT

Emily® the Strange

FAKE MONEY!

cut here

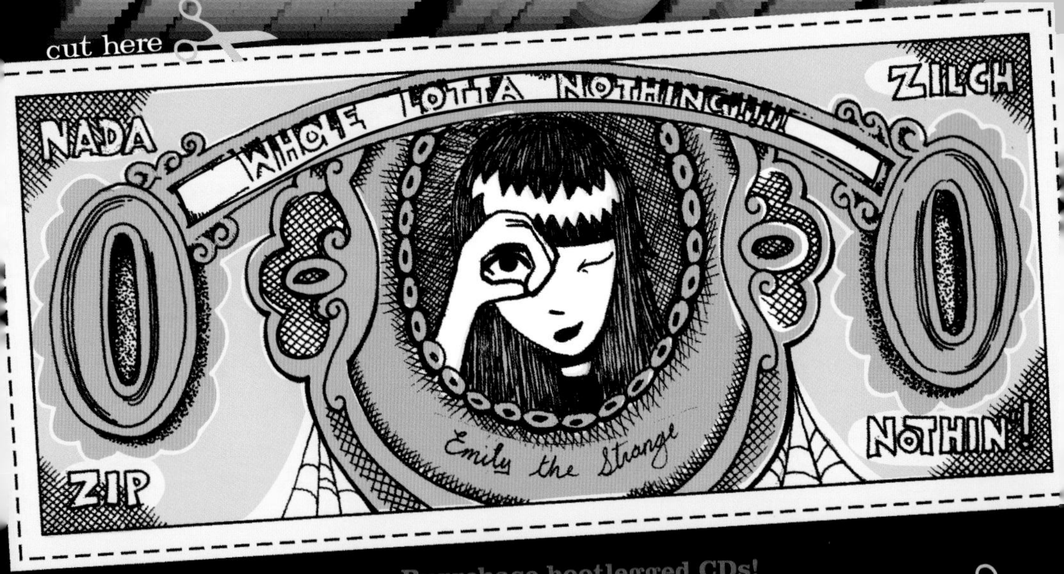
WHOLE LOTTA NOTHING!!!
NADA
ZILCH
ZIP
NOTHIN'!
Emily the Strange

Purrchase bootlegged CDs!

cut here

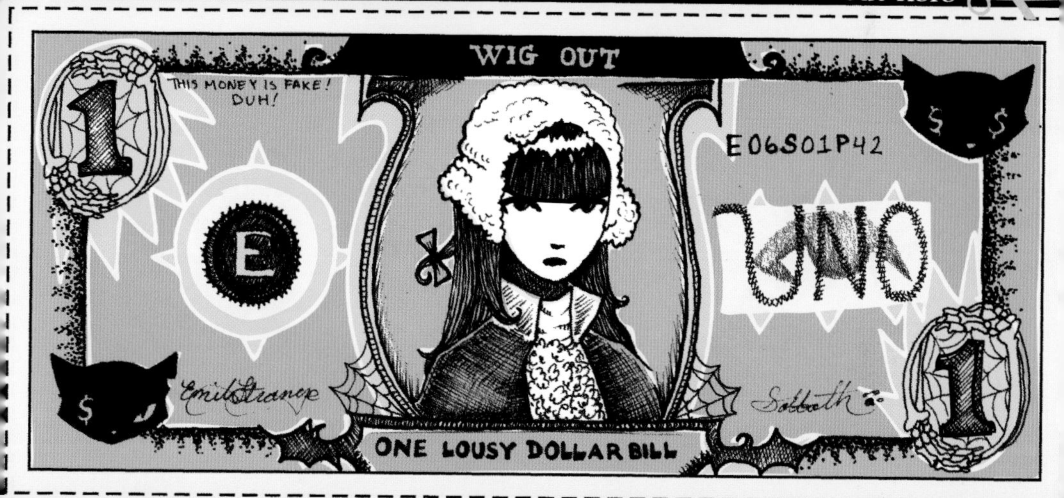
WIG OUT
THIS MONEY IS FAKE! DUH!
E06S01P42
E
UNO
ONE LOUSY DOLLAR BILL

Fake tip for your stylist giving you a bad faux-hawk!

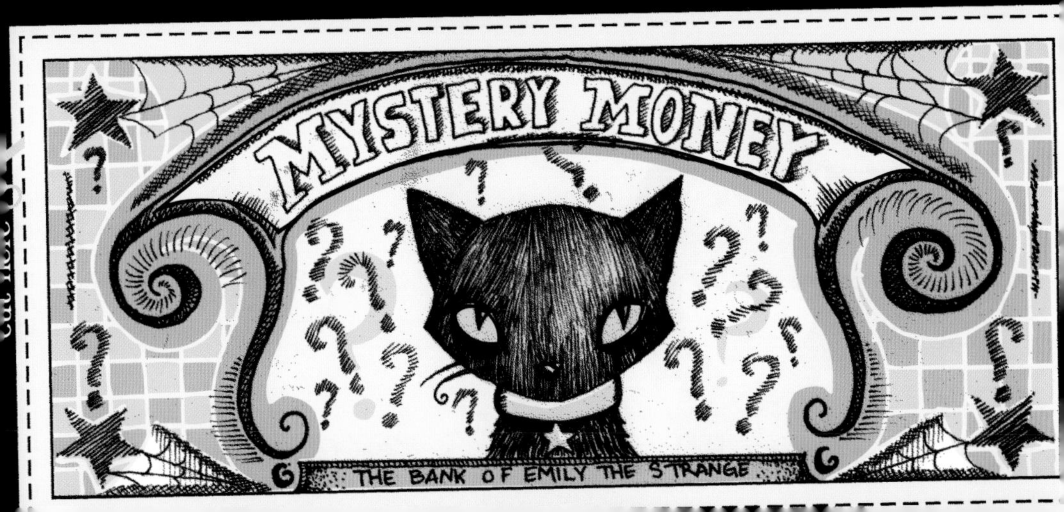
MYSTERY MONEY
THE BANK OF EMILY THE STRANGE

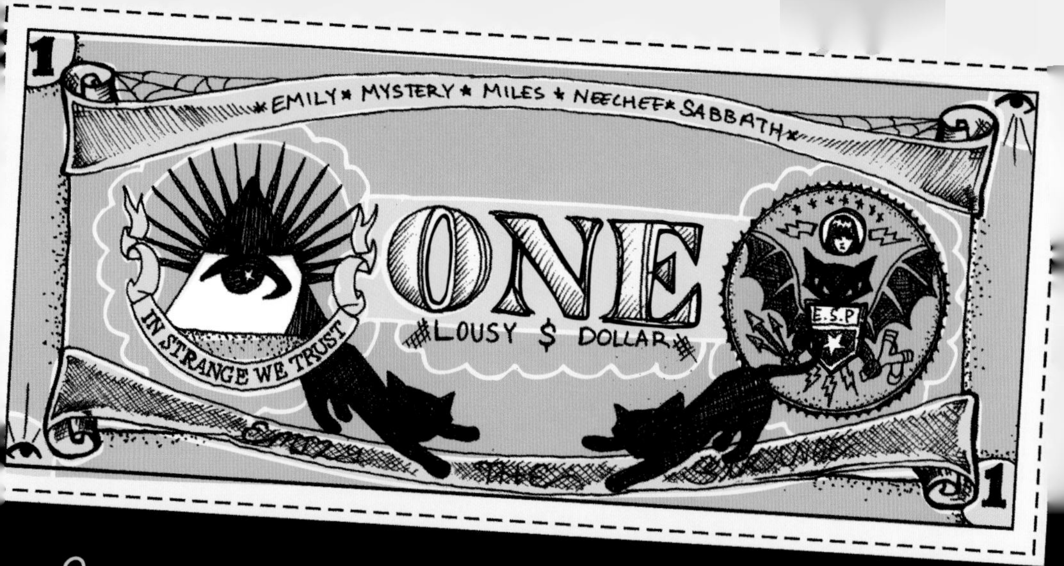
1
EMILY * MYSTERY * MILES * NEECHEE * SABBATH
IN STRANGE WE TRUST
ONE
LOUSY $ DOLLAR
E.S.P
1

cut here

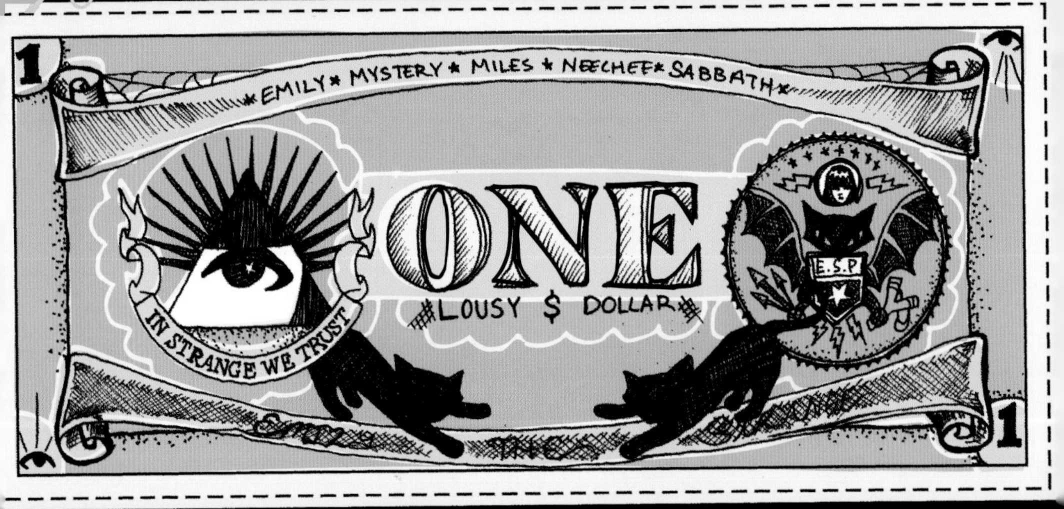
1
EMILY * MYSTERY * MILES * NEECHEE * SABBATH
IN STRANGE WE TRUST
ONE
LOUSY $ DOLLAR
E.S.P
1

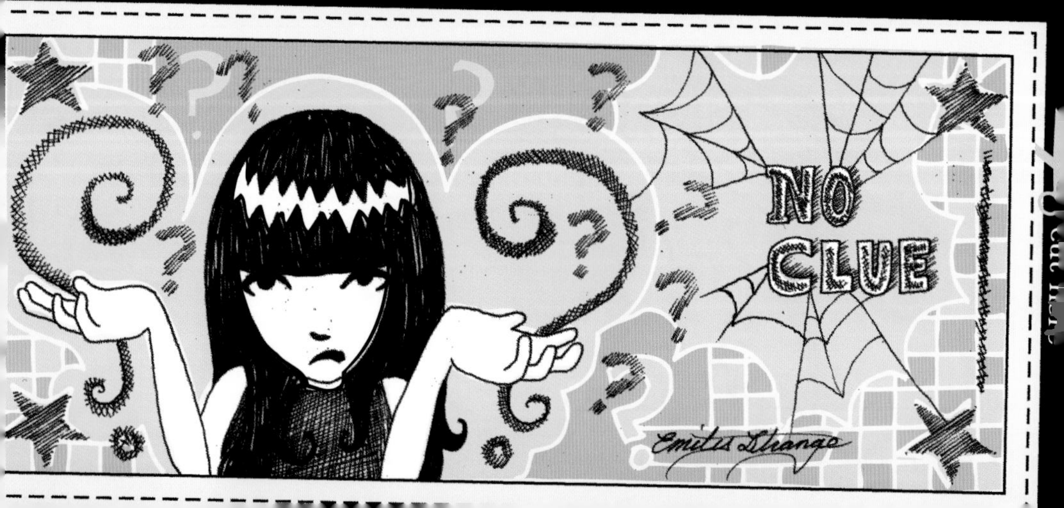
NO
CLUE

cut here

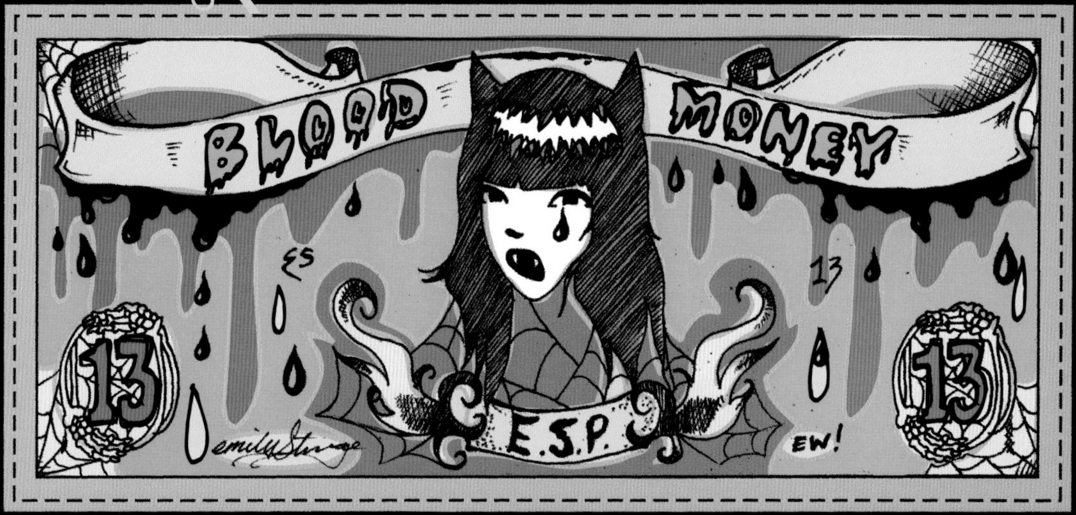
BLOOD MONEY
ES
13
13
13
emily Strange
E.S.P.
EW!

No blood for oil! Or real money, either!

cut here

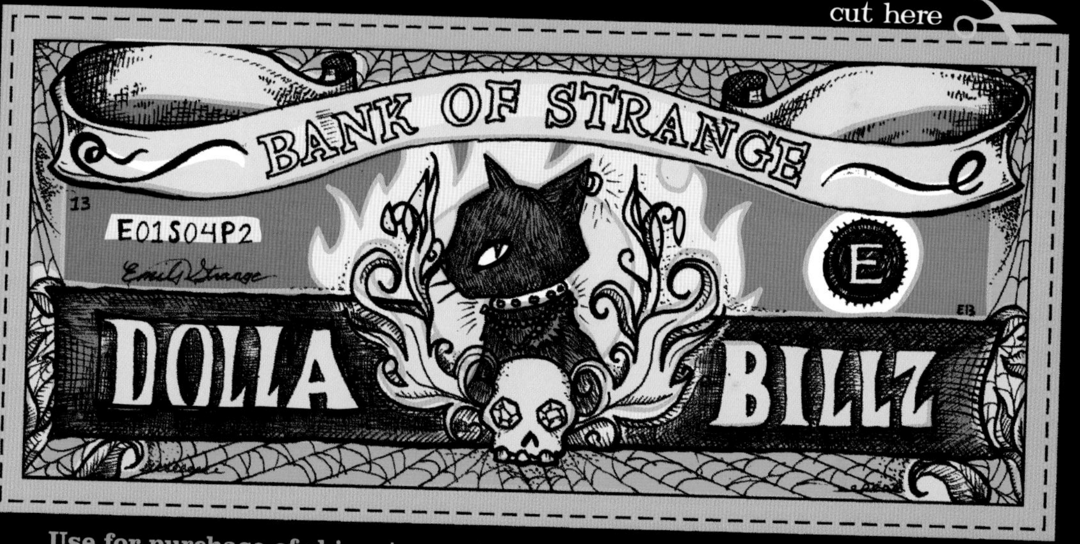
BANK OF STRANGE
13
E01S04P2
Emily Strange
E
E13
DOLLA BILLZ

Use for purchase of rhinestone collar for your stuffed kitty!

cut here

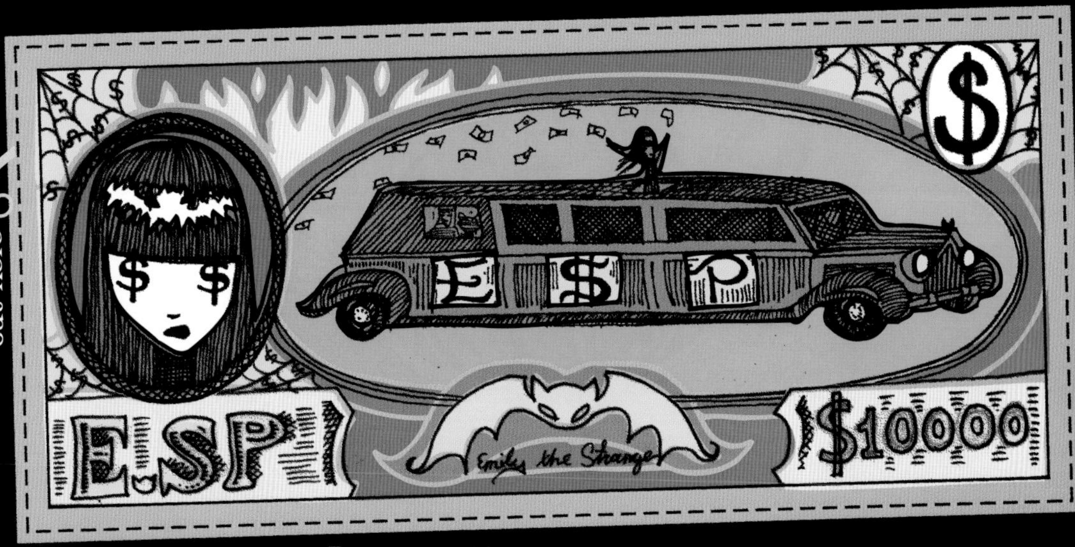
$
E S P
ESP1
Emily the Strange
$10000

Buy yourself those fake gold teeth you've always wanted!

cut here

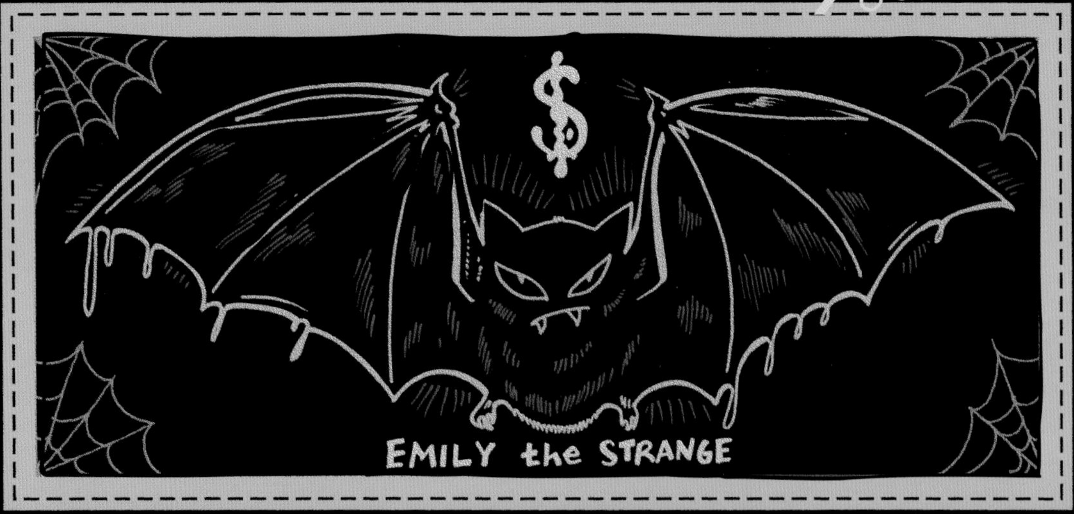
EMILY the STRANGE

cut here

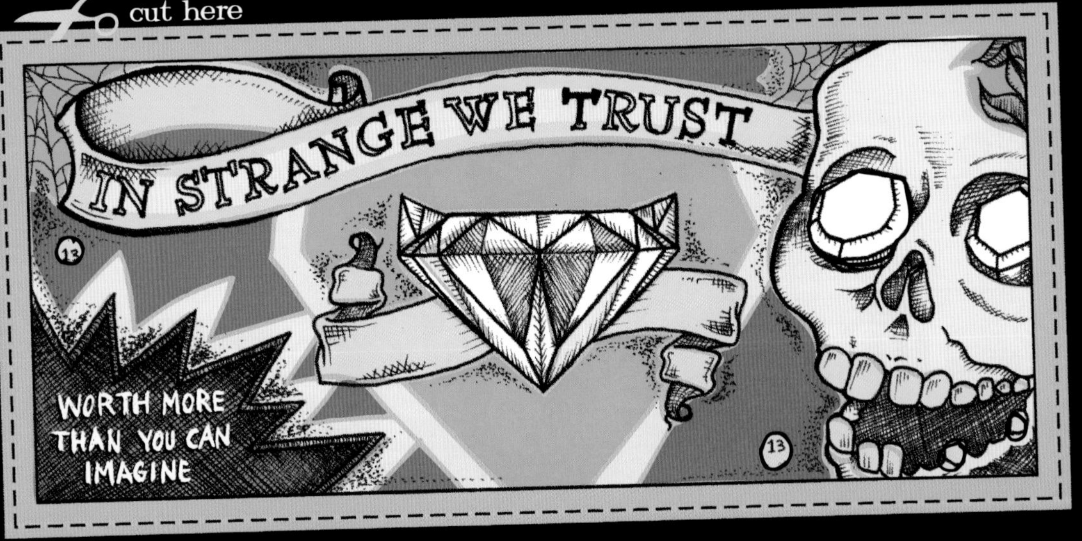
IN STRANGE WE TRUST
13
WORTH MORE THAN YOU CAN IMAGINE
13

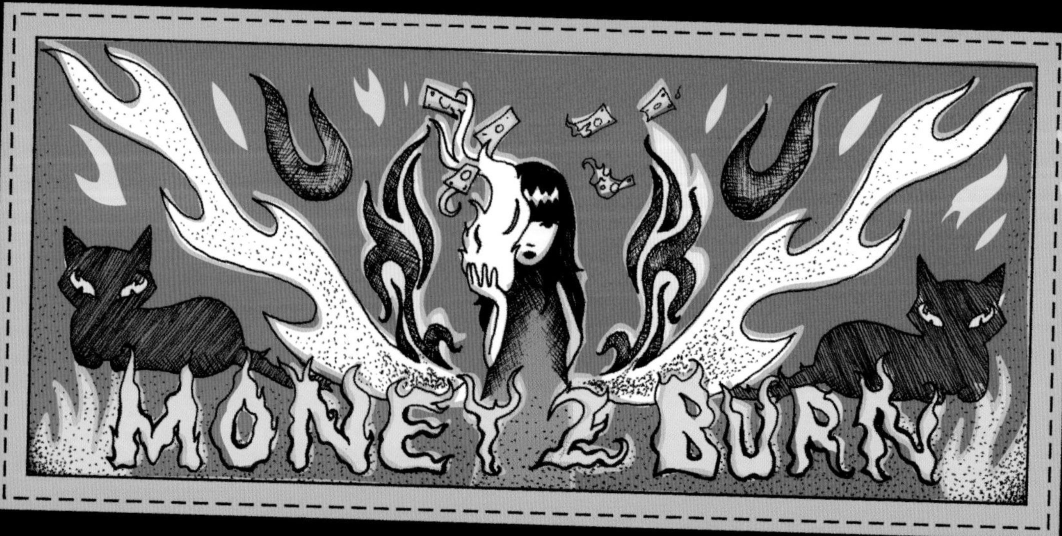
MONEY 2 BURN

cut here

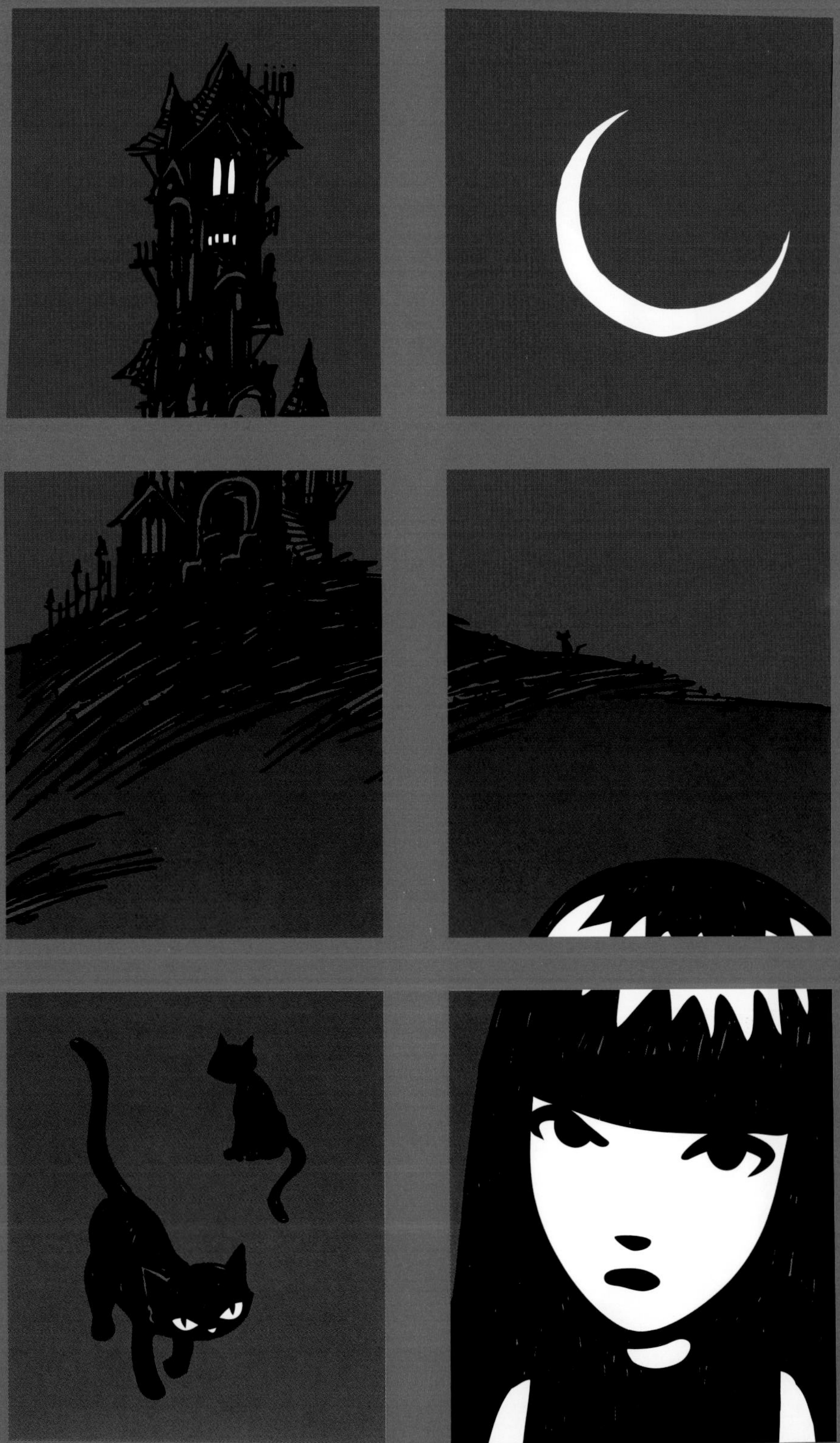

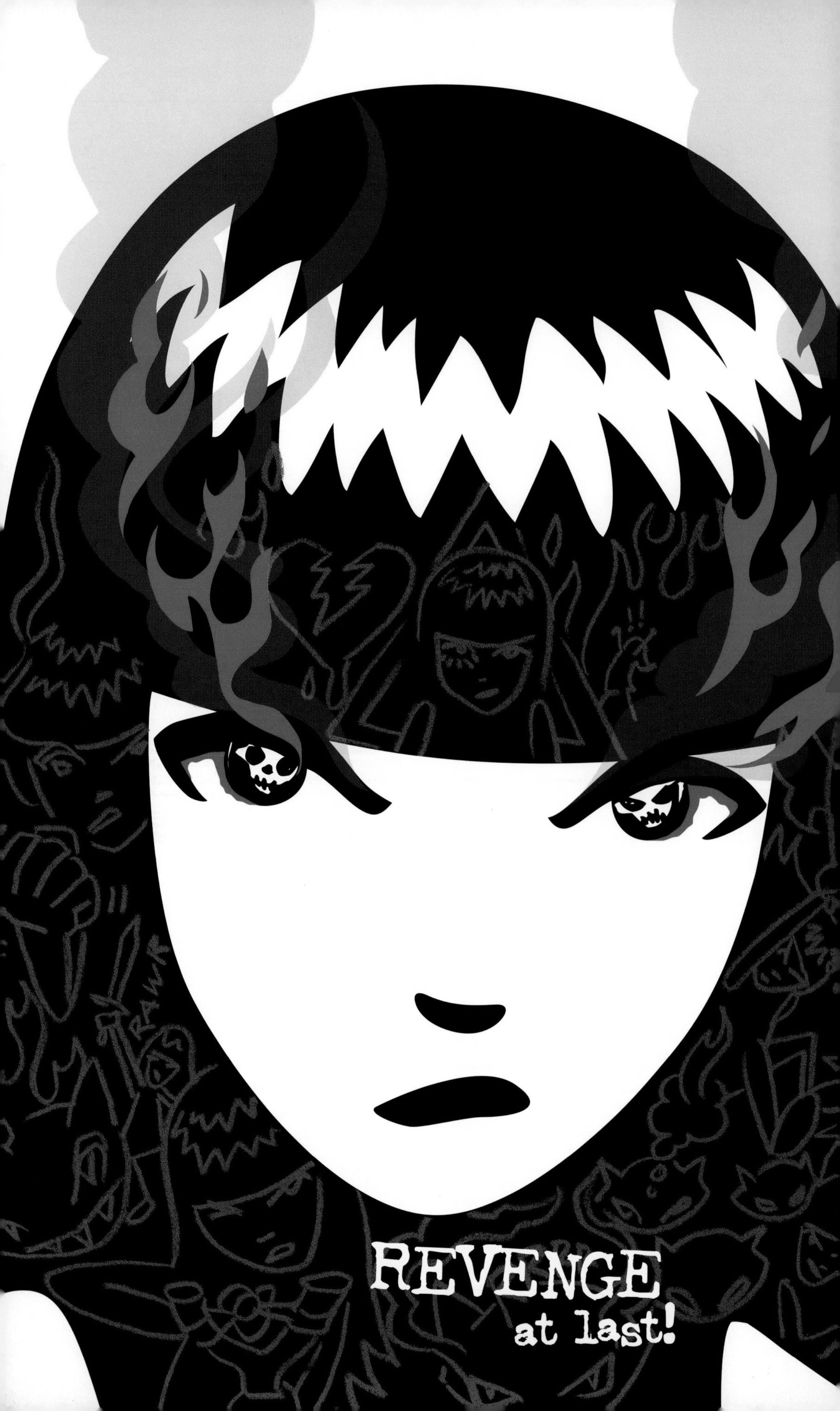
REVENGE
at last!

Emily's Top 13 Methods of REVENGE

1 Put stink bugs in shoes

2 When cats are bad, switch out their cat food with shredded wheat

3 Put revengee's hand in warm water while sleeping ("urine for a big surprise, bub.")

4 Banana in tailpipe (save for SUVs who run bikes off the road!)

5 Replace Starduds self-serve sugar-cube jar with starch cubes or rock salt

6 Issue fake parking tickets! with return address to neighbor's address for your sneaky pickup. SEND CASH ONLY!

7 Switch all the keys around on Mom's keyboard

8 FAKE CAT POOP IN CEREAL

9 Underwear in Freezer

10 Apply "I EAT WORMZ" gag bumper stickers on all cars in Wal-Mart parking lot

11 Make up goofy stuff about Rob Reger and submit daily dirt to Perez Hilton

12 Develop Flow-chart for REVENGE. Psst! See page 126...

13 Hand out fake movie passes to the global blockbuster "Dogs Are the Best Animal on the Planet"

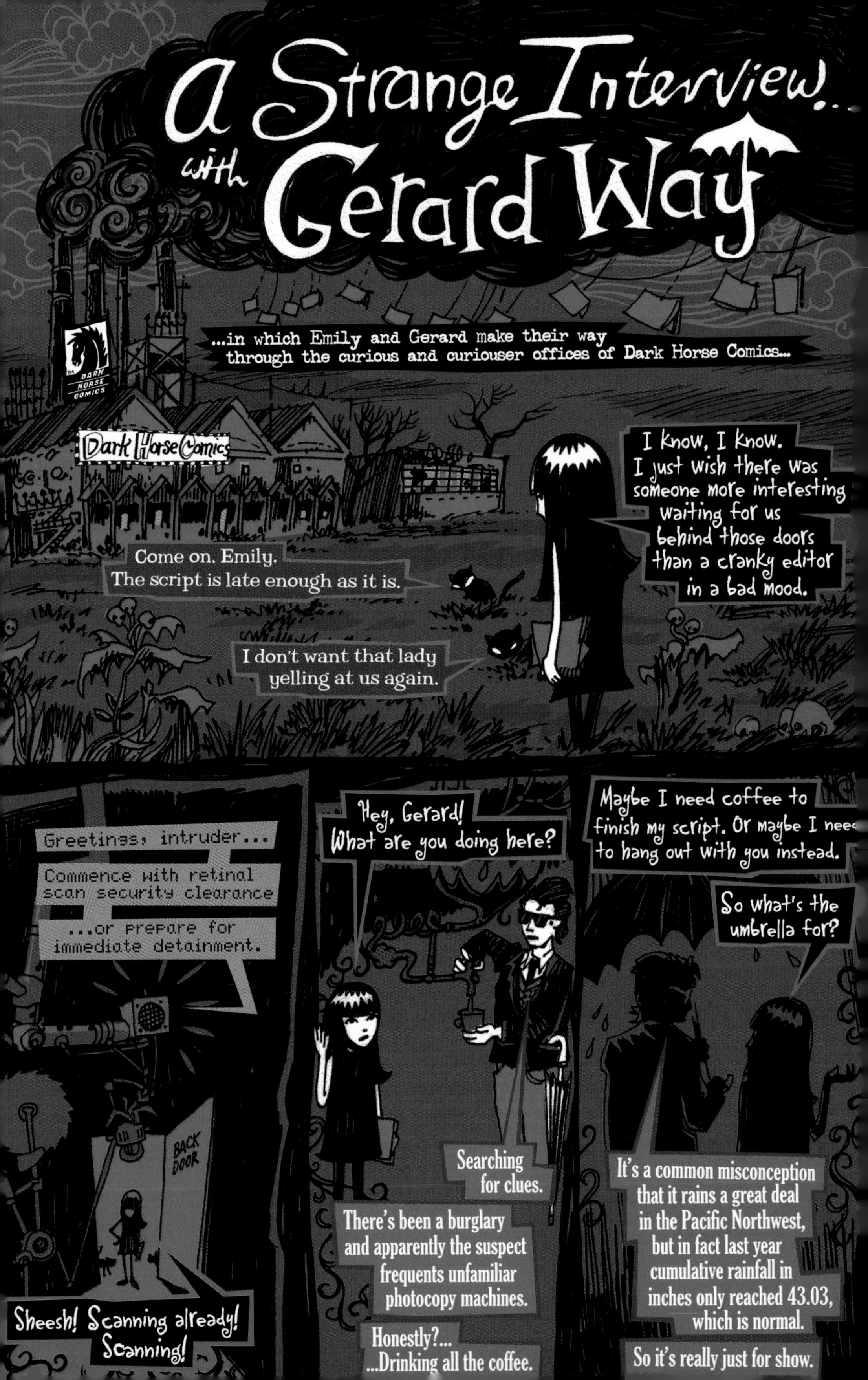

A Strange Interview...
with Gerard Way
...in which Emily and Gerard make their way through the curious and curiouser offices of Dark Horse Comics...
DARK HORSE COMICS
Dark Horse Comics
I know, I know. I just wish there was someone more interesting waiting for us behind those doors than a cranky editor in a bad mood.
Come on, Emily. The script is late enough as it is.
I don't want that lady yelling at us again.
Greetings, intruder...
Commence with retinal scan security clearance
...or prepare for immediate detainment.
BACK DOOR
Sheesh! Scanning already! Scanning!
Hey, Gerard! What are you doing here?
Searching for clues.
There's been a burglary and apparently the suspect frequents unfamiliar photocopy machines.
Honestly?... ...Drinking all the coffee.
Maybe I need coffee to finish my script. Or maybe I need to hang out with you instead.
So what's the umbrella for?
It's a common misconception that it rains a great deal in the Pacific Northwest, but in fact last year cumulative rainfall in inches only reached 43.03, which is normal.
So it's really just for show.

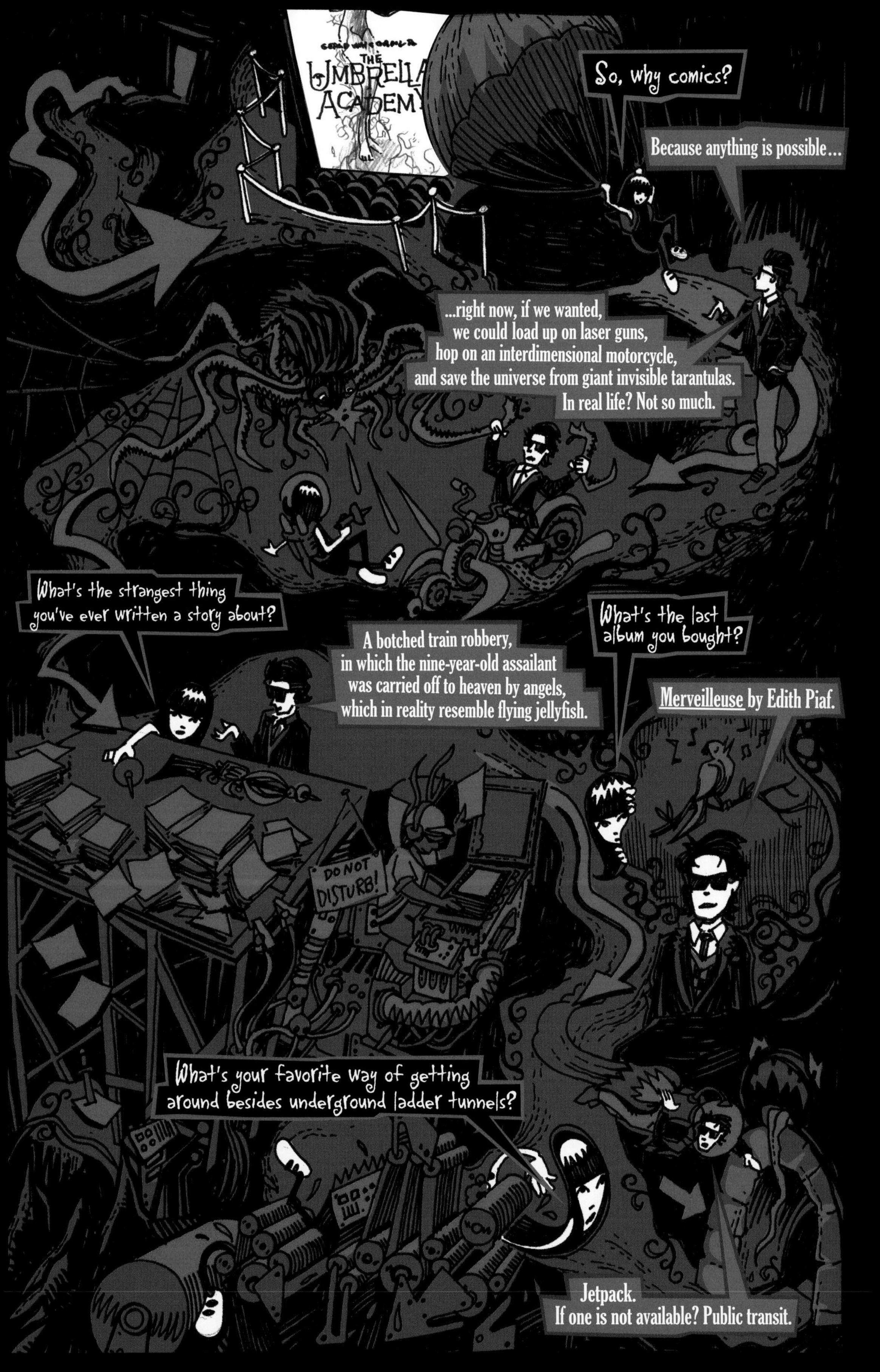

So, why comics?
Because anything is possible...
...right now, if we wanted, we could load up on laser guns, hop on an interdimensional motorcycle, and save the universe from giant invisible tarantulas. In real life? Not so much.
What's the strangest thing you've ever written a story about?
A botched train robbery, in which the nine-year-old assailant was carried off to heaven by angels, which in reality resemble flying jellyfish.
What's the last album you bought?
Merveilleuse by Edith Piaf.
DO NOT DISTURB!
What's your favorite way of getting around besides underground ladder tunnels?
Jetpack.
If one is not available? Public transit.

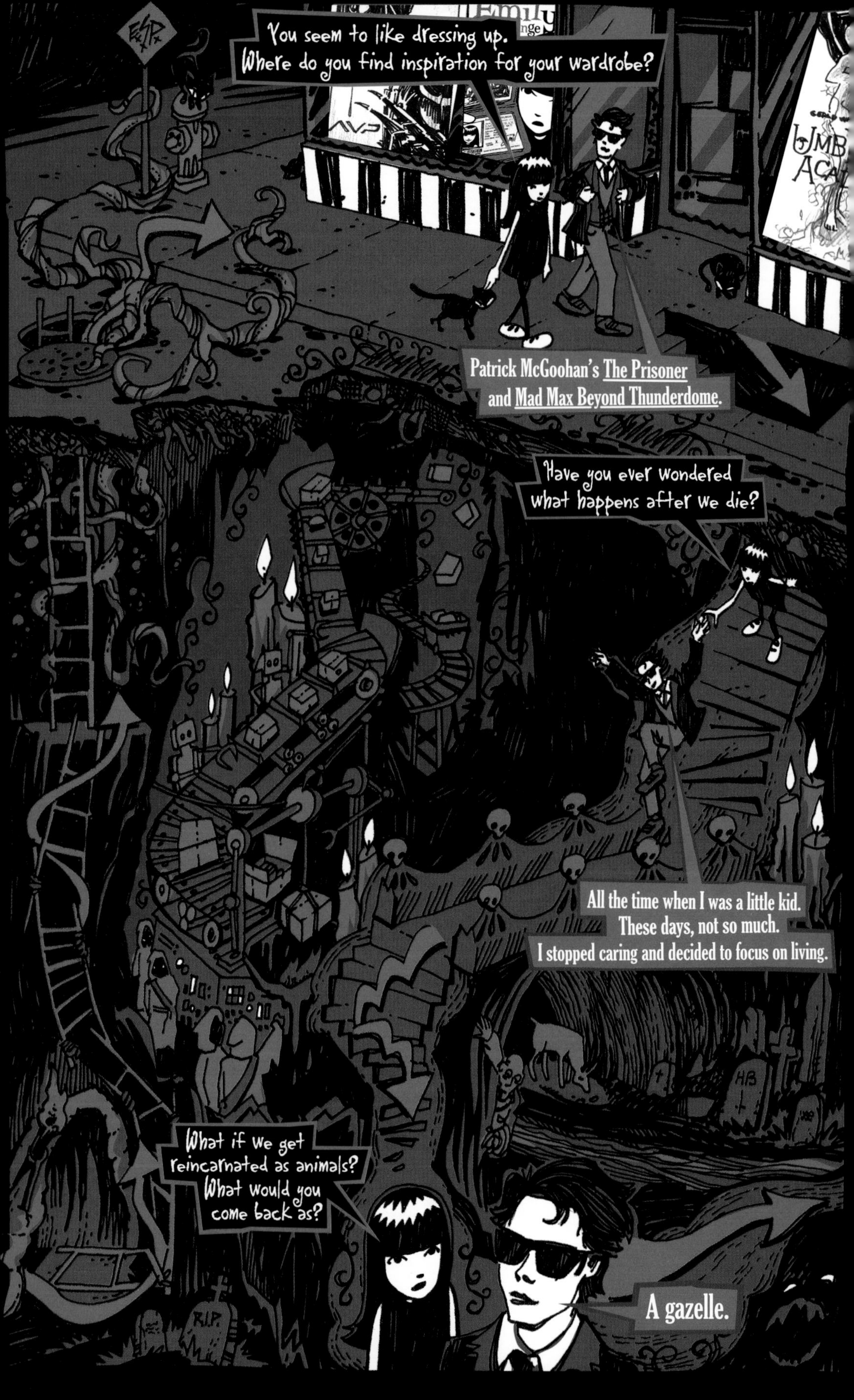
You seem to like dressing up. Where do you find inspiration for your wardrobe?
Patrick McGoohan's The Prisoner and Mad Max Beyond Thunderdome.
Have you ever wondered what happens after we die?
All the time when I was a little kid. These days, not so much. I stopped caring and decided to focus on living.
What if we get reincarnated as animals? What would you come back as?
A gazelle.

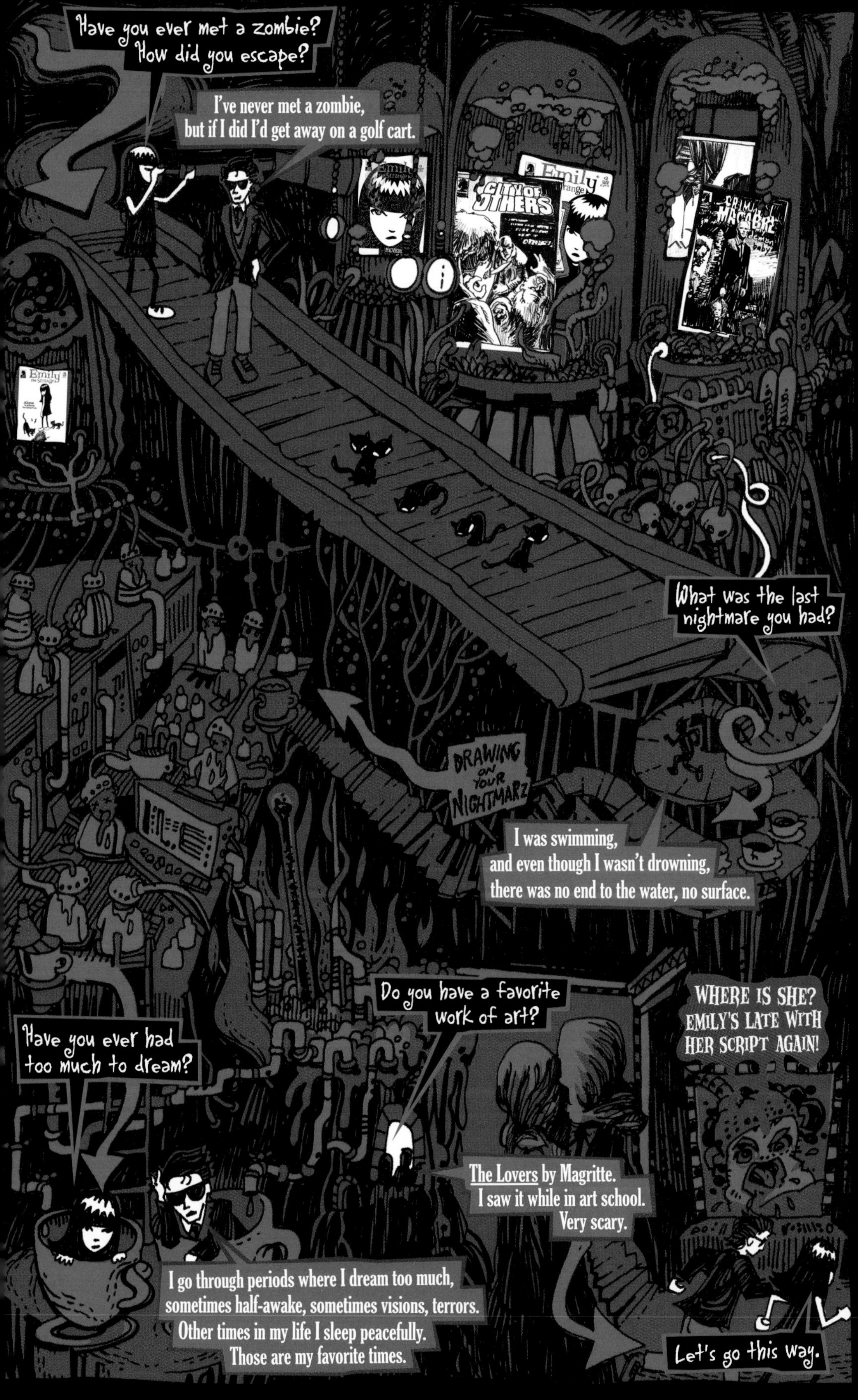
Have you ever met a zombie? How did you escape?
I've never met a zombie, but if I did I'd get away on a golf cart.
What was the last nightmare you had?
DRAWING ON YOUR NIGHTMARZ
I was swimming, and even though I wasn't drowning, there was no end to the water, no surface.
Do you have a favorite work of art?
WHERE IS SHE? EMILY'S LATE WITH HER SCRIPT AGAIN!
Have you ever had too much to dream?
The Lovers by Magritte. I saw it while in art school. Very scary.
I go through periods where I dream too much, sometimes half-awake, sometimes visions, terrors. Other times in my life I sleep peacefully. Those are my favorite times.
Let's go this way.

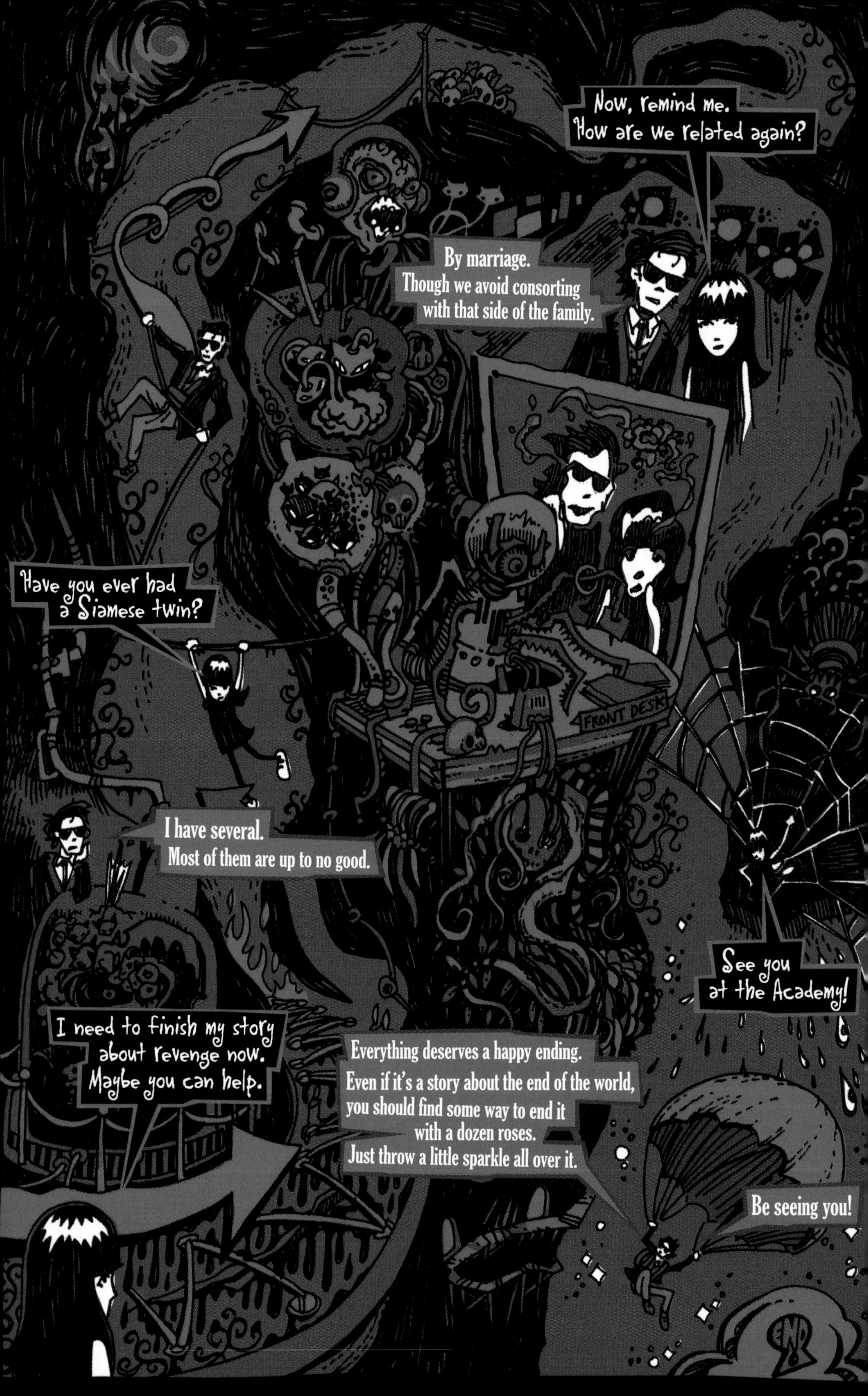
Now, remind me.
How are we related again?
By marriage.
Though we avoid consorting
with that side of the family.
FRONT DESK
Have you ever had
a Siamese twin?
I have several.
Most of them are up to no good.
See you
at the Academy!
I need to finish my story
about revenge now.
Maybe you can help.
Everything deserves a happy ending.
Even if it's a story about the end of the world,
you should find some way to end it
with a dozen roses.
Just throw a little sparkle all over it.
Be seeing you!

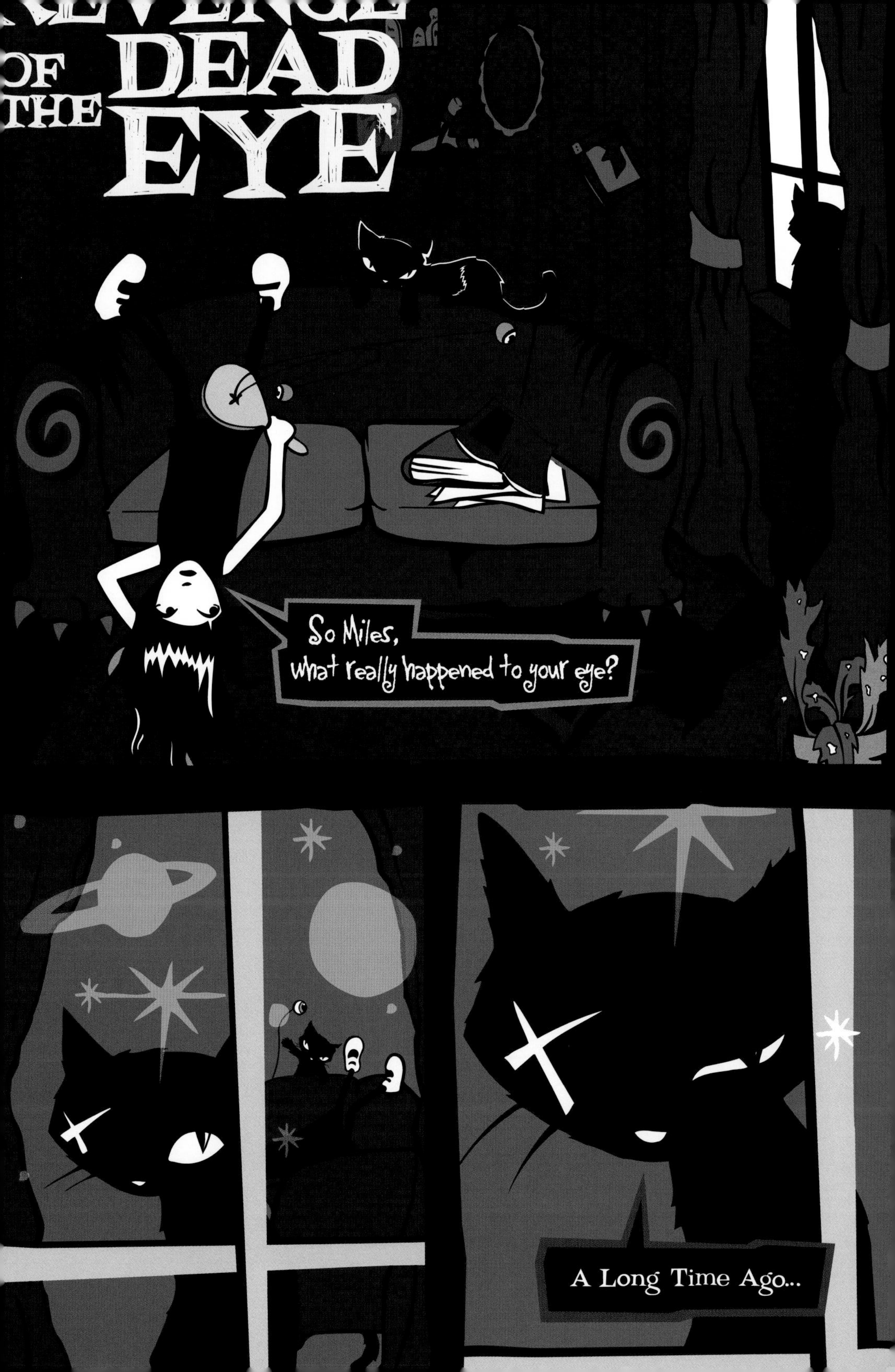
REVENGE OF THE DEAD EYE
So Miles,
what really happened to your eye?
A Long Time Ago...

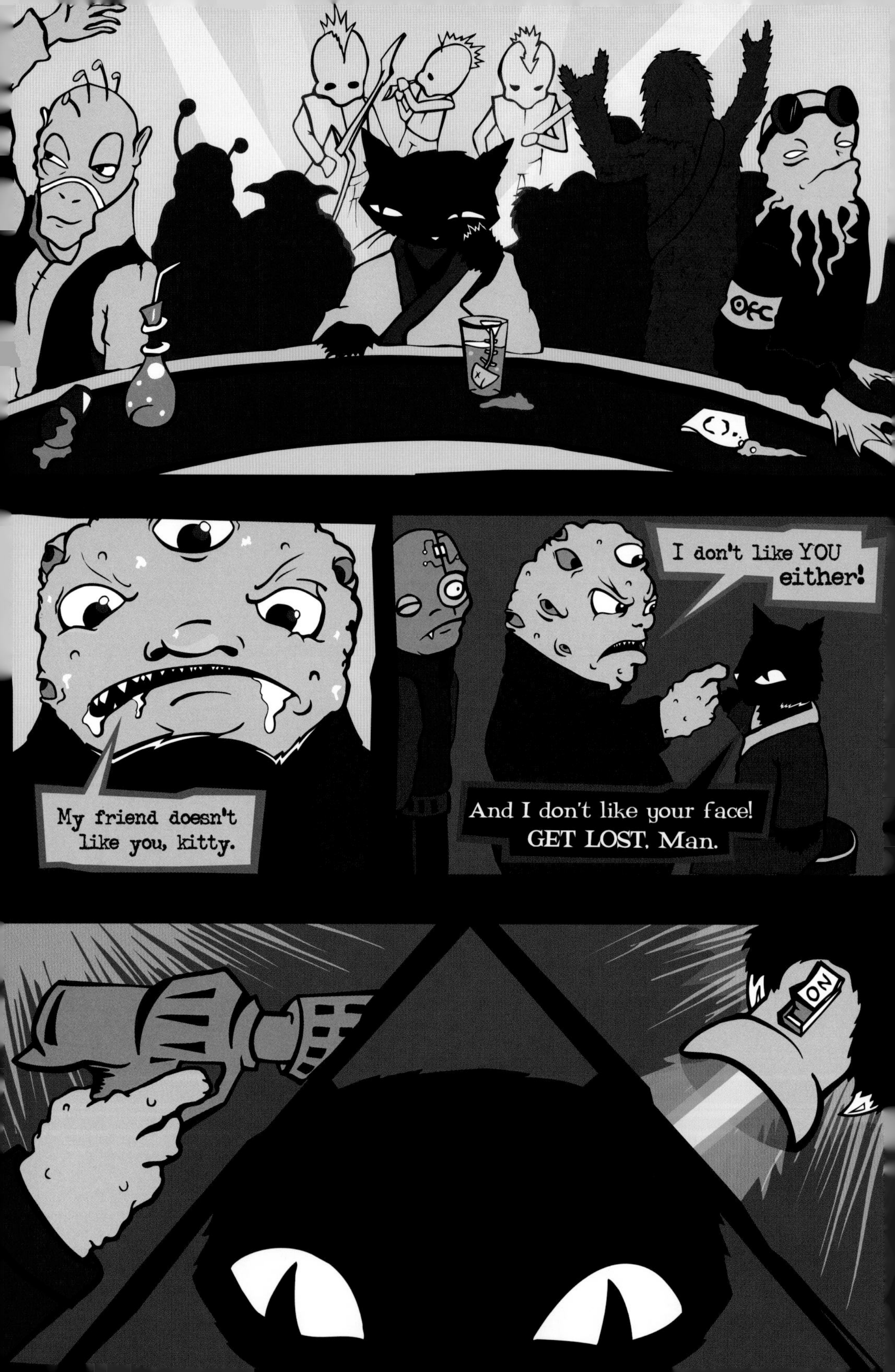

OFC
My friend doesn't like you, kitty.
I don't like YOU either!
And I don't like your face! GET LOST, Man.
ON

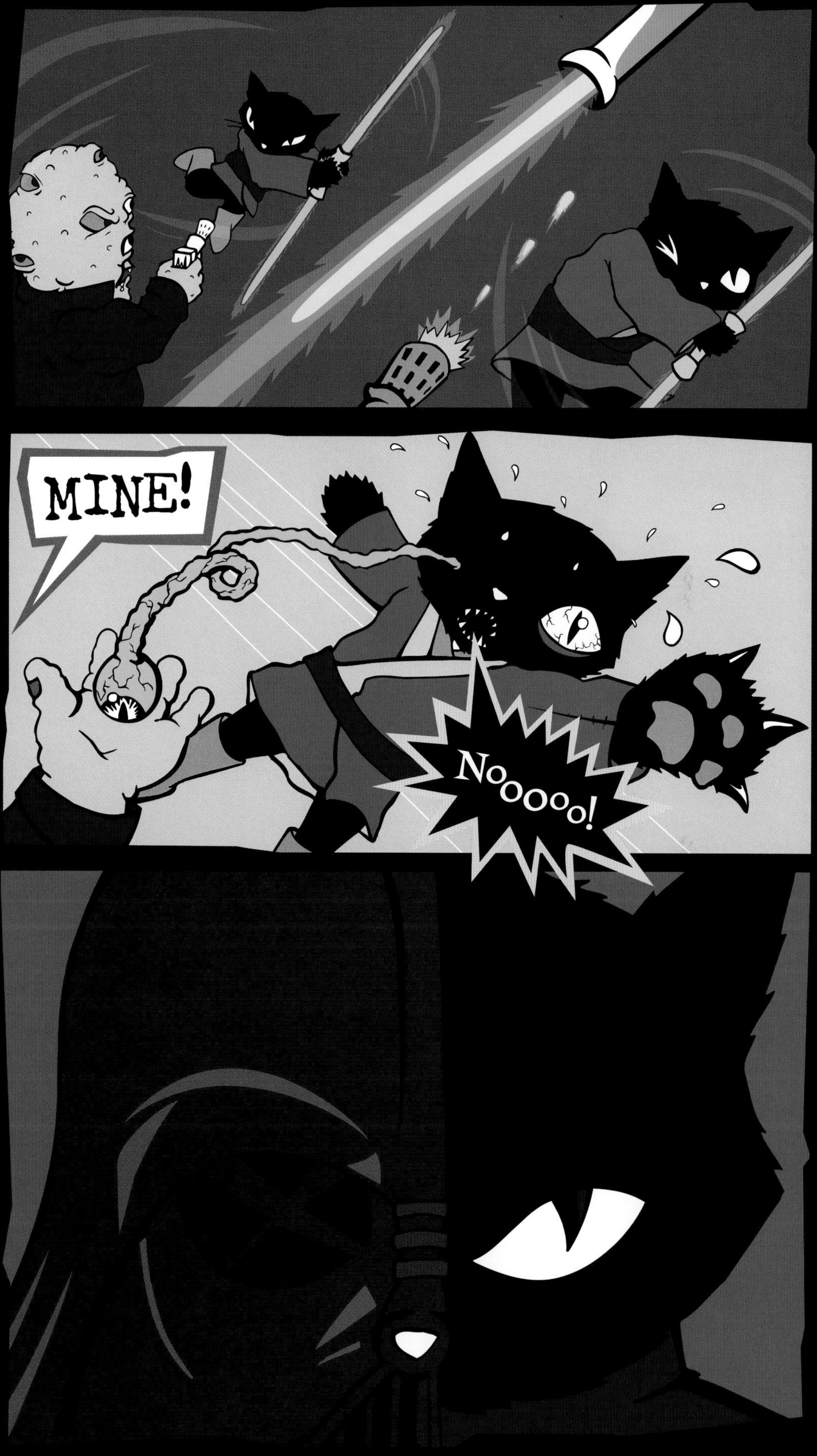
MINE!
Nooooo!

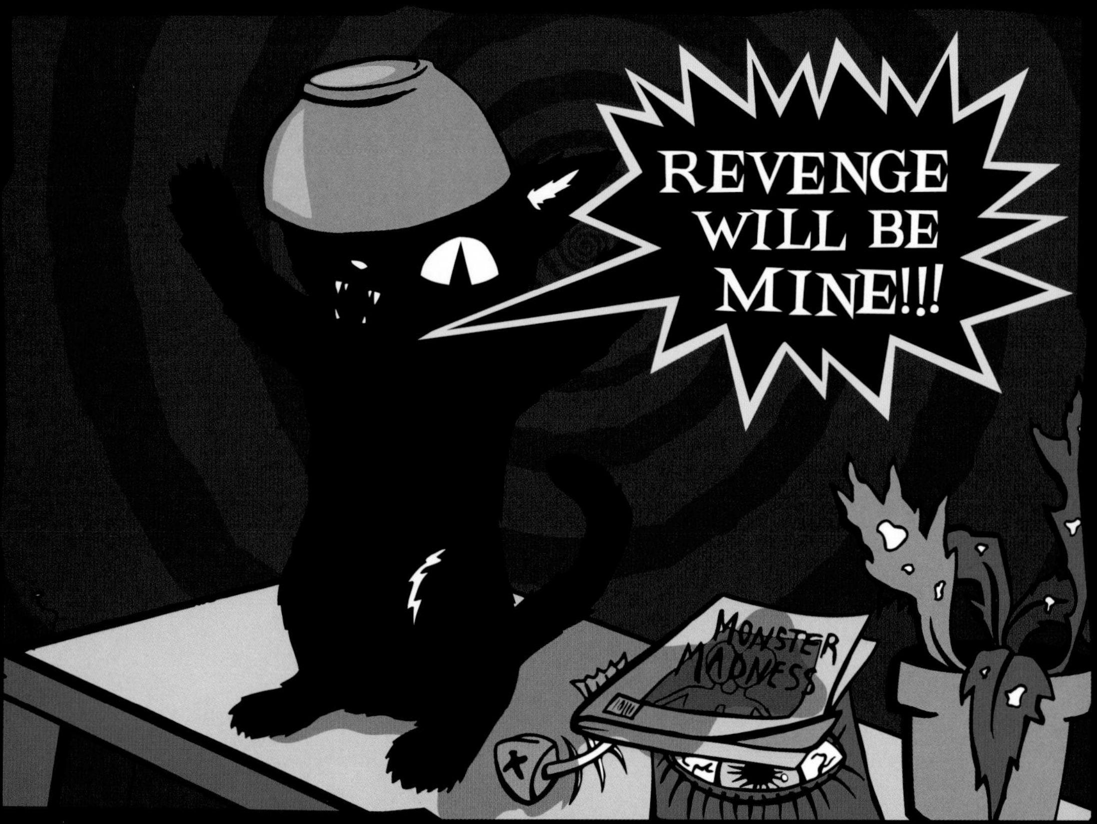
REVENGE WILL BE MINE!!!
MONSTER MADNESS

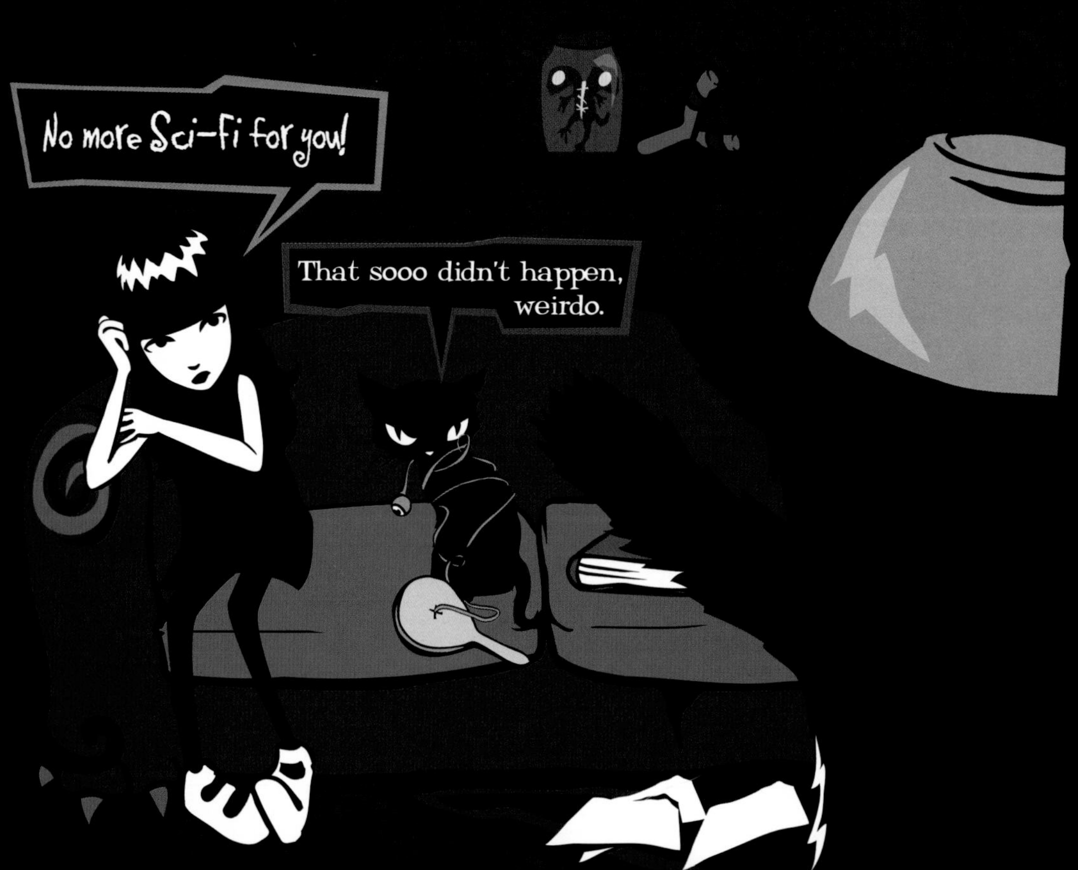
No more Sci-Fi for you!
That sooo didn't happen, weirdo.

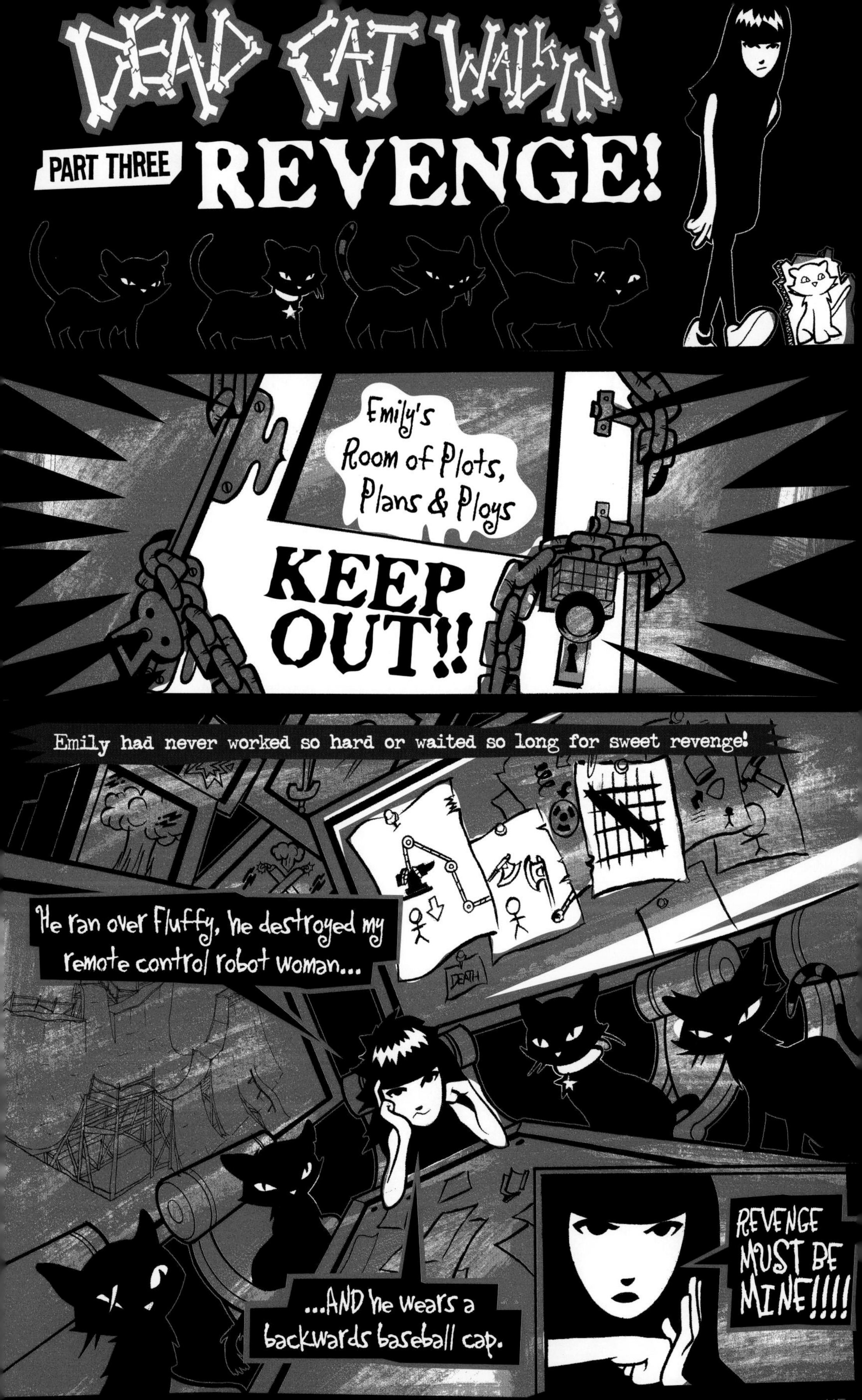
DEAD CAT WALKIN'
PART THREE REVENGE!
Emily's Room of Plots, Plans & Ploys
KEEP OUT!!
Emily had never worked so hard or waited so long for sweet revenge!
DEATH
He ran over Fluffy, he destroyed my remote control robot woman...
...AND he wears a backwards baseball cap.
REVENGE MUST BE MINE!!!!

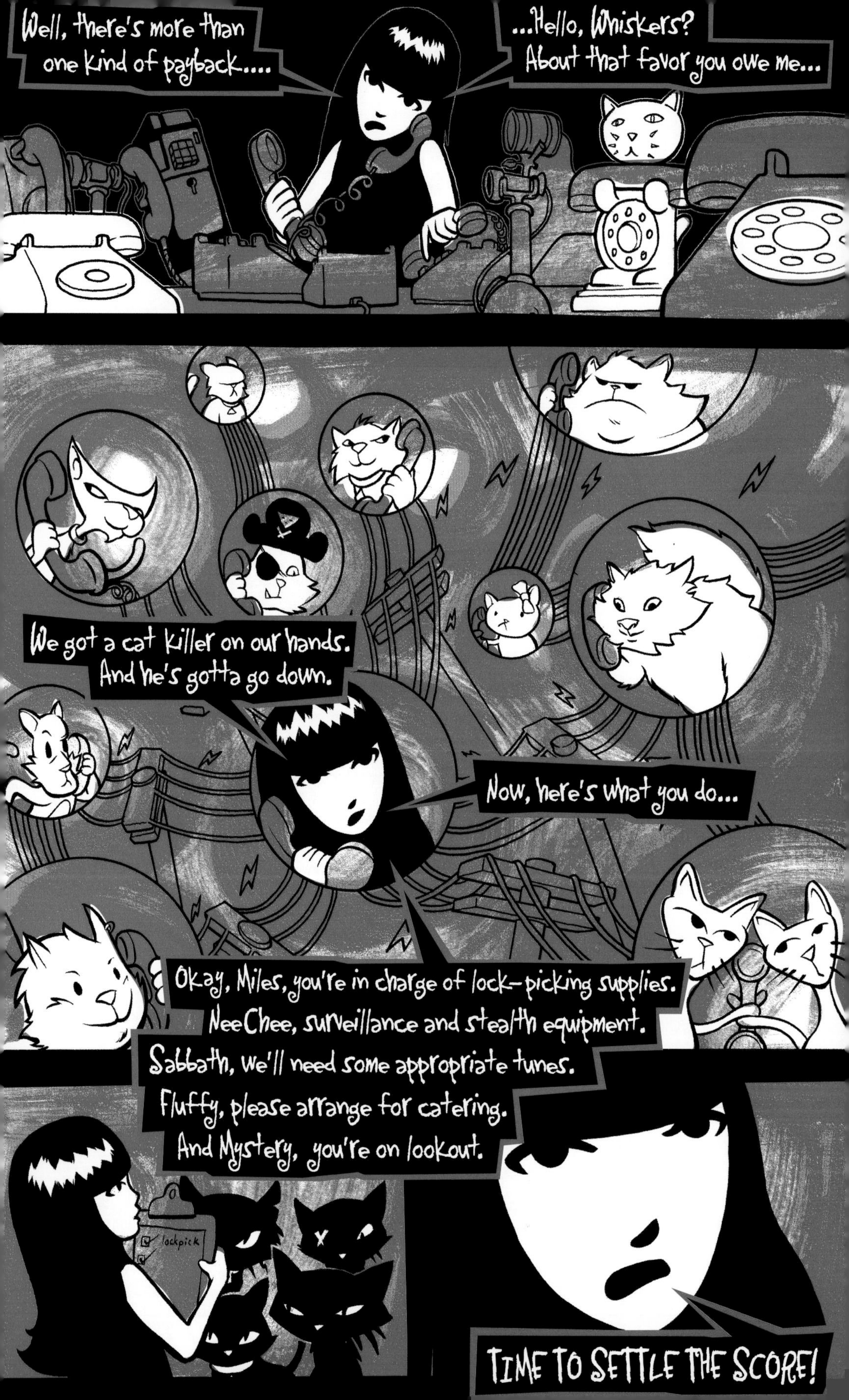

Well, there's more than one kind of payback....
...Hello, Whiskers? About that favor you owe me...
We got a cat killer on our hands. And he's gotta go down.
Now, here's what you do...
Okay, Miles, you're in charge of lock-picking supplies.
NeeChee, surveillance and stealth equipment.
Sabbath, we'll need some appropriate tunes.
Fluffy, please arrange for catering.
And Mystery, you're on lookout.
lockpick
TIME TO SETTLE THE SCORE!

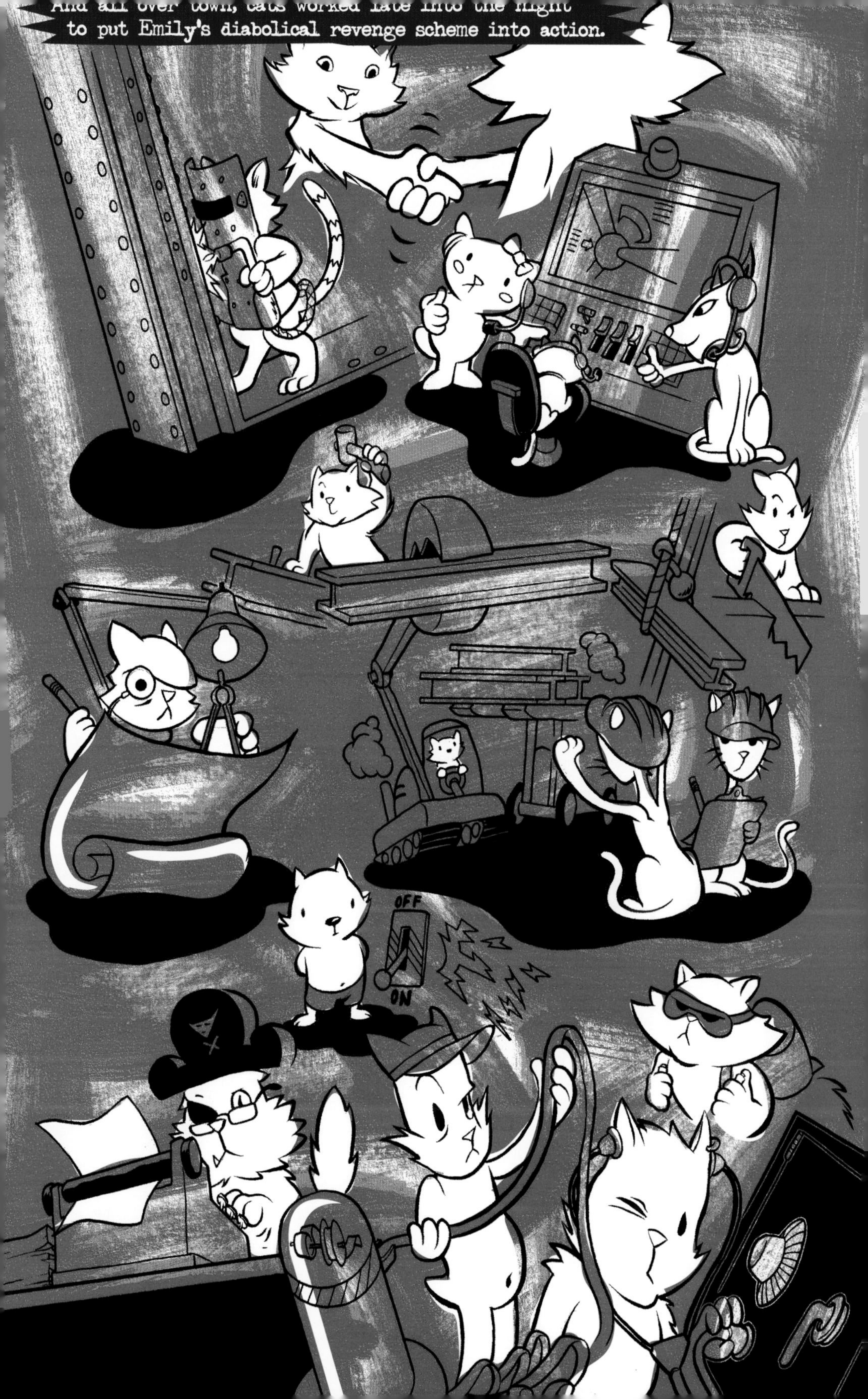
And all over town, cats worked late into the night
to put Emily's diabolical revenge scheme into action.
OFF
ON

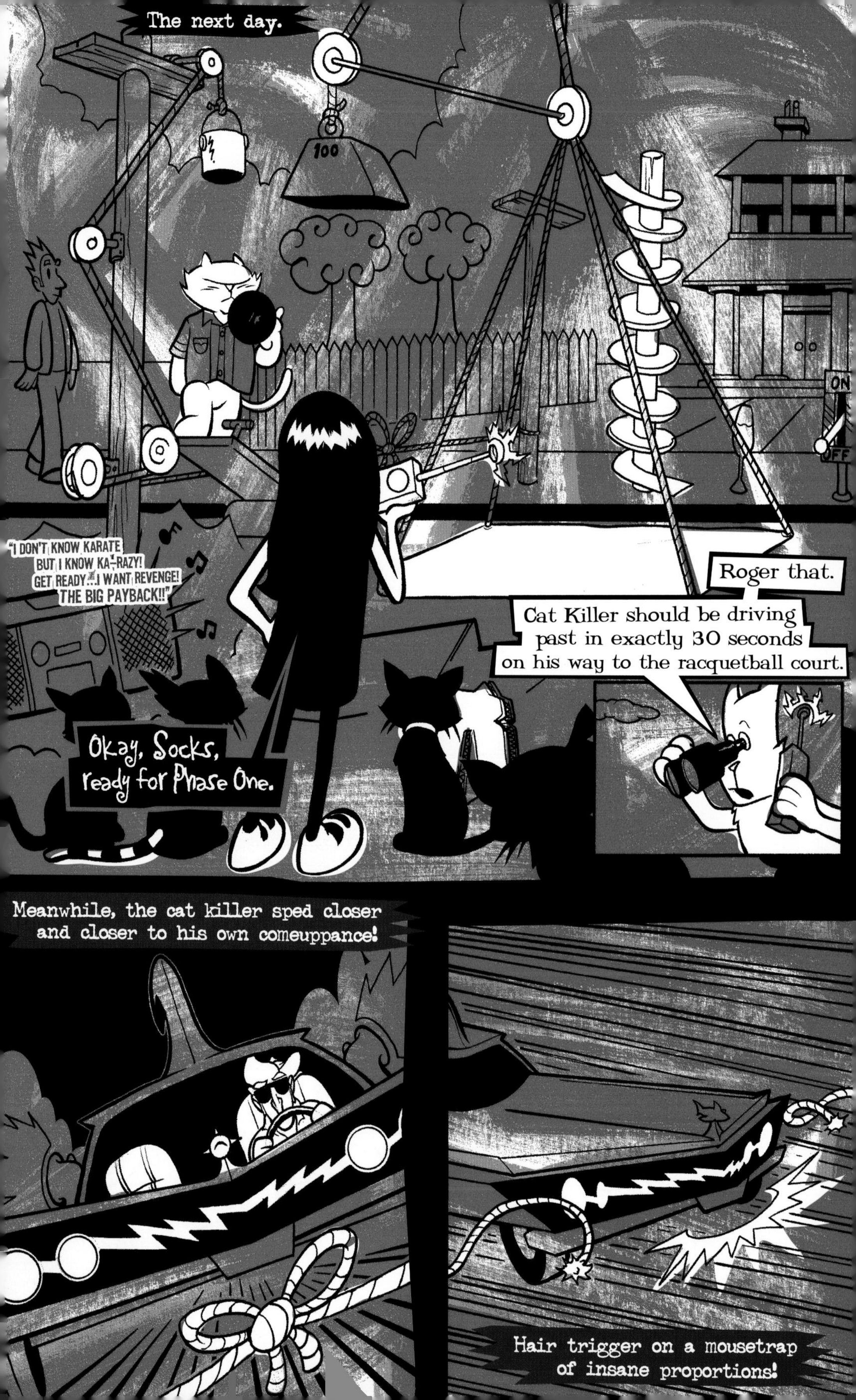
The next day.
100
ON
OFF
"I DON'T KNOW KARATE BUT I KNOW KA-RAZY! GET READY... I WANT REVENGE! THE BIG PAYBACK!!"
Okay, Socks, ready for Phase One.
Roger that.
Cat Killer should be driving past in exactly 30 seconds on his way to the racquetball court.
Meanwhile, the cat killer sped closer and closer to his own comeuppance!
Hair trigger on a mousetrap of insane proportions!

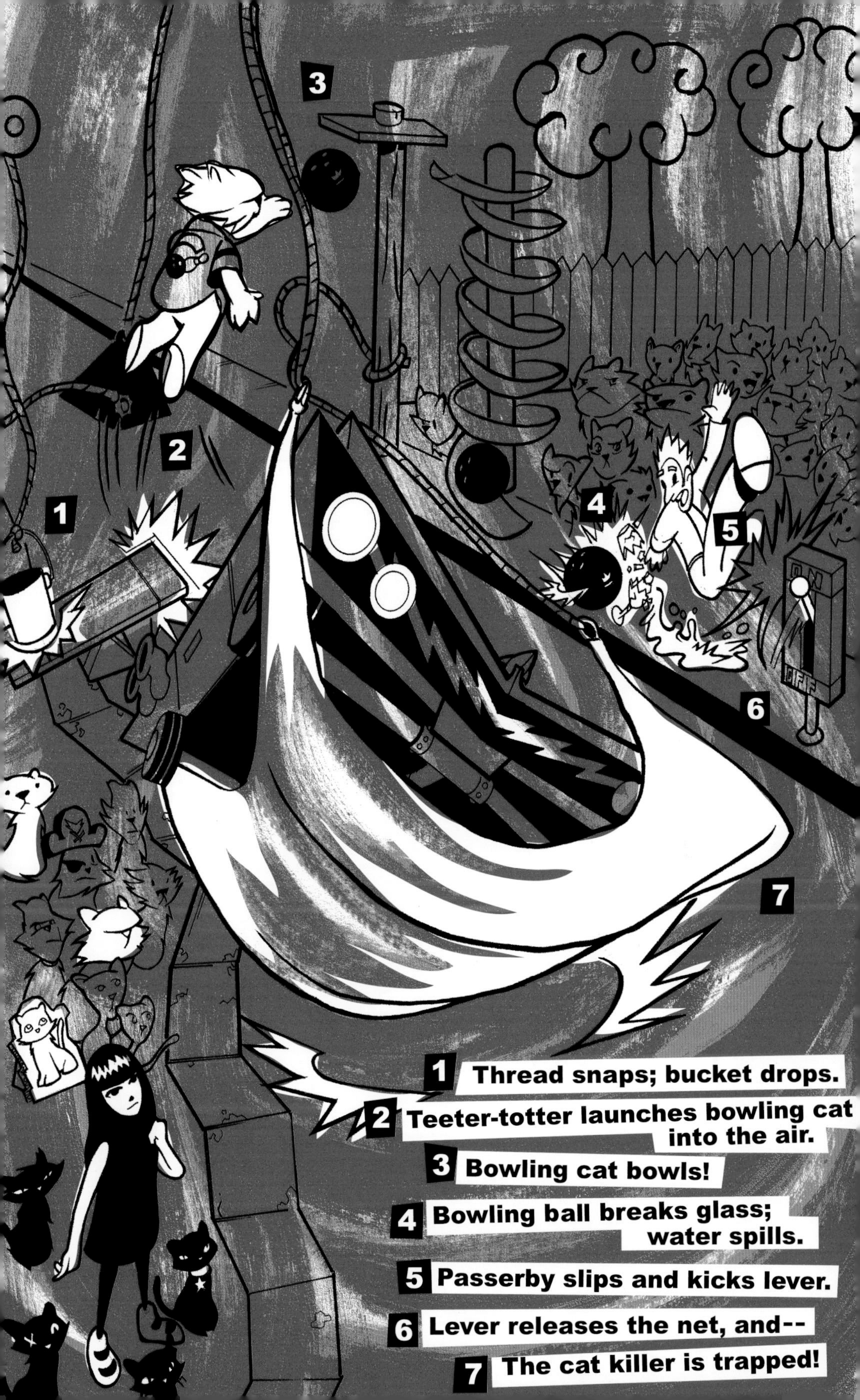

3
2
1
4
5
6
7
ON
OFF
1 Thread snaps; bucket drops.
2 Teeter-totter launches bowling cat into the air.
3 Bowling cat bowls!
4 Bowling ball breaks glass; water spills.
5 Passerby slips and kicks lever.
6 Lever releases the net, and--
7 The cat killer is trapped!

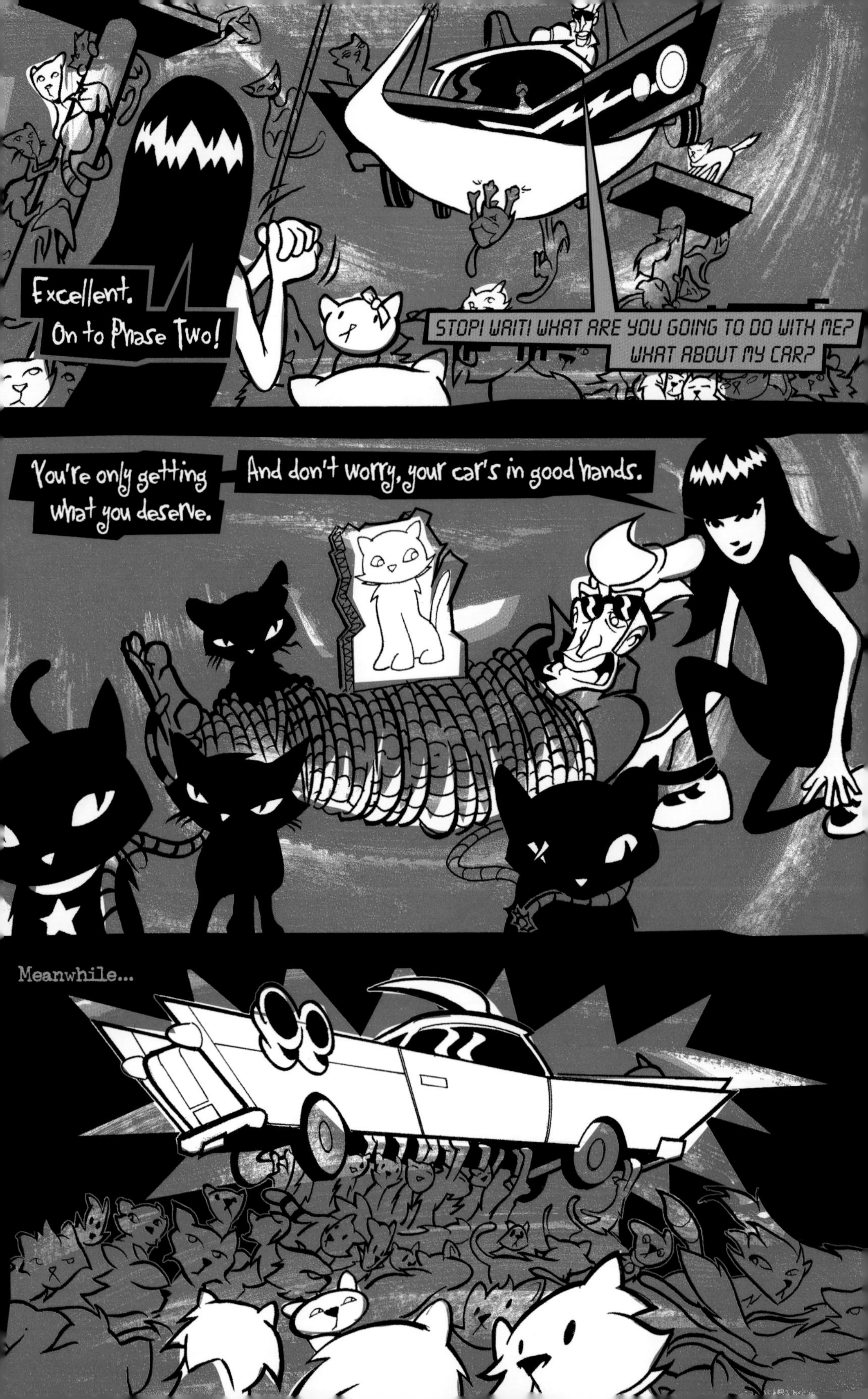

Excellent. On to Phase Two!
STOP! WAIT! WHAT ARE YOU GOING TO DO WITH ME? WHAT ABOUT MY CAR?
You're only getting what you deserve.
And don't worry, your car's in good hands.
Meanwhile...

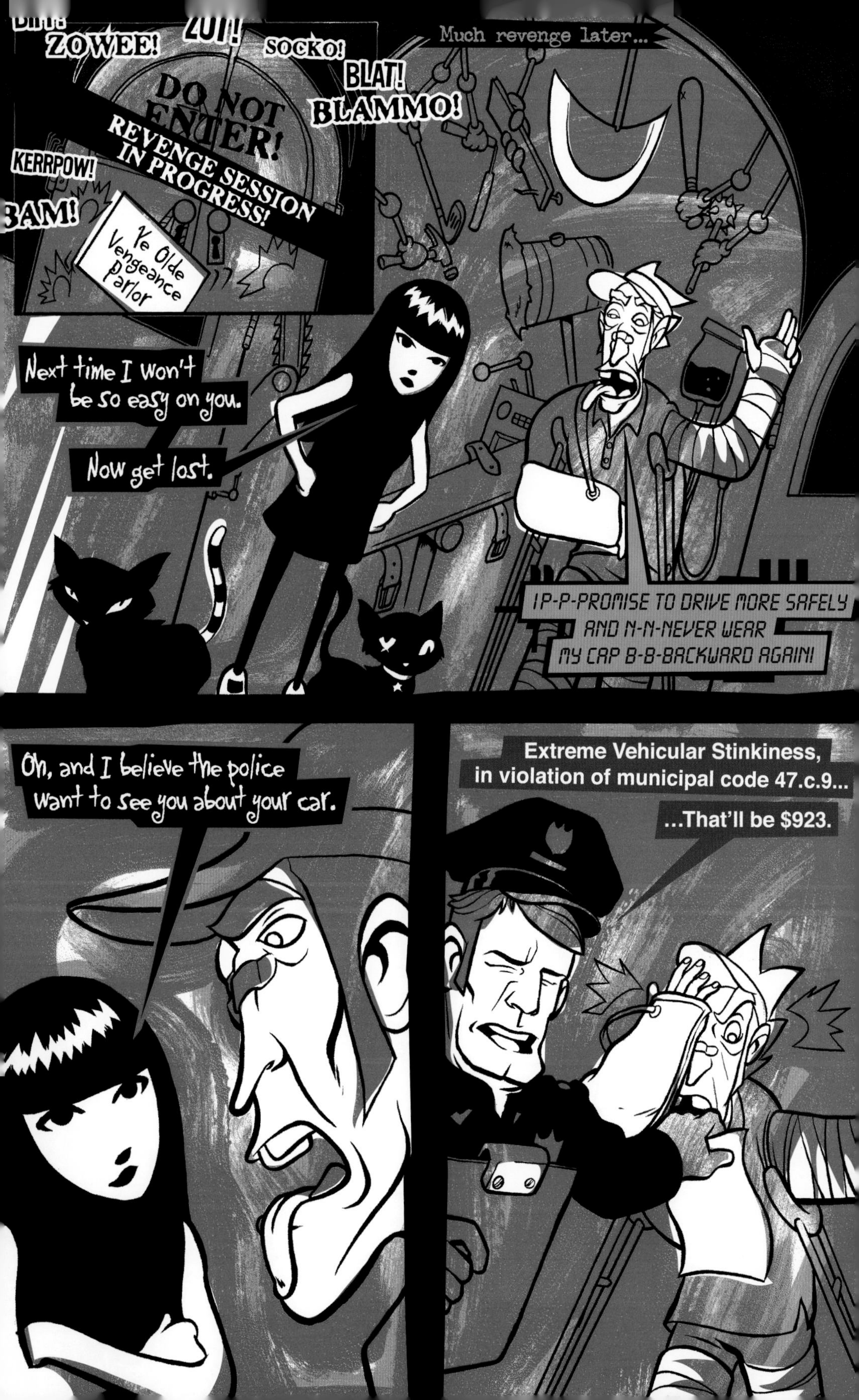
ZOWEE!
ZOT!
SOCKO!
BLAT!
BLAMMO!
DO NOT ENTER!
REVENGE SESSION IN PROGRESS!
KERRPOW!
BAM!
Ye Olde Vengeance Parlor
Much revenge later...
Next time I won't be so easy on you.
Now get lost.
I P-P-PROMISE TO DRIVE MORE SAFELY AND N-N-NEVER WEAR MY CAP B-B-BACKWARD AGAIN!
Oh, and I believe the police want to see you about your car.
Extreme Vehicular Stinkiness, in violation of municipal code 47.c.9...
...That'll be $923.

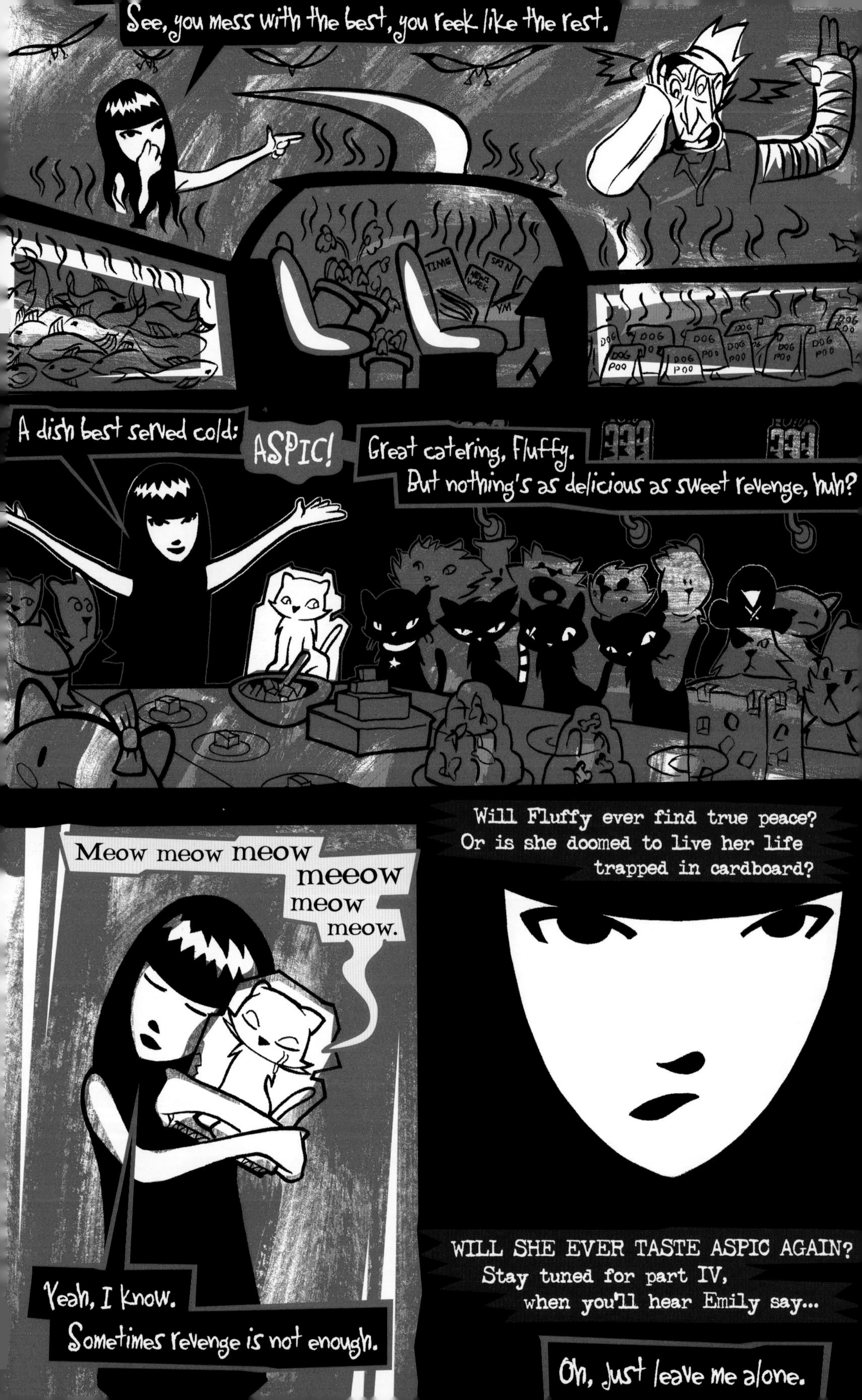

See, you mess with the best, you reek like the rest.
TIME
NEWSWEEK
SPIN
YM
DOG POO
A dish best served cold:
ASPIC!
Great catering, Fluffy.
But nothing's as delicious as sweet revenge, huh?
Meow meow meow meeow meow meow.
Yeah, I know.
Sometimes revenge is not enough.
Will Fluffy ever find true peace?
Or is she doomed to live her life trapped in cardboard?
WILL SHE EVER TASTE ASPIC AGAIN?
Stay tuned for part IV,
when you'll hear Emily say...
Oh, just leave me alone.

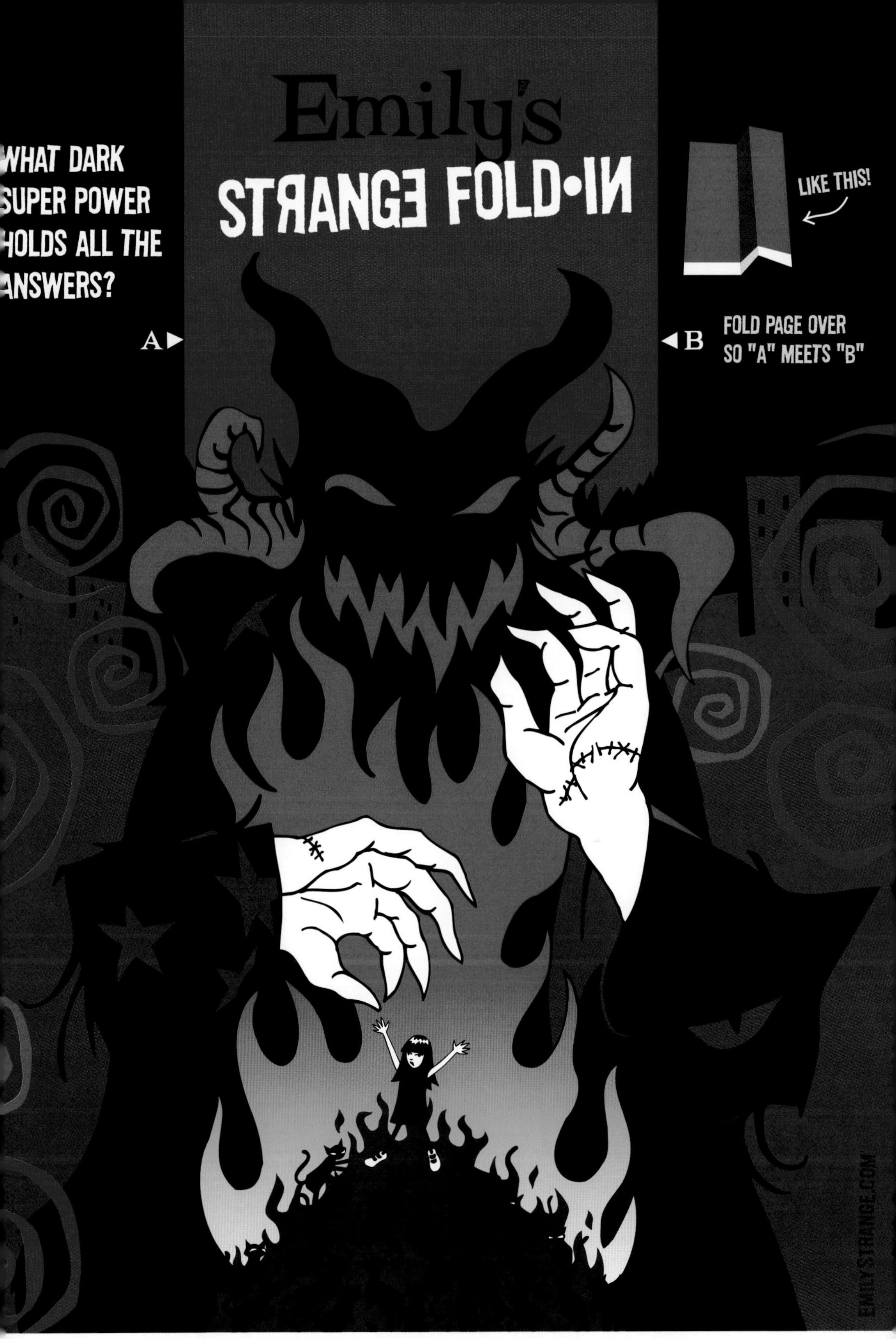
Emily's
STRANGE FOLD-IN
WHAT DARK SUPER POWER HOLDS ALL THE ANSWERS?
LIKE THIS!
A▶
◀B
FOLD PAGE OVER SO "A" MEETS "B"
EMILYSTRANGE.COM

MYRIADS OF EMILY'S POSSE HAVE SEARCHED TO BE LOST–
SO WHAT STRANGE BEAST CONTROLS EMILY'S EVERY MOVE?

A▶ ◀B

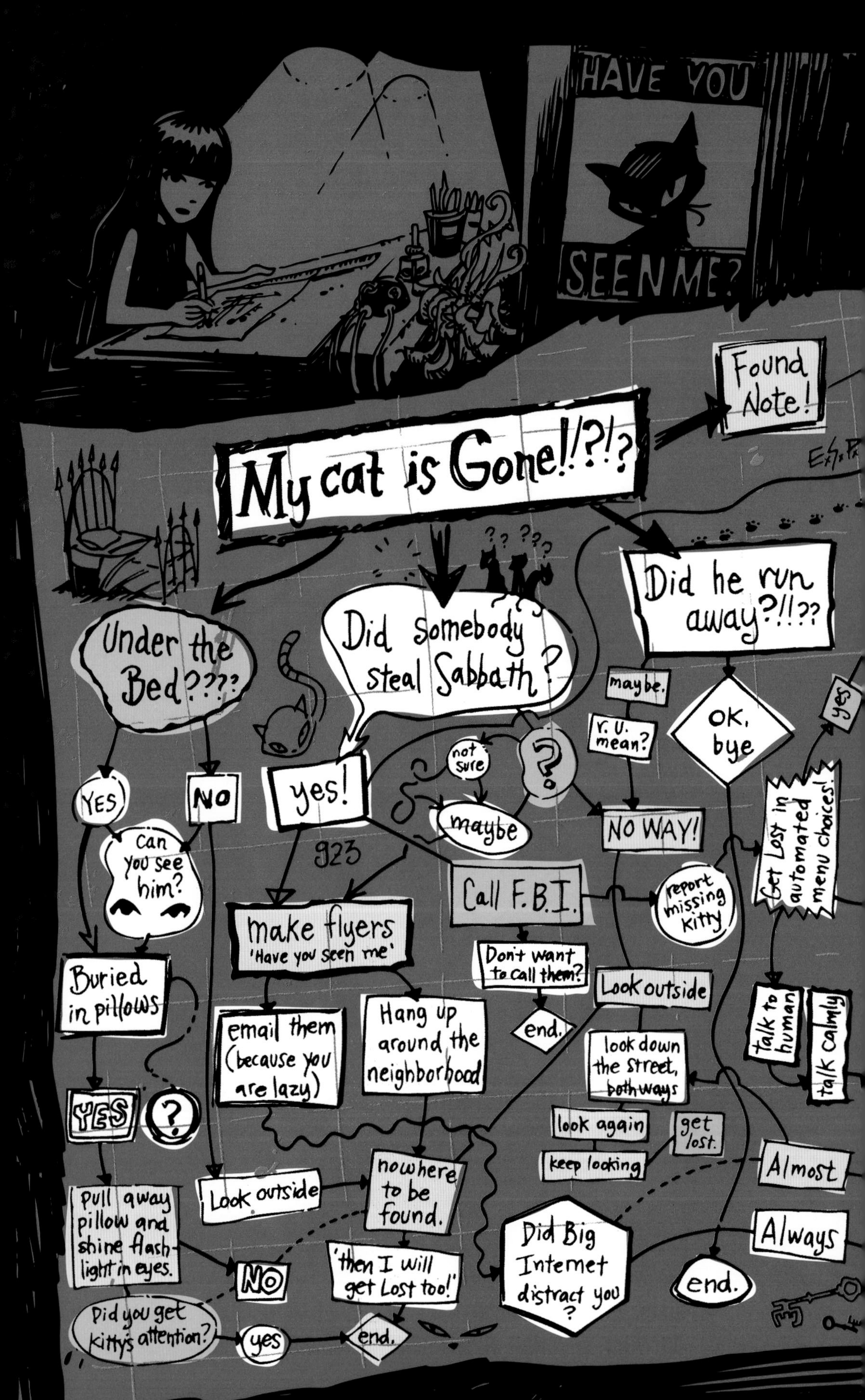
HAVE YOU
SEEN ME?
My cat is Gone!/?!?
Found Note!
E.S.P.
Under the Bed????
YES
Can you see him?
Buried in pillows
YES
?
Pull away pillow and shine flash-light in eyes.
NO
Did you get Kitty's attention?
yes
end.
NO
Look outside
Did somebody steal Sabbath?
yes!
923
make flyers 'Have you seen me'
email them (because you are lazy)
Hang up around the neighborhood
nowhere to be found.
'then I will get Lost too!'
end.
not sure
maybe
?
Call F.B.I.
Don't want to call them?
end.
report missing Kitty
Did he run away?!!??
maybe.
r. U. mean?
NO WAY!
OK, bye
Look outside
look down the street, both ways
look again
keep looking
get lost.
Get Lost in automated menu choices!
yes
talk to human
talk calmly
Almost
Always
Did Big Internet distract you?
end.

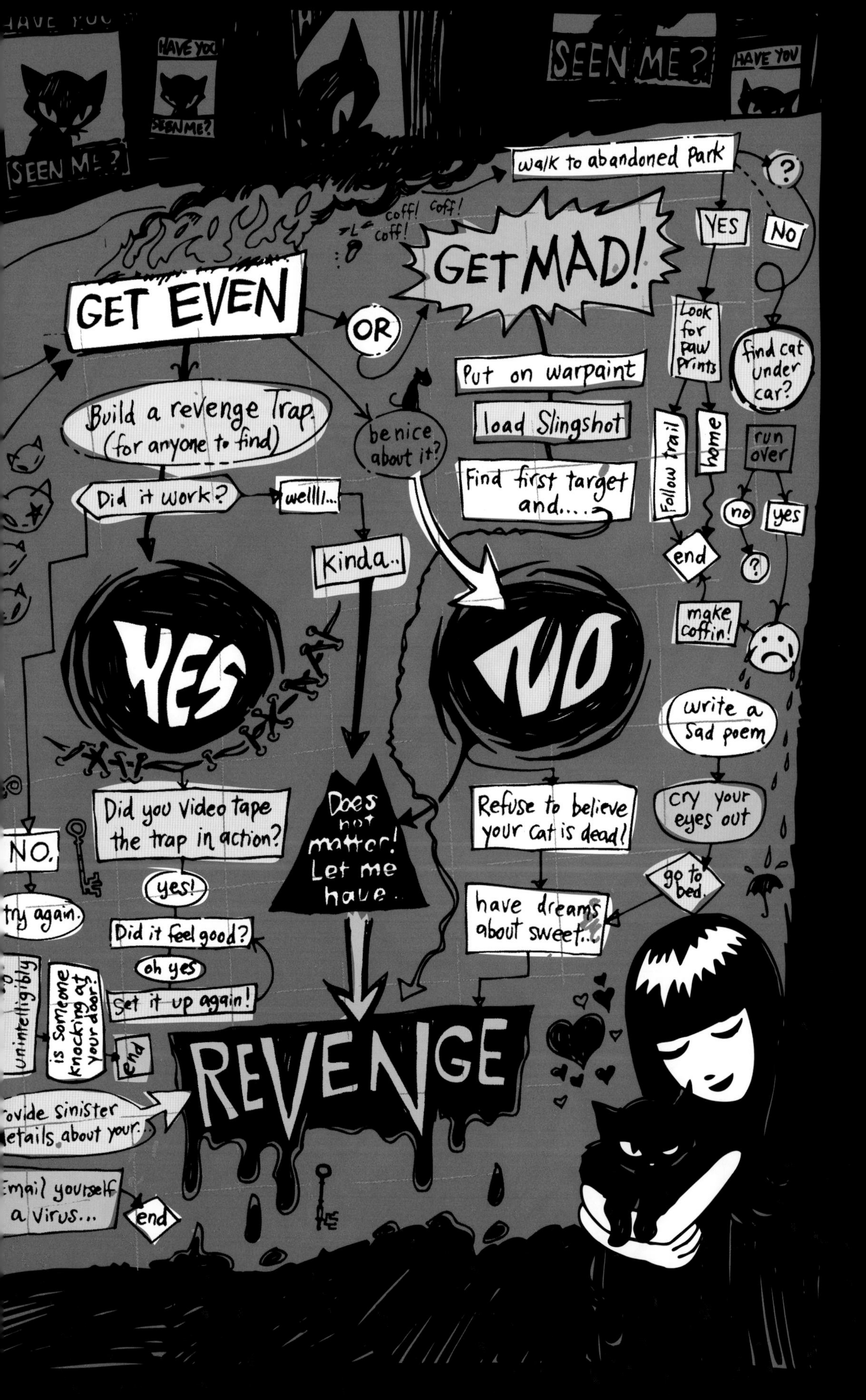

HAVE YOU SEEN ME?
HAVE YOU SEEN ME?
SEEN ME?
HAVE YOU
walk to abandoned Park
?
YES
No
coff! coff! coff!
GET MAD!
GET EVEN
OR
Look for paw prints
find cat under car?
Put on warpaint
load Slingshot
Find first target and....
Build a revenge Trap (for anyone to find)
be nice about it?
Follow trail
home
run over
Did it work?
welll...
no
yes
end
?
Kinda..
YES
NO
make coffin!
write a Sad poem
Did you Video tape the trap in action?
Does not matter! Let me have.
Refuse to believe your cat is dead!
cry your eyes out
NO.
yes!
go to bed.
try again.
have dreams about sweet...
Did it feel good?
oh yes
Set it up again!
unintelligibly
is Someone knocking at your door?
end
REVENGE
rovide sinister etails about your...
Email yourself a virus...
end

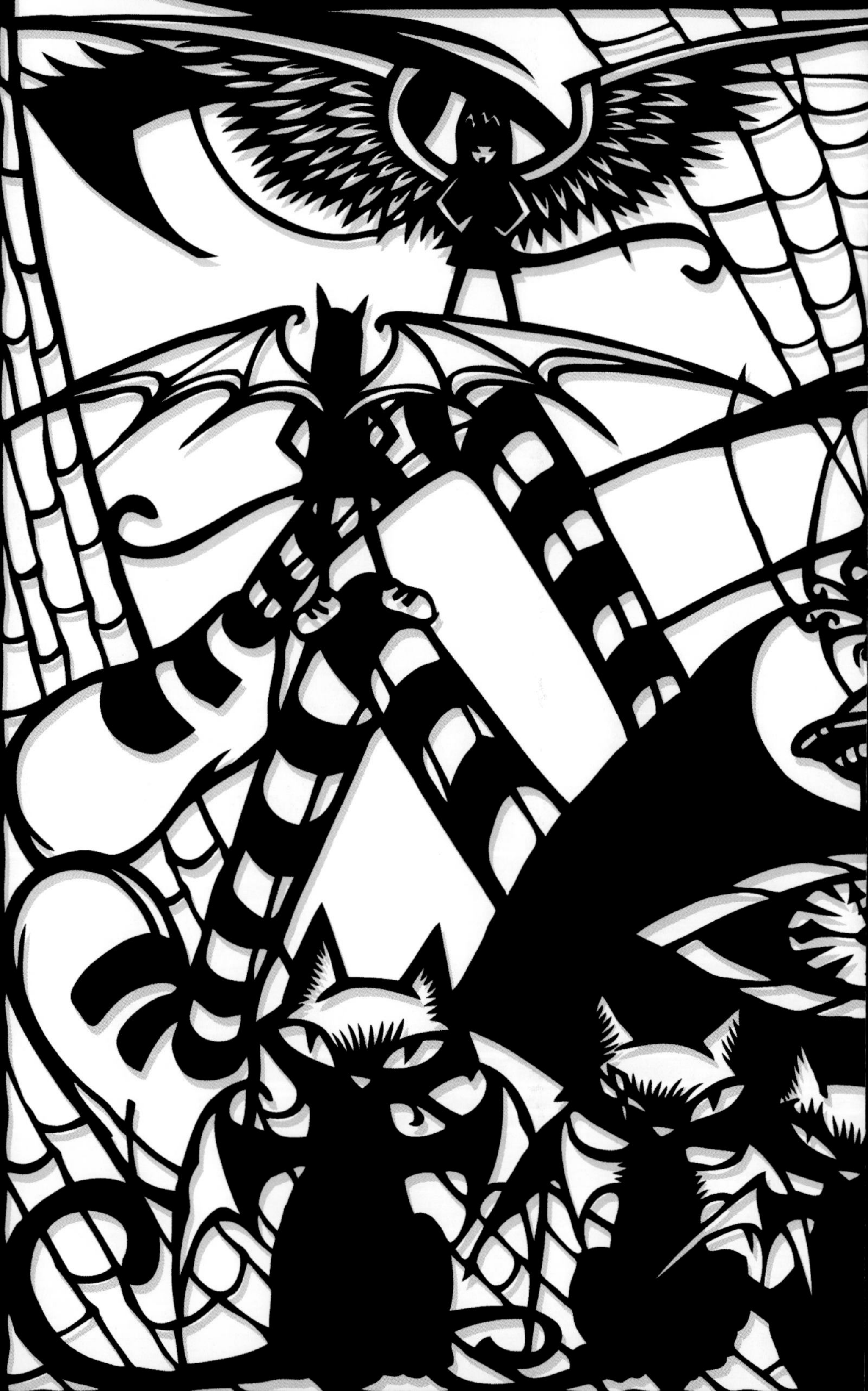

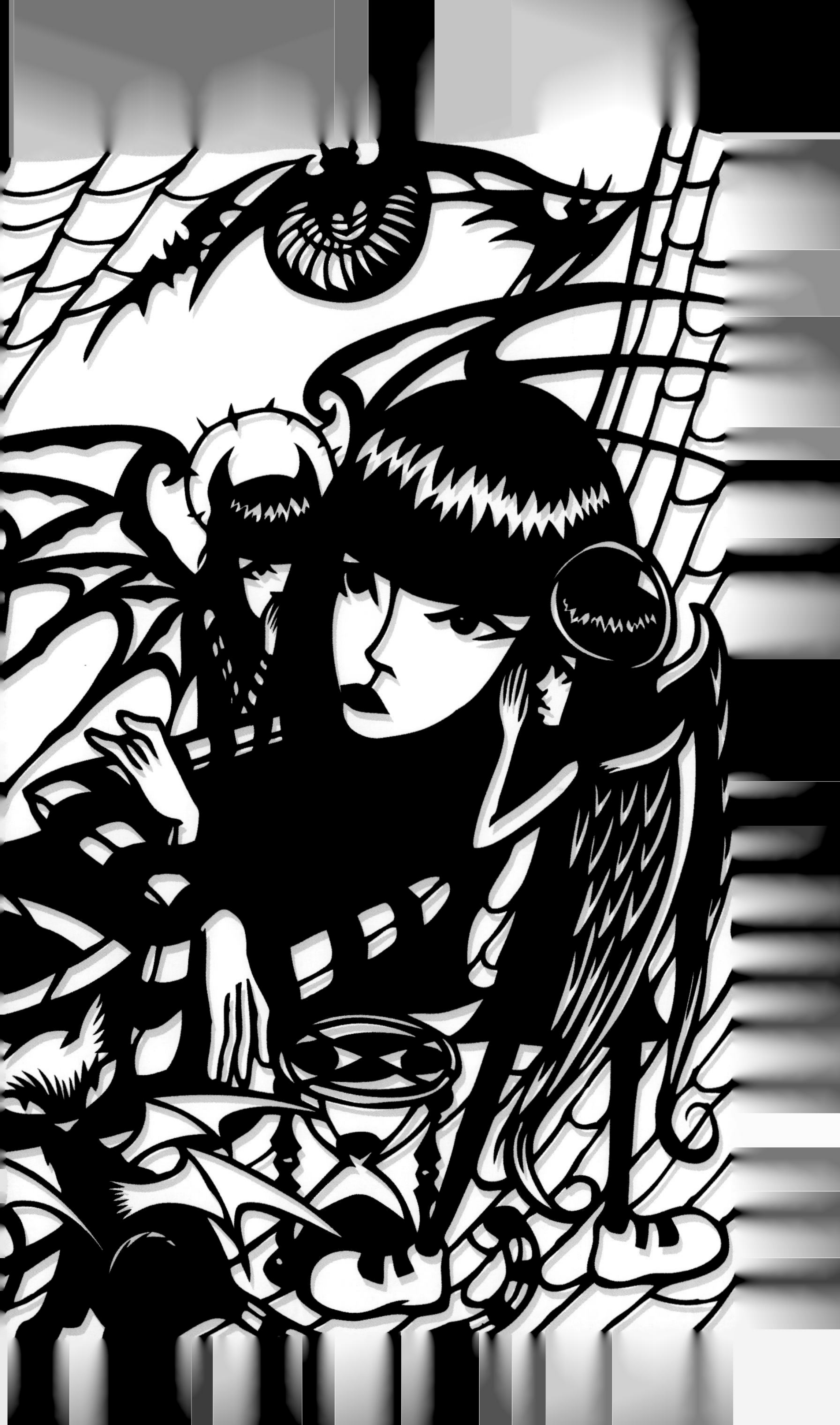

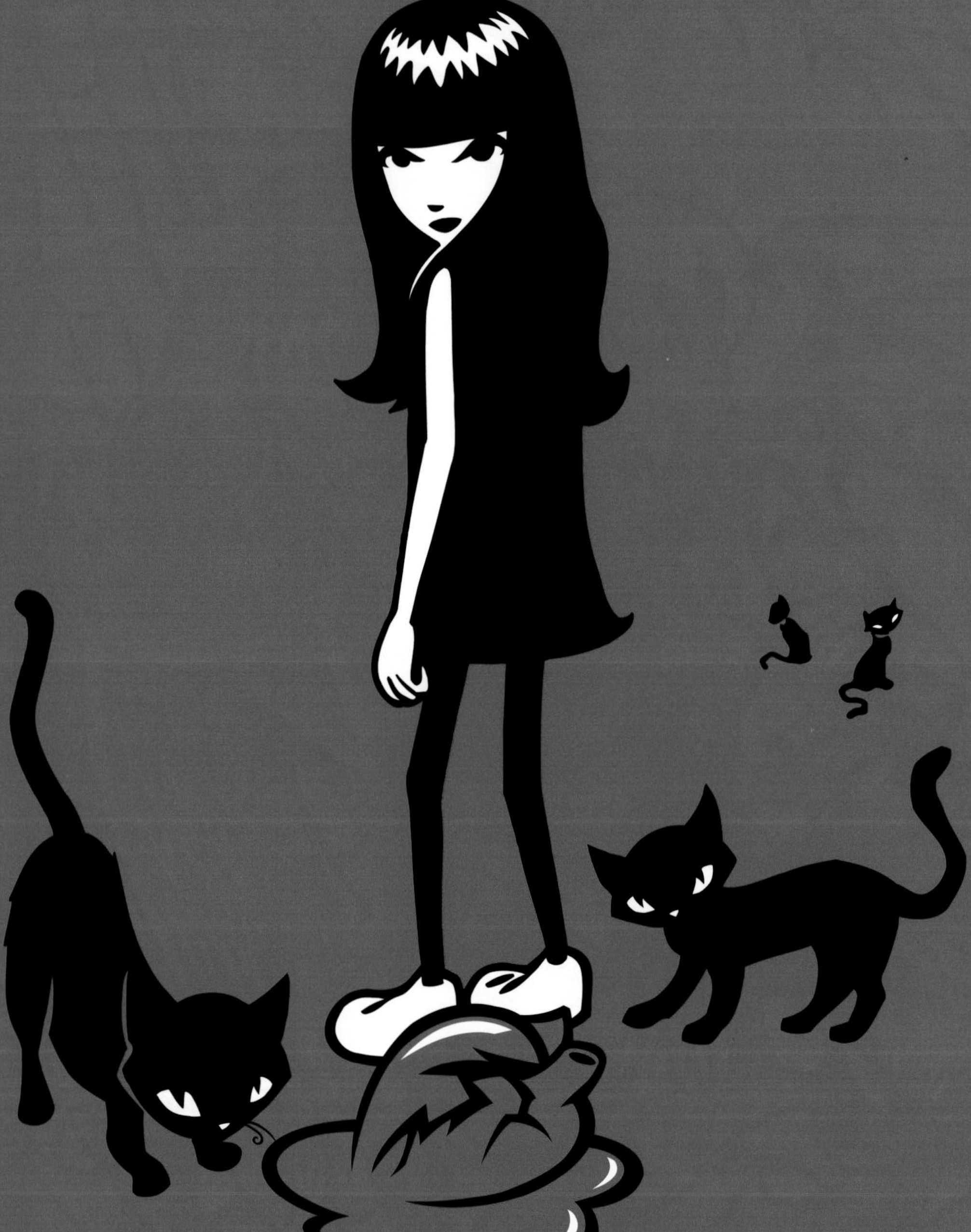

Alone is where the heart is.

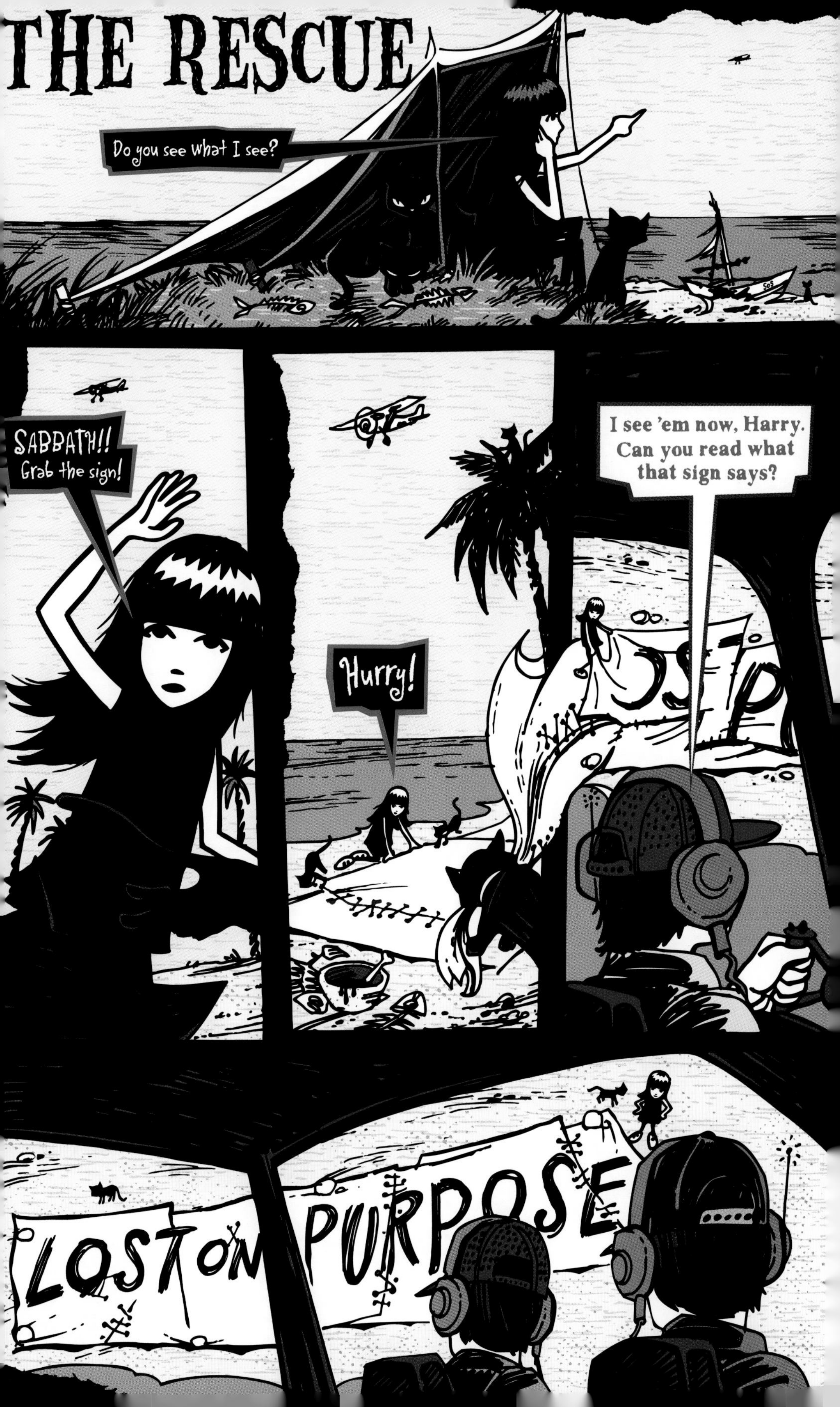
THE RESCUE
Do you see what I see?
SOS
SABBATH!! Grab the sign!
Hurry!
I see 'em now, Harry. Can you read what that sign says?
LOST ON PURPOSE

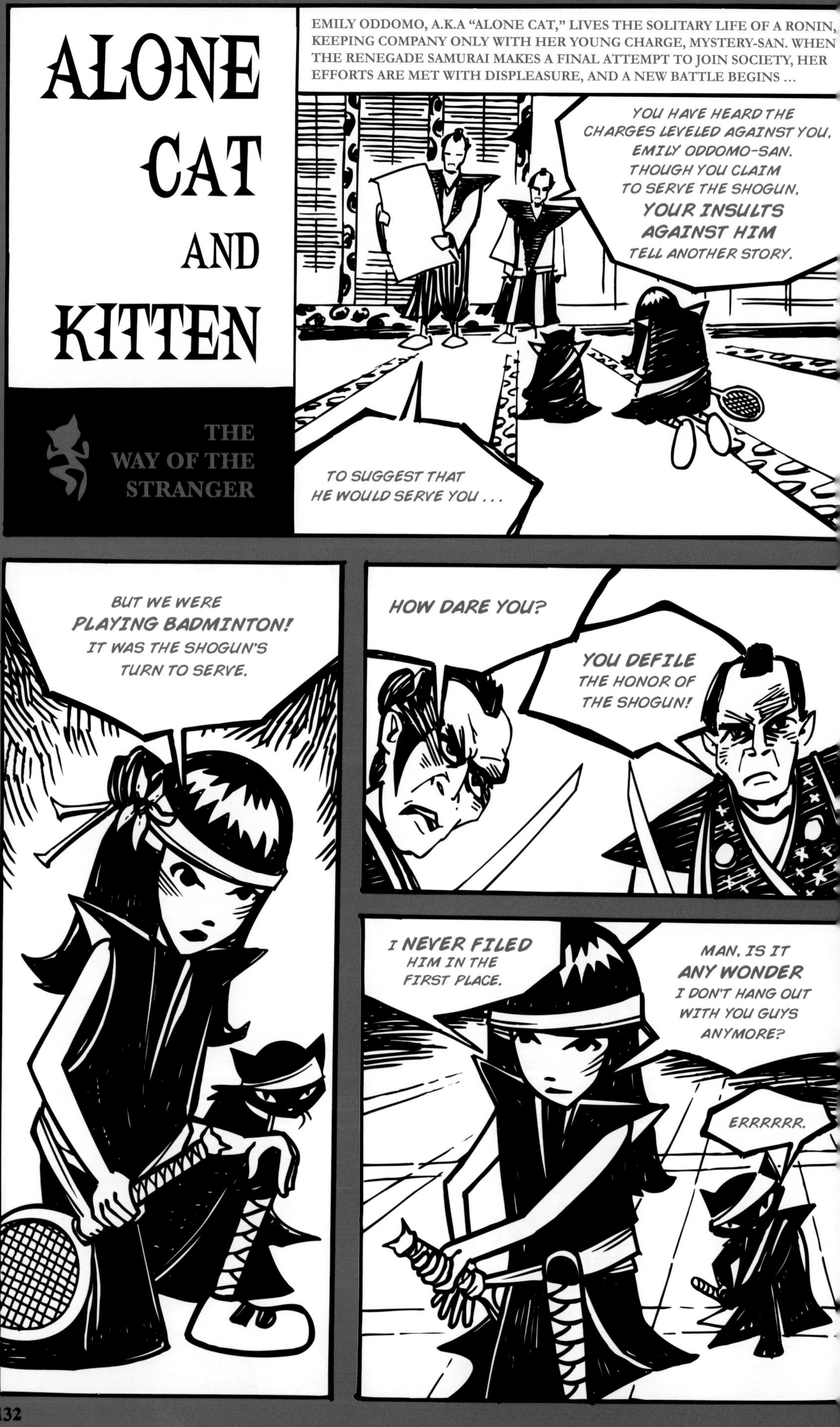

ALONE CAT AND KITTEN
THE WAY OF THE STRANGER
EMILY ODDOMO, A.K.A "ALONE CAT," LIVES THE SOLITARY LIFE OF A RONIN, KEEPING COMPANY ONLY WITH HER YOUNG CHARGE, MYSTERY-SAN. WHEN THE RENEGADE SAMURAI MAKES A FINAL ATTEMPT TO JOIN SOCIETY, HER EFFORTS ARE MET WITH DISPLEASURE, AND A NEW BATTLE BEGINS …
YOU HAVE HEARD THE CHARGES LEVELED AGAINST YOU, EMILY ODDOMO-SAN. THOUGH YOU CLAIM TO SERVE THE SHOGUN, YOUR INSULTS AGAINST HIM TELL ANOTHER STORY.
TO SUGGEST THAT HE WOULD SERVE YOU . . .
BUT WE WERE PLAYING BADMINTON! IT WAS THE SHOGUN'S TURN TO SERVE.
HOW DARE YOU?
YOU DEFILE THE HONOR OF THE SHOGUN!
I NEVER FILED HIM IN THE FIRST PLACE.
MAN, IS IT ANY WONDER I DON'T HANG OUT WITH YOU GUYS ANYMORE?
ERRRRRR.

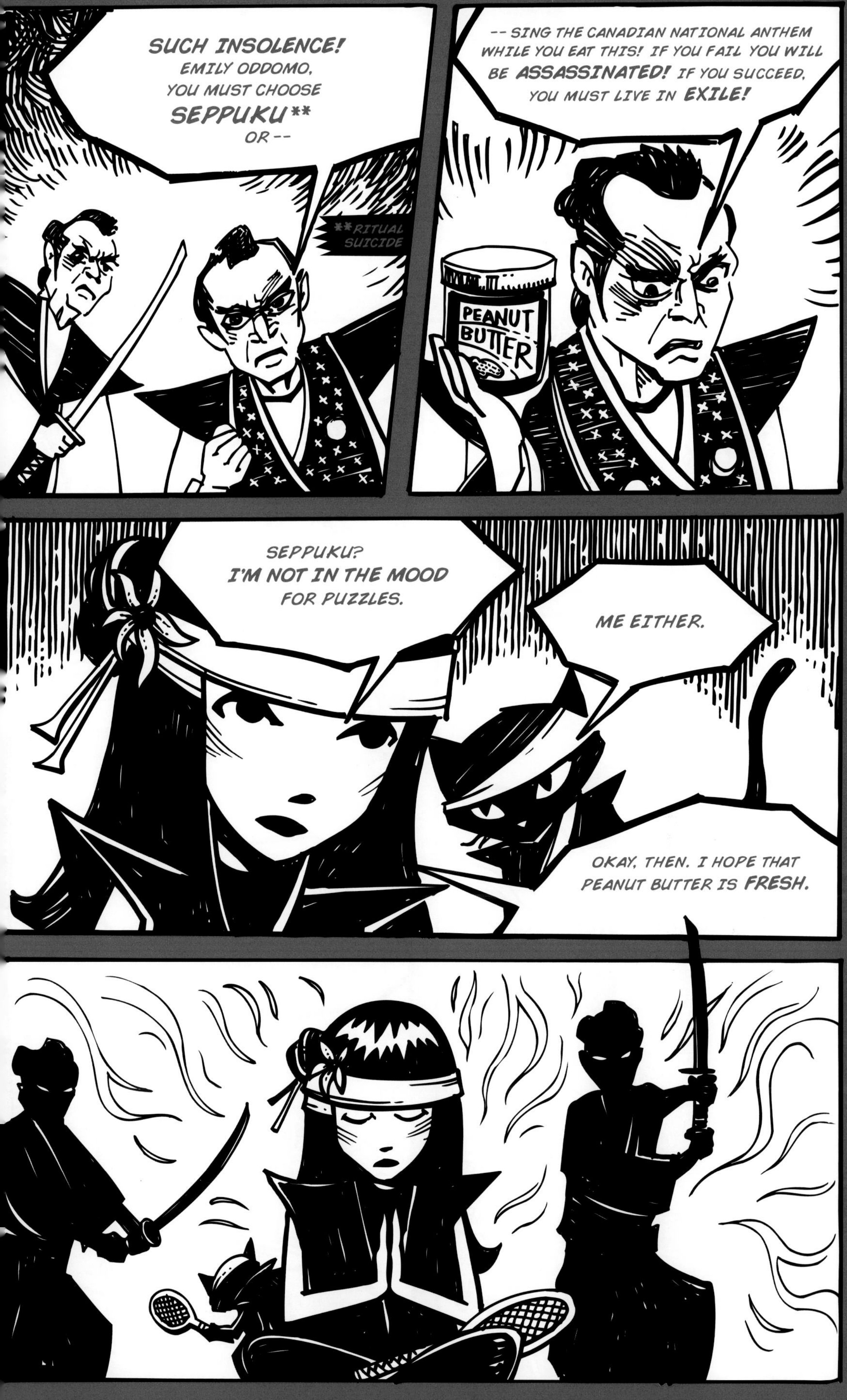
SUCH INSOLENCE! EMILY ODDOMO, YOU MUST CHOOSE SEPPUKU** OR --
**RITUAL SUICIDE
-- SING THE CANADIAN NATIONAL ANTHEM WHILE YOU EAT THIS! IF YOU FAIL YOU WILL BE ASSASSINATED! IF YOU SUCCEED, YOU MUST LIVE IN EXILE!
PEANUT BUTTER
SEPPUKU? I'M NOT IN THE MOOD FOR PUZZLES.
ME EITHER.
OKAY, THEN. I HOPE THAT PEANUT BUTTER IS FRESH.

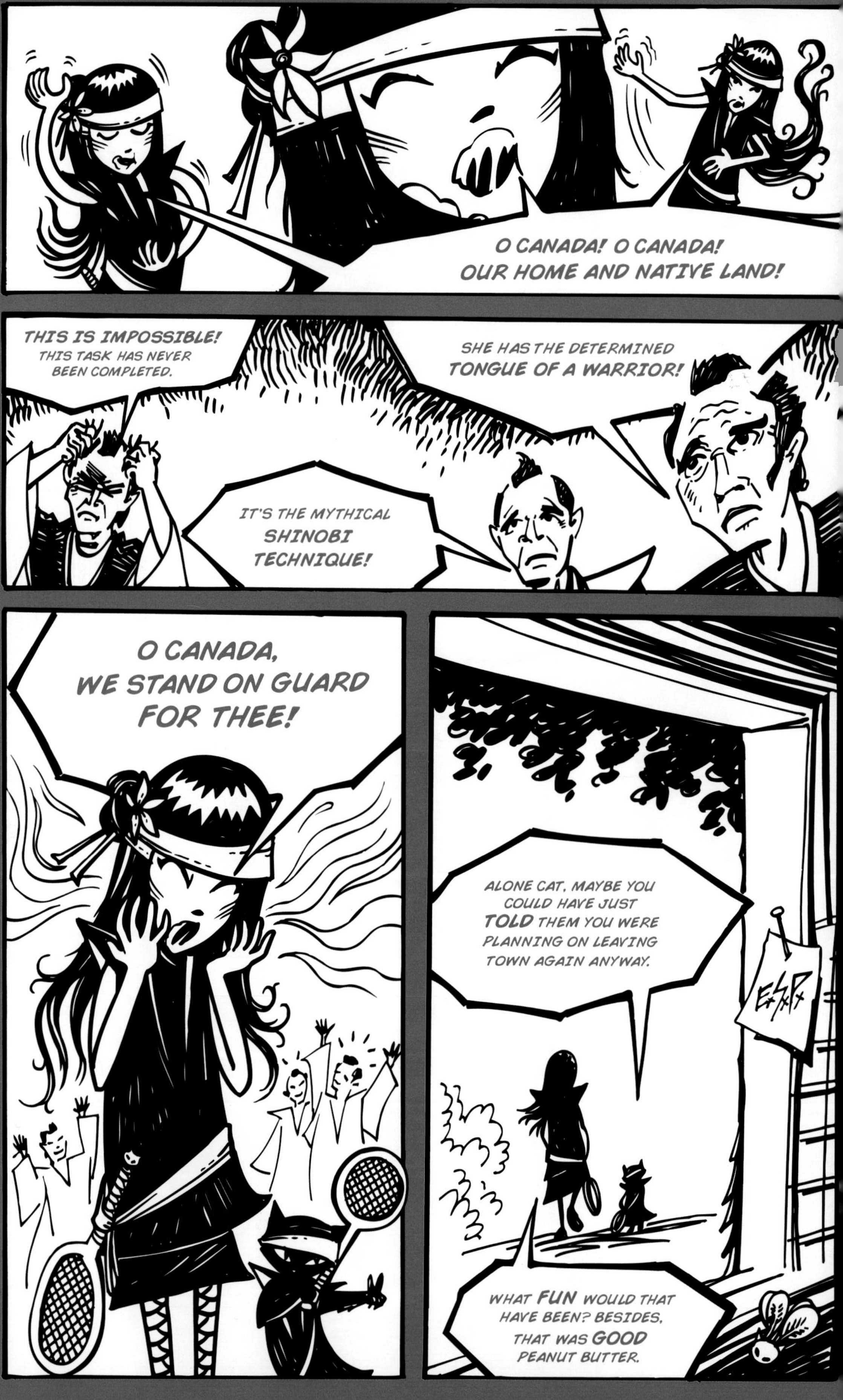
O CANADA! O CANADA! OUR HOME AND NATIVE LAND!
THIS IS IMPOSSIBLE! THIS TASK HAS NEVER BEEN COMPLETED.
SHE HAS THE DETERMINED TONGUE OF A WARRIOR!
IT'S THE MYTHICAL SHINOBI TECHNIQUE!
O CANADA, WE STAND ON GUARD FOR THEE!
ALONE CAT, MAYBE YOU COULD HAVE JUST TOLD THEM YOU WERE PLANNING ON LEAVING TOWN AGAIN ANYWAY.
WHAT FUN WOULD THAT HAVE BEEN? BESIDES, THAT WAS GOOD PEANUT BUTTER.

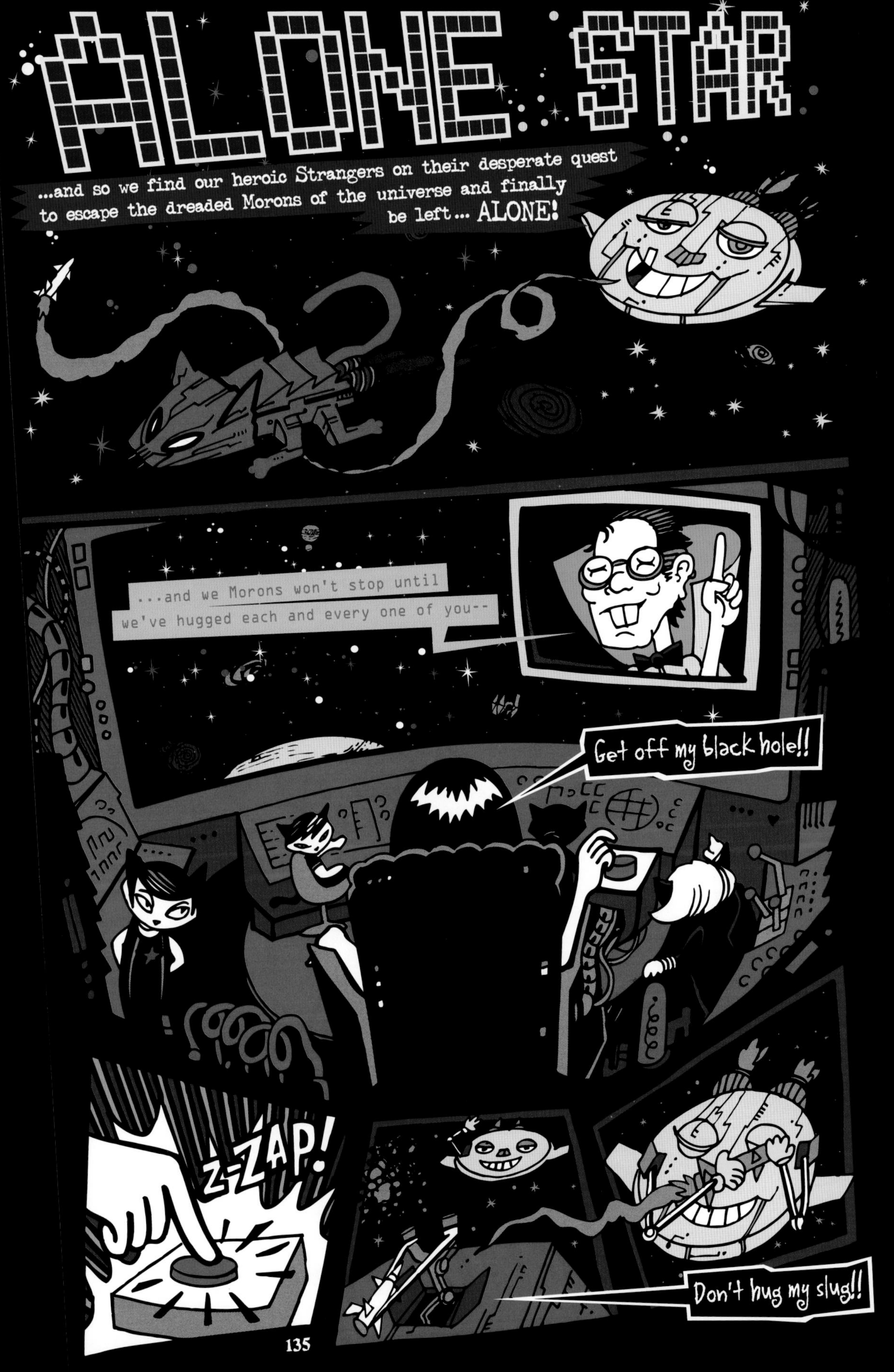

ALONE STAR
...and so we find our heroic Strangers on their desperate quest to escape the dreaded Morons of the universe and finally be left... ALONE!
...and we Morons won't stop until we've hugged each and every one of you--
Get off my black hole!!
Z-ZAP!
Don't hug my slug!!

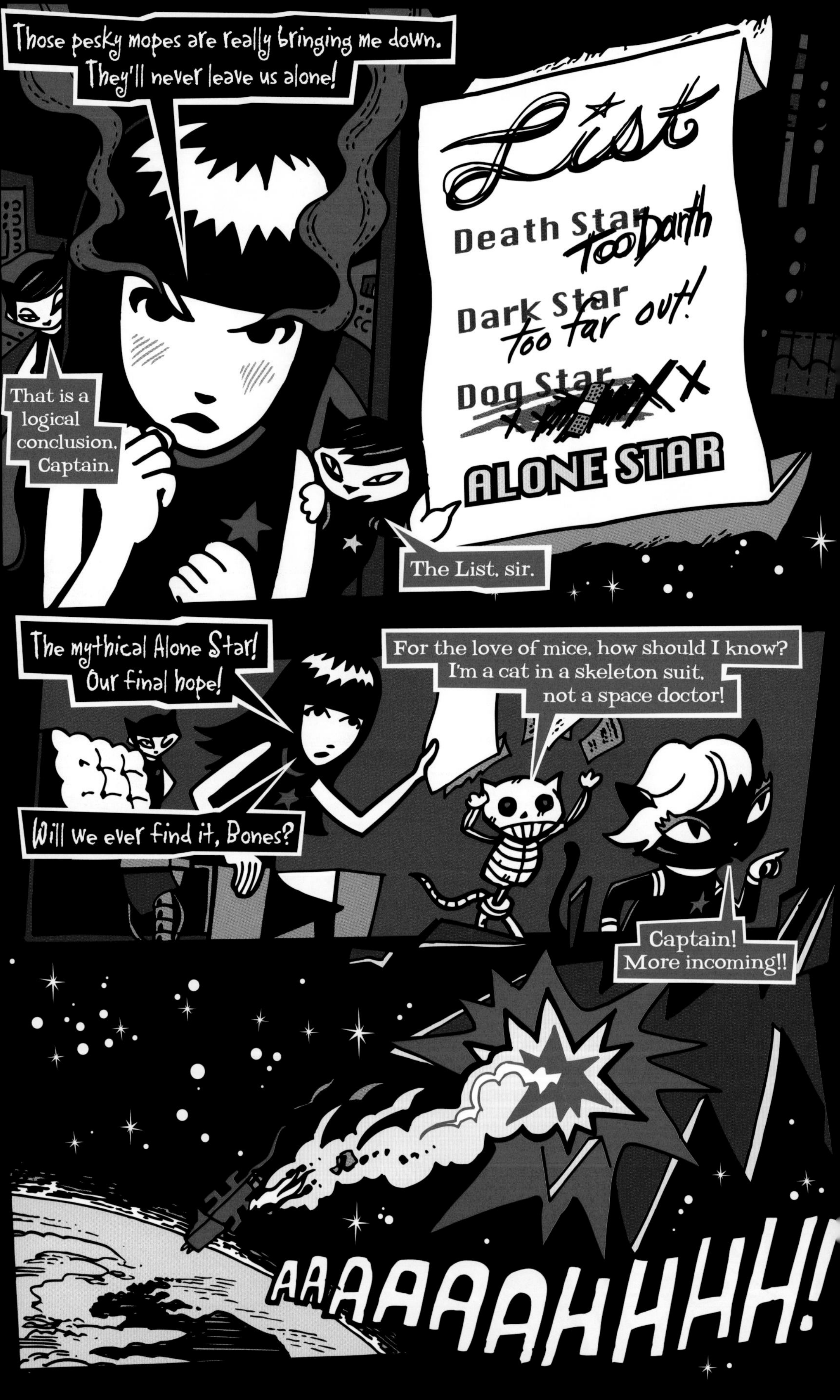
Those pesky mopes are really bringing me down. They'll never leave us alone!
That is a logical conclusion, Captain.
List
Death Star Too Darth
Dark Star too far out!
Dog Star XX
ALONE STAR
The List, sir.
The mythical Alone Star! Our final hope!
Will we ever find it, Bones?
For the love of mice, how should I know? I'm a cat in a skeleton suit, not a space doctor!
Captain! More incoming!!
AAAAAAAHHHH!

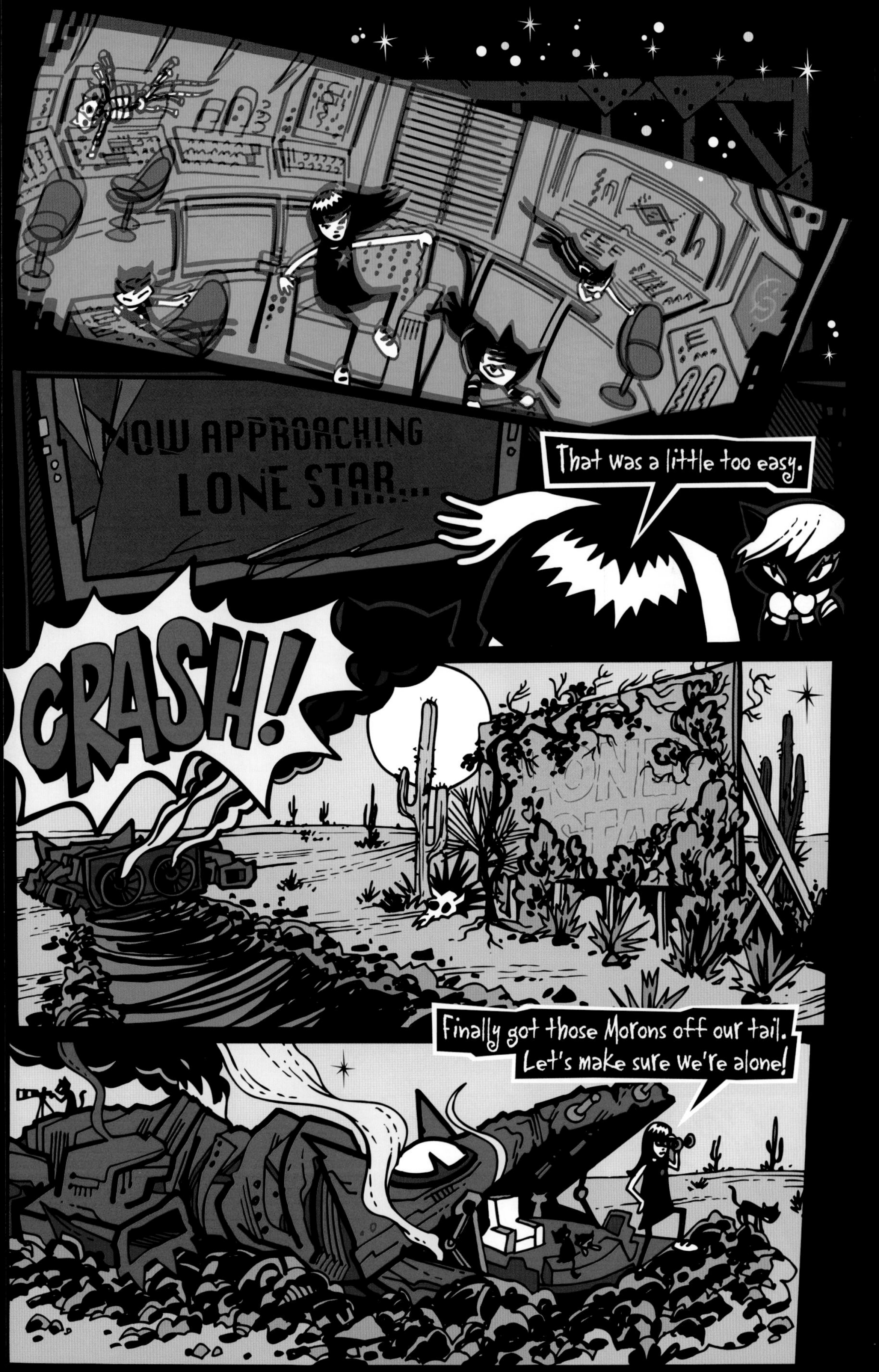

NOW APPROACHING LONE STAR...
That was a little too easy.
CRASH!
LONE STAR
Finally got those Morons off our tail.
Let's make sure we're alone!

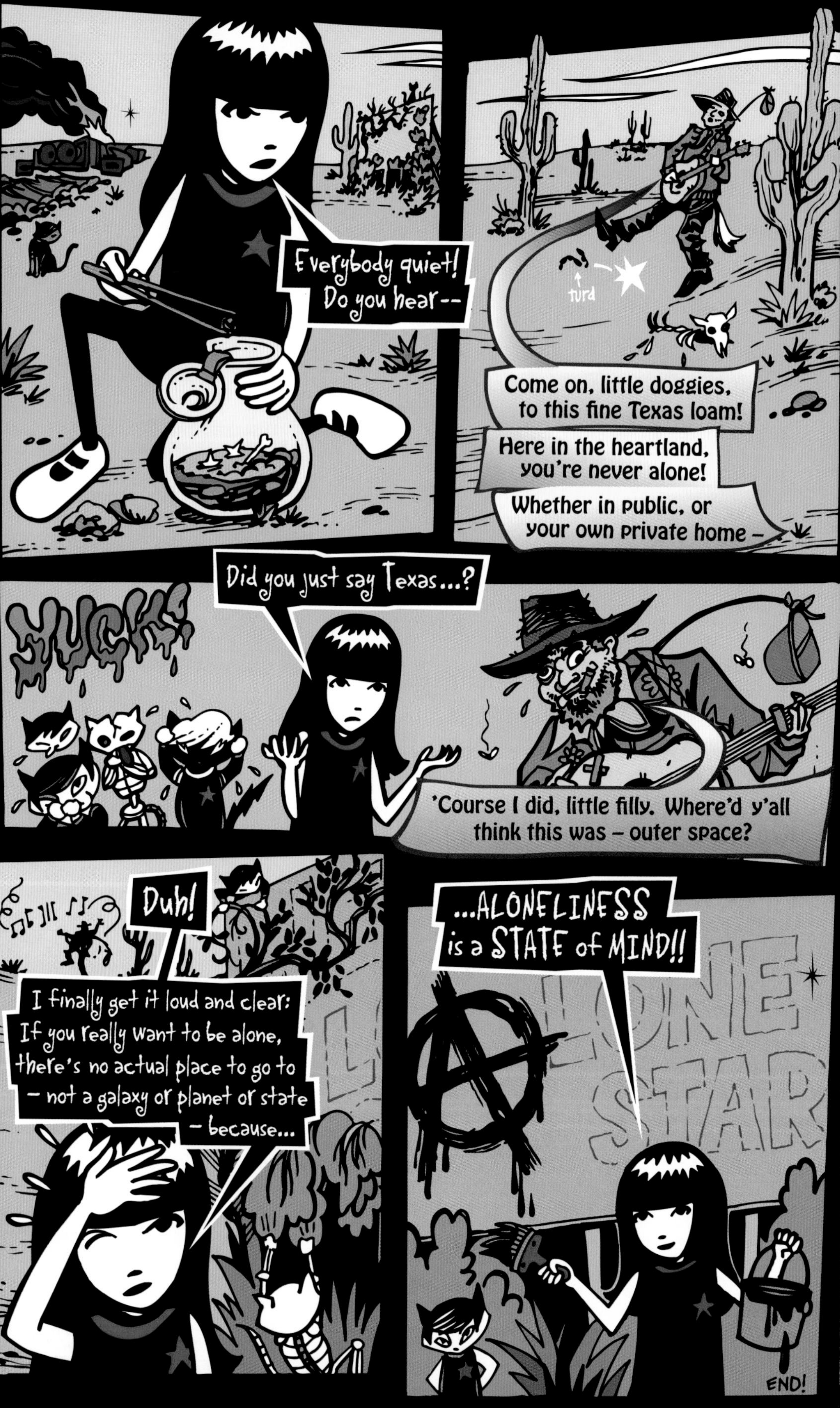

Everybody quiet! Do you hear--
turd
Come on, little doggies, to this fine Texas loam!
Here in the heartland, you're never alone!
Whether in public, or your own private home –
YUCK!
Did you just say Texas...?
'Course I did, little filly. Where'd y'all think this was – outer space?
Duh!
I finally get it loud and clear: If you really want to be alone, there's no actual place to go to – not a galaxy or planet or state – because...
...ALONELINESS is a STATE of MIND!!
LONE STAR
END!

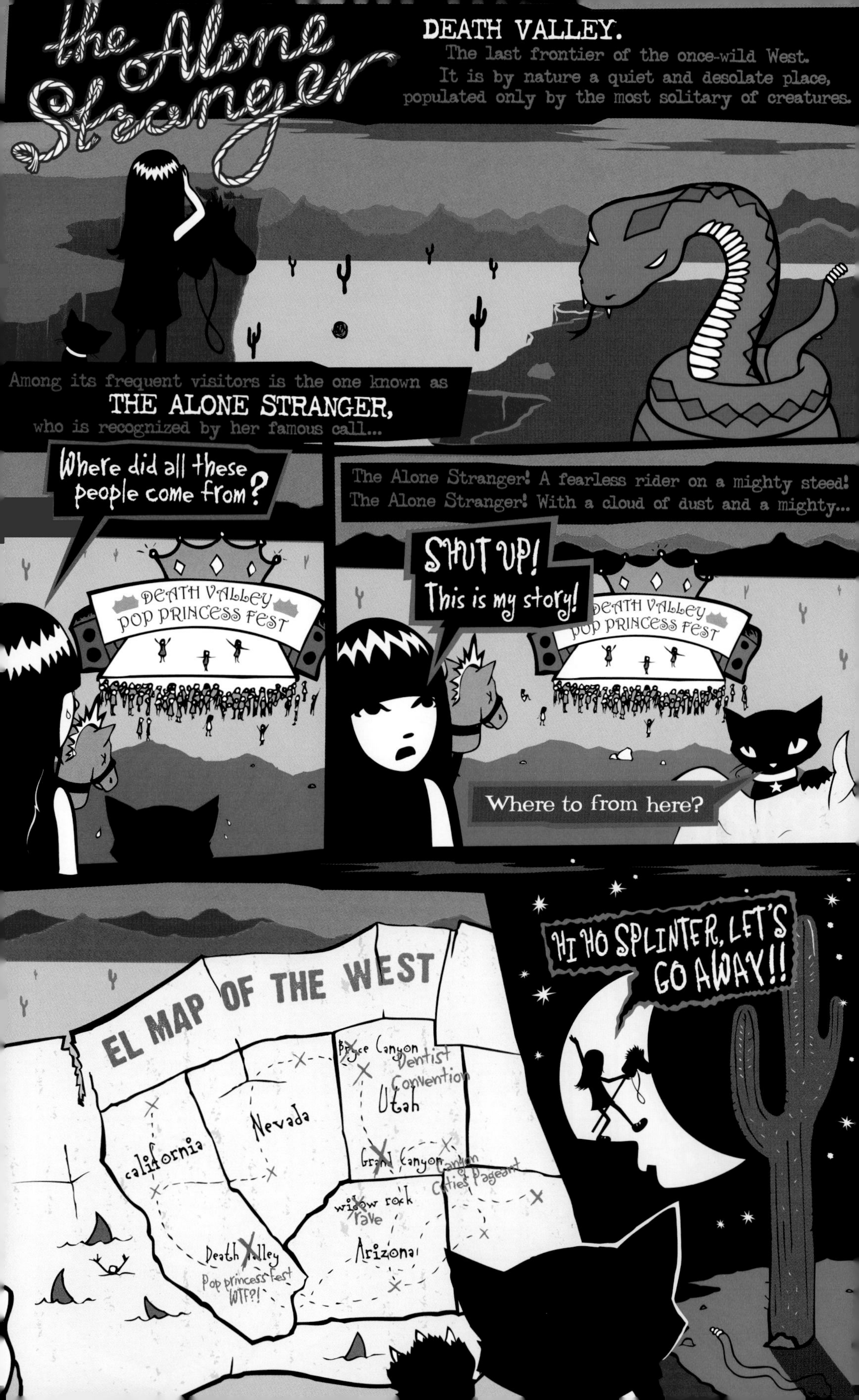
the Alone Stranger
DEATH VALLEY.
The last frontier of the once-wild West.
It is by nature a quiet and desolate place,
populated only by the most solitary of creatures.
Among its frequent visitors is the one known as
THE ALONE STRANGER,
who is recognized by her famous call...
Where did all these people come from?
DEATH VALLEY POP PRINCESS FEST
The Alone Stranger! A fearless rider on a mighty steed!
The Alone Stranger! With a cloud of dust and a mighty...
SHUT UP! This is my story!
DEATH VALLEY POP PRINCESS FEST
Where to from here?
EL MAP OF THE WEST
Bryce Canyon
Dentist Convention
Utah
Nevada
california
Grand Canyon
Canyon Cuties Pageant
widow rock
rave
Arizona
Death Valley
Pop princess fest WTF?!
HI HO SPLINTER, LET'S GO AWAY!!

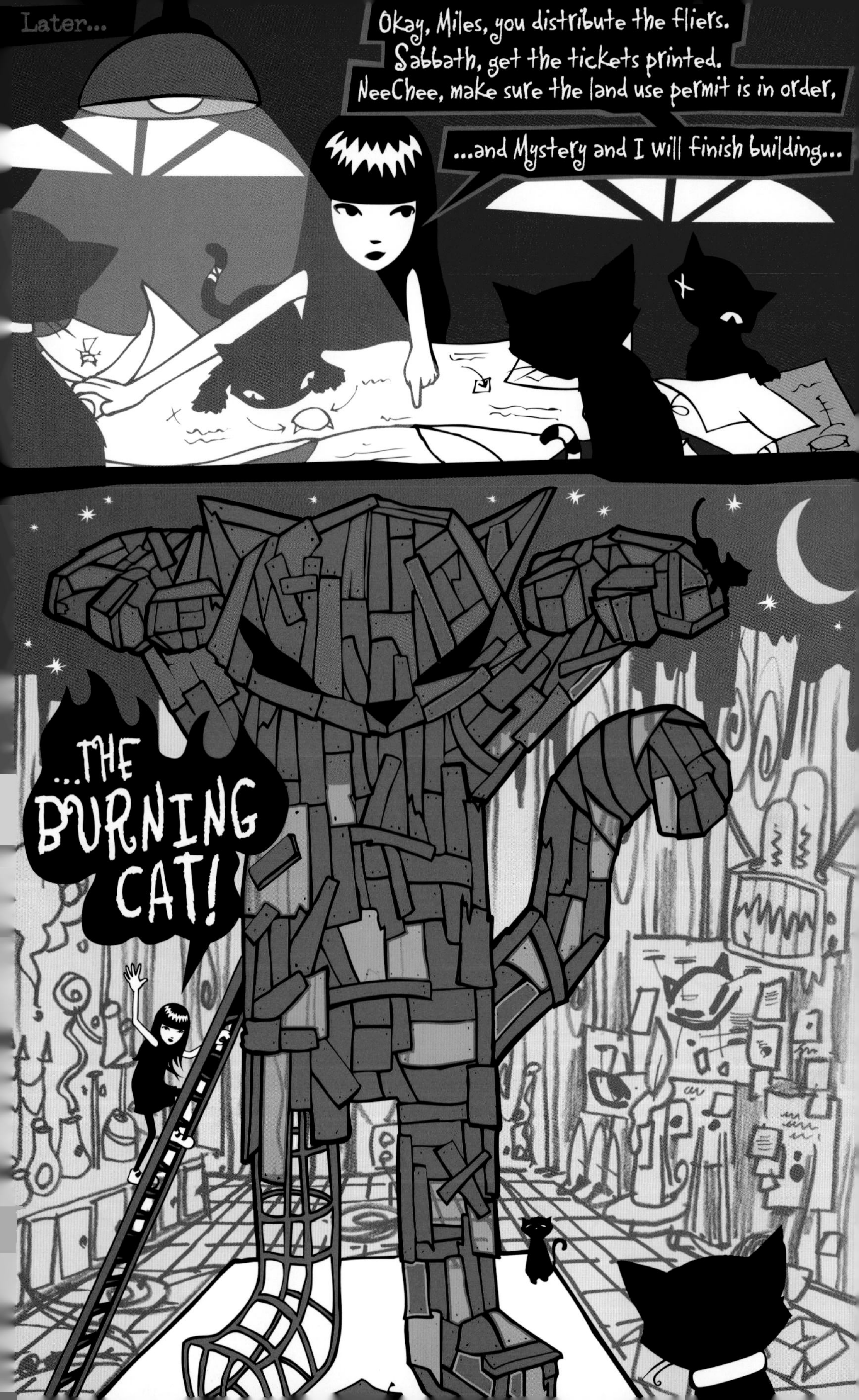

Later...
Okay, Miles, you distribute the fliers. Sabbath, get the tickets printed. NeeChee, make sure the land use permit is in order,
...and Mystery and I will finish building...
...THE BURNING CAT!

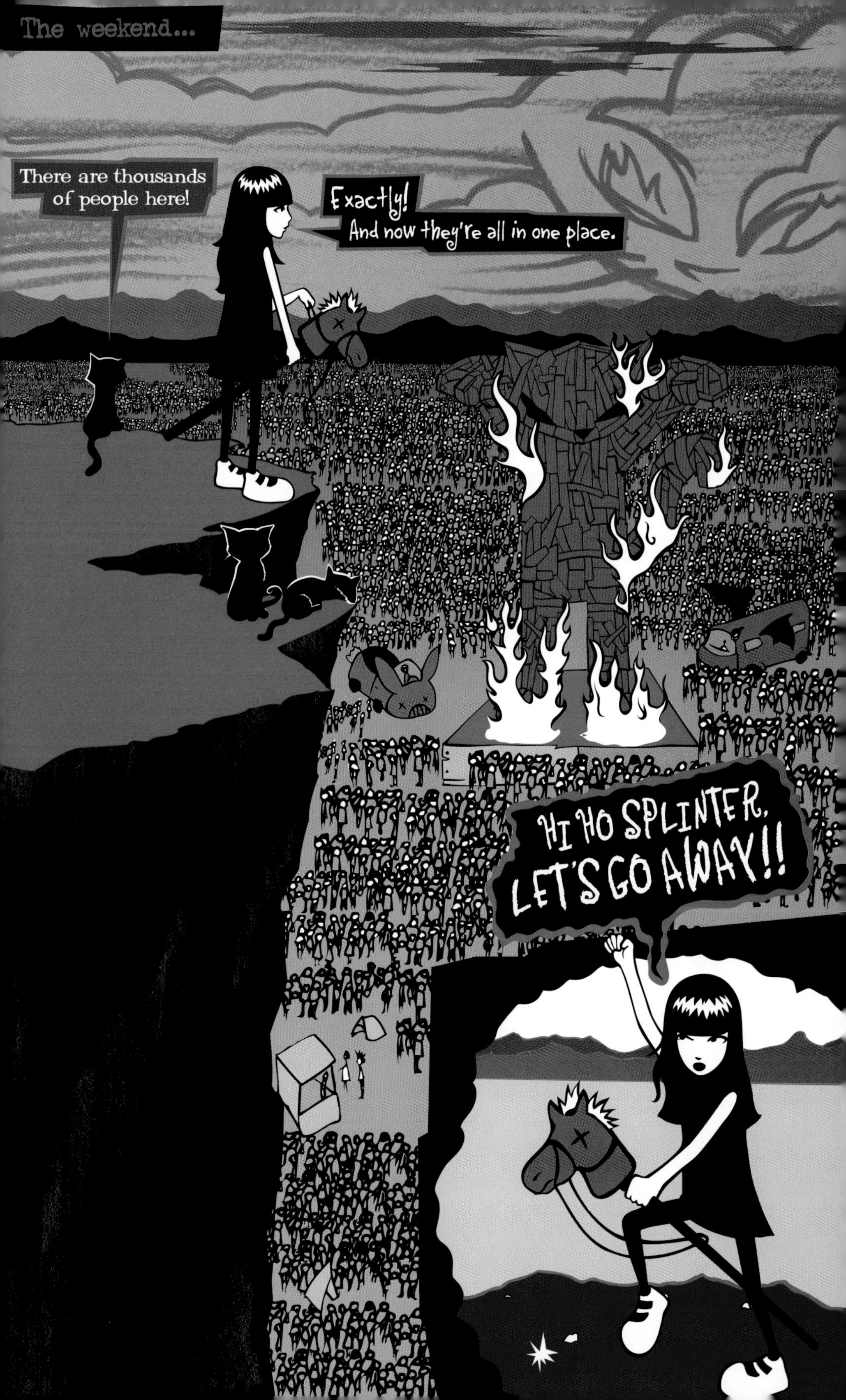
The weekend...
There are thousands of people here!
Exactly! And now they're all in one place.
HI HO SPLINTER, LET'S GO AWAY!!

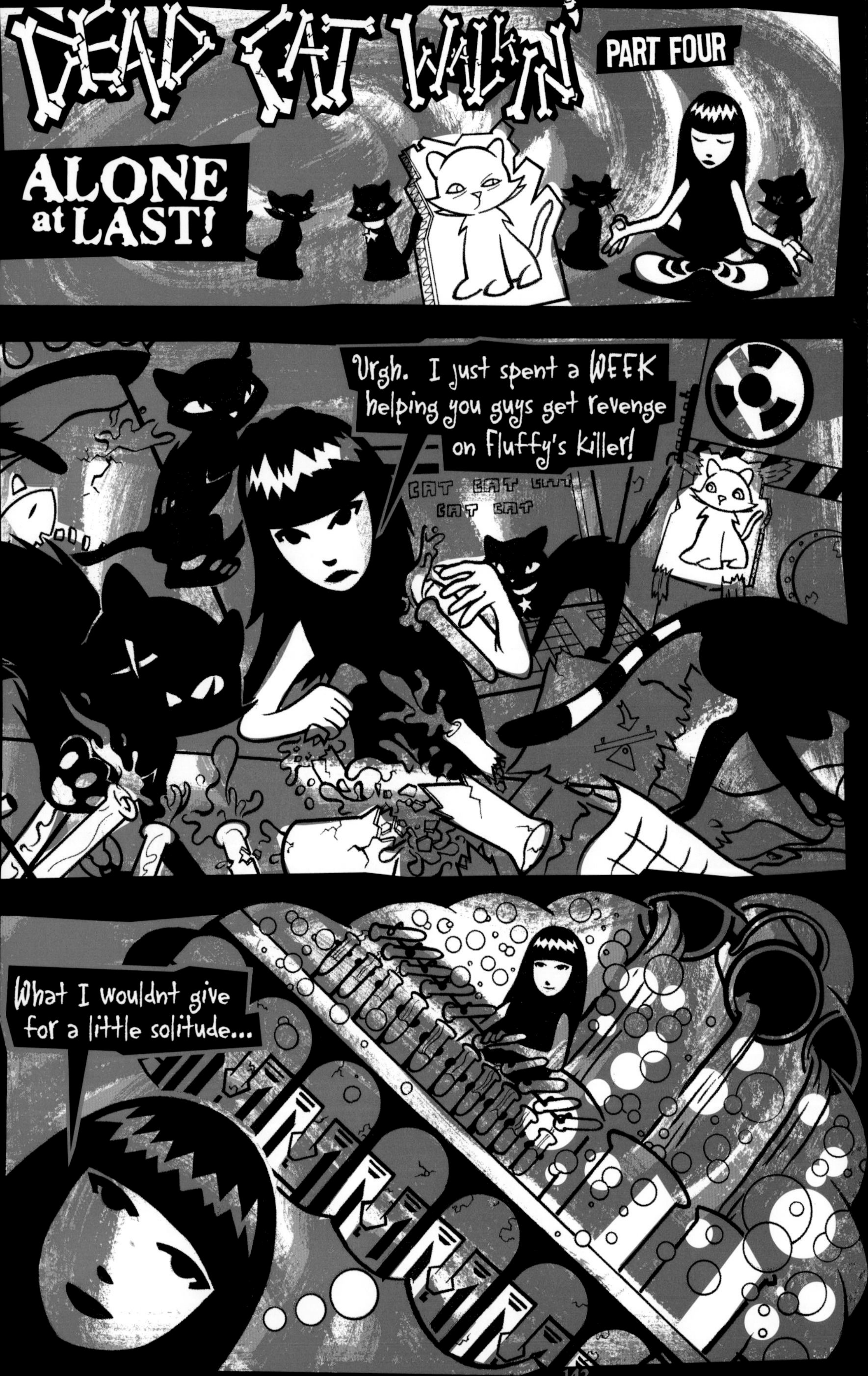
DEAD CAT WALKIN'
PART FOUR
ALONE at LAST!
CAT CAT CAT CAT CAT
Urgh. I just spent a WEEK helping you guys get revenge on Fluffy's killer!
What I wouldnt give for a little solitude...

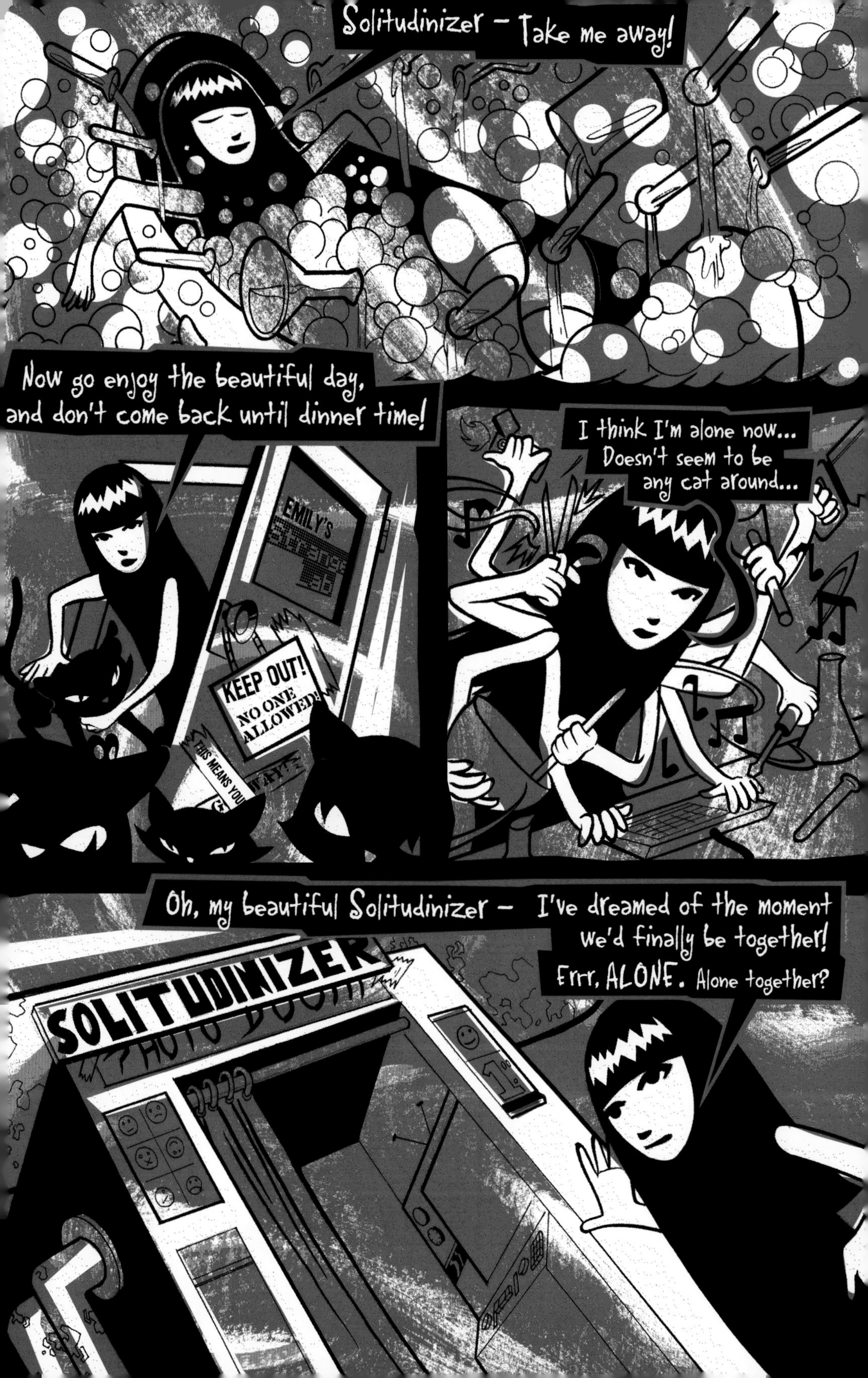
Solitudinizer – Take me away!
Now go enjoy the beautiful day, and don't come back until dinner time!
EMILY'S
KEEP OUT! NO ONE ALLOWED!
THIS MEANS YOU
I think I'm alone now... Doesn't seem to be any cat around...
Oh, my beautiful Solitudinizer – I've dreamed of the moment we'd finally be together! Errr, ALONE. Alone together?
SOLITUDINIZER

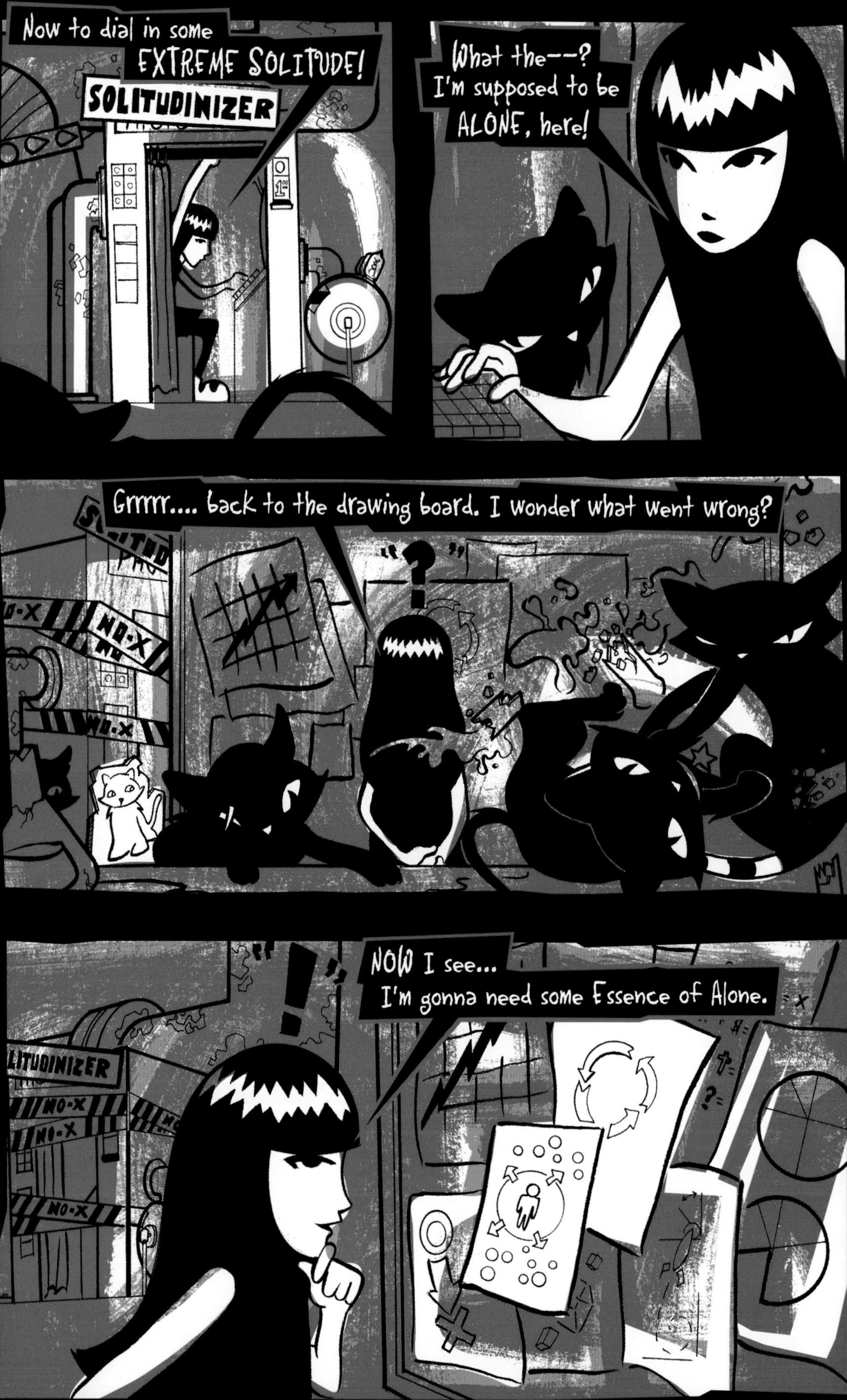
Now to dial in some EXTREME SOLITUDE!
SOLITUDINIZER
What the--? I'm supposed to be ALONE, here!
Grrrrr.... back to the drawing board. I wonder what went wrong?
NO-X
NO-X
NOW I see... I'm gonna need some Essence of Alone.
LITUDINIZER
NO-X
NO-X

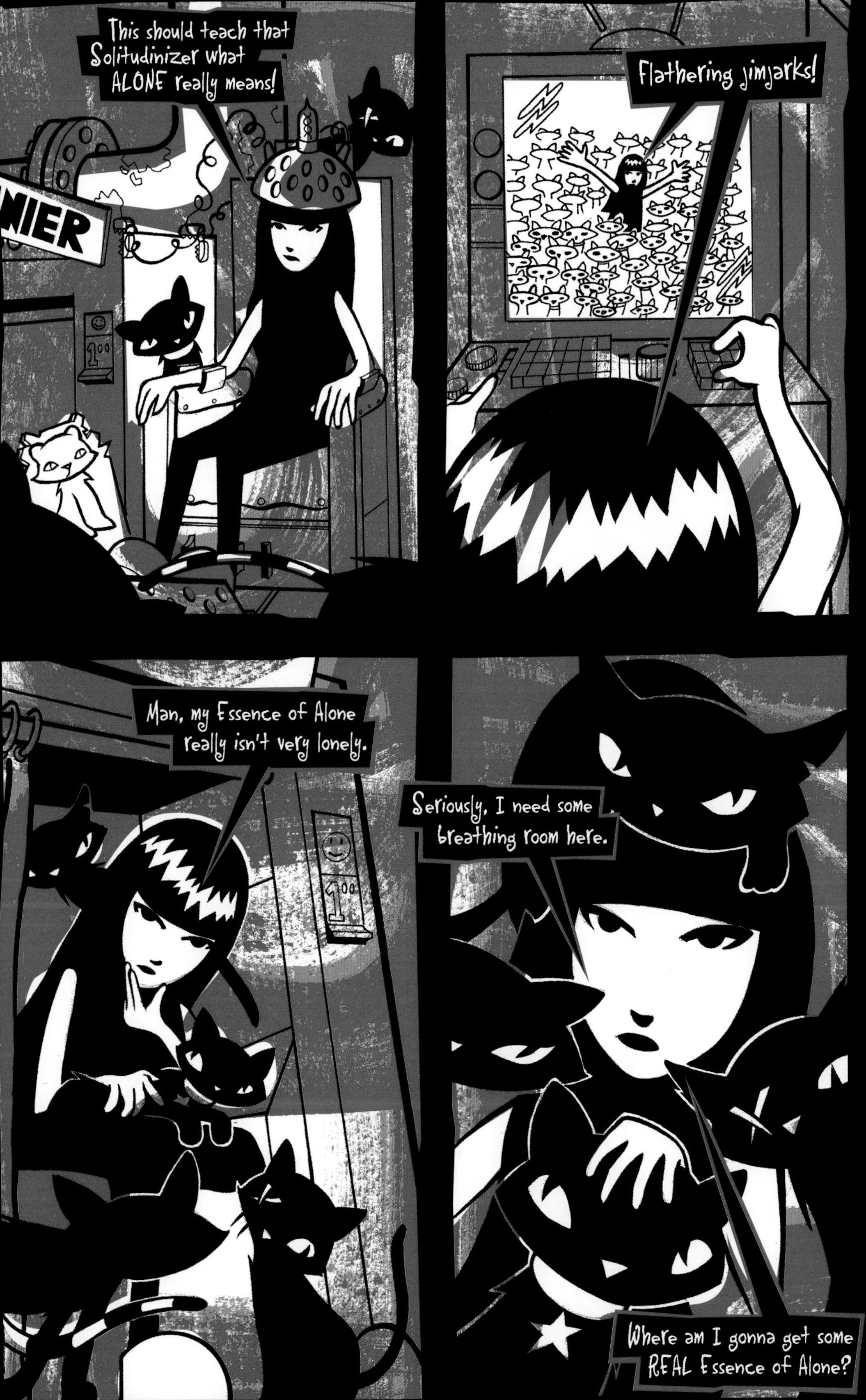
This should teach that Solitudinizer what ALONE really means!
NIER
Flathering jimjarks!
Man, my Essence of Alone really isn't very lonely.
Seriously, I need some breathing room here.
Where am I gonna get some REAL Essence of Alone?

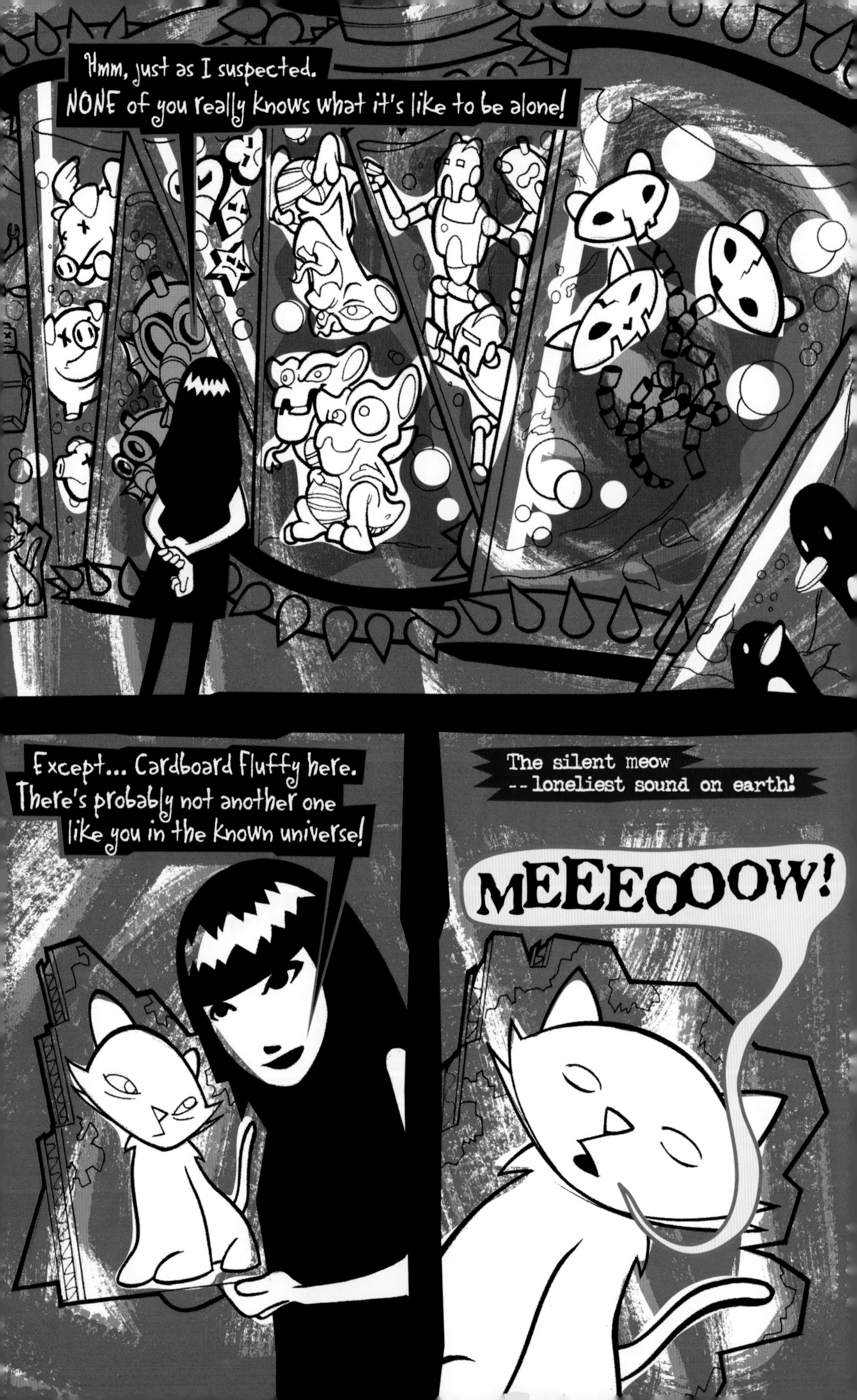
Hmm, just as I suspected.
NONE of you really knows what it's like to be alone!
Except... Cardboard Fluffy here.
There's probably not another one
like you in the known universe!
The silent meow
--loneliest sound on earth!
MEEEOOOW!

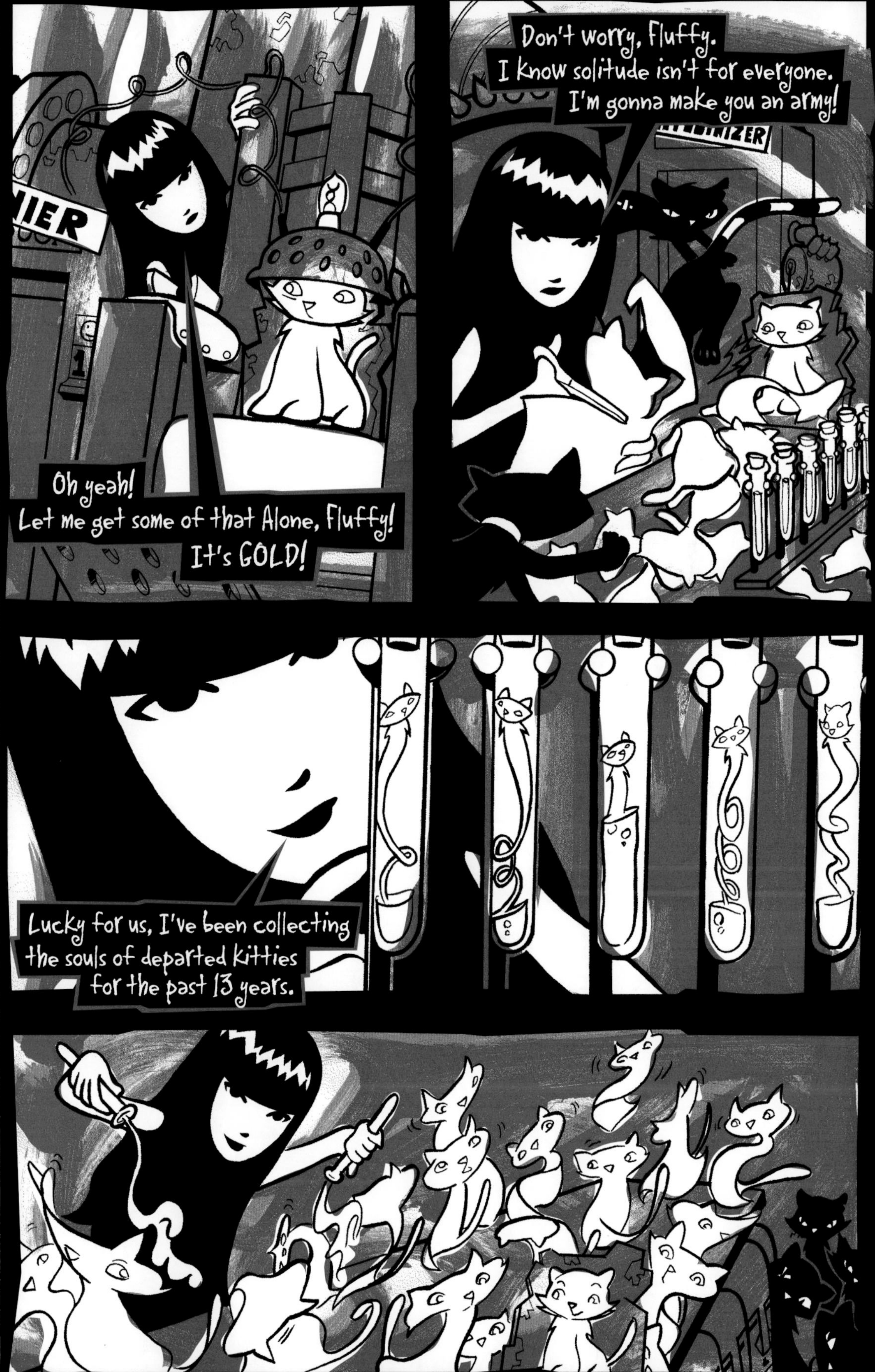

Oh yeah! Let me get some of that Alone, Fluffy! It's GOLD!
Don't worry, Fluffy. I know solitude isn't for everyone. I'm gonna make you an army!
Lucky for us, I've been collecting the souls of departed kitties for the past 13 years.

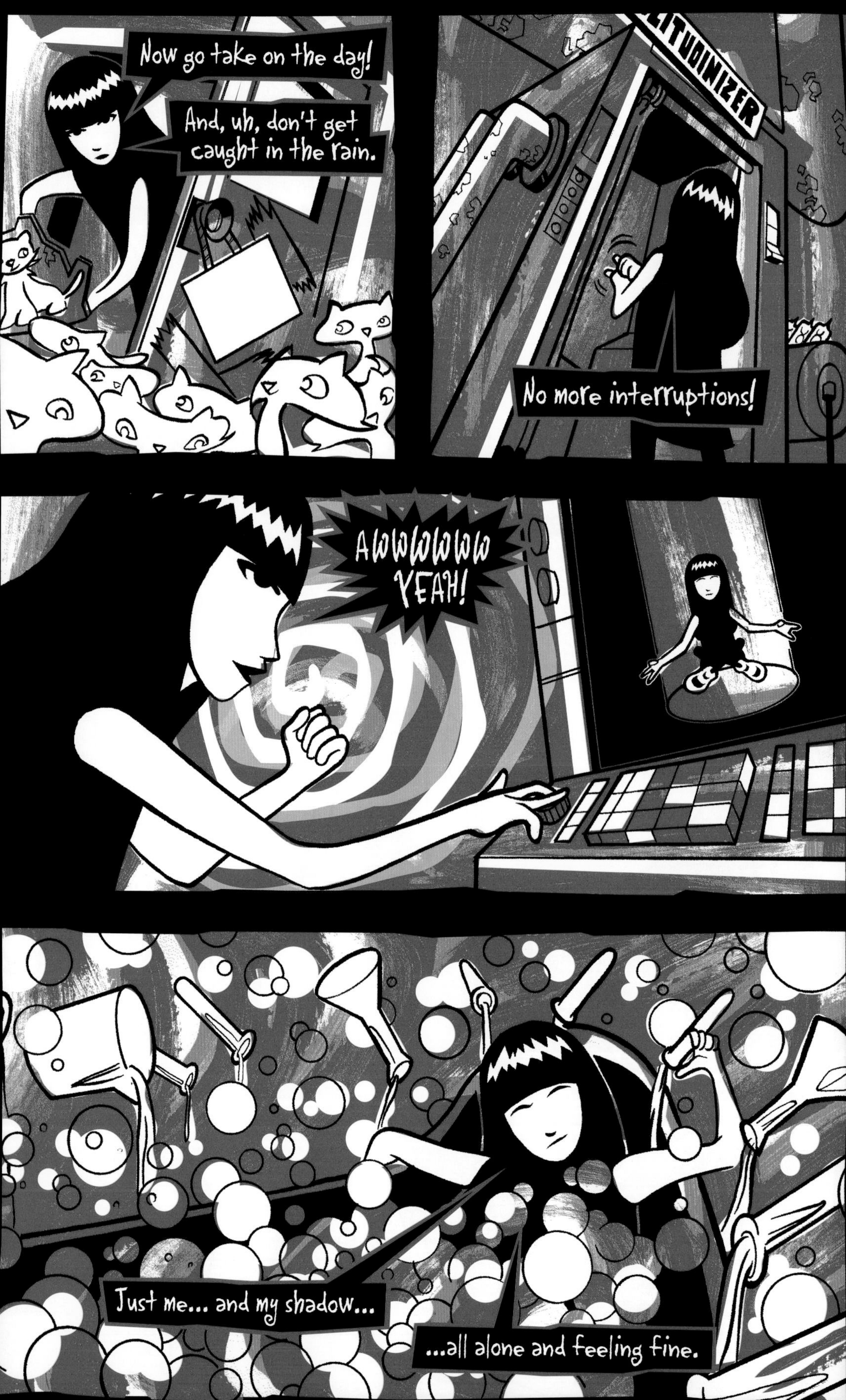

Now go take on the day!
And, uh, don't get caught in the rain.
No more interruptions!
AWWWWWWW YEAH!
Just me... and my shadow...
...all alone and feeling fine.

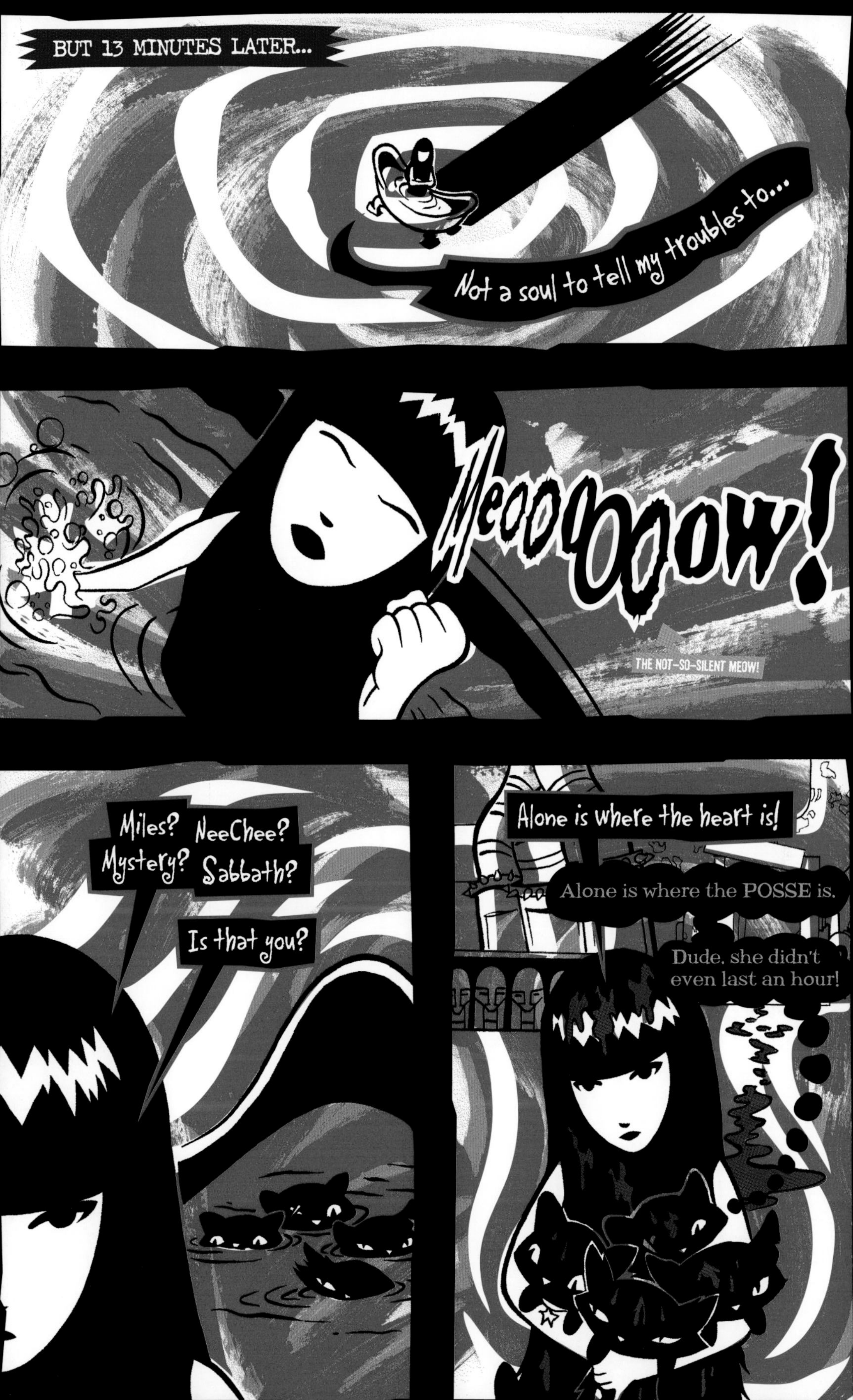

BUT 13 MINUTES LATER...
Not a soul to tell my troubles to...
MEOOOOOOW!
THE NOT-SO-SILENT MEOW!
Miles? NeeChee? Mystery? Sabbath?
Is that you?
Alone is where the heart is!
Alone is where the POSSE is.
Dude, she didn't even last an hour!

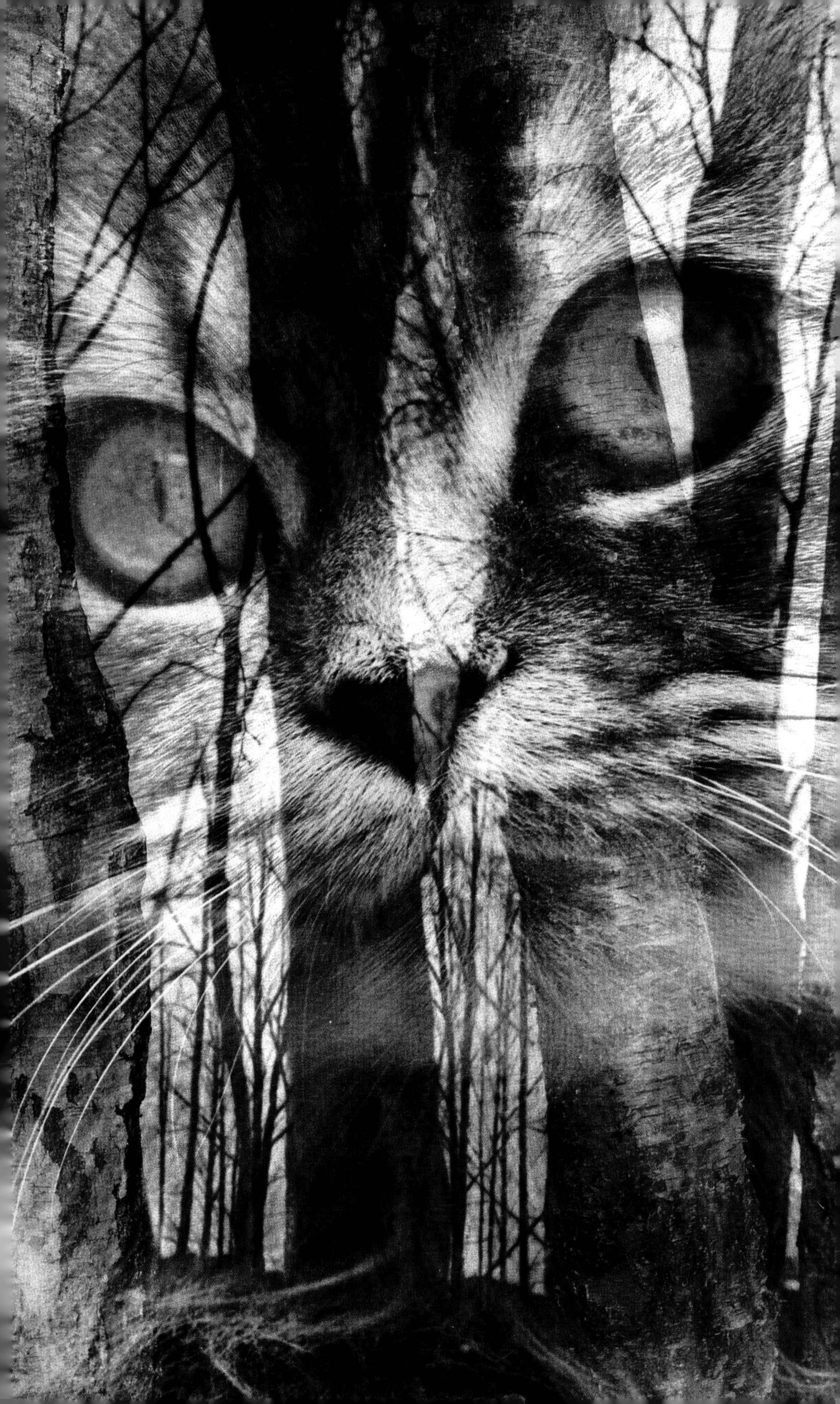

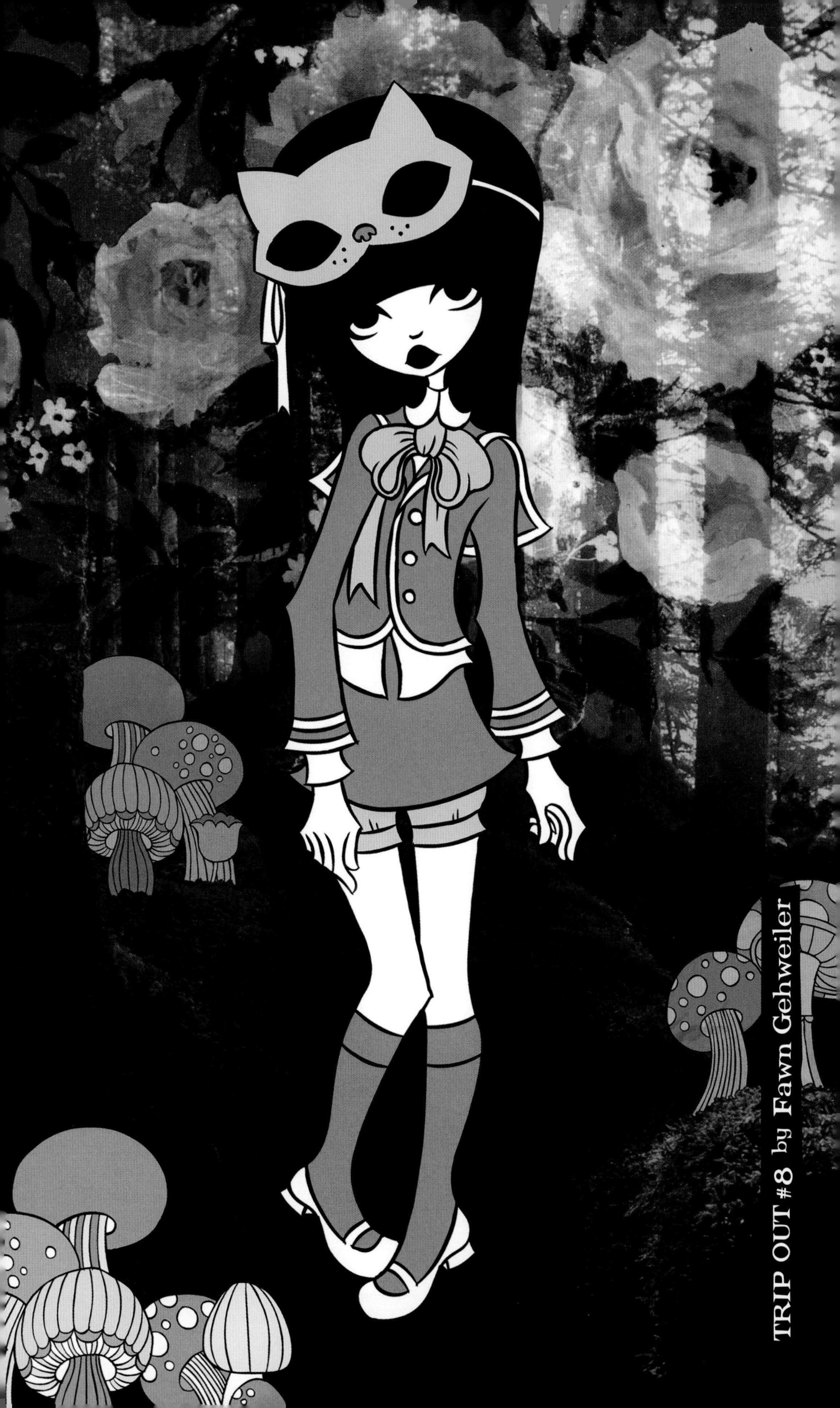
TRIP OUT #8 by Fawn Gehweiler

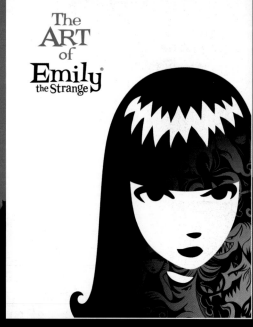

EMILY THE STRANGE VOLUME 1

Emily the Strange is not your ordinary thirteen-year-old girl—she's got a razor-sharp wit as dark as her jet-black hair, a posse of moody black cats, and famous friends in very odd places! This volume collects the first three issues of the Dark Horse *Emily* comics series—"The Boring Issue," "The Lost Issue," and "The Dark Issue," and includes one brand-spankin'-new story that you've never seen before!

ISBN 978-1-59307-573-6
$19.95

COMING SOON!
THE ART OF EMILY THE STRANGE
ISBN 978-1-59582-371-7
$22.95